NAPOLEON'S
LAST
ISLAND

Also by Thomas Keneally

An Angel in Australia

The Tyrant's Novel

The Widow and Her Hero

The People's Train

The Daughters of Mars

Shame and the Captives

NONFICTION

Outback

The Place Where Souls Are Born

Now and in Time to Be: Ireland and the Irish

Memoirs from a Young Republic

Homebush Boy: A Memoir

The Great Shame

American Scoundrel

Lincoln

The Commonwealth of Thieves

Searching for Schindler

Three Famines

Australians (vols. I and II)

FOR CHILDREN

Ned Kelly and the City of Bees

Roos in Shoes

NAPOLEON'S
LAST
ISLAND

A Novel

Thomas Keneally

ATRIA BOOKS

NEW YORK   LONDON   TORONTO   SYDNEY   NEW DELHI

ATRIA BOOKS
An Imprint of Simon & Schuster, Inc.
1230 Avenue of the Americas
New York, NY 10020

Copyright © 2015 by The Serpentine Publishing Company Pty Ltd
Originally published in Australia in 2015 by Vintage
Published by arrangement with The Serpentine Publishing Company Pty Ltd

First Atria Books hardcover edition October 2016

ATRIA BOOKS and colophon are trademarks of Simon & Schuster, Inc.

For information about special discounts for bulk purchases, please contact Simon & Schuster Special Sales at 1-866-506-1949 or business@simonandschuster.com.

The Simon & Schuster Speakers Bureau can bring authors to your live event. For more information, or to book an event, contact the Simon & Schuster Speakers Bureau at 1-866-248-3049 or visit our website at www.simonspeakers.com.

Interior design by Devan Norman

Manufactured in the United States of America

10 9 8 7 6 5 4 3 2 1

Library of Congress Cataloging-in-Publication Data

Names: Keneally, Thomas, author.
Title: Napoleon's last island : a novel / by Thomas Keneally.
Description: First Atria Books hardcover edition. | New York City : Atria Books, 2016.
Identifiers: LCCN 2016015139 | ISBN 9781501128424 (hardcover)
Subjects: LCSH: Napoleon I, Emperor of the French, 1769-1821--Fiction.
  Abell, Lucia Elizabeth Balcombe, -1871--Fiction. | Saint
  Helena--History--19th century--Fiction. | Families--Saint Helena--Fiction.
  | British--Saint Helena--Fiction. | Friendship--Fiction. | BISAC: FICTION
  / Historical. | FICTION / Literary. | FICTION / General. | GSAFD:
  Biographical fiction. | Historical fiction.
Classification: LCC PR9619.3.K46 N37 2016 | DDC 823/.914--
dc23 LC record available at https://lccn.loc.gov/2016015139

ISBN 978-1-5011-2842-4
ISBN 978-1-5011-2844-8 (ebook)

To Clementine and Gus,
my American/Australian grandchildren

Terre Napoléon

To me it was a discovery, though it was known to others. On a steely winter's day in 2012 in the city of Melbourne, I was offered tickets for an exhibition at the National Gallery of Victoria. There I visited a collection of Napoleon's garments, uniforms, furniture, china, paintings, snuffboxes, military decorations, and memorabilia.

Melbourne happens to be the capital city of the state of Victoria, but fourteen years before the queen honored by that name was even born, a French naval explorer, Nicholas Baudin, sent to Australia by Napoleon, reached Sydney in a period of peace between the Great Powers, having surveyed the coast of the later-named Victoria and labeled it *Terre Napoléon*.

There is something ruthlessly enchanting about Napoleon. We are told he was a tyrant, but we do not listen. We hear him labeled with the "Hitler" tag, but it does not take root. Counting in the blood and waste and all, the late phases of the French Revolution, the consulate and then the empire have an ineffable style, in ideas and new politics, in art and human venturing, which still compels our imaginations. Style in clothing too. For there were women's garments (Josephine's and Marie Louise's) in the exhibition, and I, like the Englishwomen of the island of St. Helena when they saw the two exiles, Albine de Montholon and Fanny Bertrand, believed these could not have been reproduced by anyone who was not French and of that period. I was as bowled over by what I saw on the mannequins

1

in the NGV as the population of St. Helena was in 1815 by those two friends and companions of the exiled Emperor.

The furniture the Emperor and Josephine had commissioned from Jacob Frères, who might have come as close to Heaven in their creation as any furniture-maker of history, was interspersed with porcelain and plate and paintings by Jacques-Louis David. We people of the globe's southernmost regions are used to going to Europe on interminable, brain-numbing flights to gawp at such items, but to be able to do it in Australia was a delight. For everything in here came from Europe, surely—that was my postcolonial assumption. It turned out not to be the case. Some of the material, including a *Légion d'honneur*, a swatch of the Emperor's hair, and a death mask of the man showing the mutilation of his head, were from an 1840s homestead named The Briars, located thirty kilometers away from Melbourne on the lovely Mornington Peninsula, a rectangular limb of earth that stretches southeast out of the city and ends in a narrow foot, which runs west to include Port Phillip Bay on its instep. That was where the Emperor's mask of mutilation came from!

And there, in the catalogue, was a name. Betsy Balcombe. Someone called Betsy was a familiar of the Emperor? And ended up in Australia? And her family had brought Napoleon relics with them, and the relics had been added to by a wealthy descendant.

So items from down the road had a connection with a young girl who had lived on St. Helena when the Emperor was stuck on that high mid-Atlantic rock of exile, and who—it was said—had become his intimate friend and annoyer. On St. Helena the Emperor specialized in giving people he liked enameled snuffboxes and other mementos, including—in the case of the Balcombe family—a Sèvres plate painted with battle scenes. And the Balcombes, ultimately exiled themselves, to Australia, had brought these memorabilia with them to O'Connell Street in Sydney and then into the Monaro bush and finally, with the most successful of the Balcombes, Betsy's youngest brother Alex, to the Port Phillip region.

Alex's robust and wealthy granddaughter Mabel Balcombe, who became a so-called leader of Melbourne society and was known as Dame Mabel Brookes, a woman born in 1890 and living until 1975, had increased the collection with purchases made in Europe and elsewhere. And here were the Balcombe-Brookes items, interspersed with those shipped especially from Europe for the exhibition. It may be worth mentioning that the husband of Dame Mabel, Norman Brookes, was an Anglophile and a supporter of private anti-Communist (that is, anti-malcontent) armies in the 1930s. That is, he should not have taken a shine to a man such as the Emperor. What did he have in common with the Emperor?

Before I proceed to tell my construction of the story of that lethal charming, I must emphasize I am not myself a person who has ever carried a torch for the Emperor Napoleon. On the one hand, he produced the *Code Napoléon*. He was not a tyrant in the notable way of Roman Caesars and totalitarian leaders, more an enlightenment man and man of destiny, but in the twentieth century we would discover the foul places men of destiny could take us. I am an Australian bush republican and was involved in the attempt to make Australia a republic by purely amiable and constitutional means. So the word "emperor" holds no allure for me, and I find Bonaparte's pretension of becoming an emperor to save the republic preposterous. I was always surprised the idea was accepted with enthusiasm by the revolutionary French (though Napoleon's brother, brave Lucien, had his doubts).

But the story of the Emperor's friendship with a girl who ended up in Australia, with a family destroyed by its association with said Emperor, gripped me. Australia was the netherworld of the nineteenth century, as close to being another planet as was possible then. People, under a cloud in Europe, fetched up here or were sent—not convicts alone: two sons of Charles Dickens and one of Anthony Trollope, for example, plain nonacademic Englishmen conveyed to a place where the rules were upside down and where even the feckless, it was believed, could find their fortune. The Balcombes were sent, damaged goods, from St. Helena, with their Napoleon memorabilia, sentenced by no law court, but duped into it and conveniently excised from the main British polity. That's a tale!

So how can an aged Australian writer credibly render a girl, and a Georgian one too, with the justice and the affection that, having read her journal, no doubt flawed like all journals, I feel for her?

As strong as was the impetus that arose from my encounter with Betsy's journal, I felt impelled also by Surgeon Barry O'Meara's two volumes on the experience of being the Emperor's doctor and intimate. With his capacity for eloquence and palaver, his keen eye for the inhabitants of the island, and his sense of grievance, burning with a furious vivid flame on the Emperor's behalf, O'Meara inveigled me.

The journals of the Emperor's friends on the island, Comte de Las Cases, General Gourgaud, Comte de Montholon, and that of the valet, Marchand, did not temper the fascination. Neither did the *Cahiers* of General Bertrand, nor the polished reports written by the Russian Count Balmain.

Secondary sources that tried to interpret the conundrum of Napoleon on St. Helena include Desmond Gregory's *Napoleon's Jailer: Lt. General Sir Hudson Lowe, A Life* and *Napoleon and His Fellow Travellers*, ed. Clement Shorter, and others too numerous to name.

This fiction purports to be a secret journal, the one hidden behind the real one published in 1844. Like Betsy's, it plays fast and loose with the strict historic chronology and suits its own convenience, but my no doubt mistaken intention is—in some way—to tell the truth by telling lies. In that regard, I have to say this sort of fiction sees the unspoken and the unexplained in journals and makes guesses, even wild guesses, when it comes to explain them. There is a scene involving the Emperor's suite and Betsy's mother which you will know to be a guess and a fiction when you come to it. I apologize to Betsy's lively ghost for my impudence.

And as a last waiver, I do not subscribe to the theory that Napoleon was murdered on St. Helena by Comte de Montholon, or anyone else. One murder mystery less, however, still leaves space for the abundant mysteries of St. Helena, the answers to some of which I have made guesses appropriate to the novel, and have still been left with plenty of others that defy explanation.

AFTER
THE ISLAND

Our Balcombe family

I had just met my husband-to-be when we had word from the Exmouth newspapers and from the harsh cries of coachmen that Our Great Friend had died on the island. This was of course impossible to believe, but we believed in it sufficiently to wail communally and privately. We saw all too sharply in our minds the rooms of Longwood, and that squat, exiled figure peering out of his windows towards the Barn, or Deadwood, or Diana's Peak, in a manner that foretold a bewildered death. Old family wounds gaped anew, and ghosts of varying colorations were released.

Eventually, something like the true circumstances of that death came to us from the mouth of an old friend, the Irish surgeon Barry O'Meara. Even though the great loss had occurred, it was temporarily an invigorating thing for our Balcombe family to see O'Meara, up from London, flaws and all, and to look to him to interpret the event and help us drink the chalice of bereavement. When we sat by a fire on a rainy day in June at the Swan's Nest, my father and the Irishman smoking pipes, and a bowl of punch before them, a couple of cups of which my mother was persuaded to take, we glowed with a familial anticipation that despite the circumstances felt like glee. To us, O'Meara had always been a sprite, so we felt strangely eased by the truth that he shared our onus of mourning.

He had arrived in our town the day before and sent us a note inviting us to the Swan's Nest. When my father received it, he went sallow with rage. On the island he used to get rubicund with irritation, but in England he turned less healthy colors. In the letter O'Meara raised the question of his naval agent, Mr. William Holmes, a man my father suspected of dishonor. Given the risks my father had taken in order secretly to ship off money drafts drawn by Our Great Friend, the idea that some had stuck to Holmes's hands on the way to Laffitte's bank in Paris was something odious. None, however, seemed to have stuck to O'Meara's, and O'Meara defended his friend in any case, saying that Holmes was about to go to Paris to introduce himself to Laffitte and allay suspicions the bank harbored about the origin of the money bills. My father was not utterly convinced, yet in the flatness and desolation of our lives, we were still pleased to see the face of a fellow conspirator from the island, a face rendered grayer, and his gray suit, familiar from the island, older.

By then it was three weeks since the news of OGF's death had come to us by way of the papers, and we were hungry for salient detail, to serve as palpable shelves on which we would stack our grief. Like soldiers of the *Grande Armée*, who had reportedly, on hearing the news, limped forth into town squares in France, looking about in shock, unable to accommodate themselves to the obliteration from the earth of that Force, we too were shocked. The newspaper accounts, even the well-meaning, progressive scribes, did not always avoid false premises concerning the Emperor and his exile, and were unable to recount credibly what had happened at Longwood House weeks before, since none of them had ever seen the island. We were consoled by the honest accounts of the *Morning Chronicle* when it arrived in Exminster from London. The *Chronicle* had the advantage of sources amongst those not rancorous to the Emperor, his admirers and in some cases old friends. But we were appalled by other at best grudging reports, such as that in *The Times*, which purported to recount the death of a man we could not recognize from the text. All this had deepened our familial depression, of course. We had been suffering for allegiances and services of various kinds to the living Emperor, and now he was gone, our suffering lacked meaning. Most of the time we crept about each other, being terribly kind, even me, the sort of kindness that confessed vacancy at our hearts, and a sense of the meaninglessness before us.

And then there came the letter from O'Meara promising to settle with my father the question of Holmes—and that he could give us the truth of OGF's expiring. With these offers O'Meara raised hope that he might return to us our meaning. He told us he had heard from surgeons still on the island the circumstances of the Emperor's death.

O'Meara drank up his cup of punch with relish, and that oval, beaming face with the curly black hair now touched with gray seemed to revive before us, and thus a little of the island and the times of promise were restored. There was no layer of despair over his features. He was writing a book, and he believed that would redeem him. My father served him a second cup with a ladle, and he raised it and said solemnly, "I propose a health to the memory of Our Great Friend, whose constitution was destroyed by the Fiend, Sir Hudson Lowe!"

Jane, my sister, and I were restricted to tea, and my brothers to cherry sodas. I suspected all at once, unlike our parents, who had been cosseted by the punch, that O'Meara might alter things for us; that the Fiend and the island might now become the one dream, and that all the questions arising from that time might be swallowed in the ocean of OGF's demise. But it could not happen until the matter and process of death was detailed for us.

"I once took out a septic tooth from the Great Ogre," declared O'Meara. "A canine tooth. And now I scrape a crust of bread, and let me tell you it is a thin enough crust, out of the septic teeth of Edgware Road—an Indian, Jewish, and Arabian clientele by and large. I am limited to places beyond the eye of the College of Surgeons, and must proceed carefully and modestly if I am ever to be reinstated. And that is the work of Lowe by Name and Nature."

"Ah," my father said, warmed by the punch and by an animosity not native to him. "I know, though, that you write pieces in the *Chronicle* and *The Times*, Barry, still hammering that man, and justly so. And declaring other things as well."

"The men who read that don't know I am a dental surgeon. The people from whom I draw teeth and the men who publish and read don't know each other. It is incumbent upon me . . ."

Here the Irish surgeon realized he was speaking rather loudly, and dropped his voice, but there was still color in his face, as if he were being criticized. "It is incumbent upon me to strike that fiend, Sir Hudson, who has violated all human expectation. None of it makes me a rich fellow, but it sustains me as a poor one."

My father raised his hand appeasingly, palm out. "You realize that for my part I am with you in the proposition that there does not exist sufficient ink in this world to supply an appropriate condemnation of Lowe by Name and Nature."

"The Fiend and Our Great Friend," murmured O'Meara, making the implicit contrast between the small, mean man with all his petty civil and military titles and the small, spacious man with all his flaws. "Do you know that when I left the island they gave him a Corsican horse doctor? You heard that?"

"I had not in any detail," my father admitted. "We are far from reliable intelligence in this little town. I have had a few letters from islanders, some intercepted by the powers of the earth along the way, and some smuggled out without interference by store ship captains of my old acquaintance. But even now these missives are a peril to them. Even here, I believe I am subject to a degree of scrutiny."

Barry O'Meara nodded ponderously and, with a vividness typical of him, said, "I understand well the methods of those who clipped our wings but yet still want to be fully acquainted with what we do in the chicken yard!"

"You mentioned the Corsican doctor," my mother reminded him.

"I did. Now that Corsican, the supposed doctor Antommarchi, is a prosector, a cutter of corpses! Our friend Fanny Bertrand told me that he laughs wildly when the idea of death is mentioned because he has private theories about what death is and he won't share them with others. Likewise pain. They are both some sort of human delusion, it seems. If the man would share the secret, it would bring a large saving in opiates."

Both men chuckled acridly while my mother frowned and let a shiver move through her.

"In any case, this Corsican administered a blistering to Our Great Friend without first shaving the flesh. And to both arms simultaneously!

When the man was limp with disease! That barbarous torture brought on a burning rash and OGF cried, 'Am I not yet free of assassins?' But our Corsican quack—what does he do but get the giggles and call in Surgeon Arnott, of the infantry, a fellow I happen to know. Now Arnott was in Spain with the 53rd Regiment when they were more than decimated by OGF's Polish cavalry, with only some fifty-two men left standing at the end. And thus, you see, *that* is his measure of an emergency, and though an amiable fellow, he is so sanguine a man that he is likely to stand right at the lip of a soldier's grave and declare the poor fellow's condition temporary. And so it was Arnott who was brought to see OGF and afterwards reported to Governor Lowe at Plantation House that the Emperor was surprisingly well, given all rumors to the contrary. He said that OGF was suffering from hypochondria. He assured Name and Nature that if a seventy-four-gun warship were to arrive from England suddenly to take the Emperor away from the island, it would instantly put him on his legs again."

My mother made a sound of incredulity and O'Meara went on.

"In fact, even had such a mercy been considered by the grand Tories of the Cabinet, he would have died at sea before he reached this shore. Our friends at Longwood had long since written to the Cabinet via the Fiend to ask that the Emperor should be removed to another climate, and be permitted to take the waters at some health spa. But Sir Name and Nature refused to allow the letter to be transmitted, all under the old pretext that the suite had used the term 'Emperor' in their appeal."

I remembered that the Dr. Arnott O'Meara spoke of had once paid a visit to Longwood while my father was there, and OGF had greeted him with a jocose question: "How many patients have you killed so far, Mr. Arnott?" The surgeon replied, "Most of my patients happen to have been killed by you, General."

Already now I saw my sister beside me beginning to tremble. Her father's daughter, she was overborne by the idea of the ruthless pain to whose ambush humanity was subject, and the onset of her own congestive ailments, signs of which had become visible in the past year, sharpened that. She was more at ease with death than she could ever manage to be with pain. She had become more given to tears, though she had never considered them an enemy or a self-betrayal, even in the years we were on the island. I heard the pace of her wheeze increase now, and I saw her habitual pressing of a handkerchief to her lips. I put my arm around her and enclosed her shoulders. They were almost as thin as they had been six years earlier, when OGF first descended on our garden on the island. Her undeserved affliction was settling in, and the Fiend and great men in England were guilty in part for that too, through the imperfectly sealed cottage we occupied by their implied desire.

"And so," Barry O'Meara proceeded, "those great minds, Antommarchi the Corsican goat-doser, and Arnott the smiling fool, decided between them that Our Great Friend should be given a *lavement*. But OGF had never in sickness or health admired the suggestion that he be turned onto his stomach, which was so tender now, and be interfered with at all by surgeons with such indignity, even by those he tolerated, those he did *not* consider utter charlatans."

"Like you," said my father. "He trusted you."

"A *lavement*?" asked my mother softly. It seemed a kindly word.

"An enema," Barry rushed to say. "Certainly, something needed to be done. OGF had been sweating appallingly, and all his mattresses were drenched. My genial informants, Fanny and her husband Henri, also tell me that in the last months the Emperor was like a woman with child, and that everything he ate he vomited. So a *lavement* was chosen. It would never have been had I been there. It is like trying to erase a bruise from a fist by inflicting one with a mallet! It did nothing to ease his tender stomach. And having failed with one crass remedy, they proceeded to give him castor oil to temper stomach pain, as if he were a child who had eaten too much fruit. The treatment, of course, caused OGF to contort himself into a ball at the base of the bed. The pity of it, Balcombe! The pity! Knotted up like a child, at the base of his bed."

Jane let her most honest tears loose then—not that she had any other kind.

"Do you want some more tea?" I asked her, but she shook her

head and was mute. I dared not look at her for fear now that she would start me on the same course as her, yet I did not want to give Surgeon O'Meara a cause to suspend his report for sensibility's sake. Indeed, he asked my mother now, in a way that made me remember that he knew much about her from the island,

"Should I perhaps pursue a different subject, Jane?"

"No," said my mother (another Jane) in a breaking voice. "We seek to know all, Barry. We must go through our obsequies too. If there are moans here, it is no different from what we would have uttered had we been there to witness it all. We would like to have that death defined, for otherwise our imaginations are tempted to think of infinite pain."

"But I fear it becomes more distressing yet," O'Meara warned my mother.

"Even so . . . ," said Jane, my sister.

"Yes," my mother agreed, "even so."

O'Meara drained his punch and my father poured him another ladleful to fortify him against our distress. Then he recommenced.

"So the Corsican quack, who at least knew that things were more serious than Arnott did, sent a message to Name and Nature at Plantation House asking Short—the island's civil doctor you'd remember—and a naval surgeon from the *Vigo*, Mitchell, to be called in. But sometimes, as I know so well, a congeries of surgeons may simply confirm the party in their worst and least advised opinions. And in any case, battalions of surgeons could not argue with a system so depleted by aggravation and hepatitis as OGF's."

The committee of doctors, so O'Meara told us, reached a consensus that the Emperor should rise and be shaved. He told them he was too weak and that he preferred to shave himself but lacked the strength. When Antommarchi and Arnott prodded his liver, the Emperor screamed—it was like a stab from a bayonet—and began to vomit. "What did they all do? Why, nobody worried—they thought it a good sign. And when OGF told them, 'The devil has eaten my legs,' they thought it was poetry, not an omen. Arnott reached the dazzling conclusion that the disease lay entirely in the Emperor's mind. And when Arnott saw Henri Bertrand and the valet Marchand helping OGF walk round the room, he told the others he thought the patient was improving. Arnott did not understand that it was raw courage itself that caused his patient to walk, that he was taking his last steps up Golgotha. So, the surgeons told Sir Hudson Fiend that his prisoner's pallor and decline were deceits of a disaffected mind. Whereas OGF well knew what was wrong with him. For here, my dear Balcombes, was a great mind, vaster in gifts and power of imagination than the squalid little shambles of their intellects. Not one of them ever asked what the patient thought! For twenty days he told them that it was *fegato*, his liver. But what would he know?"

"And was it the liver?" asked my father, deeply invested in O'Meara's narration and enduring it under his conflicting identities as a man befriended, a friend betrayed, a devotee—nonetheless—to the end. My mother was for now silenced by a similar order of grief and confusion. "I mean, entirely the liver?"

"Oh, no, it was sadly the stomach too." O'Meara grew thoughtful. "Oh, how lucky we were to ride forth with him in those earlier days! I remember watching you two young women accompanying him one day over the edge of the ravine and into that abomination of boulders known as the Devil's Glen. It was a sight—the three of you, the balance of all he knew and, well, your unworldliness then, in that arena of chaos—that affects me now. As you see, I am close to tears. And to think that OGF reached a stage where he could scarcely bear the fatigue of a ride in the carriage for half an hour, with the horses at a walk, and then could not walk from the carriage into his house without support. Remember his *confiseur* Pierron, who made those fantastical delicacies for him? Towards the end all that was nothing to OGF—he could digest only soups and jellies, served in those Sèvres bowls on which were painted records of his glories. Both the contents of the bowl and the ornamentation inadequate, alas, to nourish him any further! Our Great Friend choked and gagged and starved for lack of a capacity to swallow, and like many desperate patients he said unkind things. And when he vomited it was black matter, alike to coffee grounds."

"How could that not have alerted Dr. Arnott and the Corsican?" my mother protested.

"They were associated in denial," O'Meara explained. "You must understand that each time they saw Name and Nature, he ranted with all the energy he possessed that the illness was a trick to garner the world's concern. A pretense. That has an influence on men's thoughts, on the thought of surgeons of limited skill. Sir Hudson Fiend wondered about moving him into that newly built house near Longwood, but the Emperor's suite knew his condition was terminal, and so did—in their own way—far better surgeons than the claque of asses assigned to the poor fellow. And so did Sir Hudson Fiend, because though he could not stop pretending that the Emperor was a malingerer, he knew in his waters that some fatal stage had been entered on. So he moved himself and his odious chief of police, Sir Thomas Reade, into the new house and waited there. His systems of persecution were close to bringing him a complete result."

Jane still nursed her tears. We were all pale. Even my little brothers listened soundlessly to O'Meara, to whom they had never in all our time knowing him extended that compliment before.

"De Montholon told me in a letter—I give away no secret; it has been written in the French papers that at four o'clock on one of those last mornings the Emperor called him and related with astonishing and desperate grief that he'd just seen his Josephine and that she would not embrace him. She had disappeared when he reached for her, he said, but not before telling him that they would see each other again, *de nouveau*. De Montholon reminded him that *de nouveau* did not mean *bientôt*. Then he and others set to change the Emperor's soaked bedclothes and replace the sweat-drenched mattress. This is what it had come to. Better, wrote dear Bertrand to me, that he had been killed by a cannonball, obliterated at dusk on the day of that final battle six years past than die hunched in the bottom half of his bed."

We could see that O'Meara was nearing an end to his narration. Jane's unpretentious and authoritative tears increased. My mother's face held a blue pallor, and my father glowed with a revived unhealthy ruddiness made up of bewildered and conflicting thought and brandy.

"So, OGF was persuaded to move to a new bed in the drawing room since that was more airy. He would let only de Montholon and Marchand the valet help him—a good man altogether, that Marchand. He permitted them to swathe his legs with hot towels.

"Our dear friends had had an altar set up in the next apartment," O'Meara said. "An Italian priest had landed on the island after we went. Apparently he is a clodhopper, yet the Emperor liked him. If he were not irrational in his friendships, OGF, some of us would not be his friends, would we? And the priest was ordered to say Mass every day. Well, the Emperor had never renounced the Church of Rome, even if he *had* imprisoned the Pope himself."

"Mercy, Barry," my mother pleaded. "You must take us now to the point."

Yet O'Meara, with a sure instinct, was out to make us share in every detail, as relayed by friends on the island and by the French suite. So we heard how the surgeons decided next to give OGF calomel, mercury chloride, in a desire to make the poor man vomit more black grounds, as if these too were part of a mental attitude that must be corrected. But they had overdosed him with ten grains of the stuff, which he could barely swallow and which, when he did, caused him to vomit up both the black matter and blood. After that, he refused to see the corps of attendant doctors. He began to think O'Meara was still on the island, and kept calling for him.

"He began thinking you Balcombes were still on the island too. 'And Guglielmo Balcombe, where is he?' he asked. Honestly, he had such affection for you, William, and hoped he had never wronged you. 'Has he really left? When did it happen? And Madame Balcombe too? How very strange. She really has gone.'"

My parents lowered their eyes. They did not take equal joy in the Emperor's confused remembrance. O'Meara recognized it—he had said something that meant more to the Balcombe parents, and indeed their children, than he could tell.

"They moved him to the drawing room because there was less damp. On the day before his death, he had sunk into a coma and the shutters were opened to let the light and the island's air in, which could not harm him now, it having done its damage. And off beyond the railings stood the new version of Longwood House, where the Fiend camped, biting his nails. He was so restless for *it* to happen that he rode across to the real Longwood and stood at the door listening for the advance of death inside, yet knowing he would not be admitted. He would ride off again, but be back within an hour or so. Meanwhile, my dear friends, OGF was on his camp bed, which sat so low to the ground, but which bore four mattresses to elevate him."

The green silk curtains, which we remembered from his time in the Pavilion, were now drawn. A few seconds before the time of the evening gun from Ladder Hill, said O'Meara, OGF expired. Fanny Bertrand was in the room, half-Irish, half-imperial Fanny, a woman fit for ceremoniousness, and she remembered, as he breathed out and the breath was not succeeded, to stop the clock in his room, the one he'd always shown off to us, the alarm clock. It read eleven minutes before six.

By the time O'Meara reached this stage, we women were choking and my father's head was still down, and the boys, William, Tom, Alex, were pale, old enough now to be awed out of boyishness. I thought how noble a man my father, Billy Balcombe—*Cinq Bouteilles*, as OGF called him—was. He blamed the Emperor for nothing, for no portion of the blight on our own lives.

The tale was briskly finished. O'Meara seemed to know he must get to an end if he did not wish to provoke some unpredictable contrary feeling amidst my parents—for all he knew, a frantic quarrel was possible. Marchand and the other valets had carried the body from the death bed to a new camp bed. The priest laid a crucifix on the breast of the corpse and left the room. Outside he recited the rosary. Name and Nature turned up at the door of Longwood but was denied entry by Bertrand, who told him the autopsy must proceed. This dissection took place in a room we acutely remembered— where the billiard table had once been, and the maps on which I'd stuck pins to represent the movement of hordes of men around the countryside near Jena and Auerstädt.

Afterwards, Surgeon Short, one of the group, writing that the Emperor's liver was grossly swollen, came under great pressure from Sir

Hudson, Name and Nature, to alter his report. The Fiend thought he might somehow be blamed for that distended organ. Short refused and left the report in Sir Hudson's hands, and according to Short, Name and Nature himself changed the words, crossing out Short's verdict. Fortunately, Short had the final chance to write on the document that the words obliterated had been suppressed by the Fiend's orders.

Meanwhile, the autopsy over, the dead man was moved back to his bedroom, which had been set out in the manner of a mortuary chapel and draped in black. The next morning Name and Nature came in with a posse of fifteen officials, including Sir Tom Reade, and declared the corpse was "the General," as he still called him even in death, and asked both his party individually and General Bertrand to confirm it. Reade was not fully happy, for there was no achievable happiness in such a man. He appeared in part to believe that his enemy, OGF, had taken the game to the extreme now. In a bid for world sympathy, he had died. The soldiers, the sailors, and the farmers, the Letts, the Robinsons, old Polly Mason, the Reverend Mr. Jones, keeper of the sheep and goats, the Porteouses, the Solomons, the Ibbetsons, the Knipes, the Dovetons, and all the rest were let in to see the chin-strapped corpse dressed in military style, lying on the old blue cloak from the great victory of his youth, Marengo, and dressed by Marchand and the others in the green coat of a colonel of the chasseurs of the Imperial Guard, with white facings, the sash, the *Légion d'honneur*, the cavalry boots, and with the bicorn hat across his lower stomach. General Bertrand and Count de Montholon stood by him, in their uniforms, and in a gown of mourning, inimitable Fanny, the best-dressed woman even in bereavement that the island had ever seen, and the most faithful.

I imagined the yamstocks—the island-born—processing through those rooms that were known to us, gawping at the maps on the wall, the books, the peepholes in the shutters he used for watching the garrison and to see me win the ladies' race at Deadwood from which all the glory had long since been sucked. They must have known, those islanders, that their world was about to shrink. The garrison would go, the squadron would sail away, and all items would plummet in cost.

A death mask had had to be made, and quickly. The first was not successful, so Novarrez, doorkeeper of Longwood, shaved him for a second mask undertaken with pulverized gypsum. But the processes of death were under way, and by that afternoon the body had to be placed promptly in a coffin.

Hearing this, we groaned and cast our eyes about. This was more of mortality than we could bear.

"Enough, enough," said O'Meara, as if to himself.

"You have made us," said my mother, "devour the entire bitter loaf."

"As we must," growled my father.

One quick, abominable detail: they had removed the heart to send to his wife and now placed it in the room near the corpse, with a cloth over it. During the night, a rat emerged in the room and grabbed the heart half off its silver dish. "That rat, the very image of the Fiend, then went on to devour half the dead man's ear. . . . You see? You see?"

And we did see. That representative of darkness, in eating heart and ear, passion and the senses, provided gruesome echoes of the cramping of ambitions of self-redemption on the Emperor's part by a paltry and choleric Englishman.

Finally it was easier to listen. So we heard that the soldiers of two regiments had carried him on their shoulders to the hearse, which had made its way into Geranium Valley, ever after to be called the Valley of the Tomb, with friends and servants weeping behind it. Name and Nature rampaged through Longwood, being free to do so at last, and looked at all that the Emperor had set aside before he died, including a gold snuffbox for his London friend Lady Holland. Then he rifled through papers to see if he could discover plans of escape, which could be used to justify the strangulation process he had put in place. "And the fact that he could find nothing suggestive of it goes to explain the attacks which now appear upon him, Name and Nature, in all honest newspapers."

O'Meara spoke as if he were not himself one of the chief attackers.

"*Consummatum est,*" he sang conclusively. "It is consummated."

He helped himself to more punch.

Before OGF

A deliberate exercise in
dizzying cliffs . . .

I came to our island, St. Helena, which the Portuguese had prophetically named to honor the mother of the Emperor Constantine, as barely more than an infant; three years of age. I assume I can remember our arrival sharply, but I cannot say whether some of the details later relayed by my mother have been taken by me and labeled as memory. With that qualification, I can say that when I was brought up on deck to see the island, which had risen from the sea during the night and presented itself in a brilliant dawn, I stood holding the hand of one of the young sailors my parents liked and trusted, and the closer the island got the more it looked like a deliberate exercise in dizzying cliffs, and the more their sheer faces seemed to deny any chance of a safe landing. I stared up at the huge nose of terrifying rock rising behind inner mountains, and high saddles between them. The island began to seem less like a brief interruption of the Atlantic Ocean and to occupy a major part of the sky above. I imagined we would have to pass over those peaks and precipices to get to any habitation. And if that were not alarm enough, the young man told me that one mountain beyond the astounding cliffs consisted of the face of a Negro giant at rest.

This man carried me down into the cutter, which threw itself about madly on the writhing Jamestown Roads, as for some reason naval men called not quite secure harbors, and my mother assured me I would not be devoured. The island was not a resting giant after all. But for the Balcombes the time would come when the clumsy fable of the sailor would be made flesh, and the island would become the devourer.

The chief port was a very narrow affair. Beyond the dock one crossed a stone bridge with a trickle of water below and, through an arched gate, entered the town proper. Jamestown sat in a slot that had tried its best to be a valley. But its wide main street and shallow cross lanes provided a narrow vista of sky and interior, a V of sea in a gun sight of rock. Set on an island in the mid-Atlantic, where all possibilities of wind existed, this town went for most of the year without more than an occasional breeze. Its buildings were of white stucco, but there was a serious fortification on a terrace above the port, called the Castle. My father's warehouse was here at the beginning of the town, but we did not have to live in this pocket, amongst immutable rocks, looking up at terraces where the fortresses and artillery stood. We would live in open space beyond. Meanwhile, the British cannon above us considered that strangulated town and the sleeping Negro giant worth keeping!

The slaves of the island were mostly the children of people brought from Madagascar, East Africa, or India by the ships of the East India Company. Even as we landed at St. Helena, in London slavery as a trade was about to be enacted out of existence, but it would long continue on the island. We, who had never had slaves before, would have the use of them. The town major, a tall, dutiful sort of man from the East India Company infantry, named Hodson, had gathered the five that were our lot. Our house servants were Sarah, a sweet-faced African woman of perhaps my mother's age, and two half-Malay, half-African twin boys of about ten, Roger and Robert. They were barefooted and wore canvas trousers and a jacket but white gloves. If there was an assumption by folk that Sarah was the boys' mother, she claimed to be their aunt, and they the children of her dead sister. A Cape Malay male, an older and scrawny man named Toby, was our gardener, and Ernest, perhaps thirty, limpid-eyed and with an air of caution about him, a second gardener and our groom.

We were escorted by these slaves, and the clerks of the East India

Company agency named Fowler, Cole, and Balcombe, through the town. A horse waited for my father, and there was a narrow-axled carriage for my mother, Jane, and me. I did not want to mount the carriage—I had already developed an unexplained fear of the things. The conveyance looked incapable of negotiating the long terraces of the track that led up the cliffs of rock to the broader place my mother had promised, where we hoped to breathe and spread our elbows more freely than the citizens of the port could. One of the clerks drove the trap, and behind it walked our servants, free of baggage. But there was a string of perhaps thirty other Cape Malays following with burdens on their heads and shoulders, supplies and items for our house.

Jouncing along, I was carried by a talkative slave, a tall energetic one, in a basket on his shoulder. As I jolted my way up the heights, he declared, "Oh, lady, I carry washing, I carry flour, I carry salt beef, I carry linseed. But you, my miss, are the finest load I carry. No one bake you, no one wear you, no one pour you out on the ground."

I think of slavery now, and I wonder what gave this man the goodwill to say such soothing things to the child of his enslavers. The basket was hard-edged and the sky bounced above me and home did not present itself for more than an hour. I was heaved up into a notch in an escarpment, and I saw behind me the caravan of people hauling bags and panniers. We walked in pleasant open country now, but there were inland hills, a diaphanous forest to the right, and a large white house visible beyond it. A waterfall fell into a heart-shaped bowl of rock to our right, and to our left was a wooded hill, and notable peaks lay ahead. But there was open space for gardens and orchards, pastures and slave huts, and for our house, on the level ground ahead. A nearby small stream was named Briars Gut.

The carriageway running from the road into The Briars was shaded by canopies of huge banyan trees, which imposed a sudden dusk on us, and then from the gate of the garden, a walk of pomegranate trees took us towards a long, low house with wide verandahs. I saw over the basket's rim to the side of the house what was a plentiful orchard running down the slight slope, and now Toby and Ernest peeled off to penetrate the fence and stand amidst the trees, the older man and his apprentice, making ready to go home to the slave shacks through a grove of myrtles at the back of the house.

I did not understand then that this orchard was part of the family riches. It alone would earn my father some two hundred pounds a year, with its grapes, oranges, figs, shaddock—the biggest of the citrus—and two fruits many of the passengers on passing ships found exotic beyond their dreams, the guava and the mango, whose flesh was so overladen with syrup.

Away to the left and before the house ran a well-ordered garden.

While I assumed my fear was the only one at loose in that landscape, I now wonder how my mother had endured such a journey of ill-defined prospects before riding into this reassuring place. She was then less than thirty by some years. She was practical and sturdy but had a thin elegant neck, very marked lustrous dark eyes, what I always thought of as a wise and witty mouth, and brown hair done in the modern, seemingly informal way. She was not finished with childbearing and knew she must give birth here. But the sight of the orchard must have excited her and my father, and not just for its monetary power. They could not have imagined beforehand any of the tropic luxuriance of the vines and fruit trees as they stood beneath that vivid afternoon sky.

Toby and Ernest had already placed tubs filled with fruit ready for collection by the porters on their return journey from The Briars to the port, specifically to the warehouse of Fowler, Cole, and Balcombe, agents to the Company and superintendents of its sales. That fruit would be bought by the officers and passengers of our own ship and eaten during the passage to Cape Town. Sea breakfasts and evening desserts would be thus enlivened.

The pannier containing me was let down, and, strange fruit, I was lifted out in vast calloused hands and found my parents smiling at me by the trellis gate that led to the bungalow. Its garden was full of beds of white, yellow, and red roses, hence The Briars, spelled always with a capital "T," like *The Times* of London!

Told by so many that St. Helena was a "desert island," which we

interpreted as meaning "barren," as its huge bare cliffs had also suggested it was, we were delighted by any vale of orchards and roses
on a high plain. On the African side of the island—to the east, that
is—a plateau and a great block of rock, again imitating a human
face, stopped the more unruly vigor of the trade winds reaching us.
Down an escarpment towards the South American, west side of the
island fell that thread of waterfall into its bowl of rock.

Below the house stretched the lawn, which seemed to offer limitless play. I began to run on it. I could smell Jane near me—her
child smell, enthusiasm and powder and fresh-laundered linen. We
turned to each other and smiled. It was the simplest of communications on an island that would come to harbor complex ones.

To the side of the long lawn . . .

To the side of the long lawn of The Briars and atop a knoll approached by rock steps stood a cottage, built to charm with artful wooden fretwork. It was called the Pavilion and was a sort of summerhouse, with big windows on all sides so it could be opened up and rinsed through by the kindlier winds that favored our little dale. It was ornate, a jewel of a place with a large room on the ground floor. Upstairs there were a few garret-style bedrooms. My father had already been told that people would want to rent this place. A naturalist from a ship had spent some time there, as had officers on short appointments ashore and any other visitors, military or official, to our island. Occupancy was intermittent, though, since many preferred to live down in the town, at Mr. Porteous's boardinghouse, the Portions, which rented small but comfortable rooms. It was a common axiom that the longer you spent in Jamestown, the less you felt cramped in by the great vises of rock to either side of the town. I myself came to love the place. It was the only *town* to go to town to.

The Pavilion would become the engine of Balcombe destiny, but one couldn't have guessed that to see it glimmer on its mound to the South American side of our garden. For now, the garden favored my nature and gave me room for unruliness. Store-ship captains who stayed in the Pavilion with their wives did not do so a second time, and that was probably because of me—my spying, my intrusion, my hectic and impudent nature. I was a child with the gifts to be decorative, but I did not sit still enough to adorn any scene, exterior or

28

interior. The supposed wildness and taste for frank talk I was later accused of had shown its early signs.

I accepted, as one unthinkingly accepts air for breathing, my parents' making of their way on the island. My sister Jane was a wonderful playmate, since she lacked all unnecessary competitive spirit, all spitefulness, everything that I had in abundance. She was capable of firmness, though, displayed only when essential. We were the Balcombes' two girl children, and did not question why there was no son.

Our brother William was delivered at the hands of the island's English midwife a full four or so years after we came to the island. This birth seemed at least to me to occur with no fuss, no pain, no expectation of loss of mother or child. I had not then discovered for myself that giving birth is the equator, the dangerous passage between the poles of new life and death, which participates in, and can deliver, both.

I knew nothing. I must have some form of education before I was too old. My parents had resolved that they would take a consistent line on this. No young tutor had answered our newspaper advertisement before we left England. Jane and I had an intermittent series of teachers, but tutors were not native to the island and impossible to attract from England or the Cape. At some stage, it was set in stone: we would have to go back to England to pick up some of that commodity.

In the meantime, to direct my energy and prevent me from mounting on dangerous horses, I was given a docile island-bred gelding, unimaginatively, and like half the known world, named Tom. Jane got Augustus, a horse of similar bloodlines, whose ancestors had come from Arabia to Africa, that had first grown shaggy on the African plains and then uncouth on the island. My parents had brought two English horses, a black and a bay, with them, for island horses were considered coarser flesh. But horses like Tom were fair enough for teaching children.

Until such time as we would be sent to England for our education, the Reverend Mr. Jones, the chaplain appointed to the island by the East India Company, who had a large family to support, would be our tutor.

This Reverend Mr. Jones was considered slightly odd because he felt his Church of St. Matthew, over in the direction of Plantation House, the governor's residence, was a rock of certitude attacked from two sides—not just from the direction of insufficiently reverent white inhabitants of the island, but from the paganism of the slaves as well. Major Hodson complained that he never preached on the text "Wives, be obedient to your husbands" or "Render unto Caesar the things that are Caesar's . . ."

In any case, Mr. Jones, at my parents' invitation, rode over to The Briars to visit Jane and me and quizzed us on our catechism, a few answers to which my mother had primed us with, but not sufficient to do more than annoy a clergyman who knew the entirety of it.

Mr. Jones had a strange way of showing his disappointment at the raw condition of our religious and civil education. He would sigh most frightfully and easily withdraw into sadness. Contradictorily, this little man with a furry head possessed eyes that blazed as if with evangelism in the midst of his resigned features. His only instrument of pedagogical violence was an ebony ruler he held, but it existed as a threat rather than an employed instrument of punishment. So it was the Reverend Jones who got us started on the Hebrew alphabet, beginning at the summit of scholarship and not in its foothills. I soon knew *aleph, beth, gamel,* before I properly knew A, B, C.

Under the shadow of our Bible studies and our growing acquaintance with the Hebrew alphabet, we learned to read of our own accord. I kept my eye on that ebony ruler and never wanted to come in contact with it, and Mr. Jones, having children of his own, was not affronted by some of my more eccentric questions.

"If you are teaching us, Mr. Jones," I asked, "who teaches your children?"

"My dear wife, of course," he said, but he did not want to enlarge on that gray, worn woman. He had been in the midst of telling us about the Council of Nicea and the great argument that had rejected a heretic named Arius. His appearance of disappointment became more intense as he continued, and loaded down his jaws, and he tapped his ebony ruler reflectively twice on the back of a chair. Meanwhile, I hoped he had explained all this shadowy theology to his own children and not imposed it on us alone. "But you have a school at the church," I said.

"Aye," he admitted. "But for yamstocks, and the children of slaves and freed slaves. The islanders and the slaves are so sunk in heathenism I would not have young women such as you share a classroom with them, nor would I have my children do it."

This fascinated me. Heathenism was a word with a red glare of allure around it.

"They believe, those others," Mr. Jones told us, "in the powers not of the bread and wine and body and blood of Christ, but in the worship of the myrtle tree, the tree of rebellion as the American revolt shows us, and they believe too in the spreading of chickens' blood. Even my sanctuary has been broken into, and I see the signs where they have placed their own pagan symbols—the blood, the leaves, and a pot in which a chicken's head is buried facing towards Mecca—all around the bier of a dead man."

"You should put guards on the door at night," said Jane.

I should tell you something about Jane. She was an earnest girl and would never achieve guile in her lifetime. That she had a more solid and admirable character than mine was obvious to me from my infancy and helped color my definition of my flawed state. Jane was a child from before the Fall. I seemed to be one from after that event. But once a vein of questioning was opened up for Jane, she was as willing to take advantage of it as any child would be.

"Oh, my dear young lady, the night watchmen themselves are frightened of ghosts and of the coming and going of the supposed priests and priestesses of the Malay and African religions."

"But why are there myrtle leaves?" I wanted to know. There were myrtle trees behind the house, but I had not suspected them of any magic.

"The myrtle is beloved by God since he grew it miraculously in the middle of the desert and the Israelites used it to make shelters.

But the Devil claims the myrtle too. He will always be defeated, yet he favors its leaves as if he needed them for very life. Through Christ, God has won the battle in your souls, since you have been baptized, and have a desire for the light. But there are those who seek salvation in myrtle leaves."

And so The Briars took on for me a dual condition. I wondered if Sarah and the two boys, and Toby and Ernest, believed in the myrtles as belonging to God or the Devil, as trees to be contested for, a battlefield unto themselves. I watched the slave boys at dinner, watched their white gloves, inspected Sarah's smile. There was no evil in them, and they did not go to the yamstock school anymore, and I hoped that when they saw the myrtle grove, they saw God.

I liked the doleful Reverend Mr. Jones, but while his counsels concerning myrtle made me merely careful, and obscurely excited me, they weighed on Jane in a way that began to interfere with her appetite and her dreams. The casual tap of the ebony stick against furniture could bring tears to her eyes, and to Mr. Jones's credit, he saw this.

"Why are you distressed, my child?" he asked.

We began to notice that our mother paced outside the window of the classroom, seemingly back and forth on some adult duty, but I realize she wanted to hear what Mr. Jones was saying. Perhaps Jane had confided her terror of the myrtle to her mother.

Soon he had us reading aloud sections of the New and Old Testaments, which were a more useful form of education, for the measures of the Bible were eloquent and of exquisite structure, and of use to a person for life (at least in conversation). We had begun by reading Revelation, a book that seemed to suit Mr. Jones's melancholy. ". . . wheat, and beasts, and sheep, and horses, and chariots, and slaves, and souls of men, and the fruits that thy soul lusted after, are departed from thee."

"Ah," he interrupted softly with a tap of his ruler, "why are slaves and horses and beasts equated together, when horses are especial animals and slaves are as human as are we?"

Of course neither Jane nor I could answer.

"Believe me," he told us, "it is God's irony. The rich man will be deprived of slaves because he sins by lusting after them. I must baptize the children of slave women. Where are their fathers? That is what I ask. Where are their fathers?"

He spoke as if to himself now, his conversation a private one in which Jane and I were eavesdroppers.

"You should thank God that your boy servants here were born before your father arrived, that they are some other man's sin . . ."

At this point my mother appeared at the classroom, or parlor, door.

"Mr. Jones," she said with a severity we could not understand. "I think you have strayed into areas that are not of use to my daughters' education. I wonder, may I speak with you?"

Mr. Jones looked at us with infinite sadness in his eyes. He turned to my mother. "Dear lady, please realize that if you report me to the Council of the East India Company, you will not be the first to have done so."

"I am not interested in reporting anyone," said my mother. "But I have noted a decline in at least one of my daughters." She stepped back into the hallway, and he squared himself off manfully and walked out into the corridor. I have been all my life a passionate overhearer, but did not want to be—for reasons I could not understand—that day.

The upshot was that Mr. Jones was dispensed with, said a polite goodbye to us, and rode away with his ebony ruler in a satchel hanging from the saddle of his rough-coated island horse.

My parents redoubled their efforts now to find a tutor, and advertised in Cape Town, and in the meantime my mother took up the task. She said, "I do not say that everything Mr. Jones taught you was wrong. But the Hebrew alphabet is more appropriate to students at Oxford and Cambridge than to you."

"And Arius?" I asked.

"Yes," she said, "that too. If you remember it all, well and good, but what he told you about slaves is rubbish. Look at Sarah! Does she seem unhappy or debased?"

We both agreed she didn't.

No one responded to my parents' advertisements, and we began our reading and mathematical tasks and occasional sums involving pennies and shillings, which my mother demonstrated with items of family revenue, showing us modest bills from Solomon's store in Jamestown and counting out the shillings and pennies in front of us. She began on French grammar, having enough French of her own to make it credible. I loved the language and used its words in the midst of my conversation. When my mother took us on rides, I called out to Robert and Roger, about whom Mr. Jones's remarks had been incomprehensible to me, "Bring round *mon cheval aussi*."

We had biblical readings but poetical ones as well, and I think my mother was rather a good teacher, but with a small boy to attend to, her classes became more and more haphazard.

Lack of educational
and social polish . . .

My mother's concerns about our lack of educational and social polish led to a bitter result. It was decided that Jane and I must return to England to attend an academy for young ladies.

My father wrote to a patron of his, Sir Thomas Tyrwhitt. Sir Thomas, of whom I came to hold certain conclusive but unprovable theories, was a fellow whose name was occasionally mentioned in our house because he had helped my father get his present position as superintendent of the East India Company stores and sales. He would run it by way of an entity in which two islanders, Messrs. Cole and Fowler, had invested. They were sleeping partners and rarely contacted my father. Sir Thomas had once been the secretary to the Prince Regent himself and thus was wisdom incarnate on every aspect of the social life of Great Britain. He was also, mysteriously, the supervisory and benign figure in my father's childhood and youth. He was like a potent deity, or interventionary saint, and we children accepted his distant and unseen power as a given fact of our lives. Apparently a reply came from Sir Thomas recommending an academy for the polishing of girls. It was located in distant Nottingham.

When I reached eight years and Jane ten, we were put aboard a ship under the care of a wife from the East India garrison who was returning to England permanently. I enjoyed the journey because I was the sort of child just forward enough to be the object of teasing affection. I liked to imagine I was one of *them*, a girl sailor: I began ascending the mainmast rigging on a bright, calm day, and was swiftly brought down and spoken to severely by the first mate, who nonetheless wore a suppressed smile.

I was a sea urchin by day, but became a frightened child at dusk and spent the nights at sea in Jane's arms in her narrow bunk, while my own was abandoned and grew cold. I had heard the woman who minded us speaking to other passengers about the prospect that we might encounter the French, but the blockade by our navy was so severe that they considered it an extreme unlikelihood. But for a child extreme unlikelihood had no force compared to the power of the imagination.

I barely remember London—we must not have put into the East India Dock, for I think it did not exist then. I remember a brisk departure from the city by coach with a young gentleman who worked for Sir Thomas and had a letter of welcome and advice written by our uncle, my father's brother, who worked as a clerk in the city somewhere. It became apparent that we lacked much of a Balcombe family in England—at least, no grandparents had presented (nor did we expect them), and no flow of aunts. And it seemed perfectly reasonable that a fellow of such importance as our uncle should not appear.

I had not been sick at sea, but was ill twice during the three-day journey to Nottinghamshire, where we arrived at last on a hill above a pretty market town named Mansfield. Here was the large, drafty house called the Academy for Young Ladies, owned by a woman named Miss Clarke. What wisdom had chosen this place for our betterment, we did not know. Miss Clarke, who was warm towards her pupils, believed that it was good for a girl's constitution to be acquainted with cold, and in the dormitories we became well acquainted with it. Since the academy was a large building with plentiful grounds—in which Miss Clarke took some pride—we were sent outside in all weathers to run and play. She believed in outlets for a girl's energies as being essential to enabling decorum at the times it was required. We were aware her theories were considered experimental by some.

My misery was illimitable, and was more intense as I could not comprehend the necessity my parents felt to subject me to all this. In the first night I crept across a hallway from my dormitory into my sister's bed, but one of the young lady instructors discovered me on her patrol on our third night. I was taken to a cupboard with a blanket and locked there for the rest of the night and, to emphasize the matter, for the next night as well. That second night seemed to stretch ahead infinitely. I had no light, and for consolation had to concentrate on a small gap at the bottom of the door along which a slightly bluer and more amiable form of darkness could be seen. I had whimpered the first night and began to whimper again the following one, and then I had a revelation, an angelic visitation—though I would not like to name which angel—that whimpering was not the right tack for me. It would satisfy the expectations of the dormitory mistress. The right ploy was not to creep and seek caresses or bleat. The right ploy was defiance. This was so obvious that I found it hard to understand why it had not occurred to me sooner.

It would be unjust, however, to depict Miss Clarke and her teachers as monstrous beings, though the principal and proprietor herself was contradictory. I saw her, with an air of practical and forthright kindness, bind up the chilblains that girls had acquired through play in the cold gardens and, during sleep, in the Arctic dormitories. Whether it was kindness to keep the girls of the academy in conditions encouraging to chilblains was a question she never asked.

So we began our introductory classes in Scripture, the basic principles of mathematics—algebra and trigonometry would have cost my parents more, and they had decided we would not need them—and fine needlework. My father had paid a premium on our fees to ensure we received instruction in French, dancing, and music. These three happened to provide the chief consolation of my days. My tendency to substitute French words for English ones amused the other girls. I was not subjected to mockery, since they could tell I would exact a notable, unpredictable price for it.

I became a determined and cunning delinquent, though more subtle than unruly. I would ask questions with feigned innocence. I once asked our Scripture teacher, was it true that Miss Clarke intended to let her go? The—in all senses—poor woman was angry, but above all fearful, and I was malignly satisfied. I was careful to sit in chapel by the sort of girl who in somber situations could be set off into hilarity by a mere dig in the ribs. I was a watchful rebel, took what I could, and, for the rest, kept myself warm with contempt. I did not evade complete censure and was frequently asked why I was not more like Jane. The question seemed to cause her more pain than me. Yet she was the one who seemed to be able somehow to sustain herself calmly through the chilled nights of the academy, whereas I still shed secret tears.

Miss Clarke and her ladies read our letters home and became aware that mine were a continual plea to my mother and father to let me come back. The delay with letters was not too great since many ships on their way to Cape Town and India put into Jamestown in those days. I could play the piano, I told my mother. I could read. I knew French, which was partly true and, by the time they received the letter, would have become even more of an accomplished fact. So I was ready to resume my island life.

As in any history of misery there were hopeful moments. We were permitted to march down to the town in two columns, like troops, as if to check on its defended condition in this era of war. We would proceed by the Buttercross market and on past the new weaving mills by the River Maun to the village of Market Warsop or to a hill nearby, from which we could see the grandeur of Newstead Abbey. Boney in Dieppe had his eye on such wonderful structures, said Miss Clarke; his heart yearned to get his troops to Nottinghamshire, but he was prevented from doing so by the merciful God of the Anglican Church and the valor of the Royal Navy. When some companies of the Nottingham Regiment paraded on the market square with their baggage train, I was quite surprised to be told that they were bound not for Dieppe, the center of the Bonaparte evil, but for Spain.

Old Boney was an immanence that did not frighten us much when we stood in daylight above the collieries and the threatened opulence of Newstead Abbey, but the thought of him was sufficient to raise night anxieties. If we were back on the island, I wrote to my parents, we would be far from Dieppe, where old Boney was.

Miss Clarke called me to her Spartan office, where the fireplace was unlit, and told me that my parents deserved more than to hear me plead for a return. It is a normal thing for girls who write letters to their parents, she told me, to comment on their studies, the subjects in which they are doing well, and the respect they have for their teachers. My next letter was fulsome and declared these things to excess and declared also that I did not know what I would do when the time came to leave the academy. I then sprinkled some water mixed with a little salt onto the letter and was confident my mother would realize that I had written it under coercion, and while in tears, and the lies I told were a measure of my distress, not of my happiness.

Jane, meanwhile, was put into the sick bay twice with congestive illnesses, and I was allowed to miss certain classes to sit with her and hold her hand. She would always be susceptible in this regard. I was happy for this form of sanctuary after making other girls laugh at the French mistress, and being caught and roughly shaken for satirizing the steps of the dance master. I rejoiced in the anguish in a strange way, as if I were proving to myself how uninhabitable the academy was. I was ordered into the closet again and told myself, in its unique air and coldness, that I was a night closer to liberation. It was meant to reduce me, but I would not be reduced.

Jane sometimes interceded for me and was allowed to take me into the garden and beyond, to the height above the river, so that she could remonstrate with me, beg me to show respect and remind me of the family honor. All that should have coerced a child but didn't coerce me. I did not want to placate the academy: I wanted to escape it. In that objective, I wrote my parents other letters than the ones I sent through official channels, and paid the gardener to post them.

"Mama, I am crying to you out of a deep pit," I told my mother in one such.

Christmas was a terrible day, spent at Miss Clarke's table with girls whose parents were in India and teachers who had no other home. Our uncle, whom we never met, sent us a brief message of greeting and a florin each.

How long, oh, Lord, how long? All through the residue of winter and the first buds of hawthorn—that was how long! Then a cold spring emerged and the promise of a lukewarm summer. An astonishing thing happened one day in late June when the young man representing Sir Thomas Tyrwhitt, the same one we'd met all those months before at the boat, appeared. He seemed rather more tubercular than he had earlier, which explained why, when dozens of his countrymen were risking themselves against Old Boney in Spain, or Dieppe, or wherever Old Boney was (Boney was in fact in Germany most of this time), he was able to pursue a nonmilitary life.

He told me that Sir Thomas and my uncle were rather disappointed in me. The irony was that, as he informed me of this, my mother was nursing a new baby brother of mine on the island and had christened him Thomas Tyrwhitt Balcombe, to honor the known and unspecified services that this great man had done my father at some stage. "And," the young clerk or aide told me, drawing in a breath, "there may be men of far greater eminence even than Sir Thomas who will hear of your behavior and be disappointed in you—those who are interested only in your education and yet have seen you behave like a Mohammedan towards it."

This proposition, that I offended men on high, was appalling. Yet there was in me a calm level at which I did not care as long as I was back on the island, where distance would reduce their voices to nothing. They had not tasted the island, the earth's center, the yardstick of what was to be desired. Nor were they here at Miss Clarke's. They did not understand what it was like. Above all, words break over an unhappy child like surf above a drowning person. They become irrelevant to her condition. She is below them, gasping and gulping.

"So," he ended, "I expect you to promise—"

"I will not promise, sir," I told him in a fury. "I do not make promises."

This was an impudence that so far exceeded any measurable scale that he asked, "Are you saying *that* to me? In saying that to me you are saying it to Sir Thomas Tyrwhitt, patron to your uncle and your own father!"

I had tears stinging in their ducts but maintained my drastic intention that they shouldn't flow even for such augustness. I told him I didn't want this level of education. I wanted to go home. Thank

God he left then, after some negative remarks, and I let my tears fall on the books open before me, on the Hittites and the Persians, on Darius and the great runner Pheidippides.

My mother would show me much later, for amusement's sake, the letter Miss Clarke had written both to her and to Sir Thomas Tyrwhitt laying down the proposition that I could not be educated. Her opinion, she said, was that had we lived in biblical times, the concept of satanic possession would perhaps have been invoked in my case, but it would have been excessive to pursue such ideas in these progressive times. As it was, my parents were advised to think of me as if I did not have a particular essential faculty, the equivalent to the power to talk or walk, and they must perhaps consider for me accordingly the sort of indulgence that is directed at those who carry a great handicap. They were pleased to understand, she exhorted them, that they should in no way consider me lacking in native cleverness. However, in me, obduracy was like a disease, and I would be permanently disabled by it unless some later recovery took place on my way to womanhood.

Sir Thomas Tyrwhitt's man arrived and accompanied me back to the south, to the house of some elderly people who at last claimed to be distant relatives of my father and who lived in Sussex near the Downs. I was allowed to go for walks with a young maid. The elderly relatives were benignly gruff and willing to leave me to my devices for the month I spent with them in their house near Lewes, cared for by a kindly housekeeper who kept two cats and a retriever.

Then the great Sir Thomas visited the house unexpectedly, on business. He wanted to see me in the company of the elderly relative, the slightly distracted householder. Sir Thomas himself was a very small man, for all his power, and carried himself like a victor, cheeks clear and chin raised above his stock, brown hair still in place atop his head.

He said to me, "So you could not take to school, Miss Balcombe?"

I wanted to say that school could not take to me, but for once, perhaps with a small surge from the dormant veins of wisdom within me, I did not. With a smile I never trusted, he told me that I was required to answer him directly.

"Sir," I said, "I want to go back to the island."

Sir Thomas and the elderly male relative exchanged looks. "The father's daughter then," Sir Thomas said, smirking. "Fit for islands and secluded posts."

Then he undertook a long study of me, one more extensive in its searchfulness, I thought, than there was material to justify it.

"Does it worry you," he asked me, "that you will grow up a savage?"

It didn't worry me at all. I said, "If it pleases you, sir . . . no!"

"And your sister Jane has been so happy at the academy."

"She has a bad chest because the academy is cold. But she is not impudent, sir."

He laughed drily and scanned the ceiling and returned large almond eyes to me. "Impudence is not a disease you catch," he told me, with his gnome-like infallibility. "Not like your sister's bad chest. It is a chosen condition. And you have chosen it. And now or later you should un-choose it, miss, if you do not want to be a savage on an island."

I could see that the dour but tender relative had put his head to the side like a questioning, honest hound, and was beginning to feel sorry for me. He said, "Perhaps the experiment could be tried again, Sir Thomas, in a year or two. Perhaps she will grow to be more like her sister. That sort of thing has been known to occur."

"I don't want to anger great men," I declared, in what would have been total bemusement, except for the fact that beyond this sea of humiliation and disapproval glimmered the island. It was a fit landscape for my fallen state. Surprisingly, this contrite or at least sincere utterance seemed to disarm Sir Thomas. His laughter at it sounded authentic and no longer a form of judgment.

"I found you," he said, "the wife of an East India Company garrison surgeon on her way to India by way of the island. She will look after you on the voyage back."

And so I had achieved my aim through defiance, and on the island I would be saved by distance from the disappointment of great men. I was allowed to write to Jane and ask her to forgive me for being so bad and leaving her behind. She wrote back declaring herself quite happy for the time being to stay with Miss Clarke. She existed there, after all, in a comfortable net of admiration woven of teachers and other pupils alike.

Sir Thomas's tubercular young man took me to Portsmouth in a carriage and I returned home on a naval vessel of seventy-two guns, a most sleek ship that would achieve the passage in seven weeks. Aboard, I met the surgeon's wife, who had two girls younger than me and to whom I knew at once I must be kind and companionable. For the woman meant me nothing but good and was very handsome in a darker, watchful, ample way. Her name was Mrs. Amie Stuart; she was Canadian-French and had met her husband, Surgeon Stuart, on what she called "the Nova Scotia station," where Stuart had supervised the hospital of the naval squadron and the garrison. I learned her unmarried name was Troublant and heard her speaking in French to her two young daughters—the older of whom, the six-year-old, shared a cabin with me. At a specially blocked-off table in a mid-ship saloon, a rare enough thing in a ship of war, we all spoke French, and it was from her tuition that I learned much more of the language, reading from her daughters' primers and from French histories of the Angevin Age or of Charlemagne she had in her possession.

On the morning we at last stood in the Jamestown Roads and waited to be taken ashore in the cutter, I did not feel that there were so many grounds now for men of great power to be disappointed in me, and in any case their disappointment was remote. Admittedly, my French was only partially accomplished, but what I had, I somehow had to the full, in a way that promised future and perfect facility if I simply pursued my native interest.

I had composed an address to my parents, who, I knew, would be at the pier. They were not the kind of people who exercised punishment by absenting themselves from the ritual of welcoming one of their children. There might be chastisement later in the day, but I was confident enough in their affection to know that whatever had been communicated about me, however my character had been traduced, it would be swallowed up in their relief at seeing me again.

So it happened. I came ashore with Mrs. Stuart and her two girls, and when I climbed up to the dock from the cutter I found my mother and father. They looked to me like all I desired: abundance and forgiveness and repatriation—as if I had survived a battle and were to be celebrated for it. Sarah was there, carrying my plump new brother, Thomas Tyrwhitt, and it would turn out that Mother was pregnant with baby Alexander. My enlarged family seemed to promise an enlargement of the terms of life. It was 1811, I would soon be ten, and I was home for an indefinite future. My mother thanked Mrs. Stuart and invited her to The Briars, then knelt and said, "Oh, my Betsy," and took Thomas Tyrwhitt Balcombe from Sarah and enclosed my new brother and me in one long-armed hug.

In the shadow of the warehouse of Fowler, Cole, and Balcombe, I uttered my first long French salutation, and I could see that it eased something in my father's fraught eyes. He said to my mother, pointing to me, "You see, Jane. We are what we are, and in that we may well be superior to those who seek to tut about us."

Mrs. Stuart and the girls were to stay overnight with us, in the house, not in the Pavilion. They were astounded by the journey from Jamestown up the precipitous terraces to The Briars, where the girls and I ran madly on the lawn and called out in French to each other. We stumbled for lack of land legs, and the two Stuart children still had far to travel, through rough waters, which would be succeeded by torpid ones, and then India. Late the following afternoon, they were warned by a seaman sent from the ship that they should be prepared to get aboard, for the captain intended departure as soon as favorable.

We went down with them, and returned to the interior of the island in the near-dark, and I informed my mother of the Medes and Persians, for her pleasure at what I *had* learned outweighed the displeasure of the so-called greater folk who hadn't liked my English performance at all. My parents were delighted to find that I was willing to stay in the parlor of The Briars for three hours a day absorbing books. I engorged *The Pilgrim's Progress* and thought it a very sensible religious fable indeed. I delighted in *The Vicar of Wakefield*, and the humanity and sense of the vicar, Dr. Primrose. My mother was busy with Thomas, and had trouble finding a wet nurse for him amongst the slaves of the island, which was extremely bad luck given their rate of pregnancy and the fact that it was known their milk was plenteous. Sarah was on daily watch to report the birth of a slave baby or the sad death of one, and thus the emergence of a potential nurse.

Meanwhile, I had heard my father complain to my mother, "What will happen when these girls no longer live on the island, Jane? I would like to see them lead a fuller life, and exercise fuller skills." But he was a man easily comforted, and I continued with my own education, reading occasional French novels my mother borrowed, with strong assurances of their propriety, from Mrs. Wilks, the wife of the governor of the East India Company, or from the bookish wife of the commander of the East India Company artillery.

My mathematics remained serviceable for daily use. I could not have made a sextant reading, but was happy to leave navigation to officers of the Royal Navy. My self-education in music advanced, and when I applied myself to the spinet in the drawing room I found myself naturally impelled towards making music. One of the first songs I could fluently play—and sing in full—was "Ye Braes and Banks of Bonnie Doon." It spoke to me so powerfully and melodically of losses I could not understand yet instinctively knew I might suffer at some time.

Jane returned to the island the following summer. The family was complete and little Thomas Tyrwhitt so charming we used to play with him as he sat on a rug in the garden, he making speeches in the language of infancy, we answering him in French and English and always indulgent. Soon, it seemed, he was joined by Alex, of questioning eye and roguish smile. A decent fortress seemed our family on the island of St. Helena. The education of the Balcombe girls was marked by fits of well-meaning parental supervision, and my father was exercised by the new question of who would educate his sons.

When I was twelve years, Boney fell from his height of power. That was a distant drumbeat. And he returned from an exile and imposed himself on Europe once more. But this was an irrelevance to the rock we inhabited amidst the primeval waters.

The last day of
my accustomed life . . .

One day when I had reached the uncertain age of thirteen, I went off on Tom the horse, with Jane on her horse, riding at my mother's insistence with a lady's saddle, which while it sat aboard the creature also cleverly prevented women from riding astride. When I reached home on the last day of my accustomed life, the life I wanted, I spotted in the V in the mountains a ship newly anchored in the roads, with a few lumpy store-ships I had seen around it the day before. This new ship was a sloop, fast and sleek.

By the time I reached the house and had taken Tom to the stable and put him in the care of Ernest, I found that there were two naval gentlemen on the verandah speaking urgently to my father. My mother was there with little Alex in her arms and she intercepted me. Her face was aglow, and when I asked her what was happening she said she did not know, but something was wholly out of the ordinary. In fact, from that point on, we would never know the ordinary again.

And yet she asked me, in her innocence, "We need something a little unusual, don't we, Betsy?"

Her full smile transcended her fraught condition, the inroads made on her tranquillity by baby colic, and Jane's occasional asthma. I thought then with some amazement that the island might not be to her what it was to me: sufficient. Now, in any case, she confided in me, "Those gentlemen are officers from the frigate *Icarus*. They have come ahead of their squadron."

At last my father asked the two officers to sit down. My mother and I passed indoors, but she called to Sarah to go and ask if the gentlemen wanted anything. We could see from the drawing room that they asked for brandy and water, but they also went on talking at length.

In the remnants of the dusk, they sat at the table in the garden as the two boys in white gloves served them their refreshment, and then after some time both officers went off on the horses they had hired or been loaned in town. My father, etiquette's child, waved them out of sight from the carriage gate before bounding across the lawn and up the steps and into the house.

"Jane," he called out. "Jane!" We were all instantly in the corridor.

"I have a very large provisions order before me," said my father. "I should tell you that. I have a *very large provisions order.*"

And then his florid face broke into giggles like a schoolboy's. He had not a malicious crease in his whole face, and later I would wish he had some armor against the world. "Very large," he declared, choking on laughter. "You wouldn't believe . . ."

"Tell us, for dear Heaven's sake," asked my mother.

"I am to provision the party, the entourage, the suite of the Emperor Bonaparte."

My mother laughed at this—it was hilarious to all of us—and said, "On what invasion is he now embarked?"

And my father said, "Why, it's the invasion of our own island. Of St. Helena!"

These propositions were beyond our powers to accommodate. We stood stupefied. I could hear my sister Jane breathing earnestly.

And he said, "That was exactly how I felt, that such outcomes were too great for our geography. But those two gentlemen who rode away . . . they have warned me that the Great Ogre of Europe is two days off, aboard the *Northumberland*, Admiral Cockburn's flag aboard, Captain Maitland commanding. They are coming *here*. And I am to be the provedore to the entire party of Bonaparte and not only that . . . But that is enough for now!"

"But what is such a being doing here?" asked my mother.

"The captain . . . the man who just left . . . he told me that this is to be a new Elba. The Ogre is to be placed halfway between Europe, Africa, and South America. This is the deepest pocket they could find to put the Universal Demon in."

"Then he is very lucky," I, St. Helena's greatest patriot, asserted.

My father said, with a laugh I can hear down the years, "And it is more than that, more than that."

"It can't be him," said my mother. "Does he even exist?"

It was as if her world were becoming glutted with more meaning than she wanted it to contain.

"The gentlemen tell me that his intended residence here on the island is not ready."

"But surely that would be Plantation House?" This was the congenial English-style house where Governor Wilks administered the island on behalf of the East India Company.

"Oh, no, that is reserved for the governor, by specific order of the British Cabinet. They are building the Ogre a house at Longwood. Or they intend to."

And we all said, "Longwood?"

Longwood was a mix of farm buildings off to the eastern end of the island—not so far from us, in fact, and yet in the zone of blightedness. The northern, western, and southern ends of the island were delicious with plantations and places where the arid and the verdant played with each other harmoniously. Longwood was where the fun stopped: a series of poor farmhouses and cow byres belonging to, originally occupied, and then neglected by Major Skelton, lieutenant governor. Now they were going to combine these into a residence for the Great Ogre, said my father. But until then, the naval gentlemen had asked, could the Emperor use the Pavilion in our garden?

This was like inquiring whether Zeus might use our grape arbor. But my mother asked, reasonably enough, "Did you say yes?" She did so, I remember, in a way that acknowledged there must be some danger in saying yes to such an explosive commodity.

"Of course," said my father. "Of course I said yes. This extraordinary man of destiny!"

Men talked like that about the Great Ogre, even though we had gone to such national anguish and expenditure of blood to stop him. He was still "this extraordinary man of destiny."

"And an enemy of England," said my mother. And we all became quiet.

"There is a line regiment that will come ashore to guard us," said my father.

This was too vast an item of news to be digested. Boney from Dieppe? Who wanted to stay in the Pavilion? It was apparent, if you could believe it, that Jamestown would be like Lilliput, with the giant landing amongst us, and we holding him in place by our combined flimsiness. Except that Gulliver had been a decent fellow, and this was Boney from Dieppe. And he was to stay in *our* Pavilion. To stay like men who aren't extraordinary? To sit. To sleep. To eat food with a fork?

The improbability made me dizzy. My mother set Sarah and the twins to clean the Pavilion.

My father told us when he came home the next day that the town had been crowded, though there was nothing in sight, no naval squadron, no *Northumberland*. People had come to town simply to test out what it was like when such a vast possibility lay close to our horizons. They knew that bearing south on them was the force of Europe, the bull Europa fell in love with, up against our plainness and the geologic fastness of our cliffs. Thank the dear Lord at least for the latter.

ADVENT

Unkind to those
who sought sleep . . .

The night before the arrival was warm and moonlit and unkind to those who sought sleep, given that the crowds of constellations seemed to pause above us, as if to herald the most exceptional day that was coming, its dread and wonder and melancholy. We were awakened the next morning by the usual ragged fusillade from the guns atop Ladder Hill. Sound sleepers could remain unconscious through this dawn thunder, but none of us had been sound sleepers that night. We rode down to the town the next morning, hastening on the way, I ahead at what my mother considered an unwise canter. The island and the town and the familiar hills seemed new, as if a certain pulse of the earth had created them afresh. We had left the babies, Thomas and Alex, with Sarah, and William, now seven, rode in front of my father's saddle.

When we got there, the town appeared struck by a kind of dread. A squadron of newly arrived ships crowded the water. The question was, how could that massive advent be contained in Jamestown's narrow span?

Little more than thirty steps from the East India Company dock were my father's warehouse and his office. A crowd was gathering along and around the dock, and the East India Company gunners ignored their cannon on the height and were looking down the terraces for the apparition.

Early in the day, as we watched from the windows of my father's office, everything—any signal from an island official, any sign of activity

53

on the largest warship that was said to contain the Ogre—fascinated us and churned our stomachs. A shore party of sailors landed from a cutter, and from them everyone wanted to know the entire subtle history of the Ogre's transportation to the island. Boatload by boatload a regiment landed in red coats with black facings and pipe-clayed belts and fresh-laundered breeches and elegant black-and-white leggings, and every soldier who clambered up the steps drew heightened cheers.

The numeral 53 was on the soldiers' collars, and this number evinced more interpretations in the crowd than even the cabalists of Poland could bring to bear on a five and a three in combination. The soldiers of "53" formed up in the main street of the town, while their band stayed at the dock and played a medley of patriotic airs. Company by company they continued to land, doubling the population of the island in three or four hours. Some of the young officers, waiting for their horses to come ashore on barges, bowed to us in our window at the warehouse, a few so extravagantly that it was like a dance step: one foot before the other, a movement whose rhythm looked very French, as if in conquering that nation they had seized its habits as well. Their swords rose high behind them as some tried to get their head down to the level of their knees. It struck me for the first time that the English had won the military battle but the French had conquered English bluntness by imposing on it certain affectations. Older officers, more weary of foreign parts and customs, were satisfied merely to salute.

My father stayed at the window with us, for the young men were flamboyant with Jane and me, and full of compliments, and it was clear that he did not want us to be toyed with on such an overheated day for the imagination. So he introduced himself, and occupied them in talking about their recent service.

They were a Shropshire regiment, and people called them for some reason the Brickdusts, and these younger men could have been with them only for the last year or so of the war, advancing through the Pyrenees to the last battle at Toulouse—the young men, boys plus a year or two, were willing to mention Toulouse, as if it were there that they had learned the scope of the world and the intersection between military plumage and carnage. They told us it would be a time before we sighted the Great Ogre. First they would be marched to Deadwood barracks, they told us, where they would set up the rudiments of their camp, and return to town that afternoon to line the way for Old Boney.

"Have any of you spoken to him?" asked my father.

"We were not encouraged to, sir," said a forthright young man. He was an angel of war, as they all were. Their faces and bodies seemed made for their uniforms in some cases, and others were recent to the ranks and the reverse could have been said of them.

"But we've seen him once or twice, sir," said another. "However, we were not on his ship."

"*Northumberland?*" asked my father.

"Yes. But we rowed over there for a visit midocean. The colonel knew we all wanted to get a sighting of him."

A young man who could not have been more than eighteen and whose uniform seemed massive and drooping, his epaulettes hanging down his arms, declared, "He seemed very pensive, sir." This stylish and gestural young man we would get to know later as Lieutenant Croad. Another, older subaltern declared, "Yet in his mood he can be very jolly indeed. Very jolly nearly to a fault. I mean, a man who has set Europe by the ears . . . does he have the right to be jolly? I don't know, sir."

Then commands were shouted and the fifes began again and they were off, and people cheered them out of town and up the terraces. Wagons and slaves carrying impedimenta made a banal tail to the advance of the 53 men into the interior. The air of the spring afternoon grew dense now. The mood of the crowd was occasionally revived when this or that braided naval officer came ashore, tight-featured from the day's tension, from the business of conveying history's Demon to this little socket in the midst of the ocean.

A man my father identified as Admiral George Cockburn landed with his aides, and Mr. Porteous came out of his boardinghouse, the Portions, and shook his hand and took him to that establishment which was deemed the finest hotel of the island, with its big bulk and its narrow balconies—the place that most gentlemen stayed. Porteous had a daughter of fourteen named Adela, whom I despised, and she pranced on the edge of the group. The admiral and his party went into the house.

"So, he is staying at the Portions tonight," said my father.

I was relieved that the weight of the phenomenon had been lifted for now from the Pavilion's slender frame and from mine.

Soon after, Governor Wilks turned up at the same door on horseback and dismounted, and he too went in with an earnest tread.

My father claimed, "He's gone to say, 'You can't put poor Boney up at Porteous's place tonight. Bring him over to Plantation House.'"

We saw Miss Esther Solomon and her mother, both wearing mantua lace, witnessing things from the dock near the warehouse, and they called up to us and invited us home for tea. I was reassured by Esther's laughter; it was a comfort, a girl who was not argued out of her sameness by the scale of events. My father said to go with the Solomons, for all activity had slackened now, as if the deity was not coming. There were no further boats from the ships. History had frozen on its path.

The Solomons were the chief shopkeepers of the island; some people complained about their prices and—in the same breath—their Jewishness. But my father admired Mr. Solomon as a man of decent repute, and my father of all people knew the high price goods achieved on their way to our island. Mr. Solomon was something of a scholar too, and had a fine library, and on top of that produced the island's news sheet, whose next installment would of course be devoted to the general enthusiasm for, and the arrival of, the monster.

We went and drank tea with Mrs. Solomon and her daughter Esther in their house above the Solomon establishment, in which Mr. Solomon had throughout the day attended levelheadedly to the needs of come-to-town householders and farmers combining their purchases with standing in the foreshadow of the colossus. The furnishings where we sat were very somber and the curtains of deep damask or velvet, and silverware and the candlestick of seven separate candles—a Jewish mystery—stood on the sideboard.

Suddenly it was darker, for it got dark early in this slot in the cliffs. The sun was still high enough for most places and, no doubt, still shone on The Briars.

"Surely soon," said Miss Solomon.

Into that afternoon torpor came, with fast steps on the Solomon stairwell and appearing in the door, Adela Porteous. On her reddish complexion there sat a layer of sweat. She was a girl of neat bones and a confidence I did not know how to imitate but passionately wished I could. I know she thought me crass or stupid or vile, and I had been told to be wary of her by Esther herself. Adela also seemed, ridiculously, to think that because we lived in the hinterland we were somehow debased, and it was true that a lot of Jamestown's gossip was about improprieties, references that sometimes surpassed my understanding, in the inner reaches of the island.

Something else had stimulated her today, though, and she was willing to include the Balcombes in what she had to say to the Solomons. She gasped twice to show that this was not normal island news.

"My father found out this morning that Boney and his Frenchies are to be accommodated at our place. The admiral has arranged it. We are all in a confusion, with the maids, stupid creatures, and the slaves who think Boney is an incarnate devil, and men moving some of our best furniture into the chambers where Boney will stay. We'll have detachments of guards on the door to save us from being murdered in our beds."

"I thought that the Ogre was staying with us," said my mother.

"Oh, I don't know about the future," said Miss Porteous airily. "But the Portions will be first!" She shivered theatrically. "Thank God for the soldiers."

"Wouldn't their first task be to guard against General Bonaparte's escape?" asked my mother, who had a clear disdain for this boastful news. I believe we were suddenly quite jealous my mother and I. Even in the midst of our fear of this grand advent, we wondered why a vapid girl like Adela had such prime and casual proximity to the Ogre. Besides, visitors who came to The Briars always exclaimed what a relief it was after the cramped Portions. Something in us wanted to hear that sentiment from the lips of the Ogre.

Any further conversation with the breathless girl was cut short by the sound of the returning band leading a regiment who had seen Spain and Toulouse and left their dead brothers on that alien ground, and had gone up to pitch tents on Deadwood Plain. There was a determined, far-from-routine booming from the cannon up the many-stepped ladder above the town's roofs, and answering fusillades from the Castle Terrace. Soldiers lined up either side of Main Street and you could hear the thunderous smartness of their boots in the heavy air.

We stood up from the teacups and walked downstairs, proceeding behind the backs of the lined-up infantry, Miss Porteous, mouth agape with her grin of anticipation on her way to her father's balcony; and we set off towards the warehouse where, to return the Solomons' kindness, we had offered mother and daughter a view from the window of our father's office.

We found his clerks had crowded into that office too, and the business of the world had ceased. All attention was directed on the great experiment that would begin when the Ogre trod on the first step of the dock. Would the island sink under the weight of his deeds and crimes, the weight of the decisions he had brought down on Europe?

There were two naval surgeons there, in our warehouse, Surgeon Warden and Surgeon O'Meara, and my father seemed to know them already, given his talent for bonhomie. It was the first time I saw Surgeon O'Meara, with his piquant Irish face, eternally amused with an irony lacking in ill will, and acute in his judgments . . . though I am rushing things—I would find all that out only after a time.

The more clerkly Surgeon Warden declared of the Ogre, "He likes band music. I don't think he has an ear for more delicate airs. He used to ask for the regimental band to play him patriotic tunes, and ours—not theirs."

"And the thing that astonishes me," the Irishman joined in, "is that the French do everything backwards from our point of view. The Emperor, he prowls the deck by night, and sleeps late. And then what does the man do but demand a large breakfast full of all manner of things we would consider appropriate for supper—even chickens we collected in Tenerife. And he imbibes claret with it! In the evening he champs down a brisk little meal, no lingering over the plate and taking a sip or two of wine. The man's virtue exists at the wrong end of the day."

"That wouldn't suit me," my father asserted.

"It doesn't suit the wardroom, let me tell you," said Dr. Warden. "Your average naval officer likes a long dinner more than your average citizen."

They seemed delighted to have license to off-load their items of witness on solid ground, for this passage to our island had transcended all the passages they had ever made, even in the time of war. The afternoon stretched until its warmth had utterly congealed in Main Street and the sun was being lost from the eastern precipice above the town and the Castle Terrace. Still the Ogre's cutter didn't leave the *Northumberland*.

The gossip of the two men moved on to the man's entourage, the subdemons. There was Count Bertrand, loyal and sensible, O'Meara said, and his wife—a tall lump of a woman, the daughter of an Irish general who had fled to France in disaffection. He should have fled again but was caught by the Terror of the Revolution and Robespierre beheaded him. The Revolution was incarnated in the general, perhaps, said O'Meara, but he had hated the Terror and thus Fanny Bertrand was herself also a disciple of the Great Ogre and Universal Demon.

When her husband, Bertrand, had decided that it was necessary for him to be with the Ogre, so it became necessary for her. "She is a good wife," declared O'Meara, "if one with her own opinions. A big, raw Irish girl." This was an unknown woman we might or might not sight within the span of the remaining hours of light.

It was from these gentlemen too that I first heard the names of Count de Montholon and his wife—"Looks meek but would fight a tiger with a twig," as O'Meara summarized her—and of their small son, Tristan. De Montholon himself, as a child cadet, had been taught the principles of artillery by an older cadet—yes, Emperor-to-be. So he was solidly loyal too, and his wife, though pregnant and not in the best of health, was less noisy about her destiny than the Countess Bertrand. Albine de Montholon, the surgeons told us, sang Italian tunes, the kind the Emperor liked, in a high voice that seemed strange at first but became appealing.

A chamberlain of middle years named Las Cases, and his son, Emmanuel, were also in the party of French, and then, said the surgeons, "there's Gaspard Gourgaud." They didn't get round to describing Gourgaud, except for both of them to toss their heads in an eloquent way. They gave us no clue to his nature or the register of his voice, and the same applied to the chamberlain Las Cases and his son.

For they were now interrupted. I saw the two surgeons stand stiffly and formally, and then in the doorway their tall admiral and behind him a large woolly-haired dog.

"This is ridiculous, Balcombe," said the admiral, as if my father and he were intimates. "It is Balcombe, isn't it? You provisioned me four years back. Remember? Yes, you remember."

My father of course said how pleasant it was to remake the admiral's acquaintance. Indeed, had he been here alone, had every islander's expectation not been fixed on, to use O'Meara's term, the Universal Demon, Cockburn's advent would have been considered momentous, though in a normal way, a way that did not threaten to sink the island under the weight of its own significance.

"The map we were given," said the admiral, as the Balcombe and Solomon women stared at him stupefied, "suggests that a fit dwelling for Bonaparte would be Plantation House or else the Castle across the way. Now I'm told that this has all been ruled against by a higher power. Poor Wilks himself is embarrassed by it all."

My father coughed a little and said, "Some of your officers visited my house . . ."

"Yes. I shall point it out to the General when we ride out. I have heard good things of it, Balcombe. But for the moment there's Porteous's establishment. Looked it over earlier. Not of an appropriate standard! But what can be done?"

We were all quite impressed at the Castle, a structure of some pretended grandeur that stood on a terrace above Jamestown. At the top of the opposing steep cliff stood the most handsome house other than The Briars on the island, Plantation House, a "country seat" style of house, squirely, large-gardened and in kindlier territory towards the South American side. Both had been denied to the island's improbable visitor. The Great Ogre and all those counts and their children and two countesses and a further grand figure and his son seemed to have no other option than to become boardinghouse inmates.

As we waited, the sentinels on the dock and all the way up the street remained silent, but there was an eloquent hubbub from the crowd and it mounted now because, after a day of waiting, the party of all parties was declared to have left the *Northumberland*. Eyeglasses were screwed to eye sockets, but my father felt the necessity of offering his to the admiral.

"No, thank you, Balcombe," said the admiral softly. "I know our visitor's features very well."

So it was my father who swung the glass over the roads and the late afternoon meeting between air and light and water, and was the first of us to report he was sure he could see the man, in green coat, amongst others in the midst of the cutter. The glass was then passed for verification to everyone in turn—my mother, Mr. Solomon, who had closed his store by now and joined us, Mrs. Solomon, Jane, me, Miss Esther Solomon, and on to my sweaty little brothers.

I could not see anything during my turn—the high color of the moment made my hold on the thing skittish, but if I found the cutter for an instant, the light swell in the roads lifted it out of my sight. I wanted anyhow to see the corporeal Emperor with the naked eye, not distorted, flattened, and hazed by distance and the imperfection of lenses. As I waited and others exclaimed, "I see, I see!" I closed my eyes for half a minute at a time, in a sort of dread but in the most intense and aching curiosity I have ever felt.

The admiral excused himself to go down and greet the Emperor on the landing.

The dread that seized the port in that instant was not only for the man's devilish reputation, not only for the fact that he was the Great Ogre, but once more that his tread would rock the earth, and that the escarpments above Jamestown would shatter, and boulders the size of God's hand would descend on the town's humble roofs. Many indeed must have felt like that, since when the cutter was not so far off, the crowd, which had been vocal all day, grew near to silence, and what had been shouts became whispers, and as the air grew reverent and fearful I noticed near the archway to Main Street, behind the dock and the little bridge, an island character named Old Huff. Old Huff was an English gentleman and something of a scholar, enduring exile—it was said—at his family's demand, to expiate some offense committed when he was young. My father had recently employed him to tutor my sister and me occasionally, but especially my younger brothers, William, Thomas, who was five, and Alex, who was nearly four. Now, eccentrically dressed, slightly mad-haired, Huff dropped to his knees and raised a pained, reverent face to Heaven as if it was from the clouds that the Ogre would reveal himself.

"Old fool," I heard my mother whisper. "Someone should send him home for his own good."

For his posture was that of a papist in front of a saintly statue, not of a sensible man.

My father murmured, "Always odd," and then, after a while, "but erudite."

No one came up to trouble Old Huff for his excessive reverence and try to drag him upright. The silence, if anything, intensified and one heard the bump of the cutter against the buffers of the stone dock, and after a few seconds, feet could be heard ascending the step of the dock. A banal British naval officer and coxswain were seen first. We had beheld figures like these two all day and so were disappointed.

But then the Ogre appeared, revealing himself step by step, a fellow of unremarkable or even diminutive height, but with a marked ceremonial walk. He wore the same hat that was depicted in all the cartoons of Boney, his green coat with white facings, and over his vest a sash with one single vast starlike decoration, its symbols and validity as mysterious as, say, a headdress of the Incas. And he had a paunch. His breeches and knee boots were unremarkable. He stood on the stone dock and looked about at Jamestown's architecture and the cliffs that so aggressively contained the modest town. Thus he read the geography we already knew by heart. How we all wished in that second that we had something vaster, something of metropolitan or imperial scale, to present him with.

He waited in that spot with the naval officer standing by, and the old admiral, his dog at his heels, greeted him and bowed to him, even though they knew each other so well from the voyage, and they exchanged salutes, and the admiral moved his hand towards the inland, offering the Emperor the hospitality of the place.

Others arrived on the dock. There was a serious-looking man wearing a brown morning suit. His combed black hair did not quite cover his brow. At his shoulder was a boy about my age, a miniature version of the unimpressive father, dressed identically in brown, outfitted by the very same tailor with the very same cloth. The father led his son and they stood with purpose by the admiral, as though the father—Las Cases?—perceived himself to be an intermediary between the big naval Englishman and the Great Ogre. Then a tall, well-fleshed woman with her little boys, and a diminutive, plump woman, also with a young son, appeared and stood gracefully on the dock after the months they had been at sea since their capture. No sooner did they reveal themselves than we saw they were dazzling, long-necked women, the diminutive one in a gown of russet roses on white and with a vivid green shawl on her shoulders, the taller, apparently the half-Irish woman Fanny of whom O'Meara had spoken, in blue and saffron. "They are court dresses," my mother whispered with assurance and uncertainty at once. Both wore about their shoulders long necklaces of cameo and gold. Veils framed their faces, but I could tell that Madame de Montholon's was oval and dark. Their husbands, one neatly made (Bertrand, the grand marshal, as it turned out) and his colleague de Montholon, wore uniforms of a bluer hue, their jackets severely cut away from higher than the navel and long-tailed behind, all of it saying most emphatically, "French! French! Alien!" A fussy young officer in frogged green jacket and the hat they called a "shako" was the last and edged himself amongst the others till he was close to the Emperor.

"He wore that coat to Moscow and back," whispered O'Meara, pointing to the Emperor's uniform.

Women in the crowd were voluble, but in whispers, discussing the exiled women's clothes, full-bosomed, high-waisted, sweeping down, a cut that, they told each other, as we did at the warehouse, as if to exempt ourselves from competing, only the French could achieve. This mixture of the natural and the elegant, even in their hairstyles, seemed beyond the skills of the island. They were exquisite. The smaller one seemed the more classically so and had that gift women talk about of "carrying things off." The strangeness of the newcomers was such that they might have come not from another country but from another star.

It was time to begin some progress from the dock, and Admiral Sir George Cockburn, accompanied by his dog, and the senior officers of the regiment, raised their hats to the Emperor with a broad gesture. The Emperor, frowning, unsettled his own black hat on his brows. The regiment was stridently ordered to present arms, and did it.

They, the powers of the earth, still allowed the Ogre to wear his sword, my father observed, and we were astounded, since that sword had dominated the Continent and could easily dominate eight miles by five. "That is the sword he wore at Waterloo," the Irishman told us.

I wondered was it so or if the surgeon was exaggerating his intimate knowledge of the man's garments and accoutrements.

"We look upon the habiliments and the implements of great histories," O'Meara reminded us, though he did not need to.

We all gazed. "You see that little man in the green uniform, the young one with the exceptional hat atop?" O'Meara hissed. "That fellow would volunteer to be the Demon's literal shadow if the laws of physics permitted such a thing. And, like most French generals, he's scarcely a year my senior. A general named Gourgaud! Could you imagine a fellow like that, that size, that age, a restricted intelligence for that matter, commanding thousands?"

My mother said, "He is not much smaller than the Emperor."

O'Meara conceded, "Yes, that is acutely observed, madam." He beamed as if proud of her. "But the Emperor is the Emperor. Sure, this crowd around the Emperor are baby generals—you see Bertrand, a man now of decent age but a general when a child, and de Montholon—generals before they were out of their swaddling clothes. It's the way the Emperor's always done things."

I could make out Gourgaud maneuvering to be close to his master, with the tall figures of the Bertrands bulking behind him.

For those of us who had waited the entire day, it was an exotic procession that now took place. The Emperor was escorted by Admiral Cockburn and that gentleman's huge dog, and the colonel of those who wore the number 53. The slight general, Gourgaud, followed as close to Napoleon's spine as if he actually wished to assassinate him or prevent someone with the imminent intent to do so. Behind them trod the trim figure of Bertrand with their little girl, Hortense, and his wife with her hands out to their two little boys, using no nursemaid for the purpose this afternoon, for surely no nursemaid would be adequate to the experience of these children. The chamberlain and his son followed, the son with his head thrust forward as if to study the earth now he had been reunited with it. General de Montholon supported his wife by the elbow as if she were lame. A French maid followed, holding by the hand the son of Madame de Montholon, Tristan, a handsome boy of five or six.

Our curiosity was endless, and the procession had not satisfied it when the admiral and the colonel stood by the door of the Portions to allow the Ogre the first entry into that honest but very ordinary establishment.

From our position we could see, just inside the door, the gleam of Mr. Porteous's bald head, and it rose and fell, rose and fell again, doing the Great Ogre serious honor, more than he would later be instructed by the representatives of the British government to offer. The Emperor vanished from sight. So did the rest of his stately and fashionable suite, and Miss Porteous was now reduced to waving to the crowd. A sergeant's guard moved into the doorway of the boardinghouse, but it did seem that their task was not to keep the Ogre in but the crowd out.

We fell back again on the gossip of the surgeons, O'Meara and Warden, and they were willing to rehearse various scenes aboard the *Northumberland*. Previously the Emperor had been on another vessel of war, named the *Billy Ruff'n* or more correctly the *Bellerophon*. It was there that he wrote his appeal to the Prince Regent asking that he be let live as a private person in the English countryside. He received no response. Aboard the *Northumberland*, the news about his being consigned to our island had become definite. The Emperor had sickened straightaway, and it had taken him a week of seclusion in his cabin, with his valet Marchand as his chief company, to recover.

There was some talk between my mother and Mrs. Solomon about Countess de Montholon's magnificence and the statuesque appearance of Countess Bertrand and the dignity with which she had progressed with her two children, looking over the heads of the populace, refusing to be weighed by the eyes of the St. Hélènes and the yamstocks. But the only new thing added was an aside by O'Meara, addressed to Jane and myself. He welcomed us into an exchange of views by extending his arms. "Be careful of General Gourgaud," he warned us. "He kept on asking me whether the island has any *femmes jolies*, and I am delighted to say that you Balcombe girls are as *jolie* as would be required by any island or, I do not flatter you, any continent."

O'Meara did flatter us, of course, and we were both flustered and excited by this compliment. He withdrew his arms and stood straight and returned to conversing with our parents. We noticed Huff was still on his knees, though somehow he had moved around to face the Porteous place, into which the object of his veneration had passed. No one disturbed him, the soldiers thinking he was the town's problem, and the town the soldiers'.

We thanked the Solomons for their hospitality. They were people who were careful of their repute and in a way kept separate from us, to give no offense. They would never have paraded on a balcony like Miss Porteous, or like, had I been Porteous's daughter, I must admit I would have.

Expiring at the first sight . . .

Returned up the terraces to The Briars in late light, and after eating a modest dinner, we slept once more fitfully. That squat giant lying in his room at Mr. Porteous's house was on our mind. The tension of seeing him and not expiring at the first sight had tired us. I slept late. At breakfast my father said it was as if the entire town were exhausted, for he had already been down there and seen but a gathering in the street watching the window behind which, it had been decided by someone, the Ogre lay and now began to engage himself in preparing for his first island day. Yet no blind was raised; indeed Porteous's entire upper floor refused to open its blinds to look down upon the avid, restive townspeople. And as during yesterday there was more than a vulgar curiosity in the crowd, though there was that as well. Above all, there was an attempt to work out the great cipher, the small man in the boardinghouse who was somehow taller than the Pyramids. They had been set by God or the heavens or the British Cabinet a puzzle beyond their means to resolve, and yet they felt they must not evade the duty.

My father rode over to Deadwood, the area grazed clean by the island's goats and subject to high trade winds, where the regiment had its tented cantonment. Wagons were dangerously creeping up the terraces to reach inland and turn for Deadwood, and behind them came a string of Chinamen and slaves carrying the high-priced goods of the East India Company provided from the warehouse of Fowler, Cole, and Balcombe. As we watched the wagons crest the escarpment in unfamiliar profusion, we felt the same puzzling burden as my father had observed in people in town. My mother said we should not go to town at all that day. She meant to keep us at home for obvious fear that in some way our brains might be disturbed and an eternal restlessness set in. Old Huff came along and taught my brothers some Latin vocabulary and my sister and I some French and a little Greek. He had been warned not to talk of the Phenomenon, the Great Ogre, but to keep us on the plain fare of pedagogy. My mother knew Huff needed too, for his own sake, to avoid the burden of the imagination that had made him drop to his knees on the pier, an action I had somehow understood. I was rather pleased someone had done it, as shockingly venerating a posture as it was.

Afterwards, as Old Huff was fed refreshments by Sarah, my mother sat us down to sew on the verandah, but the endless passage of wagons, slaves, and Chinamen in the middle distance distracted us. In late morning we saw a group of horsemen come over the saddle and keep on towards us under a great inland cliff and in bright sunshine. We could see scarlet in there amongst the file of horsemen and were sure, even at that distance, that a darker one was Admiral Cockburn, for we could see his dog, Pipes, running behind his horse. It must be remembered that we were girls unaccustomed to seeing such traffic, for until now we could remain at The Briars for days without our vision being teased by any distant human movement.

We went inside and combed our hair and washed ourselves from a basin of cold water brought in by Sarah and a new younger maid, Alice. She had been granted to us by Plantation House in view of the pressures about to be put upon our family. Her slightness and delicacy of movement contrasted with the heavier household tread of Sarah. As the admiral's cavalcade neared the crossroads below The Briars, navy blue manifested itself more clearly, and my mother decided for certain it must be the admiral. They passed on eastwards.

At my mother's insistence, we went to our rooms to rest, and we swooned away and woke at an hour when hints of a blue dusk were spreading eastwards from Plantation House to Deadwood. When I went out to the verandah, my mother and Jane were already there, and they were standing as the cavalcade, seemingly the one we'd seen that morning, picked up the main track that ran down to Jamestown and, instead of taking it, turned to The Briars. Then we saw a preposterous streak of green hedged in amongst the rest of the horsemen, in a position of imprisonment or at a center of honor.

Nearing our carriageway, the individuals became discrete from each other. Green there—beyond dispute! As the party turned into the carriageway amongst the trees, I felt an impulse to flee. At the gate, most of the gentlemen of the party dismounted, and Toby and Ernest ran from our stables to take the bridles. One presence remained on its horse.

I, supposedly the bolder and crasser of the Balcombe girls, reputed to be willing to say anything and to ride astride horses, stood on the balls of my feet and took a half step sideways, like a restive animal, and my mother could read the urge in me to be gone, to flit under the pressure of the fear that this man would take my air away from me.

My father had emerged from the house now, and indicated with some urgency that we should line up with him on the lawn. A young officer was opening the gate, and it was apparent that old Admiral Cockburn and the regiment's Colonel Bingham were amongst those who had dismounted. But the Emperor was not required to, and when the gate was open, Cockburn and Bingham accompanied him through, one at either stirrup. The mountings on his horse were crimson and gold, as was the saddlecloth, on which stood an embroidered golden bee, which I would discover was the Emperor's most admired creature—small and effective, I suppose you could say of him and the bee both.

The Ogre was rendered grander by the men who accompanied him at his stirrups, and by those who followed. The jet, imperial horse, big-hoofed, was tearing the family's cultivated lawn and my father was advancing warily, an Englishman ready to defend his home, beginning with his turf and his wife and daughters.

Sarah and my three brothers also broke from the house now. The boys, too young to be impressed by omens or to know the man's record, were unafraid, as if, on a dull day, they had discovered that there was a sort of fête in the garden. The bulky admiral with his huge face shook hands with my father first, and his great shaggy dog grew familiar with my father's scent and gave his left boot a lick. Next the admiral removed his hat ceremoniously in our direction, as did the colonel.

There was an awful gravity in the two of them still and in the party, as if they wondered whether or not the green man would deign to debouch from his saddle and need to be seduced by courtliness. He did not. I could see his eyes were dark and feminine, and with them he took in the scene and weighed it, and only then—with a surprising equestrian agility and in one fluid movement—did he descend from his saddle.

He did not seem happy or, once his feet hit the ground, as grand anymore, but I still suspected that a predator might have been let loose, a man who could disorder the world from a height of five feet five inches.

"May I introduce you, Mr. Balcombe," the admiral ground out, "to the General Bonaparte."

My father would of course find out, as we all would, that Cockburn's orders from the home government were such that the detained Ogre on the island should be called "General" and never addressed at a higher rank, and certainly not as "Emperor" or "Majesty." For that reason, in my account I will use the contrarian "Emperor," unless I remember slights, in which case I will fall back on the term "the Ogre."

I watched my father reach out and shake the small hand and engulf its tapered fingers. The Emperor's complexion, I now saw, was sallow, perhaps from the sea journey.

"I have heard of you, sir," said the visitor with great conviction, directness, and glittering eyes. The interesting thing was that I could tell he meant it. The bestrider of worlds had been on the island less than a day, there were many inhabitants to hear about, yet he had heard of my father. Other than that my father might supply groceries and candles to him, the question was: Why?

With an embarrassment he covered by adopting a basso voice,

the admiral stated, "In company with the General, we have been to see Longwood and it is—as you no doubt know, Balcombe—neither fit nor ready. It will need to be rendered suitable but that will take months. I have already instructed the ships' carpenters to get to work on it. In the meantime, the Emperor . . . the General . . . would like to be accommodated at The Briars."

As my parents exchanged looks, I raised my chin towards the Frenchman and felt immediate resentment. His dark, gravid eyes rested on mine, and despite their fame—I had seen them depicted in journals as the eyes of a tyrant or of a hero martyring himself for *gloire*—I would not look away. This was characteristic, of course. I would not let my sight slew off to uncontested ground. He who had sought to seize Russia now wanted us to surrender the whole Briars to him, not simply the Pavilion. Of course he would expect that. Let him bring up his cannon, I thought. But I feared him too, just as much as I had earlier. To have him on the island was peril enough for me. To have him at The Briars was beyond tolerance.

My father must have felt the same because he was left muttering, in a numbed voice, "Of course the Emperor is welcome to The Briars. When would he care to take occupation?"

"No, no," said the Emperor/General. It sounded like, "Nor, nor." He smiled quite attractively then, a smile drawn into being, it seemed, by a sudden innocent whimsy at the corners of his mouth. I did not quite believe in it. Cockburn and the colonel both laughed as if they did.

"The General does not wish to incommode you to that degree, Balcombe," the admiral assured us.

The Emperor lifted a feminine finger, which had somehow directed the movements of hundreds of thousands of men and compelled the fealty of millions.

"Là, le Pavillon seulement, monsieur."

He pointed to the little knoll atop which stood the summerhouse, and then he brought his eyes back to my father's face and tried his smile, and to clinch matters tried to encompass us all with a glance, as if I could so readily be rendered loyal.

"Well, we were told as much," said my father. "But now he is here, I see that the Pavilion is hardly large enough for the . . . the General."

Indeed we knew it to be a mere eighteen by twelve feet. Upstairs were two small bedrooms, hot when it was hot, damp when it was damp. Having got to an island five miles across, did the Ogre wish to reduce his scope further to eighteen feet by twelve?

Now the man was about to speak, and I will not fill this account for readers of one language with discourse in another, just to show that I had a certain competence in French. It would turn out that the General claimed to speak French, Italian, German, and English. But his French and Italian were the better of the four. And his English would prove the worst.

So he turned to Jane and me and said with his Satanic smile—for the Universal Demon always has a good smile, fleeting light on darkness, a bird skimming the night—"Speak do you the French, young ladies? The admiral tell me you did."

Jane was dumbstruck.

"My sister speaks it better than I do," I assured him.

I must make another aside here. I know that any compiler of memoirs likes to enlarge her part in encounters with the renowned. But I assure you I am not doing this now, for it is a despicable conceit and in any case invites contradiction. He happened to begin with Jane and me because he saw that we had followed a conversation he had been having with Colonel Bingham, sotto voce, about servants and accommodation. But it soon became apparent too that he was likely to try to win over the person in any company who exuded most suspicion or contrary feeling towards him. And, last of all, he liked directness, and since I had looked at him so directly and ferociously—or at least I liked to think so—I had presented him with an obvious mark.

He looked around and remarked to us that it was very quiet and pleasant, as if the metropolis of Jamestown was raucous by comparison. We were proud to hear him say it nonetheless. We stood in a basin on a desert island, on a plot that my parents and the gardeners Toby and Ernest had transformed into something creditable.

"Does the General have a large establishment?" asked my father nervously.

"Considerable," said the admiral. "He even has a *lampiste* to illuminate his quarters. But surely only a few can be accommodated here."

Already some of Bonaparte's servants or attendants were riding or walking across the upland towards us, summoned from Jamestown. A group of five male servants now passed through our carriageway gate, carrying various items of furniture. Their leader was a darker man, and another had a wizened face and a crankily tied neckcloth. The rest were young and well dressed: their hair was groomed with care, and beneath their hats they seemed to be laying their own claim to the place. A wagon followed the servants, and there were some crates of goods aboard it, which a party of Admiral Cockburn's sailors were set to unload. As the admiral's attention was now absorbed by the servants and the first items of toiletry and pieces of furniture to enter the Pavilion, we Balcombes became hapless witnesses to it all. We did not know whether to go into the house or remain in the garden. Mattresses and a camp cot, commodes and a washstand were now being hauled across the lawn and into the Pavilion. The admiral began to discuss with my father the necessity for erecting a large marquee as extra accommodation for the French, while inside the little house the young *lampiste*, Rousseau, began to illuminate it with lamps and candles brought up from Jamestown. A sour-faced cook whom we would get to know as Le Page was led to the kitchen at the back of the house by Sarah to inspect the site of his labors. We could see two other household servants unpacking the chests on the knoll, taking out books and china.

My father occupied himself in discussing with the admiral where the proposed marquee should be located. We watched through the drawing room window, beside which we had settled as an uneasy compromise, and my mother asked Jane to go and invite the Emperor to dinner and, since she had made her own assessment of the items of furniture, to ask if he might need a dressing table we had to spare. She had used the term "Emperor," and the idea of uttering such a sentence amused her. "Oh," she asked us, "doesn't it sound like a line from a drama on Roman potentates? But tell him the dressing table is very plain and not up to usual imperial standards."

Jane returned with the message that the Emperor had said he would be delighted to dine with our kindly parents—"as long as you and your imp of a sister are also at the table, mademoiselle." Jane had met Marchand, the valet, a young man of noble features who wore a trim navy-blue suit, and another, a Corsican, an intense man, very formal, much older than Marchand. We learned their names at once, as a person seeing previously unknown and questionable beasts moving in a forest learns and never forgets their exotic names. The Corsican was the maître d'hôtel, Mr. Cipriani.

I wanted to pass up and down the corridor to hear what else was happening in this overcrowded universe of The Briars. I heard the Emperor's cook in conference with Sarah, who had trouble understanding Le Page's fractured English. He was concerned with two things—chickens for the Emperor's breakfast and adequate hot water for his washing basin: he liked his bathwater extremely hot, said Le Page, tossing his head. He was a man who had once worked for the Emperor's brother Joseph, the one now in America, and could have been in America himself, and seemed, as he tossed his head in our kitchen, to wish he was.

Jane, having overheard Le Page, told me with her solemn air, "If he eats chickens for breakfast, nothing but sides of beef will suit him for dinner."

My father came back inside with the admiral, who was also staying for dinner.

"It is a plain and ample British dinner," my father warned him.

"Precisely what *I* need, in any case."

"Does the Emperor like port?" asked my father. For port was my father's passion and brought out the gout in his left foot, the one Pipes had licked.

"Perhaps some Bordeaux?" murmured the tactful admiral.

"Oh, sir, I have some stored, but the conditions of this island . . ."

The admiral said he would send one of the sailors to fetch some from the *Northumberland*.

Dusk fell, and men of all complexions kept coming back and forth between the town and there, delivering the Emperor's impedimenta. At the back of the house, my mother was speaking in a loud, fluting voice with Le Page, his communications with Sarah having broken down. He was not happy with the lamb that had been prepared but could not say exactly why. Perhaps the French did not eat lamb. Even the admiral could overhear Le Page, and sent a message to him that all would be well, for Le Page should remember General Bonaparte was a tolerant eater, and, the admiral whispered to us, if he put up with Le Page's cooking it was an exemplar of his tolerance.

The Emperor had told Cockburn that he wanted to see the orchard, and in the last of the day's light the old admiral and Pipes, and the Universal Demon—surely not the Emperor, I thought, at least judged from behind, by his narrow shoulders and his pear-like shape—walked amongst the trees with my father, Jane and myself trailing behind with the young grandee General Gourgaud, who still stalked the little man's spine. An English officer named Poppleton, who had been appointed as England's answer to Gourgaud, a sort of Emperor's bodyguard or supervisor, followed.

The Ogre told the admiral it refreshed him to be in such a place, and began to discuss the species of oranges grown.

My father said, "Oh, sir, it is Toby who is the orchardist." He pointed to Toby's hut beyond the rear boundary of the orchard, up the hill a short distance.

The admiral turned to Poppleton and told him to run to the hut. The Emperor stood and discoursed in French with the admiral, and absently patted Pipes's ears as old Toby emerged and walked towards us at Poppleton's side. He held a straw hat in his hand by way of reverence.

The Emperor reached out towards him and made putting-in-place gestures, installing him emphatically as the informant and then pointing to a particular bush.

"Shamouti?" he asked, fondling the leaves of a tree, rubbing a thumb along the skin of one of the fruits.

Old Toby said, "Jaffa orange, Your Majesty."

The Emperor nodded, and the word "Majesty" was forgiven in

Toby. He had only a selection of broken teeth left in his mouth but was known as a great eater of his produce—given my father's agreement that he should eat his fill.

"Palestine," said the Emperor, though he pronounced it differently from us.

"They are oranges from Spain, Your Honor," said Toby, pointing to another bush. The slave looked at Jane and me, whom he considered scholars, to see if he'd done well in his answer, and Jane nodded at him.

Poppleton declared, *"Espagne, Général."*

The Emperor seemed more curt in acknowledging this than he was with Toby and kept his attention determinedly on the orchardist. "Valencia," he murmured. And then he moved his hand to another bush. *"Bionda Comune?"*

"The plant come by ship, Your Honor," said Toby, looking at us now, my sister and me, as if requiring further support.

"India?" asked the Emperor, assisting Toby with a kind of respect. "Or *Bretagne?"*

But Toby did not seem to know and he painfully let his silence hang in the air. Jane suddenly declared in French that she believed they came from India, but that the orchard had existed long before our family came to the island.

The Emperor was delighted to see a mango tree and stood admiring the subtly colored hanging fruit, but did not take anything, even at my father's urging. Gourgaud had turned from his place at the Emperor's right shoulder and placed his placid dark eyes on Jane. His collar held his chin high and his hair was dark and there was something not to be depended on about the overall features. A hunger resided too obviously there, like a child's smear of jam on a man's face.

I said in praise of the slave, and to diminish Gourgaud's place in the landscape, "It is Toby who made them perfect. *Parfait."*

The admiral, Colonel Bingham, and Captain Poppleton all looked at me as if to say, "We have encountered the Universal Demon's devouring curiosity before." It would certainly prove to range wildly far beyond questions of fruit and extend, as his now quenched ambition had, to the world.

The Emperor said to Jane and me, in his oddly accented French, "I should know the botanical differences, but campaigning absorbed a great deal of time that should have been given to the study of nature."

"Well, you'll have plenty of time now," I told him. "But there's not so much nature here as in other places."

Jane nudged me as if I had said something too sharp-edged, and I felt the bewilderment of being unable to judge that myself. This was the directness, apparently, of which I was always accused. I never quite understood when people laughed, as the Emperor and the admiral both did now, as if remarking the flatly obvious was funny. The laughter of the Ogre sounded less affected than that of Admiral Cockburn.

I had noticed that so far his discourse had been with a slave and two young girls, and it did not escape me even then that he might have been making a point, declaring he knew the men of influence had orders that made friendship with them dubious. But then he was exclaiming again, moving on to the guavas and further on to the shaddock trees, with weighty citrus hanging from them big as balloons, and Toby was not further questioned and was allowed to return to his hut.

The orchard having been adequately surveyed, the Emperor turned and began to tread his way down the slope. My father moved uncertainly. Was he courtier or guard? Was he the friend of the admiral or had he encompassed the Emperor into his circle of connections and loyalties?

"Well, I have some good Bordeaux," he boasted too loudly.

It seemed that every lamp and candle we possessed was burning within The Briars, and in the Pavilion Rousseau had been so skillfully at work that the summerhouse looked itself like an ornamental lantern. The pulse and flicker of light through our windows was so intense it seemed that The Briars was about to consume itself—in delighted anxiety, I thought, for I had noticed that my mother, in instructing Sarah and other servants, had been more fearful than I was, and her pale, pretty face was shiny with hope and endeavor.

She greeted us when we all reentered the hallway from the orchard and announced, "Dinner is in advanced preparation," then asked the Ogre in French if he would like to sit in the drawing room awhile. And so he and Gourgaud approached the room with the admiral, the colonel and my father following, and there was suddenly no sense, after his toddle in the orchard, that the Emperor's radiant renown would consume the place. His thin shoulders and large head, which seemed to advance ahead of his body, bespoke a being more alert than inflammatory.

My father had lined up Sarah, Alice, and the twins with their white gloves, a small corps of servants for the visitor to inspect. In the drawing room, where we had by now been marshaled, my mother presented us in order of age and we rose. The Emperor took Jane's presented hand, and kissed it. Then mine, as I flinched, not wanting his hungry lips on my skin. Then William, Thomas, and little Alexander, who had had some solemnity threatened into them by our parents and Sarah. I felt a second's pride of kinship in these uncommonly solemn, pretty children, destined to be handsome men.

My father offered the Emperor refreshment and he raised his plump hand in refusal. He asked my father what quality of goods he stocked, and he listened earnestly as my father explained that provision supply from any direction had advantages and disadvantages—he knew reputable merchants as far away as Recife on South America's hip and had dealt with them. They were sometimes better suppliers of port than the British. But distance made it all difficult. On the other hand, he said, he depended a great deal on the storeship captains he knew, because they, and the suppliers too, would not load inferior goods for him.

The arrival of such a large garrison and a naval squadron would drive up the prices of local produce, my father further explained in English, attempting to translate this into his poor French. "I am very honored to serve the Emperor," he labored to say in conclusion.

"It is good of you to call me 'the Emperor,'" the Ogre remarked, with a kind of earnest humility, and he turned to the Balcombe women, his face immediately lightening. I would see him direct that look at many; it was a device of his to engage. He asked me in French, with that whimsical light still in his face, whether I was familiar with the outer world. I said we were familiar with England and the island, and of course the Atlantic. Jane made the same declaration.

Then he began to quiz us on the capitals of nations.

"Bavaria?" he asked.

"Landshut," said Jane, who had acquired these names of the world's cities as part of the furniture of an ordered mind.

"Württemberg?"

"Stuttgart, sir." Jane again.

"*Pologne?*"

Jane let me answer this, because she knew I knew it.

"Bravo! *Russie?*"

Jane told him that the capital was now St. Petersburg, but it had been Moscow.

Why was he doing this? Had his fall from power sent him mad? Quickly his humorous eyes fixed me because he knew I was the more intractable one, and he asked me a question, which I must give in French, despite the pretension of that, but perhaps to convey its impact on me.

"*Moscou? Qui l'a brûlée?*"

Who burned it?

I said, "It wasn't the English."

"No," he declared with false solemnity. "Whatever the faults of the English, they cannot be blamed for that. And so who burned it?"

I said, "The Russians burned it, I have heard, or the French say so."

He said, "Exactly, exactly." His laugh was intense and unmeasured and therefore startling. And he fixed me again and said I was prevaricating. "As an Englishwoman, you are required by law to be certain that I was the one who burned it."

This man was playing ducks and drakes about fires, famed as they might be, and for pure mad jollity in a room on an island of nullity!

"What I've been told," I said to him in a literal way, "was that it was the Russians who burned it down to get rid of you, sir."

My father and the admiral choked on some sort of laughter. The man wagged his finger but with a wide, alien smile.

Jane looked terrified. Huge combustions had been evoked and it was as if The Briars were not safe from them. I had found my voice with this creature, meanwhile, and I resolved not to be treated with the kind of sport he clearly saw me as good for.

My father pointed the Emperor to a chair, while the admiral occupied a slender window seat that had survived the Atlantic in a ship's hold and been carried up the terraces to The Briars without breakage. The same miracle of survival had been achieved by the slim-legged cabinet beside which the Emperor's seat was placed. The Emperor had noticed this item of furniture and, before sitting, began to exclaim how charming it was and told my mother in English, "Very good, very good!" He admired in particular the inlays. "They is the yew—*commun?* Or sycamore? Very much of English style. Very much of the English.

"A most civilized drawing room," he then told us in French, "to find in such a far place."

He still had a few pieces even now, in the last of the daylight, being carried up to The Briars, but he said they were very rustic by comparison, apart from his washstand. He stuck his hands behind his back and made his paunch notable. "Very rustic pieces," he declared, frowning at my mother, his eyes lustrous.

My mother pointed to an inlay and said, "Rosewood. *Bois de rose.*" She was doing her best, and as well as I could have done, but I don't know to this day if she got the name of rosewood right in French. At that moment the desire formed in her to offer him that dresser too, and so an ordinary item from The Briars became part of the furniture of his life. But so did we, and that's the tale.

After soup, Sarah and Le Page brought roast lamb to the table, and Sarah's twin boys in their white gloves carried around the accompanying dishes. The Emperor sat back and admired the elegant progress of Alice to mid-table with a gravy boat. He took a modest amount of cauliflower and beans and told my mother, talking while he chewed, that his *confiseur,* one of the best in France, would come up from the Porteous house tomorrow at the latest. "He is a great toymaker too," said the Emperor of his pastry cook. "He will make toys for your children."

The idea seemed improbable.

The pudding was rich with a dozen eggs, but the Emperor merely tasted it, a few mouthfuls. He had also drunk only two-thirds of a glass of the wine provided by my father.

My uneasy mother had about her a combined air of striving and shyness, which I found unsettling. She could not let her features settle themselves into those of my confident mother of the household, and I wanted her to achieve that level of ease, and found that her skittishness put a distance I did not desire between her and me.

The admiral rose and asked would the General think it improper if he proposed a toast to the King? The Emperor nodded assent. He did so from the sitting position, though; the admiral and my father and the colonel and the rest of us stood.

The admiral proposed a toast to the General.

The Emperor waved his hand. "No, no, no, no," he said briskly. "I do not drink to generals. Even a grand marshal like my friend Bertrand must be fortunate to find me raising my glass to him."

Cockburn arched his shaggy eyebrows in the direction of the colonel, who shrugged.

"I hope you understand, sir," said the admiral, "that that is as far as we can take the toasts, in that case."

"I have never been fond of drinking toasts," said the Emperor, quite pleasantly.

Suddenly he stood. There was no time for my father to begin the passage of the port around the table; nor had the time arrived for my mother, my sister, and me to withdraw. My mother said fretfully that had we known we would have such eminent company she would have contrived to serve something more delicate, but the Emperor said the meal had been all delicacy. He noticed the piano and turned to me, and said with a sort of playfulness that he assumed I had not managed to learn the piano.

"You are mistaken, General Emperor," I told him. "I have six songs over which I have utter control."

"Six songs?" he asked, his eyes glimmering and his mouth moving into a Gallic rictus that was mildly satiric. When his name had frightened us in our babyhoods, we had not imagined this whimsy of the eyes, or the particular way the corners of his mouth operated as the most subtle foreign machinery for a smile.

"Is it possible that I should hear one of these six songs?"

The adults laughed with him, as they would not have laughed for an older woman. I would come to be irked by that indulgent laugh, the indulgent smile. I looked at my mother, who nodded too urgently, sitting straight-backed still, every muscle clenched. Jane said, "'Ye Banks and Braes.' That is your most accomplished."

I took to the piano seat and raised the lid and began. My father and the officers politely suspended their conversation, and I let go of the doleful lyrics, as if laying down flowers on a current, strewing them freely, learned lines that had no real connection to me, the plangent tune and the rhymes of loss. Since I did not know of what I sang, the poet's lyrics served the undeniable vanity of a thirteen-year-old girl, as well as providing a means for her to assert herself in the face of that smiling magisterium.

Ye banks and braes o' Bonnie Doon
How can ye bloom, sae fresh and fair?
How can ye chant, ye little birds,
And I sae weary, fu' o' care.
Thou breakst my heart,
Thou warbling bird,
That wantons thro' the flowering thorn.
Thou minds me o' departed joys,
Departed never to return . . .

The Emperor spread his hands as if exhorting the world to listen as I made a smooth passage between verses and raised the register. When he stood at sudden song's end, the admiral did too, and the other men, and all applauded. I explained, "Those are the words of Robert Burns. Have you heard of him?"

Laughs, brief. Then the Emperor declared that this was the prettiest English air he had ever encountered, and he did not believe that it could come originally from them, since their songs were all about the military.

"The reason may be," I said, standing, "that it is Scottish."

"Now that explains it," he told me. "Not that I dislike martial songs. Do any of you here know '*Vive Henri Quatre*'?"

"You test our limits, General," said the admiral amiably, his cheeks a little aglow by now since my father had contrived to get the port circulating.

"He does test them," my father said, nodding in the early stages of tipsiness. "All of our limits. He does that. No fool, he."

Bonaparte raised his hand and keeping time began to deliver, in an off-key series of la-lahs, the burden of "*Vive Henri Quatre.*" It was an unaccustomed French song, ancient, and I heard Henri referred to as a demon four times over. It was also heavy, turgidly military, but the Emperor rose and marched around the room keeping time with his hand. The tune was so mauled by him that all this should have been comic, not least because the song showed the very faults with which he had labeled English music. But I think we were too astonished. Only my mother ventured a little and uneasy *heh-heh* at the end.

Then he stopped and lowered his heavy cheeks over his stock. "I know it sounds bad," he admitted, "because French music at its worst is nearly as bad as English. For the true songs let us all go to Italy! Madame de Montholon will at some happy time perform them for us."

He began to sing a theme from *Orpheus and Eurydice,* something so lyrical from the hand of Gluck that it was difficult to understand how he could maul it. But he managed it, and subverted Gluck's divine melody.

He declared tiredness now. He said the Count de Las Cases would come up tomorrow to the Pavilion, and that Las Cases's son would be good company for Jane and me, being just thirteen. Admiral Cockburn clucked almost like a nursemaid and agreed that he must be tired, and then in the corridor and on the verandah we made an informal guard of honor and Captain Poppleton and Le Page accompanied him out of the house and down the steps, across the lawn and up through a rockery towards his glittering cage. Poppleton was required to sleep near him to make sure that on his first night on St. Helena there should be no escape. Gourgaud accompanied his Emperor too, a step behind.

I could see the glow of a pipe at the end of the carriageway where sentries were placed, but the admiral did not seem too anxious that the prisoner might flit—certainly not a prisoner who had laid down the ponderous sounds of *"Vive Henri Quatre"* in our drawing room.

Contemplating what
person he was . . .

We now knew that the Emperor was not the sort of monster who in fact and deed devours a person in the night. This again did not make us sleep easier. Indeed, I was awake to a late hour contemplating what person he was. This conundrum who liked "Ye Banks and Braes," and who spoke to girls and slaves!

As well as that, he was down there, in unimaginable sleep, entertaining unimaginable dreams in the Pavilion, which was as close as the stables. There had been two servants waiting for him to return there—we had seen their shadows—Cipriani and Marchand. It was a heartbreaking scene, his sauntering to his camp bed in the Pavilion. No wife with him, no son. His little sister Caroline, Queen of Naples, had surrendered of her own accord to the Allies with her husband Murat, in hope she would be allowed to keep the throne he had put her on—that was something we would hear about. And his brothers scattered across the world from America to Italy.

As for his mother, Madame *Mère*, the matriarch of such a brood of generals and conspirators and princes, I realize now that she lived in the Roman hills, as the admiral himself had mentioned, where she could be visited often enough by her friend the Pope, about whom—of course—our family as decent Protestants felt an ambiguity. But the admiral said that the Pope's friendship with Mother Bonaparte was all the more interesting because her great son had kept the Pope nearly a captive, and thus a victim, and now the Pope, who was no longer a captive, visited the elderly Corsican mother of the man who, on an Atlantic island and as a prisoner now, had made his way alone (let us not count Captain Poppleton, and the one young slave that lit his way) across the lawn to our Pavilion.

We were awakened the next day by the sound of sailors and soldiers on the lawn and found them erecting a vast marquee on the sward below the Pavilion. The morning air was full of their curses as they struggled to put it up and blamed each other for its failure to ascend. Count de Las Cases and his son, both in brown suits, emerged, and the count began, with an air of uncertainty, to assess the men, and then to wander about the parts of the garden.

The son, having dressed appropriate to a man over fifty years of age, looked like the paragon of courtliness the Emperor had promised us.

"What a foolish little boy," I said impotently, and my sister Jane replied, "But you don't know him."

We watched him taking exaggerated notice of the limits of our garden. I could tell I would not find him a welcome presence. On the edge of womanhood, when one is capable of becoming interested in certain men, it is also easy to have an enhanced revulsion. I felt that revulsion for the boy, who prowled the garden wearing the same scholarly frown as his father.

I was the kind of child, no longer fully a child, old enough but not too old, to whom visitors addressed the sort of tale they wanted the entire company to hear and respond to with jollity. It was as if I were the necessary medium or filter that justified the irony in what they were saying.

"Well, imagine this, Betsy," the Irishman Surgeon O'Meara told me at dinner one night, the Emperor being over in his Pavilion, a circumstance we were still amazed by. It was clear that the matter Surgeon O'Meara was addressing was not merely for my sake but for the full table's. "Imagine a French doctor surrendering such a choice! For there was a young surgeon called Maingaud to do the job, a florid young fellow, thin-lipped and priestly in appearance, and dressed like it in a tight black suit. He had come with the Emperor from France and foresaw a life as an English gentleman's physician. But he had this horror of the tropics, you see."

We were used to maritime narratives at my father's table, for he entertained every storeship captain that put into Jamestown Roads, but even by those highly colored standards, the Irishman, himself tickled by his own tale, had the table thoroughly tickled as well.

"So picture your humble servant taken to the cabin of Admiral Keith, where the pale little French surgeon told the big-nosed English admiral that he had a terror of tropical diseases and that he was not so certain of his allegiance to the Emperor anyhow that he didn't want to follow him into the torrid zone."

"Yes, but don't call him the Emperor, surgeon," said our admiral leniently. "Remember to call him 'the General'—according to Cabinet instructions."

O'Meara, as would become apparent, was determined to call his patient "the Emperor." It was not out of contrariness, it would turn out. It might have been vanity. Anyone could have generals as patients, but who had ever had an emperor? However, it might have been his semiradical Irish politics. Even when "the General" surrendered the first time, before repenting of exile and unsurrendering, the British had still addressed him as "Emperor." So how could they now demote him from that omnium compendium of a name to the title of a mere officer?

"There must have been many unattached Frenchmen who would have taken the job in this little fellow's place," the Irishman went on to assert. "But this young man was ready to go back to the France that would come after the Emperor . . . or *the General*. The France without color, or fraternity, or imagination."

The admiral was willing to laugh and say, "By God, O'Meara, you sail close to the wind. You may call him by that name for the rest of this anecdote but then change, and for good."

The Irishman bowed to Admiral Cockburn and finished his glass of port, uttered a little "Um" of sugary appreciation, and continued. "So I inherited France's dying color, and I inherited the care of its imagination."

Admiral Cockburn wasn't as happy now.

"You ought to look out for subtlety, my boy. There's no promotion in it. Is 'the General' the earth's imagination? And does the rest of the world now lack imagination because that quality has been concentrated in this island in the person of the Emp— the General?"

"Aha!" cried O'Meara. "I had you nearly say it, sir! That wee British Cabinet has to be informed straight off, wouldn't you say, Balcombe?"

My mother and my sister Jane laughed as merrily too, but looking as women do for confirmation and almost for license from the convulsions of the men. In matters of hilarity, though not in all matters, my mother always bowed to my father. Men owned laughter, it seemed. I always liked if not envied the way Jane laughed, without artifice, generously but not just to please. It ran like a warm flame beneath the skin of her face.

Admiral Cockburn shook his big, meaty head, a head that appeared to have become more reinforced by the habit of command. "You see that United Irishman there," he said, pointing at O'Meara further down the table. "He is a serpent from the wrong end of the garden! You understand the Irish pretend to be with us when they need a post. But their impulses run to dangerous spirits!"

O'Meara was delighted to be thought of in such complimentary terms and felt entitled to continue. "So, after the little French surgeon had bolted, my superiors came aboard the *Bellerophon* and asked me would I consent to leave the ship and come aboard the *Northumberland* and do the duty of physician to . . . well, to him . . . to the Great Ogre and the Savage in Chief. I should serve here as well, with regular naval emolument. 'Milord,' says I to Admiral Keith, 'an O'Meara *may* speak to an emperor.' At that stage I was ignorant of the great policy regarding names, and I used the word for the sake of historic accuracy. And then Lord Keith said to me, 'I'm afraid, O'Meara, he has great contempt for your profession.'"

"Sensible man!" said my cherub-cheeked father, genial lover of the table and of all these naval fellows.

"Indeed, Billy," O'Meara familiarly told my father. "If he didn't despise surgeons he would have accepted neither the little priestly Frenchman nor myself, both of us men worth avoiding and far from the apogee of our profession. The upshot, in any case, was that I transferred to the *Northumberland* to accompany the Ogre and his entourage to this place. The man's servants were already aboard, but I saw the Ogre himself and his suite ascend the gangway, and engage in energetic and jovial talk with the admiral, who showed him round the ship and brought him at his own insistence back to the poop deck. Then . . . 'All right now, surgeon,' Captain Ross of this ship-of-exile told me. So I went up myself to the poop. Below us, I could hear all the Great Ogre's retinue settling into their quarters. And I could hear the lovely Countess Bertrand, as Irish as me, calming her three questioning children, and General Bertrand calming her. And Madame de Montholon, quieter but as bewildered as she was entitled to be! Until then they had thought they were to be exiled to, at the worst, Scotland. I heard her husband tell her, 'Fear not, my darling. I shall write a book on our desert island life and it will make us wealthy.' I should have laughed, but it made me sad—that it was all he had to offer."

The table grew wistful.

"Madame de Montholon had a little boy with her, but it was to Fanny Bertrand and her sons that my heart went out, big sturdy whack of a woman as she is. Yes, her father was Irish—did I say that?—name of Dillon. But he lost his literal head years ago, in old Robespierre's day, after earlier fleeing Ireland because . . . well, you know why men flee Ireland!"

"To escape embezzlement charges," suggested one of the other guests, Mr. Ibbetson, a newly arrived military commissary.

"Yes," said O'Meara, rushing to get his riposte out of his mouth. "Embezzlement that should so frequently be charged against Dublin Castle! There, I uttered sedition and am guilty, milord!" O'Meara offered his wrists for cuffing. "The charge of United Irishman proven! Yet before I go to my death for the Rights of Man and of the Great Ogre, may I finish the story?"

Permission was granted.

"So onto the poop went I, Mrs. O'Meara's witless son, and saluted the little portly man standing there alone. I reintroduced myself under the new species of being his *personal* physician. I was aware that this fellow on the poop had tried twice to send armies to bring revolutionary principles to my homeland, and that is no small gesture to my mind. Come now, rally yourselves! No sour English mouths there!"

He looked around comically—like an inspector—to ensure we were obeying him, and laughter again abounded.

"Says O'Meara," as O'Meara told us, "'It has been suggested, sire, General, Your Imperial Effulgence, that I might have the honor to be your surgeon on board and, if you choose, on shore.' Says the Effulgence in reply, 'Are you a *chirurgien-major*?' Says I, 'I am that very object.' He asked what country I was a native of—was it Scotland? Perhaps the fact that we were speaking Italian at the time might have excused his mistake. I replied that I was from . . ."

"Ireland," we all shouted, as he had invited us to do by a choirmasterly sweep of both hands.

"Indeed. And he asked where I had studied my profession. 'In Dublin and London both,' I replied."

O'Meara's part-foxy, part-bearlike brown eyes still held mine. I remained the filter and the conduit.

"'Which of the two is the best school of physic?' the Great Ogre asked me. I told him Dublin was best for anatomy, but London was the better for surgery. He smiled at me with the smile that had captivated Europe but not, of course, our admiral. You will be a captive of that smile too, little Bet."

My face blazed. I would not let myself be written off as an easily-dealt-with child. That was, to too great an extent, the law of my blood. "Only if I choose to, Surgeon O'Meara," I told him.

"That's true," cried my father. "That's Betsy. Only if she chooses. Believe me, believe me."

He'd learned that much. I looked at my father's large, flushed, and very trusting face. It tended to sunburn, but he wore big straw hats on the island, and his cheeks were nearly as rosy and untouched by sun as they would have been in England. They shone so genially that he would have excelled anywhere on earth as a host in those days, before doubleness and tripleness in men and women became as apparent to him as later they would.

O'Meara continued. "'Anyhow,' says the Grand Ogre, 'you praise Dublin for anatomy just because you're an Irishman.' I begged his pardon but insisted I'd said it because it was true, and that there was a reason for Dublin's anatomical prowess. The poor of the Liberties in Dublin dug up buried bodies for us every night for a living, and there was a queue of disinterrers and their wares each morning outside the School of Anatomy at Trinity College. A corpse for dissection could be obtained in Dublin at a quarter of the price you had to pay in London. A case of market price favoring scholarship!"

For some reason the idea of cheap Irish corpses made the entire table break out in merriment. Even I let loose a small stutter of laughter, though I thought the story horrible. But at least now O'Meara dropped the affectation of addressing the story as if entirely to me. He raised his eyes to take in the entire table.

He recounted how the Grand Effulgence had asked him about his service—navy and, before that, it seemed, army, because O'Meara was talking about his time in a regiment of foot in Egypt days. "I told him that the officers of the old 62nd messed in a house that had formerly been a stable for his cavalry. He was hugely amused at this. From Egypt we moved on to the topic of bleeding as a remedy, which the Great Ogre considers a laughable English fashion, and soon we were interrupted by Count Bertrand, the *grand maréchal* of the palace, which at this stage had shrunk down to a number of small cabins on a British seventy-four. And to accommodations no better than mine."

"Hmm," said my father, turning philosophic, and now all at table seemed to pause, and to reflect on shrunken majesty.

*T*hat same night Count de Las Cases was invited to the table. He arrived late since he read to his son each evening. Las Cases seemed externally a dry man, but when he began to speak in his careful English, he could not be called a bad narrator.

"Yes, I lived in London for nearly twelve years," he explained; the Las Cases were ancestral nobles and thus he'd had to flee the Terror, but ultimately he had renounced the title so he could return to

France. "Then the revolutionary government gave us an amnesty and back went my wife and I, to make something out of our estates, after the—forgive me—poor quarters we had lived in in London. I know Wapping, I know Shoreditch, and I can still smell Thames mud. It was all better than death."

This was not much of a compliment, but in fact the English officers did not seem offended and uttered comradely groans to think that such a fine man had been excluded from his inheritance until the revolutionaries came to their senses and allowed his return. Then it was revealed that he had written while in England a renowned historical and geographical atlas that most of the officers at the table had studied, and that explained the reverence they had shown when he entered. I was now torn between scorn and reverence for him.

"Then, sir," a lean officer named Major Fehrzen politely asked him, with an unmilitary sensibility, "your devotion to the Emperor . . . ? It is true, isn't it, that early in your English exile, you were encouraged to take part with others at the landing of émigrés and British soldiers at Quiberon, by which you hoped to restore the French monarchy? Yet now the monarchy is restored, you are here, not with your monarch but with the deposed man, and determined to serve him. I simply wondered . . ."

"Because I chose in the end to take my oath to him—to *your* guest, Mr. Balcombe. Yes, when I was an émigré and fled to England, I hated the Revolution and the poverty it had reduced us all to. But being reduced to the masses by the confiscation of my estates, I knew that the Revolution, though brutal . . . well, I must admit I could see where it arose from. Just the same, I felt that it was right for me to end the Terror some twenty years past, indeed. So, not knowing that the cure already lay in the heart and intentions of an obscure officer named Bonaparte, we all set off for Quiberon, that debacle of a landing in which I was involved as a former French naval officer on one of Lord Hawke's ships. Being of naval background I was able to escape when our troops ashore were encircled. It was a sad business. There were betrayals within."

They showed an interest in his being a former naval officer, and he said that, yes, as a young officer, he had been considered for the role of assistant astronomer on the expedition of Lapérouse, whose ship had been last sighted by the officers of the convict station at Botany Bay, New South Wales, and which had then, on the eve of the Revolution they could not have foreseen, disappeared utterly in the South Seas.

It was thus from the mouth of dour Las Cases that I heard the name of one place, Botany Bay, which would appear in my later history.

"I am the ghost of that expedition," said Las Cases. "I was chosen but was then serving in the waters off San Domingo. I missed Lapérouse's departure! If I had not, I would have been amongst the dead, and we do not even know whether they were drowned or massacred. So to me it is no hardship to be here, since I am not in that sense entitled to be on the earth. Back in France, I could see the signals of coming savagery and got away to Koblenz and then to your country and thus averted my appointment with the blade. I say this because no more than you, gentlemen, do I believe I am entitled, having made an oath, to abstain from observing it when affairs become difficult. I was his chamberlain when he returned from Elba, and I am his chamberlain still. For he redeemed us from the Terror, and he became a monarch, yes, but one whose reign encompassed the masses. I cannot resign from my undertakings. I do not advance that proposition as if it were one of remarkable virtue. I do so in the awareness that you are fulfilling similar undertakings."

There was applause after this declaration, and it made Las Cases uncomfortable. He made apologies and rose, saying that he had to attend the Emperor early. He departed in a cloud of general approval. But I still felt there was something too mechanical in him, too dry and inhuman.

No one had asked him why he had insisted on bringing his son into exile.

Two French ladies down
in Jamestown . . .

It became known that the two French ladies down in Jamestown, Countess de Montholon and Countess Bertrand, were both anxious to meet well-disposed islanders. My mother dispatched a formal and nervous invitation to them at their quarters in the Portions, and acceptance, written in English by Countess Bertrand, came as easily and punctually as if my mother had invited Mrs. Solomon or Miss Knipe of Horse Pasture Farm to visit. Even though we were making an attempt at treating the Emperor as a normal person—I certainly deludedly thought that I was doing my best, even though I now see I was overreaching in my impudence as others overreached in their efforts of hospitality—this advance of the two elegant women, whom of course we saw as unanimous in intent and fashionable sisterhood, created total ferment amongst us. On the morning of their visit we spent a great deal of vain time having Sarah and Alice set our hair according to instructions, and then resetting it according to our vapid revisions of intent.

Warned that the Frenchwomen's barouche was visible topping the saddle out of Jamestown, we were tormented by spasms of inferiority. Mine centered on the English pantaloons I wore, according to custom, not being yet a woman, those satin stovepipes of immaturity in which my legs were encased. At the news of their approach, Jane and I both energetically moved the shoulders of our dresses down, to expose as much throat and collarbone as possible, in a final attempt to answer the invading French elegance.

The Frenchwomen were helped from their carriage by two young liverymen, French brothers, who had ridden the horses that had dragged the ladies here. I was pleased to see the women wore ordinary bonnets, that they could not, any more than we could, transcend the reality of tropic sunlight. My mother rushed too effusively to the gate, opened by Ernest, and the women entered, the lofty Madame Bertrand in white, and the small, full-bodied Madame de Montholon in a magnificent white bodice intersected with lines of blue, and a dazzling blue sort of reversed apron with a bow falling behind her.

"*Mesdames,*" fluted my mother, "*bienvenue chez Balcombe.*"

I blushed at this, for my mother was trying to please them, but to an embarrassing degree. Here before these elevated French personages, décolletage looked all-conquering, and my mother's simpering could not steal any of that away and endow us with it.

"Mrs. Balcombe," said Countess Bertrand in English only faintly accented with Irish, "I am Fanny Bertrand, and this is Albine de Montholon, and we would seek to be your friends." She opened her arms to the sky above The Briars. "You look upon two exiles."

Madame Bertrand's eyes moistened, and she explained what she had said to her smaller companion, who nodded and bowed sagely, and in a form of gratitude took my mother's hand, and then Jane's and mine in both of hers, one after the other, and declared in French that she was delighted to be in our house.

"Please," said my mother. "I don't know where the Emperor is at the moment—perhaps in the grape arbor, dictating to the Count de Las Cases."

"Don't disturb him," said Fanny Bertrand, fairly promptly. "He is well used to our company."

The women crossed the lawn and ascended to the verandah, Albine looking around her with genuine interest as if entering a much more elevated habitation. It was hard not to like her for making the effort. She was trying to trim herself, as they all must, to her island. We drank tea in the drawing room, and Albine seemed a model of reticence while Fanny Bertrand discussed with us the fact that the sea voyage had worn her children down: she had seen her sons' arms, little Henri's—he was three—and the seven-year-old Napoleon's arms get thinner, she said. And young Tristan, his arms too. Fanny Bertrand's five-year-old daughter, Hortense, must have been robust, for she was not included in the lament. To be the mother of boys is to be by nature in a special position, and Madame Bertrand and my mother discussed their sons, their raucousness and charm, at considerable length. Madame de Montholon did not seem to think having a male child was such an enchanting thing and spoke only occasionally, nodding in a seemly way, and contributing a few words on Tristan.

I had until now been taken by the serenity in Madame de Montholon. She glowed with it, and I was of a mind by then to wonder whether such a seamless emanation was reliable or a mere trick. I knew it gave her advantages over the big, plain-boned, and frankly passionate Fanny Bertrand.

There came a time when, after various signals to her maid, Madame de Montholon needed to withdraw. She disappeared into the house. Suddenly the décolletage front of Madame Bertrand and Madame de Montholon was unexpectedly split.

Madame Bertrand leaned forward, so vast that she seemed to cast a shadow over all three of us Balcombe women. "She is *enceinte*, you know," she said. "It doesn't show yet. She is an adventurous woman, but this time it is certainly her husband, since it was conceived on board, without latitude for adventures."

Jane and I looked at each other beneath the startled demeanor of our mother. Did women away from the island normally speak like this? Was it a matter of comment if a child *was* the child of a woman's husband? Madame Bertrand's eyes settled on us and she could sense at once that she had created a sensation, at least by our standards. It was clear she was fairly pleased she had.

"I have to say," she pressed on, "that she has taken to this business of exile very bravely. We have been on the road together in France, and then at sea, racked with anxieties day by day. And then the thunderclap as the gods announced we could not enter England!

And then at sea yet again. . . . You know, we never quarreled, but in all the indignities that usually make women sisterly, we never became close friends of each other either. She is . . . she is *careful*. She is *very* careful in movements, and in what is said."

"She is very contained," my mother agreed.

Madame Bertrand at least lowered her voice. "And she has a power over men I cannot understand. She's such a little rump of a thing. Yet de Montholon went crazy for her, and she's three years older than him! Her boy Tristan is from an earlier marriage. . . . She came *here* with a better grace than I. It should make us sisters. But it hasn't."

How could we not be grateful for gossip frank in a way island English gossip was not? It was not all gossip, of course. That was the thing. It was open confession as well. About the time of Russia, she said, confident that we knew what "the time of Russia" was, Madame de Montholon's first husband, a banker, had sought a divorce because she was already living with de Montholon, then in the Duchy of Würzburg, which is some sort of German principality where de Montholon was the Emperor's legate. The Emperor had made it known to de Montholon, so said Madame Bertrand, that he didn't think it was a wise marriage, but when he passed through Würzburg on his way to Russia, de Montholon had asked him would it be all right to marry a niece of one President Séguier of the Supreme Court. The Emperor agreed it would be. This was a trick—for the niece was Albine. "De Montholon married Albine then, as if it could not wait a day. Such fools we are. Indeed even in Moscow that October, when the Emperor had better things to think of, he wrote very angrily to de Montholon about this trick of his and sacked him from his post. But things would narrow down, and de Montholon, like my husband, would rally to the Emperor in the last days. I don't want my husband and I ever to become as close as they are to the Emperor, or in the same way, for there's a sort of pretense in it. The Emperor *became* the Emperor so that people would not have to go through that sort of slavishness they bring to their behavior around him. I don't want us to be an imitation of them or of that fool Gourgaud."

And then, not aware that she had in any way startled us, she threw her head back and became pensive, looking west towards High Knoll, on top of which a garrison, who could scan the entire island and semaphore their observations to Deadwood, had been placed.

"Third marriage," confided Madame Bertrand of her absent friend, drawing her large head back to us and gazing at us one after the other for emphasis. "What do you think of her earrings?"

We are to comment? I asked Jane with a look. I had noticed the earrings as I had noticed everything. They were confections of gold and a good-sized pearl was attached to each.

Fanny Bertrand carried on. "The Emperor's gift. He doesn't give me any gifts, but then I tell him the truth about himself."

So already it was obvious: the women who had come up here in their fabrics and their shoulder scarves, their bonnets and under their parasols, were not the right and left of the united French line. They were, Jane and I were astounded to find, set against each other by a margin of doubt. In twenty minutes, Fanny Bertrand had given us her map of the divided French entourage. She would continue to supply us ever afterwards with amusing supplements. I admit I looked across the garden to the grape arbor, where the Emperor might be, and at the marquee and up to the Pavilion itself, deserted at this time of day. It was hard to see how this grand scale of gossip could continue in such confident voice within the shadow of the Emperor. Yet, as she said, she was not afraid of him.

"Now, I think she's probably being sick, poor thing," Fanny Bertrand said suddenly, as if remembering an oversight. "Call me Fanny. Do you Balcombes have any Irish connections? I must say I was charmed on the ship by Surgeon O'Meara, whom I consider my countryman and fellow United Irishman. I think it is there, under the skin—the republican fervor. And the Emperor did send two armies to Ireland, you know—for the great uprising seventeen years back."

My mother's eyes widened at this treason talk about Ireland and the United Irishmen. O'Meara had made a joke of it some nights before. But it was no joke to Fanny. I'm sure that is why the Irishman and the Emperor got on well from the start.

Madame de Montholon returned and bowed to my mother. There was a strong whiff of rosewater about her as she approached. My mother and Madame Bertrand got up and made sure her seat was pulled out from the tea table, and Fanny Bertrand was a paragon of sisterhood.

Madame de Montholon nodded contentedly, though after all this time of shared change and difficulty she must have known that her co-exile was an artiste at nuance. She turned a half smile to us, a smile that was like a secret, for it conveyed something that Fanny Bertrand, beside her, could not quite see. A smile of complicity, a smile that said, "I know *you know* how much to believe."

At last it was Fanny Bertrand's turn to seek the services of her maid and of the chamber pot—the impact of the tea, which we Englishwomen had, almost without being told, learned how to cover up, to wait to relieve ourselves until guests had left. But the French were franker in their needs.

Abruptly I said to Madame de Montholon in French, with a sudden onset of adolescent madness, "Countess, Madame Bertrand told us how you met your husband, the count. It was fascinating. Very dramatic. Like a novel."

She thanked me with no trace of doubt on her face, and began to supply us therefore with information about Fanny. Did we know, she asked, that Fanny was the daughter of a Creole mother? Hence the relationship to the Empress Josephine. So, the implication was, not French at all, but Irish-Creole.

"The dark eyes," said Jane, thoroughly delighted now that I had instigated this further stream of what passed by English standards for a gush of scandal.

"Fanny frequently spoke to her cousin Josephine about her own difficulties in finding a husband," Albine smoothly told us. "And the Emperor heard and mentioned his chief of the engineering staff was a single man." Again, the benignity of her sweet plump oval face remained unaltered as she continued. "They were a perfect couple, since Comte Bertrand was not greatly sought after by women, and Fanny, quite handsome in her way, was yet somewhat intimidating to many men. After some resistance from dear Fanny, it became a perfect marriage, and they are a great succor to each other."

All this was said with such an air of subtle condescension and a gleeful, unimpeachable contempt that even Fanny Bertrand herself, had she been present, would have found it hard to complain.

Fanny Bertrand now returned, a galleon in the doorway. She knew of course she had been spoken of, and my mother managed to say we had been talking of what a splendid mother she was to her boys, and Fanny pretended to believe it. That was the thing about both of them: acceptance. It satisfied them so well.

After they engaged in plentiful kissing of our cheeks, they went companionably to the barouche and were driven away, back towards the rock cleft of Jamestown and the Porteous house.

My mother said to us, "Do not forget that, though they might be worldly, they are both very brave."

Walking in the hinterland . . .

ertrand and de Montholon would come up from town to visit the Emperor, and when they did Gourgaud loomed jealously about the door of the marquee or the Pavilion or the gate of the grape arbor at the side of the garden. He wanted to be a high counselor. He seemed visibly anxious that he was not. It was at his urging that Marchand the valet or one of the other servants had dug in the floor of the marquee the outline of a large crown, so that anyone who entered under that canvas roof had to cross it and could not avoid acknowledging majesty. The admiral seemed to tolerate this as a fairly innocent assertion of vanished power.

On days when Gourgaud's spirits about being supernumerary to the governance of the Pavilion improved, he asked Jane and me to go walking or riding with him in the hinterland. He liked striking towards High Knoll, marked out by the semaphore station on its summit and set to the South American side. That country was designed for an invigorating ramble, up the slopes of a great cup of rock the waterfall had cut in the base of the mountain.

Gourgaud always seemed socially clumsy with us. He would greet us and compliment us on our dresses but without actually seeing them. His compliments came in little spurts, like lines remembered by a bad actor, in jumbled and inept order. "Mademoiselle Jeanne," he would tell Jane, "your handsome neck maintains, in this climate, the complexion of a lily." And then, "Let me tell you about the fever hospitals in Pomerania, and the quarrels between the surgeons on the two chief methods of treatment." Without easing us towards the idea, we would hear how dysentery had pervaded the Emperor's army even before it entered Russia, and while it was recovering from the previous winter in East Prussia and the Duchy of Warsaw. And then, camp fever!

He had, in a different sense from the one in which the Ogre managed it, become a military child, as Emmanuel de Las Cases was a secular one. All with him was therefore a strange, distracted intensity. He had no sense that we might not want to be entertained with fever wards, and it is therefore just as well that I was fascinated by such details.

On the march into Russia, it seemed Gourgaud was in charge of the ordnance and had had to manage the conveyance of cannonballs and muskets to the front. Noble horses broke their hearts hauling cannon through Lithuania, he assured us, and he told us solemnly he numbered the conscripted farm horses of Pomerania and East Prussia amongst the heroes of France.

My sister Jane would tell me she was touched by this noble feeling of his, as if it had not been the sacrifice of involuntary horse-flesh on Gourgaud's and the Emperor's altar, and as if Gourgaud had expended his own heart as well. And though I was beginning to suspect, like my father, that the Emperor might deserve an altar, I was not so sure that Gourgaud deserved the one Jane seemed willing to create for him. Nonetheless, as we strolled through the island's verdant belt and into its more arid regions of spiky plants, he strewed the strange bouquet of the Russian campaign at Jane's feet. I say "at her feet" because he would bend forward continuously, his hands open, as if laying the facts down for her, and even me, to tread on. He progressed in this flattering manner to tell us of the wounded at Borodino, who lay for five days untended and who carved meat out of the corpses of fallen chargers. He declared that the town of Mozhaisk became so foul with the *Grand Armée*'s dead that the capture of Moscow grew to be a medical necessity, the army needing to escape the putrefaction of its own advance.

To give him credit, he did not try to woo Jane with anecdotes of his own valor or suffering. The army and he seemed to share the same mind. Though the quartermasters failed, he had, it seemed, nourished it with his supply of cannonballs. This gave him strange conviction as, in the ferny though scree-strewn foothills of Diana's Peak, he told us how the cold had set in on the great retreat, and how this or that man had suddenly staggered about as if he were drunk, and his face had grown swollen and red, just like that of a drunk, but only because all the blood had fled there, into the head, the central citadel, abandoning other parts of the body. The stricken soldier could no longer hold his musket but let it fall from benumbed fingers. Unable to feel his feet, he dropped to his knees, and when he wept, tears of blood came from his eyes. Gourgaud's voice broke at this point. He suddenly became august.

"It was a beautiful army," he said. "Sons begotten from Europe's seed! Some of them had fortunately plundered women's clothes from Moscow and were now, in the great cold, saved by these layers of warmth. And some had stolen shoes, even from the servants' quarters of houses, and were spared from the freezing of the extremities that brought men down into the snow."

I could see that Jane was horrified and entranced. It was strange to observe one's sister, for the first time, become subject to *that* sort of attachment, one different from friendship, one aimed at other indefinite and portentous outcomes. "The Emperor," he told us more than once, with a conviction that enchanted Jane, "was maligned. Some asked why he allowed foreigners remaining in Moscow to follow us out in our retreat, and why he let them pile our wagons high: even some English with us, certainly Germans, Swedes, and Poles, carried on wagons all their earthly goods, from pianos to bookcases laden with classic authors in vellum. But you see the wisdom of that. He knew that the weather would make them lighten the load as the season advanced, until the goods on each wagon were used to make fires and the wagons themselves were entirely returned to the accommodation of our wounded and sick. He always knew what he was about. Even in ill fortune he had a plan. He sees ahead of us—he leaps ahead of the path we ordinary people can see, to the path only he can see."

Something in Gourgaud's bombast riled me, given that I had not finally decided to welcome the Ogre, or in what sense to welcome him. I interrupted his gush by asking, "Can any man have as much foresight as you say the Emperor has? If he's so clever, why didn't he go into Russia earlier in the year? Or not at all?"

The painful adoration in his eyes dimmed as he turned them with a frown—with disbelief, in fact—on me.

"Our army was delayed by an outbreak of spring fever, and these things are not organized overnight, young Miss Balcombe. Our first troops entered Russia in late June. No one could have guessed that was too late a date."

"If I'd been in command," I said, "I would have made sure I was ready two months before. He must have had very bad quartermasters and surgeons to be held up so long."

Gourgaud looked up at Diana's Peak to the south and his eyes were slits. "It is easy to be wise on St. Helena," he said. "But I can say that for good reason the ordnance had been ready to move in April!"

I almost hoped I had made him fall out of love with Jane, just by marring his story, his Genesis and Exodus. Jane did not want him distracted, however.

"Please," she said. "We live such restricted lives. Tell us more about the sad retreat."

She too frowned at me in a way that said, why are you such an awkward and contrarian child?

"Oh, the most sad, dear Miss Balcombe," said Gaspard Gourgard, returning to his text, "the most sad was when we passed back through Borodino again, where the battle had been, and we were nearly grateful to the wolves for devouring the unburied and for doing the service we had had no time for. By now the horses of the cavalry had been either eaten or sequestered by myself to haul the guns. And in even greater numbers men would fall to their knees in snow and remain there for a long time as if pondering, trying to decide whether to rise again. But I never observed a case where they managed it. As if they were campaigning in Egypt, some took their uniforms off. Boys came to resemble eighty-year-old cretins, but sometimes as they shed their clothing it was snatched up by those who needed it. How relentless the Cossacks and Russian peasants were! Hacking with sabers and billhooks at the solid bodies of frozen soldiers, and so infused with demonic hate that our deaths were not enough for them! Oh, no, these barbarians wanted to penetrate our outer layers and discover the soft organs and let blood flow from them and freeze into huge clots of ice they would raise and bite into."

By now I knew that at base I was as fascinated by this horror as Jane.

"And you, General," asked Jane, "how did you live through that terrible cold?"

Gourgaud pulled in his chin to consider this before the tribunal of his own military conscience.

"I was fortunate, mademoiselle, that I had a specific task of saving the ordnance. Unlike the infantry I had a carriage and traveled close behind the Emperor's coach. I would fill it with suffering artillerers, but most died there, on my seats, for it was cold enough even within the conveyance. I would say that hundreds of men were hauled into my coach as a mercy, and when one died, another from the roads was dragged aboard at my order. When we reached the Berezina River the Emperor asked me to stay there and to see our troops across and, of course, the ordnance too. I had a purpose, you see, other than mere escape. And whenever I found sufficient horses to haul what was left of our guns, I felt warmed by a sense of triumph. Other men were not sustained in that way. Mind you, I was as mad as the rest, but my madness was salutary, you understand, and kept me breathing. Even so, while my officers were away from me one day—they had gone off to persuade the Württemberg artillery not to abandon their guns—I sat alone on a birch log surrounded by the mounds of frozen corpses and all at once had a terrible desire to sleep, to slide down the stump. I was awoken by some nearby soldiers quarreling over the butchering of a dead horse, and struggled upright, then drank some of the sweetened brandy I always carried from my flask. Becoming upright after the snows had decided to suck you down—that was the trick."

Jane said, "We are very pleased that you rose."

By now he had become encased in his own memory and was distracted from Jane.

It was in its way an astonishing story—as I had to admit at a deep level—and he recounted it well. In that quiet bowl amongst mountains, on a silken October evening, Gourgaud summoned up memory of the Russian attacks on the rear regiments, those still armed, those still subject to their officers. Gourgaud could muster only forty cannon to face the Russians' hundred at Viasma, but the men who stood there, he said, were the cream of men, the oldest, the best, the foredoomed. Ferocious Russian peasants waited at the edge of the battle to move in and avenge themselves on the French wounded, and to chase after the Emperor, who was not far ahead.

I was characteristically awed and contemptuous as Gourgaud rounded out his tale. "So what is it to be?" I asked him suddenly and with the archness of a nearly but not fully grown woman. "Are we to sympathize with those who just fell over, or admire the old guard who dropped over in the snow anyhow? What about those who were killed by cannonballs? Or what if they were killed by Russian peasants? Are they more heroic or less so than the rest?"

He looked at me with a kind of reproof. I was blasphemous. "But that's right," I wanted to say. "Woo Jane and you'll always face these eyes of mine!" I would not believe, as did he, that it was all somehow of the same cloth, that the Ogre's destroyed army was one thing. I believe that each category of misery must be weighed in its own right and—like all great sins—independently repented of and regretted. To Gourgaud, there was no coming judgment, neither of himself nor the Emperor. But if the Emperor was to be praised for being in close touch with the rear guard, why was he not at the same time to be blamed for the rest? I knew that Gourgaud would not understand. He had been a soldier since an age younger than mine and his whole mind had been the function of soldiering. It had all been one thing there, one glory and one tragedy, but the tragedy served the glory and was its own justification.

"The Emperor was in no way to blame," he explained in a calm, ferocious voice. "How could you say he was, Miss Balcombe? You have met him. You have dined with him. You have seen his humanity."

He had by now left Jane's side to surge forward and rein in his horse directly in my path.

"How could any of it be the Emperor's fault?" he challenged me. "Any sane nation would have made peace with us after Borodino. If anyone is to blame—anyone—it is myself. I provided summer shoes for the horses, for there was never an idea that we would return whence we came in midwinter. Will you have me shot, mademoiselle? The heavy-shod Russian horses came on through snowdrifts and across ice—do you think I did not notice that difference, while ours skidded and slipped and broke their legs? I have apologized for this to the Emperor and it is always on my mind. And yet he says to me, like an honest friend, 'Gaspard, you should not have been expected to know what I did not know myself.'"

Tears began to form in the eyes of this gallant booby, and he was more influenced by them than his anger. He had taken the crime off the Emperor's shoulders and insisted on carrying it on his own.

Jane hung her head, genuinely overcome by the pathos of it. "General Gourgaud," she declared, "I must say that our whole family is grateful to the sweetened brandy you carried, for it made possible our acquaintance with you."

Gourgaud swallowed. He made a polite if curt bow in my direction as well.

I could not let it all finish in this spate of false amiability. "What will you do to me, sir," I taunted him, "if I exercise my freedom to blame the Emperor anyhow?"

His answer yielded up the struggle to him, I'm afraid. For he said with some grace and composure, "I will lament your ignorance, mademoiselle."

My ungraciousness to Gourgaud, who after all had done nothing real to offend me, had an explanation, and arose from something strange that had occurred when the Emperor had come to dinner the night before. My father had asked the usual guests—the admiral, and of course the officer attached to the Emperor's suite, Captain Poppleton, and Surgeon O'Meara, who resided in Jamestown but came so often he was a favorite by now. The dinner had bowled along at a good pace, but in its early phases the Emperor seemed distracted. I wondered if, like a reluctant student, he was burdened by the great history he was writing with the help of Las Cases, under the man's schoolmasterly and daily urging.

But in any case, a Frenchman should have been interested in such a conversation as that which prevailed at table—wine. And how welcome Bordeaux and other wines were now that they could be shipped licitly across the Channel to England!

I watched the Ogre, his hand in the sleeve of his jacket making tiny silent taps on the tablecloth as if he were memorizing poetry to himself. He saw me watching him and turned to me baleful, distracted eyes, and then, over a second or two, revived from his dismal condition, gathered himself, sat up, and looked at me with his usual geniality—or at least I thought so. Because the sight of me had seemed to spur and incite him, and he gazed out across the table now, and coughed and began to draw invisible diagrams on the starched tablecloth with the nail of his index finger as if to draw attention.

"Madame Balcombe," he said. "Mrs. Balcombe!"

My mother raised her chin. "Yes?" she asked. "Yes, sir."

"Sir" had by now been found to be a good compromise between the form of that address the Emperor was entitled to and that which had been imposed upon us by government.

The Emperor growled in rawest English, "You are like my Josephine." He looked into undefined distance. "You are reminded me of my wife Josephine." Then in French he continued. "My poor late Josephine. At the highest of her life and beautiful."

Then he seemed to come to a sense that he was in company, and he coughed again and said, "I have remarking since the day first I came. Forgive me, Balcombe and gentlemen."

It was the kind of flattery of uncertain currency, and no one at the table seemed to know how to broker it. The men avoided each other's gaze.

My father said, "That is very kind of you, sir," but his voice was confused. The blood had come to my mother's face, and my gaze was fixed on her to see how long it remained. I did not like to think of her in any conjugal terms, even by comparison, in relation to the Emperor. Now that the Emperor had unduly elevated my mother to an imperial connubial beauty, what did not embarrass me sickened me.

The Emperor began to look around the table and smile at each one—his way of returning the guests to a more easy state of the kind my father relished, and to encourage the resumption of normal talk. At last I turned my eyes away from my mother—it was too painful to watch her slow accommodation of both the compliment and the distracted profundity it had come from.

So I stared at the Emperor and hoped vengeance was legible on my face. But his eyes reached me neutrally and his smile was mild and then broadened. If he was trying to win me to the proposition of my mother's beauty, it was a proposition no thirteen-year-old girl wishes to hear: that her mother is the object of some lonely and confused desire. I had by then read two things of Josephine—that her teeth were very bad and her breath rank, and that she had had many lovers, and thus was a participant in the game of desire, a game, again, no young girl wishes her mother to take part in.

"Your present wife, the Empress Marie Louise . . . she is a handsome woman too," my mother bravely said, though the valiant impulse seemed to trip over itself.

"The most exquisite classic features," said the Emperor in French, obviously speaking of his living wife and no longer trying to deflect that quality sideways onto any other woman in the room.

In English he said with difficulty, "They had not letted Marie Louise to join with me here. Your government has not letted . . ."

But like everyone on earth I knew the gossip about this and was tempted to get even with him by saying, "Would she have come if they had?"

I am pleased on reflection that I did not utter the words. Such a statement would have been a grenade pitched into the middle of the dinner table—the company would not have survived. Besides, my father seemed to have recovered, seeing no peril to his hearth in the Emperor's praise.

"I must say," he said, choosing to seem utterly at peace with himself, "after such a handsome compliment, you must forgive the boys for calling you Boney. I am afraid they have heard it from their elders, whom I shall not name, and it has become their usage."

"*Boys?*" asked the Emperor, struggling with the term in English. And then in French he said, "Your daughters call me that as well. Well, one daughter does."

"Betsy," said my mother, happy to fall back into the habitual stance of maternal reproof, feigned or real.

"You must understand," said my father to the Ogre, confident that the commandant or the admiral or one of his daughters would translate, "that 'Boney' is a usage for your name that we English have raised our children with. Likewise 'Prinny' for the Prince Regent. In the case of 'Boney' it is half-affectionate, but a corruption for which I apologize on behalf of all British parents and children."

The entire table laughed, we were back to normal, and the Emperor redeemed himself by saying, "And a pretty child you are, Mr. William Balcombe!"

And as everyone laughed I knew that it was true: my father still had a schoolboy face, broad and cherublike and only half-instructed.

The contradictions of the Emperor's nature . . .

I *had heard many discussions* concerning the contradictions of the Emperor's nature, and these were argued at the heart of our family on the night he mentioned that my mother looked like Josephine. I think she was still in a sort of fever about it, the casual way he had landed such a huge burden of resemblance upon her. On the one hand she was mother, a goddess of the home by my lights, but her godhead extending only to the *domus,* and on the other the supposed copy of a woman who transcended all home, and whom the Emperor had himself presumed to crown in the presence of a pope, a woman whose name was more than her dutifulness, more than the color of her hair or eyes, more than the scale of her shoulder measurements, the length of her limbs.

I believe my mother had begun by finding the comparison a sort of violation, as I wanted her to. But I think that she was contradictorily disturbed by the idea it was something he said to the wives of all the men who gave him dinner in his fallen state—that it was like passing a coin to them, ennobling them, since he could no longer endow them with titles.

I have said there was a fever in the house. My sister Jane, I think, slept fitfully, teased by the admiration of Gourgaud. In the meantime, I purposely did not sleep. The Emperor's thrown-out remark had caused a shadow to fall between my parents, given my father's fraternal habit of indulgence towards other men. I wanted to hear my parents speak in the shadow of that preposterous comparison the

Emperor had made; I wanted to hear the outcome, the argument, or the plain fare of final reconciliation.

There was a panel in our small parlor that I knew, because it was the sort of thing I made sure to know, could be removed from the wall. It had in the past enabled me to secrete myself in a space between the parlor wall and the one adjoining my parents' bedroom. The panel removed, I left it leaning in place, for I was terrified of the inner cavities on which the island rats had taken a lease. To deal with them I carried an ebony ruler, like the one the Reverend Mr. Jones had used. I let my first footfall in the wall cavity be firm, to scatter the beasts, and indeed I barely heard any scurry, as if this were no longer a popular place with them.

I entered, and appreciated the small light from a parlor candle I had lit, and knelt in that musty cavity, ready to brain rodents from whichever side they came at me. I was aware that I must be accurate in doing this—a thud through the walls would not disturb my parents, since they were used to animal activity in the space, but the impact of my bludgeon on stones and wood would certainly cause them to be suspicious and to search.

I attempted to follow the line of their conversation. It was like finding out how the gods spoke amongst themselves when they were not busy directing thunderbolts at our heads. They were talking of a fellow I'd heard a lot of recently—one Duke d'Enghien, of whom I had been utterly ignorant ten days before, and yet whose ghost ran beneath our astonishment at the Ogre and whose name was muttered as an argument against too much awe. To reduce the Emperor to scale before sleeping, d'Enghien had to be invoked.

There had been conspirators against the Emperor, I knew or had heard my parents say—the Chouans, the silent ones, the self-proclaimed Owls, wise and discreet and seeing. In my infancy, and with my country's money behind them, they had been employed to land in France to kill the Universal Demon. Our prayers and those of the girls of Miss Clarke would have accompanied the Owls, had we known what they were engaged in. A man named Georges Cadoudal was a Chouan leader, and he had helped plan an attack on the Ogre on Christmas Eve in 1800 when the Emperor was on his way to the Paris Opera. An explosive apparatus had detonated by the Emperor's coach, dealing death to dozens in the street but not to Boney himself. But then, four years later, a plot involving a more direct assassination of Bonaparte was in play. The blow would be intimately delivered, by blade as in the killing of Caesar, or by that modern-version blade, the pistol. But the conspirators were arrested after they landed and, it was said, tortured.

At this time a young, urbane Frenchman, the Duke d'Enghien, was living in a German town just seven miles from the French border and receiving a British pension. It seemed that after the Chouans were severely questioned, on the basis of their confessions French soldiers illicitly crossed the border, captured d'Enghien in his house, and took him to the fortress of Strasbourg, where a French court-martial was held. The story was that the duke's grave had already been dug before he faced his judges. In court, d'Enghien was a model of resolution, at least according to the views of our side of the wars. He declared to his questioners and persecutors that he had requested from England a commission in our army and was told that he would not be given it but should remain on the Rhine, where he would shortly have a part to play. He had not yet undertaken that part when the French apprehended him, though he was not ashamed to say to the court that he hoped one day to bear arms against the Ogre's France. He was sentenced to be shot, this honest saint, an émigré becoming by valor an honorary Englishman.

We had all seen engravings of d'Enghien, his chest stuck out in defiance, standing in a fosse in the torch-lit fortress of Vincennes, looking upwards into the barrels of a firing squad on the morning of his martyrdom.

Now, as my mother raised that name, I could hear her brushing her hair, which was a little wiry, like mine. She chastised it with her brush. She declared, "We all forget in his presence what we remember out of it. Don't we? We remember once we're away that he had been guilty of that young duke's death."

My father was sighing, presumably with the comfort of getting his boots and breeches off.

"Well," he said, and I could hear a bubble of wine-built wind punctuate his speech, "as I'm sure he would have said, it was a court that killed the duke. Besides, say, my dear, just say that an infernal machine had been exploded near the Prince Regent as he was proceeding to Covent Garden, or that Frenchmen had landed with butcher's knives to carve him, and say as well . . ."

"Say, say," repeated my mother. She was angry at his turgid equanimity and wanted him to help her dispel the enchantment by listing the Ogre's sins. She would rather have had a murderer in the Pavilion than someone who complimented her in such threateningly intimate terms!

"Well," my father said, still equable. "Perhaps. But a further question for you! Would you not have applauded any of our valiant soldiers who raided France to capture one of the radical conspirators against our Prinny, to take hold of a man who was a traitor and conspirator, self-confessed as well, to bring him back from that foreign place and punish him? And if he, the conspirator, were retrieved to England, would not he be subject not simply to a firing squad but to having his body torn apart by horses?—I mention merely what the treason statute calls for—after being hanged from a scaffold first, cut down before he choked, eviscerated then, and his bowels displayed to him while the horses . . . well . . . ? And when those four sections were taken to the four corners of the kingdom, would we not consider that adequate and just treatment?"

"I would not," said my mother, "at this stage of human enlightenment, rejoice in the barbarity of rendering a man harmless by having him tugged apart."

My father sighed again. "Oh, I think we would," he persisted. "And if our prince then called out for clemency and allowed him the sweeter death by firing squad, we would cry, 'Oh, clement Prince.'" There was another little rumble of indigestion. And my father said, as if to himself, "Oh dear, oh dear." And then, "All I say is, let us see it from the point of view of matters of state."

"There are courts higher than the courts of Europe," my mother warned, invoking Heaven's court.

I was both titillated and engrossed by this parental argument. The very fact that they said things not meant for children to hear teased me, and made a strange sensation of pleasurable intrusion swell in my skull and press against the inside of my forehead.

I know now, and even knew from Gourgaud's narration then, of the thousands—the tens of thousands, the hundreds of them—this little man across the garden had led into vastnesses in Egypt and Russia, and it was curious that he was not condemned as much for that as he was for d'Enghien. My mother did not raise Egypt or Spain, Prussia or Poland or the Steppes. She raised this one slim, fashionable martyr.

I heard my father gasp again as he lowered himself down—a certain recurrent pain in the sternum or else in his foot, or in both, the penance he did for the pleasure he took at table and while he conversed. He drank with naval and maritime men so much, and the navy in particular was well known for its leisurely meals and its circulation of the port and conversation; and the army, I would soon enough notice, were not behindhand in those same enthusiasms.

I listened to my mother, still upright as I could tell from the timbre of her voice, discuss his costiveness and gout, and then she approached the bed and lay down and, prone, her voice was different. There was a particular piquancy to listening to them speak as they were recumbent.

A dull fellow by the name of Dr. Kay was my father's favorite physician—not so much my mother's. It was Dr. Kay's theory that kidneys and other offal should not be eaten by a sufferer of the gout, and though my mother thought that nonsense, she obeyed the stricture on the chance that he was right. Though she loved a kidney pie, she dutifully did not have it prepared for meals at The Briars. As already clearly stated, my affable father did not cooperate by renouncing port. On one occasion the Emperor had raised his own little glass and toasted my father, *Cinq Bouteilles*," he cried. "My friend, Five Bottles Balcombe."

"Do you know?" I heard my mother say, though not too wasp-ishly anymore, seemingly ready for sleep. "I believe that, with half of Europe, you, Billy, are infatuated with that fellow! Like half our Whigs too! Yes, yes, you might have wanted to see him defeated in the end. You might have wanted armies to move against him. But all the time you were enthralled, and you were secretly saddened when he fell, and now that you've laid eyes on him, you've forgiven him everything!"

My father, yawning, said that he could accommodate both thoughts at once in his head—charm and the fact that the Emperor had been the enemy. These were not contradictory things, he suggested. Did my mother think it was essential to making war that one side should be considered laudable and wise, the other brutish and lacking in allure?

"He certainly has allure for you," my mother said. "Even in Cock-burn too there's something that nearly wishes our visitor would es-cape and run loose again. Because he offers you something that you don't find in being English."

"No, no, my darling," my father protested. "Everything is available to Englishmen." His voice had softened and I heard him kiss her.

My mother muttered, "No, I believe that from China to Russia to Spain there are people who pity us for our plainness." There was a rustling again, and no conversation occurred, and I was about to vacate my space when I heard her say, "There!"—as if to conclude a conversation—and heard her kiss him in return, and at that, feeling a sudden warm onset, an amalgam of bewilderment and a sort of disgust, I covered my ears and backed out of my hiding place.

A few evenings after the day of this indecorous dinner, the Emperor himself sent a message that he would welcome a stroll along the route we had taken with Gourgaud. I had seen the Ogre in the morning in his dressing gown and turban, striding the floor of the Pavilion and dictating to Las Cases, with Emmanuel as reserve amanuensis and clerk. Now, in late afternoon, the Emperor presented himself in his breeches and green coat. Gourgaud was of course close by him.

We went out by the carriageway, where two sentries, the victors of Toulon, presented arms and gawped at the Emperor as he passed. Then we turned left, before the road, onto a rough track that took us past Toby's sacrosanct garden. As the Emperor looked into the orchard, he told us, "I have spoken to your father. I wish to see Toby the slave liberated. I have never seen such slaves as you have here. Aren't slaves Africans? And Toby is not African. He seems as Malay as that pretty young maid of yours, Alice."

Pretty maid? How many women was he open to admiring? "But many Malays are slaves in Cape Town," said Jane earnestly, wanting to clear up unwarranted assumptions.

"Mention it to your father, as I have already done. That I shall pay the East India Company what they ask and we shall put Toby on a ship as a free man, to return to the Cape."

"But who will look after the orchard then?" I asked the Ogre, given the pronounced appetite for fruit he had shown.

"His younger assistant might fill that role. Toby has served long enough."

"But you are not a man accustomed to freeing slaves," I argued.

"The Republic freed them," he said, "and I represented the Republic in its highest form."

"But," I argued, "you sent soldiers to your slave colony in Dominica to defeat the slave army there."

That, I hoped, punished him adequately for his outburst about my mother. Sadly he was amused. "My heaven," he said. "You have come armed with all the arguments, have you not, Betsy? We sent an army against General l'Ouverture because he refused to ally himself with us, not because his troops were former slaves."

"You always have an answer," I accused him. "You're always blameless, aren't you?"

Gourgaud shook his head and Jane gasped. The Ogre said, "It is Toby I wish to free in any case, not the entire world of slaves, whom, after all, your government has not been persuaded yet to free. Of course, as they would say, one can make an excellent argument that slavery is one of the conditions of humankind, particularly if one studies certain verses of the Old Testament. But one can also make an even more excellent argument that it is the worst injustice in the world."

I had failed again, of course, in ambition or instinct that sought to make him lose his temper so thoroughly with me that all would change, and I would never be called on to be an ally, and I would never be teased or tease him back. I did not even want to be treated with the courtliness that was his manner towards Jane. But then I wondered sometimes whether Jane was a person as was I, or a construction of easily learned attitudes and mannerisms.

In any case, I wanted to be free and back to my old self, and I knew now it could happen only if he renounced friendship with me.

By this time, we were beyond the wall of the orchard, and the stone-walled pasture with the dairy cattle was seen, dairy cattle from the Cape, since an English Jersey or Guernsey would have found the life difficult and the pasture inadequate. These Cape cattle were, however, hardy, and the omnivorous Ogre quizzed us about them, and the incomparable Jane answered in her well-schooled and earnest manner.

"They call them Cape Holsteins," Jane told him. "They are Dutch but mixed in with African cattle. The African element makes them hardy."

"I should very much wish to greet them," he said. "I mean, we should visit them. Gourgaud, you will help the ladies, will you not?"

And so we began to scramble over the stone wall. It took the Emperor little time. He seemed very agile on his thin legs and carrying his paunch, and was over at once, while Jane and I still sat on the top stones as if mounted upon horses.

"Good evening, ladies," said the Emperor, bowing amidst the cattle.

Gourgaud took Jane's hand, standing by the outside of the wall, and vaulted it himself without losing hold of her, and helped her descend onto the pasture side. I had to manage things according to my own skills.

By now the Emperor was already advancing across the pasture for the inspection of the Holsteins. As he drew near the small herd, he joined his hands behind his back in the manner in which he was always depicted, as if he were about to inspect a regiment. I may have been the first to notice that a robust if slightly scrawny and saggy cow raised her tail like a flag and began to run towards him.

There instantly rose in me a reluctance to call out a warning, a willingness to wait and see how events developed, to see if a man who was so prompt in recognizing his empress in other men's wives might be able to deal with this hazard of nature. So I was fascinated and in terror at once, and an inevitable rush of Greek fables ran through my head. As the cow lumbered forward at a solid pace, I thought of Zeus appearing to Europa in the guise of a white bull, fragrant and roaring but in a form of divine music. Then, according to the book of myths, Zeus "had his way with her," and what his way was went unspecified. This was the reverse, a cow running at Europa's bull, emitting as it came an unmusical dairy-yard moo.

But I waited to see if it was she who had been appointed to take revenge on the new Zeus, the deity who had ravished Europa, who stood five yards from me in his green uniform jacket. Was she an instrument of the divine? It seemed there was no other explanation but the Emperor's presence that had got this languid old cow running in this way.

The Emperor saw his peril now but began laughing. Again, given his age and his portliness, he proved to be a creature of great nimbleness. And as he stepped aside and made a pirouette the cow could not reproduce, he cried out, "Retreat, ladies."

Gourgaud came running up beside him to hurl himself between the beast and the Ogre and was told, "No, Gaspard. Flight!"

As we ran back to the wall, I felt the Emperor's arms around my waist, tight, identifiably male, lifting me over the stone fence—given that the proprieties of moving in pantaloons would have delayed us—the Emperor then himself vaulting the fence. It developed that this man of such ordinary dimensions had managed to sweep both Jane and me off the wall, and I heard Jane wheezing, as she had when she was a child with a weak chest. But Gourgaud remained in the field with the cow looking at him in confusion. He stepped forward and had drawn his sword, and I did not know if he was joking, but thought he wasn't, for he cried in French, "This is the second time that I have saved Your Majesty's life!"

The cow, however, did not seem to wish to impale itself on Gourgaud's sword. Boney was panting, but absolutely tickled by the behavior of Gourgaud and, indeed, of the cow. Whether the young general's boast was serious or comic, the Emperor took it as the latter. "Remain in a position to repel cavalry, General." The closer the cow got to Gourgaud, the more impetus it lost, and at last it veered off towards a tuft of pasture to its left, finding grass more appealing than the task of impaling. I think it was to Gourgaud's disappointment that it showed such a lack of Russian and Cossack malice.

"Come, Gaspard," called the Emperor. "She's lost interest in transfixing me with her horns." He turned to Jane and me and said, "A valiant cow, young ladies, that wished to save your government the cost and fuss of keeping me!"

General Gourgaud waited a time before he solemnly sheathed his sword and still after that stood there, asserting the right to that invaded stretch of pasture. Then he turned and vaulted the fence. From the look on his face he might just have defended the crossing of the Berezina.

Jane watched him as if he had achieved valor.

Sportiveness

I am at this age embarrassed by some of the sportiveness between the Emperor and me at that time, since much of it seems so childish. My behavior varied between the blatant and the pert, with an occasional bold-faced fit if I happened to remember his unabashed compliment to my mother.

People do not believe me that, given his awful stature, his repute as the great tyrant and the devourer of bodies, he was ready as if by instinct to play children's games, by which I mean blindman's bluff and hide-and-seek, with myself and my brothers raging round looking for him, or wearing one of his own vast scented handkerchiefs as a blinder that smelt so potently of something strange, of him. Some of our exchanges could correctly be seen as infantile, as if he had never had a chance for a full childhood of his own.

My father had meantime decided that Jane and I would become even more accomplished at French, and each morning he set us a passage from a book in our library to translate, having already spoken to the Emperor and extracted from him, with ease, an offer to study the results of our exercises.

My father did not seem quite to understand what an astounding offer this was. You might maneuver an offer like that from a lodger, but it was not the sort generally made by a man faced with the task of writing not only a history of *the* domination of the world but of *his* domination of it.

I hated this translation task. It would be a cause of conflict between me and my father. Let him translate! His French wasn't as good as mine.

Jane, as well as being assiduous at her translation, was the sort of unpretentious girl who was quite admired by the yamstocks. Occasionally a farm child would come and visit her, though only rarely would a farmer be found at The Briars. My father dealt with them directly, either down at the dock or by riding up into the hinterland to buy their stocks of vegetables. In the midst of our French lesson, there appeared at our gate a girl of about ten, Miss Robinson, wearing new leather shoes. In her world, they were a phenomenon— many of the farmers' families went barefoot year-round, but the new prosperity had enabled her to receive a gift beyond her expectations, a gift from another tier of society. In her place I would have had the same impulse to show off the shoes, and Jane was a perfect, open-hearted target, I knew, for such demonstrations.

The child was still wearing a canvas dress as she rode up on her rough island pony, the shoes glittering in the stirrups. She dismounted and showed them excitedly to us at the table where we often sat on the shaded lawn in front of the house, working on Montaigne. Jane did everything the child would have wanted—exclaimed about the stitching and the leather and the buckles! We called on Alice to fetch the girl a glass of milk to celebrate the attainment of this footwear.

There was, sadly, always something about Jane's untainted goodwill that annoyed me, that rankled for being too seamless, for not presenting edges up against which one could rub. Down in the grape arbor there was no such smoothness. If one passed, one could look into that cave of vines and the seats within as the Emperor, Las Cases, and little Las Cases worked, the son occasionally escaping to transcribe, being trusted, I noticed, even to put a gloss on what had been dictated.

Sometimes the Emperor would send the Las Cases away, and Gourgaud, if at home, would be sitting there with him, watching the Ogre doze with his legs up on Las Cases's chair. Today, though, I knew, Gourgaud had gone down to Jamestown on business.

When Jane went to attend to something, I was left with Miss Robinson. To call my impulses in her absence impish was to diminish some of the severity in them, that there was a kind of strict reason to them. For they were a protest—the child should understand this, I believed, that not all young women possessed the same transparent and seamless kindliness Jane had inherited from my father.

"Miss Robinson," I said, "would you care to meet Boney, our Ogre, who is in his cave at the bottom of the garden?"

"No, thank you," she said briskly. "I came to visit you, but had I seen him on the way I was purposed to ride home again helter-skelter."

"Come," I said, "you mustn't be like that. You are of valiant stock and not to be so easily frightened."

I took her hand and held it in an inescapable manner, and she was brave enough to yield, and together we walked down the lawn past the marquee, towards the gate that gave into the arbor. I walked her quickly, before tears or stubbornness could develop.

When I got to the gateway, I yelled, "Boney, Boney, are you awake? I have brought a child who is terrified of you. Do you intend to devour her?"

I could now feel Miss Robinson pulling at my hand. I could also make out that the Emperor was standing, and brushing his hair. He began then to make peaks of his thin hair either side of his head, as if to represent horns. And thus in breeches and shirt he came running down the tunnel roaring—a Cossack yell, he later told me—and little Miss Robinson screamed as I let her hand go, and she ran for the house, and I felt something despicable. A malign glee.

Knowing that my parents would never applaud what I was doing, and could not understand the fine balance of ill will and impishness that the Emperor and I shared so thoroughly, I caught up with Miss Robinson and held her, and she sobbed into my shoulder as the Ogre also drew level with us. I could smell his scented sweat.

"Please, mademoiselle," he cried, and dropped to his knee and set to smoothing her hair. He brought from the pocket of his breeches some licorice and said in English, "You like some supplies me? Licorice are very *tonique*, I do believe."

Choking with sobs, Miss Robinson was nonetheless not going to let licorice pass her by.

"You are unkind to compel her," said the Emperor to me, but I noticed that his eyes were alight and ironic, as if he understood me precisely.

"You are unkind to chase her like a fiend," I told him.

He remained kneeling beside the child and asked in English, "Your name, mademoiselle?"

I told him in French, "She is Mr. Robinson's daughter, Anna. She came to show us her new shoes, bought because of all her father's vegetables the garrison is eating."

Miss Robinson, noticing the Emperor looking at her feet, declared, "My papa gave me these shoes, sir, because my papa loves me." She hid her eyes again in my shoulder, but her sentiment chastened us.

"Tell her I thought it was a game," the Emperor pleaded with me. "I have a little boy, you know," he continued. "More younger than you. I do not like it that a child be fearful."

And in a very short time he had won her over—of course, winning children over was his style. She chewed her licorice, raised her eyes, and looked at him directly.

"Where your father been living?" asked the licorice-dispensing Ogre.

She told him—Prosperous Plain.

"May I be a visit him?" he inquired.

"As long as you don't yell at me," said Miss Robinson.

"I am visit the farm *seulement* by the daytime," he told her seriously, "since not permitted leaving my bed at night."

"Miss Robinson has a very pretty elder sister," I told the Emperor, making mischief, selling him the senior Miss Robinson so he would no longer declare anything untoward to my mother.

*F*rom our verandah we could now see each day a parade of wagons and slaves and Chinamen making their way up to

Longwood, carrying planks and plaster and implements. That this farm had been announced as the ultimate imperial residence baffled my father, and even I was bemused about why that open plateau, beneath a dour block of stone named the Barn, which barely blocked the easterlies always blowing and frequently carrying fog on their breath, had been chosen for the Universal Demon's ultimate residence. Had the British men of power simply inspected a map, seen the house identified on its plateau, and chosen it without reference to its notable disadvantages?

It had been a gentleman's farmhouse some time back, had been lived in by the Skelton family for a while, but had since deteriorated, its inner core abandoned, its outer rooms serving as cow byres. On these decaying premises, the domiciled rats suffered little attrition to their abounding numbers. Cats' appetite for rat meat was on St. Helena in particular out-sped by rats' appetite to proliferate. If St. Helena had had a coat of arms, its heraldry would have consisted of a rat and a goat.

For now, at the Pavilion and in its marquee, the Ogre remained relatively free of the gross intrusion of rats, and we were interested in the civilities and ceremonies of the household. The breakfast that preceded the history-writing was quite modest by English standards and appeared to consist chiefly of coffee and rolls. The longer the Emperor stayed at The Briars, the more his morning nourishment seemed to consist chiefly of coffee. But even that was prepared and served with imperial formality.

Then, in the evenings, if the Emperor was not dining with us, we would hear Cipriani intone his loud invitation to his master to descend from his Pavilion and enter the marquee, and when the Emperor emerged to dine he wore uniform and decorations, and so did Gourgaud, whereas Las Cases and his son wore court suits.

There seem in memory to have been many nights when the Ogre and his suite dined, similarly adorned, with us, and accepted whatever dinner hour the Balcombes decreed. He was a lenient guest, easy with any menu that was presented.

Within a few weeks of his moving in, he sent General Gourgaud to our door to deliver an invitation to Jane and me to attend dinner, and, he declared, our three small brothers were welcome to visit before dinner as well. I discovered that my brothers had decided amongst themselves to bring with them a particular toy they thought their fellow child, the Emperor, would enjoy. It was a toy Frenchman with a big curlicue mustache, and a lever with a frog on it. When the lever was pressed, the frog entered the Frenchman's mouth, and the English children giggled and squirmed to think that this was what the French were like. William was a thoughtful seven-year-old, anxious to be wise, rather in the manner of Jane, and had asked if he could bring the toy with him, and Jane had said no, that the Emperor might be offended by it. But I argued with her and said that if our guest, who, after all, lived on our property, could not tolerate such a small dent in French amour propre, then he was not who we thought he was.

I was aware that Alexander, who was most like me in assertiveness, had another toy, which Jane and my mother had forgotten to prohibit him from bringing. I whispered to him that he should bring that one too, that the Emperor would not be offended. Even Alex frowned and did not immediately fetch it, until once more I urged him to.

"Keep it in the pocket of your dressing gown and surprise him," I advised Alex.

So we set out with our three brothers, and the French servants reported we were on the way, and Gourgaud was waiting for us near the door of the marquee. Gourgaud's eyes flicked in admiration across the face of my sister Jane, and she turned her head aside. But I could see she was not averse to him. He bent and, to impress Jane, playfully shook the boys' hands and nodded to the toy Frenchman and toy frog William carried. His English was a little better than the Emperor's, so that he could manage to say only slowly, and without full accuracy, "What is it here?"

"Something he had a fancy to show the Emperor," I told Gourgaud in French.

"But yes," said Gourgaud. Before anything could happen, however, Las Cases in a gray suit turned up with Emmanuel, similarly arrayed, who looked mournfully at us from under his brown locks. I could tell that he wanted to be led into being some sort of playmate but that he did not know the moves to go through to achieve it. A cruel negation in me prevented me from guiding him in the simple steps involved, and I sat thinking punitively, You could be your father's brother rather than his son.

Then I nudged Alexander forward, in part precisely because I knew Emmanuel would be shocked by his toy. And now the Emperor appeared, plump and uniformed, wearing his hat and striding towards the table, his teeth stained with his licorice. Cipriani stood straight, and the servant Ali St. Denis (who did not look Arabic at all yet had been given Ali as a nickname by the Emperor) prepared to take the Ogre's hat.

I would later think of his time at The Briars as OGF's optimistic period on the island. I wonder, even while he was in our garden, did he hope for deliverance? There were plans for it everywhere, closer to us than we believed, but I think he must have hoped at this stage that his friends in Parliament—and one in particular, the eloquent Lord Holland, Henry Fox, whose uncle had once been prime minister of Great Britain—would win him a decent home in an English county. I did not know then that there were plans even in America for his rescue, though I guessed they proliferated in France and Europe.

Much later I would read that five soldiers in the French Army closely resembled him and had been schooled in his mannerisms. He must have harbored this knowledge even as he presented himself to us and invited us to dinner. So was there a hope then, even at The Briars, and despite the British flotilla keeping guard, that one could somehow be landed on a St. Helena beach—Sandy Bay, perhaps, the only realistic one—and exchanged for him? To this day there are stories that such an exchange took place. As if physical resemblance could be enough to compensate for the exact balance of resentment, playfulness, hubris, humility, curiosity, and literary appetite, and all the rest of which I would, in the end, learn something more than I wished.

That evening, the Emperor declared, "I see you wear, Miss Jane and Miss Betsy, your short skirts over your pantaloons again. This is a terrible fashion your nation subjects its young naiads to. You are not at fault for it, but only the English could devise such a means of punishing young women for their beauty."

This opening, I see now, grew from his unexamined belief that one's first remarks to women of our age were teasing—that teasing was the essential path to our affections.

"What do young Frenchwomen wear then?" I challenged him.

Gourgaud stepped in and in a very courtly way, bowing, said, not to me but to Jane, "They wear long dresses, mademoiselle, with low-cut necks and shifts and other proper garments beneath."

Our younger brothers were milling amidst this parley and wanted to show their toys. But Pierron, the pastry cook, brought out for the three boys some swans constructed of spun sugar and embodied with cream, and at a side table they began devouring them, William still with his Frenchman and frog in one hand, and Alexander with his unrevealed seditious toy in his jacket pocket.

I had felt a flush of rebellion, meanwhile, against the idea that the French were superior in all their manners.

"Is there anything we do the right way?" I asked the Emperor. "You don't like our roast beef, or you say you don't, and you don't like our puddings, and you hate our music, and now you don't like pantaloons. Is there anything else to hate?"

Jane put a hand on my shoulder to restrain me.

"Oh," he said, "I am sad if I brought forth in you, Betsy, the need to be a patriot. I admire so much that is English, above all the hearts in your breasts."

I leaned across the table at which we sat and said, "Jane, the boys are finished. They wanted to show the Emperor something before they go to bed."

Of course the Ogre immediately wished to see it, and pushed his chair back to welcome the delegation of boys. This was the true aspect of the Emperor, his face full of a kind of unpretending, child-like expectation. William displayed the Frenchman devouring the frog. The Ogre hooted. Next, Alexander came up confidently and showed him a ladder with a crude wooden doll of the Emperor at the top rung. At one flick of Alex's finger, the Ogre overbalanced and went tumbling down the rungs in a clickety-clack manner, which made the boys laugh and Jane cry, "Oh, no!" When Alex reversed the ladder, the Ogre doll swung upright again, and then descended. This process was repeated by gleeful Alex over and over again.

As if he thought the Balcombe girls might be affronted by Alex's toy, the Ogre took a second to assess us, as the arrogant doll began a further clattering fall. Gourgaud stared at the apparatus with a particular kind of frown, bringing his fingers together as if he might want to pray. Young Emmanuel considered the device wanly, but it was his father who uttered a gasp and looked away into the corner of the marquee as if invoking the Muse Clio to intervene and end this vulgar atrocity.

Then the Emperor began to laugh, his hacking but musical laugh. This pacified Gourgaud but not Las Cases. The more the Emperor laughed the faster Alex inverted the ladder and doll to let the Ogre fall yet again and again. "I hope you understand," he said, gasping. "I hope you understand . . . Alex, oh, for dear Old Boney's sake, let the thing down for a moment. . . ."

Jane had gone to Alex and prised the apparatus out of his hands and gave a look of reproof in my direction.

"I hope you understand," the Emperor continued, "that to make me fall, young Alex has first to raise me up. I doubt, young Alex, that your Lord Bathurst would be as amused by that. But that *is* indeed a toy! Give it here and let me manufacture my own downfall."

Jane raised her eyebrows and passed the thing over, and the Ogre played with the tiny doll in the bicorn blue hat with a rosette on it, and laughed every time the small doll fell down the ladder.

"Oop, he's up!" he cried in English, and as the doll rattled down the steps of the ladder, "Bah, he's on the down!"

He and my brothers were by now crazed with laughter.

There had not been sufficient mischief, so I asked in French, "Do you think the ladder is Russia?"

"It is an imbecile toy," said young Emmanuel de Las Cases in English. "It is not Russia."

This did make me pause. I was not expecting commentary from him.

"It is for baby imbeciles," he asserted.

He was so certain about it that I was almost attracted to agree with him, to make an alliance now. He had been the one to attack the malignity of my question. I was hoping it would be his father.

Gourgaud was saying, "No, no, my little scholar. It is amusing." He thought that in defending me he was pleasing Jane.

Las Cases in the corner of the marquee, and his son at table, both glared.

The Emperor held the thing aloft and said to everyone at the table, "This is what they gave English children in their nurseries to ensure they would grow up and defeat me."

At last he handed the toy back to Alex.

"The ladder, Betsy," said the Emperor, "is rather small for Russia. But what does it matter? For *choc, choc, choc*, I am here!"

Jane and I ushered the boys out, and they went with the unrepentant laughter of the Ogre in their ears. The dinner was brought in—two tureens of soup and a number of dishes of meat and fish and vegetable—and served onto silver plates decorated with the Emperor's eagles under the direction of Marchand. We could smell the work of Le Page and Pierron before we saw it, for they had prepared three chickens, which had been cooked and basted on a spit Le Page had devised so that he did not need to incommode, or at least struggle with, Sarah and Alice in our kitchen.

We sat. The Emperor spooned up the soup less elegantly than the Balcombes did. When the rest of the food arrived, he ate very quickly and uttered a little murmur as he chewed. The two Las Cases men and Gourgaud rushed their food to keep pace dutifully with him.

Gourgaud asked, "How long have the charming Balcombe girls actually lived in their native land as distinct from on this island?"

The Emperor interjected, "My friend General Gourgaud would prefer to say that you had never been to your native land. That you were the unsullied product of this rock."

"We have been for some time in England," said Jane. "We were there as young children. And Betsy and I as students."

The Emperor asked, "But if asked to define yourself, are you women of Britain or women of St. Helena?"

"Britain," said Jane, without hesitation.

"St. Helena," I said, with the same level of conviction.

The Emperor held out a plump, cosseted finger and, not for the first time, looked pleased. "And there we have it."

Jane, the Englishwoman; I, the desert island savage.

"Then what can you tell me about this woman who rides to town on an ox?" he asked.

This was Miss Mason, a farmer of the island. We had heard, both Jane and I, that she was once a great beauty. Now she was a strange crone in a canvas skirt. We said what we could—she had extensive vegetable plots and dairy herds and was a rich islander but never displayed her prosperity. We were interrupted by the brisk clearing of plates, whether we'd finished or not, and Pierron brought in some chocolate and ices and spun sugar swans of the kind the boys had earlier eaten.

"Tell us," asked the Ogre, "is the Prince Regent really your grand-father?"

This was a question that routed us. Jane was stunned. By nature, I knew how to play for a little time.

"Our grandfather?"

"I don't think it can be true," said the Ogre. "Though it's said in the town."

"What is said in the town?" I demanded. The Emperor could see that we were both bewildered, and he rushed to say, "Are you not all the children and grandchildren of the Prince Regent or, as you call him, Prinny? Is that not a proud enough description for you?"

I frowned. Jane signaled with her hands and movements of her lips that we should let the Ogre's statements slide by us.

"Betsy is distressed without cause," declared the Emperor. He turned to young Emmanuel. "She laments the lack of a standard education, you understand. But the value of such things is overestimated. Have you known a standard education, my young friend? Tell the Balcombe girls."

"I was in Your Majesty's court. I caught lessons from excellent tutors as I could. I receive an excellent education but not in the usual manner."

The Ogre said, "I know. You must forgive us. You could not have been born at a worse time. A child at home in Languedoc and then, all at once, as I called on your father, at court. And the rest of your schooling?"

Emmanuel declared, "I have learned all I know by obeying and assisting my father."

"A wonderful education in itself," said the Ogre. "So, Betsy, you have little to complain of. For there is no perfect education, whether in an imperial court or on an island in the midst of seas."

I was thinking not of education but this thing he had said about our being Prinny's grand-brats.

Suddenly the conversation seemed to have been taken over by Gourgaud and Las Cases and military matters. The geography they called up evaded me, yet I was overwhelmed, to an extent I vowed not to show, by what these men had achieved and endured together. That I refused even at that age to be awed was my strength, and marred my life.

A shrug in Gourgaud's direction . . .

*A*n afternoon shower had brought my mother and me in from the garden, and as clouds milled at the top of Diana's Peak, we sat together companionably reading, an experience I valued as much as if I had her entire attention. I had presumed that my sister was in her room—I was sure I had seen her flit inside earlier. And then I heard Thomas, whose feet pounded on the steps as he entered the house, shouting, "I saw old Gourgaud. With Jane. In the grape arbor. He was feeling her bubbies!"

My mother ran into the hall. "What is that?" she asked, as if terminology was the problem. "Where did you hear that word?"

132

"They were kissing," he roared with riotous distaste.

"Go to your room!"

She pushed him down the hallway and he stumbled, but as he righted himself acrobatically he gleefully called again, "Her bubbies!"

As abominable a term as it was to my mother, it was an adventure in language to him.

I followed her onto the verandah and saw Gourgaud and Jane standing together on the lawn looking confused, Adam and Eve cast out of the grape arbor. Thomas, imbued as all boy children are with such curiosity, compounded with much animosity to the female gender, was still caroling the news indoors with gusto.

"Jane!" my mother called to my sister. And Jane came across the garden and up the steps towards her, pallid for one second and blazing-faced for the next two, without a glance towards Gourgaud. The sword of my mother's voice had easily cleaved them apart. Gourgaud now bowed profoundly towards my mother though his face did not change color. My mother did not accept his obeisance and turned on her heel and followed my sister inside.

I do not know why I then made a shrug in Gourgaud's direction. It was certainly in part to let him know that he had gone beyond the terms of our sharing our habitation with him. But I realized at once that it could have been interpreted to mean that I thought he'd had bad luck. When one is thirteen it is hard to say anything clearly, for all is ferment, and this gesture was of that order. As I felt there had been a sort of invasion, now I was comforted by how severe my mother's face had been to Gourgaud, as severe as I could possibly have wished it to be. I was also amazed by Jane. If she and Gourgaud had been close together . . . well, it couldn't be imagined. And if something had happened to Jane, then it must happen in a worse way to all lesser girls, including myself. I rushed down the hall to hear, through the closed door to my sister's bedroom, the loud and urgent counsels of my mother. Jane's shamed sobs were audible too.

"God knows," said my mother, "you are innocent enough and men of the great world take advantage of it. Men are not ruined, but a girl is ruined every minute. Men can move from sunshine to the dark at will. But women live on a knife edge, miss. You must be more careful. To go with a man like that into a hidden place . . ."

I was thrilled and appalled by this definition of my sister's folly. My mother would have been delighted to know how thirstily I drank up every minatory word. I wanted her to be harsh, to make me a safe child. I was delighted with every admonition I heard thrown in Jane's direction in the next half hour, not in this case out of some mean delight in seeing Jane threatened, but because I felt the threats enhanced and fixed me in time and virtue as well.

At last Jane was left to herself, and my mother emerged into the hallway. I had fled down the hall by then and into the drawing room, but my mother stamped in behind me and put her ferocious and seemingly bruised eyes on me. "Don't pretend you didn't listen, Betsy. You take note too. A knife edge! You are the sort of girl the world would love to condemn!"

I felt with a wave of primitive awareness that she was right.

My father, once home, was sent down to the Pavilion to ask Las Cases whether he could have an interview with the Emperor, and when he was let in to see OGF, who was reading in shirtsleeves, he outlined Gourgaud's behavior towards Jane. From what I heard, listening agape during my father's later conversation with my mother, the Ogre called Gourgaud up from the marquee, where he had been sent to wait throughout the meeting. At the end of my father's complaint, Marchand was then sent to fetch Gourgaud. Gourgaud's face did not betray the contrition my father had expected he should be suffering, but at least he showed no arrogance. He accepted the Ogre's reproof almost humbly but also, said my father, with a military dispassion. The Emperor told him that he had violated a dear friend's welcome, and then slapped him on the cheek, one deft, plump-fingered slap. My father was pleased to hear Gourgaud's breath catch, but then the man stepped forward instantly and apologized as fully as my father wished. I believed, however, that it was a soldier's apology and owed more to Gourgaud's alacritous obeying of the Emperor's orders without question than to true penitence.

Later that night I went to take some junket to my sister's room. She began to spoon it in mournfully, for she had eaten nothing.

"What was it like?" I suddenly wanted to know. I was hungry to know. What was to be avoided and what welcomed? "What did it mean to you?"

"It was terrible," Jane insisted. "It was hateful."

She thought that, under my mother's strictures, she was telling me the right thing, but I could see that she was lying. I could well believe it was horrible in some sense, that it was the awful collision of the angelic and the worldly, and terrifying. But there was something before that. Something I could not envisage—something to do with allure and a choking of the heart.

*W*hile Jane and I worked on our French translation, Jane invariably finishing first, I took every chance to move into the house, visit the kitchen for a piece of cheese from indulgent Sarah, and pause by the small parlor to hear how Old Huff was getting on with my brothers. William as the oldest was more solemn and tried to manage the other two by example, but Thomas and Alex were indulged by my parents, or else benefited from the idea that girls on the edge of womanhood needed more rigorous terms imposed than did small boys, in whose case it was accepted that they should be feral for the time being. As well as that Alex was clever and glowing-cheeked, like my father, and capable of sitting docilely on his daddy's lap and charmingly instructing him in the history of the Medes and Persians, which he had precociously learned from Huff. My father told anyone who would take an interest that Alex would be the family's scholar. Huff's exposition of any knowledge before the young meant that, as from the passage of migratory birds, a seed might drop into a pocket of rich soil and produce from it an educated being.

It was not only the Medes and Persians and the Hebrew alphabet that Huff imparted to the boys, just as earlier the Reverend Mr. Jones had imparted them to Jane and me. He had seized their imaginations with the tale of Fernando Lopez, the first man of the island. It was confidently said by the yamstocks that Lopez was out there still, that he could be heard howling from the thickets in the mountains by Prosperous Plain. Lopez, a Portuguese nobleman, had traveled with General Albuquerque to seize the port of Goa in India. He had been the man placed in command of the garrison at Goa while Albuquerque returned to Portugal for reinforcements. During that time, Lopez and his men, led astray by the beautiful darkling Moslem girls of Goa and accepting their beauty as if it were a theological argument, adopted the religion of the region.

In time General Albuquerque returned to Goa with a fleet of transports and considerable Portuguese soldiery. Now back in the hands of his appalled countrymen, amongst whom the Inquisition and its punishments were established, Lopez was tortured for his apostasy—as were his men. Indeed, many of his fellow apostates died during the torture. Amongst the spiritual cures and defacements Lopez himself suffered was the excision of his nose, cartilage and bone, his ears being cut off, his right hand and his left thumb lopped. And though he was now unspeakable to behold, his soul was returned to Christ.

All this Alex and his older brothers were thrilled and awed by.

Thomas asked my father one evening, "Is it better to have no nose and have God, or to have no God and keep your nose?"

Alex waited moon-eyed for an answer.

"We English people," my father said, "are not as extreme. We believe in keeping our God and our nose and not swapping one for another."

To the boys it was an utterly unsatisfactory answer.

Lopez, on his way home to the country of his God and his family, seeing the island and what a fortress it was with its cliffs, and how wooded in those days, and being uncertain whether his family in Portugal could still love him after taking first sight of his savaged face and body, chose to land and hide in the woods that then covered Deadwood Plain and amongst the rocks of Devil's Glen. Parties searched for him for many days, but he could not be found. So he was abandoned, though his shipmates left goats ashore to provide him with ongoing sustenance. Where Fernando Lopez's bitter tears fell, the island's fancy says, lemon trees grew.

Yet he was not an evil man, Huff argued. Not in his deep heart. He had imprisoned himself here as a penance, and with his mutilated lips and sucking breath he prayed by our streams and our mountains and rendered the island holy. Fernando Lopez bathed himself in the streams and cleansed himself in a repeated form of christening. Lopez foreshadowed the Emperor, said Huff, as St. John the Baptist foreshadowed the Lord. The Emperor, as tormented within as was Lopez, was also confined to this island and had the power to give it, said Huff, a new weight. This latter, prophetic detail barely touched the boys. They had been satisfied by nose-mutilation and were now ready to move on to other arresting tales of that kind. So plain meanings, let alone unspeakable ones, were beyond Thomas and Alex, and noise from Huff's classroom was riotous, and William was distracted by trying to act as a conscientious prefect, as Jane would have done.

Yet there was for me some mental stimulation in hearing Lopez depicted as St. John the Baptist, making straight the way, and holy the streams and mountains. For the One to Come.

Day for translations . . .

So again it was a day for translations. My father had gone to his little library and extracted a copy of Thomas West's *A Guide to the Lakes* and marked a passage for Jane to translate into French, then allocated another to me. The passages were never longer than a page, and with ordinary application I could have made a fair rendering in twenty minutes. But it was the application of the perverse soul that failed me. My father had his fixed and simple idea about what was needed of young ladies. He had randomly decided to express all his sense of parental duty into this damned daily exercise.

As we worked at the table under the tree in the garden—the very ambience should have made me more amenable—my father's horse was brought to him where he waited by the gate to the carriageway. At this second the Ogre emerged down the rock steps from his breakfast in the Pavilion, in a hurry, bearing down on the table, where he snatched my paper and, with a rogue's smile, said he would show my father how much or how little progress I had made. He took the page up to my father and seemed almost to expect shared amusement. He looked at its scatter of ill-framed phrases and dismounted. He advanced on me with the translation in his hand and told me there would be trouble if the exercise was not adequately done by the time he returned from the town. He bowed august thanks and respects to the Emperor, then was helped by Ernest into the saddle, raised his large hat, and was gone.

"Oh, my dear," the Ogre, returning, said to me, "I did not expect your father to be so very serious about this. But perhaps he understands we cannot have a young woman of your station in life unable to make a lively translation. You can express lively sentiments to me. Why can't you simply write down what is there?"

He then leaned over and murmured, "Do not forget your French is better than your papa's, so you have that advantage if you simply make it neat."

"Was it your place to interfere?" I asked him.

He made a squeak with his lips and a little shrug, very Gallic, and said, "Marchand must shave me now that I have created sufficient disorder." And he was gone, fast on his thin legs, his plump feet.

This intervention by the Emperor summoned up a sprightly riposte in me. Suddenly I could work with a will, because I was doing so to defy the Ogre. That afternoon, with the translation done and approved by the Emperor, all the Balcombe children were invited into the marquee to be served some of Pierron's refreshing ices.

Without our knowing, Alexander brought his own pack of cards, hoping the Emperor would play snap with him but also unabashed that on the back of each card the Emperor himself was depicted, his head rising upwards and wearing a tricorn, but connected at the neck to another Emperor head, upside down and wearing a Turkish turban. I could not work out the purpose of this device but it was clearly not meant to flatter.

"See, Boney," said Alexander, breathless. "This is you on the cards." To Alex, this made the Emperor a figure of true fame.

"Bony?" asked the Emperor, in mock reproof, and did what had become in a week or two the standard joke of showing his hand to prove that he lacked boniness. I found it a fascinating hand and wanted to be able to hold and study it at length, something that was socially impossible, for it seemed to possess a martial strength and yet was dimpled at the knuckles like the hand of a healthy child of two years.

I said, "I know your hand has held a sword. Yet it's hard to imagine you wielding such a heavy cavalry weapon as the one you were wearing on the day you first came to the Pavilion."

It was a harmless remark by the standards of my normal discourse with the Emperor. But with that Gourgaud drew his sword, the one with which he had attempted to repel the Cape Holstein. Did he think I had insulted the Emperor and now intend to impale me? If so, I would die laughing, for Gourgaud's steel brought out more whimsy than fear in me. I was once more amazed by this man who had managed to find more than one hundred cannon and put them in place at the frozen Berezina River, and yet had no more idea of how to behave in company than I did.

"It is not about the size of a hand or its form," he declared. "The sword glides. The sword emerges like a viper." And then, inspecting it, he became more absurd still. "You see those tarnishes? They are acidity from the blood of men I have impaled."

Again, was this meant to be a warning?

The Emperor laughed, "Sheathe the thing, Gaspard, for dear God's sake. By heaven, you have really never lived anywhere except in a barracks or a field camp, have you?"

This chiding, added to the one given in the field when Gourgaud ridiculously faced the Cape cow, brought the darkness of rejection to his face. We were getting used to this expression. Jane, who was comfortable with him now that he had been reduced to an integer in her life and affections, declared, "I doubt it would glide and emerge like a viper for me."

"Run in behind the screen, and get mine then," the Emperor instructed Gourgaud. Gourgaud sheathed his sword and proceeded with a military degree of ceremony behind the screen and came back, his face hard to read, carrying a long embossed case with a golden "B" on it. He laid it ceremoniously on the table, and backed away from it as from a bier on which lay the corpse of ambition. The Emperor approached the case, opened it, and lifted with two hands a glittering sword in a gold-and-blue scabbard. I looked again at the tortoiseshell scabbard in his left hand, all studded with golden bees, his plain and subtle symbol. The handle in his right hand was shaped as a gold fleur-de-lis.

After holding it aloft, he suddenly withdrew the blade from the scabbard, and began flicking it about in his hand and lunging with it as if to satisfy theorems of swordsmanship, and as if the friction of the thing in his hand was like a form of memory.

"It is very heavy, nonetheless, Betsy," he said, ceasing to feint, fluidly reversing the sword and passing it handle first towards me.

I felt that in receiving it I was oafish amongst masters. I was dragged forward by its very weight. In the sweaty fold of my plain hand it was a rich implement, perhaps the most valuable, for symbolism as well as for cash, that had ever entered the island. The gravity of the blade threatened to tear the gold handle out of my hand.

"I do not want to tarnish the handle," I said, with some awe and in the hope they'd take it from me.

"No, Betsy," the Emperor said. "You are designed for such implements. Or it is their duty to be designed for you."

And so my awe gave way, as he had intended it should. He wanted some gesture from me. I knew what it was: that I would threaten him with this tool of war. He wanted the craziness of such a scene. I took full possession of the handle then. "It is a matter of honor, sir," I shouted, "that my French translation shall not be mocked!"

He barked with excited laughter and began to back away as I gestured. I lunged towards him, careful not to strike him but to find empty space with the point of the thing, with which I felt an increasing contact through the haft and steel and tip. Even so, given my lack of skill, this was possibly the most dangerous thing I could do. The idea of accidentally impaling the Universal Demon excited me, and him too.

I saw Gourgaud go for his own sword and have it in his hand, half-drawn, willing to tarnish it with further gore of the Emperor's enemies.

"No, General Gourgaud," yelled the Emperor, and returned to braying with hilarity.

The measure of excited fear in the Emperor's voice made me understand it was not merely play with him. It was all to test the terms imposed on him by the island, to see if one of its daughters could be ill-spirited or accidentally exact enough to kill him in play and thus render his escape. In the way he laughed there was a sort of proposition, an invitation to give him from a risible and friendly hand what hostile hands had never been able to. And, after all, they would not hang me for transfixing the Great Ogre and Universal Demon.

So in frantic excitement I began to make slashes in the air either side of his body, and then, reaching the limits of my strength, swishes above his head, even while holding on in desperation so that the sword would not fall and harm him. A mere cut, as against a serious penetration, would reduce the scene to inanity. It wasn't what he was looking for. He was looking for something ultimate, and that was marvelous.

Not being a knowing participant in the whole gamble, Jane was raging at me in terror at the possibilities of my swordplay. The boys were cheering me on, of course, since they were creatures of mayhem. But with Jane there was the risk she would run and get Father. I was to put the sword away immediately, she screamed. I laughed in a particular manic way that made the Ogre laugh too, and I pointed the weapon at Gourgaud and yelled in English, "Come and take me!"

And the Emperor still, within easy reach of my sword—for it *was* my sword now—and in the midst of breathless laughter, kept telling Gourgaud to hold his place.

I was aware of other presences in the marquee now, a gathering of forces. The Grand Chamberlain, old desiccated Las Cases, had entered with his solemn son. I took an instant to see if they were both as wide-eyed as I wanted them to be, the scholarly chamberlain and his mannequin.

Jane was still screaming her energetic threats as Las Cases roared with surprising force, "Desist, mademoiselle! In the name of all reason, desist!"

I had become exhausted by now from holding the thing. The madness that had kept the blade horizontal was passing from me. I stepped back and with a great gasp let the blade come down towards the earth, being careful not to dent it against the ground. I managed that by holding the hilt two-handedly. This permitted them to think I could still choose to prosecute further havoc. But then, not looking at the Ogre, and certainly more clumsily than he would have done, I presented the hilt to him.

"Fair exchange, Boney," I told him, without repentance, and confident that he was the only one who understood what I was talking about.

The Emperor slowly took the sword and inspected it with love.

He said, "It has not had such a flourishing in a long time, Betsy." He passed it unsheathed to Las Cases. "Please, Comte, have the blade and handle cleaned. It is so humid on this island, and Betsy so enthusiastic."

And then he turned to me, his eyes playful, and waved his finger in front of my face as if to get my attention, and reached forward and chose an ear that happened to have been pierced the day before. He knew it had been pierced too—it had been at his recommendation that my parents let Sarah attend to it. And now he squeezed it.

Of course, I determined I would not show any pain. I gazed at him. The ear stung, but it was less intense than being impaled by Gourgaud, who would have cherished more blood-acid on his blade.

"I can't believe what I have just seen," said Jane in what sounded more like shock than chastisement. "General, you must forgive my sister. She is sometimes out of all control." She lowered her voice. "She's supposed to be nearly a woman."

I heard the soupy, regular piety of her voice and hated her for it.

"Oh," I said, "I suppose that if I were a woman, I would be so much under my own control that I'd let Gourgaud paw my body!"

She turned away, uttering a few more vapid, terse sentiments. She could not participate at the level of understanding the Ogre and I had reached. The Emperor himself was making reassuring waves of his hand. She did not understand the compact that existed between him and me; that I had particular knowledge of him, and of his impulse to play, fully as children play, inflicting pain as children do, and with the same fierce intent of children.

Antic regions of the soul . . .

he problem was that Jane, aghast and believing herself right, reported the scene to my father. Rare anger suffused his face. I began to argue my case well—or at least I thought so. "You don't know and can't judge. He wanted me to play with the sword like that. Ask him! Go to him and ask him!"

My punishment, he prescribed, was to miss the proposed ball at Plantation House, envisaged as a levee of welcome for the Ogre. But even that did not stick in the end since Bonaparte talked him round. The matter of the ball, however, would provide further asinine exchanges between the Emperor and me. If the reader believes that I am making some special claim over the antic regions of the Emperor's soul, then be assured that is precisely what I am doing. I was utterly convinced I was the playmate from the childhood he had never had and which he now possessed the time to pursue. My father's connection with him would be a far more substantial one in many ways, based on serious arrangements, and bearing serious consequences. And his connection to my mother . . . Well, that will be told.

Nor did the madness between us end with the incident of the sword. One day we had the Count de Las Cases and Emmanuel to tea, along with the Emperor, Pierron having provided the cakes even to our household and the Balcombes merely the China tea. I suggested a game of hide-and-seek, since that seemed best designed to discomfort the count, and the Emperor instantly agreed to it. There was no consultation with his chamberlain. There was no claim that he needed to get on with his history. As yet, it was rumored, he lacked all the reference books that he required, and the bound *Bulletins of the Imperial Army* that would be of great guidance and act as an accelerator of the work were still on their way to him. Thus if he might not in the future have time for us, the limitations of the library gave him the leisure now to play yet another child's game.

Later I would hear it argued, and above all see it written, that on the island the Emperor used his natural ease with other human beings as a means of gaining allies who could then plead his case in England, France, and Austria. But what power did young Thomas, Will, and Alexander have to speak for him before those high potentates? The truth was that a great deal of his ally-making was as natural to him as his own breath, and his power to win souls over had no higher purpose when they were the souls of children or slaves or servants or householders, none of whom had any management of the gales of opinion that swept the earth.

"Come join us, Emmanuel," he called to Las Cases's son, and the boy rose and did his best to be enthusiastic, ever desiring to be a good playmate.

The Emperor began to count loudly to allow us to scatter, and I saw as I ran for the back of the grape arbor that Emmanuel looked around as if he lacked the capacity to conceal himself. At last he simply descended to his knees and crawled under the table on which we had had tea, where his best protection was the neutral face his father directed at the abandoned tea and cakes.

It struck me that poor Emmanuel was no more to blame for his inability to play than the tone-deaf are for theirs to carry a song. An impulse to educate him in the automatic rituals of children rose in me as an urgent task, given his condition as a born adult and the competing fact that each morning now my mother quizzed me about whether anything had flowed from my body to signal that my childhood was over.

But with the cruelty of my years and my uncertainty about what a friendship with a boy his age would mean, I decided in the end not to give him the slightest merciful training in childhood. The Emperor, however, had plans to supply the lack. When he found me behind one of the maples, he held me by the wrist and called to Emmanuel de Las Cases, who crawled out from under the tea table, like a summoned orderly, and at a nod from his father, ran to where we were.

When he arrived, the Emperor demanded, "Kiss this young woman, Emmanuel. She is shy and pretends a lack of interest in you, my young count, even to the extent of feigned enmity."

I could think of nothing more obscene and struggled in his grasp, but he was determined to have it as a game. That was very well for him. It was an outrage for me. And with the heat of being so held, I felt at the same time the heat of rejection, in being defined as the object of kisses from a boy who had never known the gifts of childhood, when I had thought that I was somehow a freestanding votary of the Ogre himself, a votary who showed my devotion by repeated mischief. And now it was a child summoned to kiss me!

The Emperor's laughter filled the garden, and as I struggled, I could smell his particular sweat, and the amalgam it made with his perfume water. I saw his teeth, darkened with licorice, as he kept roaring in command and hilarity for pathetic young Las Cases, and in the end the strange boy did step forward and I could smell that he had had peppermint, and he lunged and laid his lips against my cheek, making a little squeak to go with it, and only to please his Emperor. The ninny was doing it like the Imperial Guards charging a redoubt, and his dutifulness made it all worse.

I felt a sense of outrage once the kiss had been consummated and I heard the Emperor hooting, while I choked on the bile of this cruelty disguised as play.

"Quick, Emmanuel, run," cried the Emperor. "Run, my boy!"

The younger Las Cases's face was flaming unattractively now. The Ogre pretended he was on the verge of losing hold of me. Whether he knew it or not, he had inflicted a scalding memory on both of us, and now the young count did turn and flee, taking to the steps, into the door of the Pavilion, and up the ladder to his room, where he knew I was not permitted to enter.

Meanwhile, the Emperor had begun to count to ten, and as he released his hold on me I lashed out at him with my elbows, then ran across the lawn and up the stairs and entered the Pavilion. I was bewildered. This had been a serious ploy of the Ogre's. Stealing his sword hadn't been enough vengeance to balance it. But I could not pursue the younger Las Cases to his room. I ran out of the Pavilion again and up the lawn and into the house, aware at every step of my awful pantaloons. I went to my bedroom, calling on Sarah to help undress me. Later Jane came in.

"Why were you so distressed?" asked Jane. "It was only a bit of horseplay."

It was as if she had been won over to the imperial side. I could not have explained to her, or even begun to explain to my mother, who came in to speak to me later and to solace me, the nature of my grievance. Nor could I understand my night tears and my sleeplessness, with that childish mark of the young count's mouth on my cheek and with the itch of vengeance crackling away under my skin.

In the morning Gourgaud was at the door with a note from the Emperor, a message of apology to my mother, saying that he had perhaps teased me too far, and in reparation he requested the company of Jane and myself that evening to play whist in the Pavilion, until now forbidden to us—though I had broken the prohibition the night before. Even so it was as if he were graciously opening up all his territory to the Balcombe girls. For though the Pavilion belonged to my father, or, more accurately, to the East India Company, it did not *seem* to do so under this new arrangement.

I could refuse to go, but my mother kept asking me to explain why I was reluctant. I was unable then to clarify my chagrin. So off I went to the Pavilion, in a strange mood of vigilance and inner sullenness with a sense of recrimination.

As we entered, we were warmly greeted by the Ogre himself and by General Gourgaud. Gourgaud was happiest in the evenings, when General Bertrand and the Count de Montholon were down in the valley of Jamestown with their wives at Porteous's boardinghouse. I noticed that Las Cases had been seated in a corner and given the job of maturing the cards at a side table, obediently spinning them out of his hand, taking the edge off them until they could be dispensed smoothly.

"My partner will be Jeanne," announced the Emperor, "because I can depend on her not to impale me with a sword."

He had already announced that we would play for money—for five-franc napoleons. He said he would have some brought to us if we needed them. But we had had a few of these coins presented to us a year before by a ship's captain who knew my father, so I brought them out of my locket and plonked them on the table, like, I suppose, a fishwife or tavern-owner's daughter.

We sat at table—I was teamed with the odious Gourgaud—as Las Cases delivered the cards.

We were in the strange situation of gambling money that carried my adversary's profile, a laurel wreath encircling his receding hair, thin in the years of power as it now was in exile. Our bets were placed and the Emperor declared, "Very well."

Gourgaud and I won the first game, and the Ogre must have considered that adequate reparation to me, for in the second he began to peep under his cards as they were dealt, held up his best ones for Jane to see, and distracted Gourgaud and me with small squeaks and moans, and sudden comic movements I did not find funny. They showed, however, that the tit-for-tat games were not done with, since in these situations the child's play ends only in the emotional collapse of one infant and the chastisement of the other. Yet there was no one to chastise the Ogre.

Now he revoked—that is, failed to follow suit, despite being able to, which I knew from having counted the cards so earnestly, like the young fool I was.

I said to him, "You have cards in that suit. I know it and so do you."

He made the normal banal denials—"Me? I am a simple fellow, Betsy." He was so delighted with himself that his laughter came nearly to choke him, and amidst it he demanded in a throttled voice that I pay up my napoleons to Napoleon. At last Cipriani entered and told us that refreshments were ready in the marquee below.

Las Cases was still sitting at the table, observing the game with all the solemnity as if his master had been negotiating a treaty with the Tsar of Russia. I was sure that he blamed the Emperor's frivolity on my influence.

The Ogre sent his servant Ali St. Denis to summon young Las Cases from his garret. "We can't leave little Emmanuel out," the Ogre told me dolefully. "He yearns for his mother, as indeed do I for mine."

I was desperate that our reciprocal madness should now end, though I could not yet see how that could be managed. When everyone was gathered, we left the Pavilion and descended the steps towards the marquee. I hung back. I refused the courtly invitation of Las Cases and Gourgaud to precede them, and left the Pavilion sullenly, behind the young Las Cases who, with averted eyes, had invited me to go ahead. Since I would not accept this graciousness, he shrugged briskly and went out himself.

The pathway down to the lawn level was of flat stones, and for decorative effect slaves had been persuaded to border the descent with the island's boulders, black and pocked. These cooled lumps of lava channeled us into a descending single file, the Emperor leading, Gourgaud, Las Cases next, then Jane, Emmanuel, and I.

As Jane went, she lightly touched the rocks on either side with outstretched fingers. I ran down a step and barged into the gray-clothed back of the young count. He fell with his hands out to protect himself, and thus pushed Jane, who collided with the back of the chamberlain, who involuntarily pushed and collided with Gourgaud, and so in that limited defile Gourgaud fell against the Ogre, achieving his normal wish of being as close to the man as possible, while I believed I had now made the conclusive gesture.

Emmanuel, who had fallen heavily not only against Jane but also against one of the volcanic rocks, righted himself, turned on me, and hurled me back against the boulders. Almost at once the boy's father loomed up behind him, glowering at me. The impact with the rock had expelled all the air from my lungs. I thought breathlessly, I haven't killed the Ogre but his stupid boy has killed me.

Getting some air back, and being convinced of my own survival, I called out, like someone who had suffered a mortal indignity, "Oh, Boney, this Emmanuel creature has hurt me."

The mood of mischief had obviously not worn off the Emperor, and he leaped up and climbed the stairs again in his normal agile way, the others, having recovered their balance, making way for him.

"Who did the pushing?" he asked. And then, his dark eyes not done with sport, he looked at young Las Cases. "This brute?"

"It was all an accident," I told him. "I tripped, and Emmanuel turned on me."

He wrapped his arms around the young Las Cases and said, "Betsy, you may punish him."

And though I knew him somehow a victim too, I began to hit Emmanuel across the face, feeling his flesh like a shock, and then to slap him openhandedly across his body, liking the impact against his clothing better, doing him no harm but immensely damaging his dignity. By the lights from the Pavilion I saw tears on his face, and felt the urge to stop and make an alliance with him against all of them, but yet again swallowed. Behind me I heard Count de Las Cases ask the Emperor, "Your Majesty?" He wanted clemency for his boy.

The Ogre let go and the young count made off to the Pavilion.

His father came up and asked the Emperor to forgive him, and asked whether he could join his son. Before he left, he turned to me and said in English, "You are a disgrace, mademoiselle. My son is in delicate health."

I felt something within me break with a snap I was sure could be heard. "Am I to blame for your own child?" I demanded.

I walked back wordlessly to the house, wanting them all dead and reduced to ashes, but not as passionately as I desired death for myself. It seemed to me that my life had become impossible since the Ogre had expanded to take up all its cubic volume, and there was no corner in which there was a remaining habitation for me, merely the bed in which I desired to expire.

I lay with a hot brow in my bed all that night, and did not sleep, then lay there through a day in which I did, in a profound slumber, and through another night, sticking determinedly to unconsciousness. I was confident, however, that I had broken the enchantment. My mother visited me regularly and stroked my brown hair, which I'd inherited from her. I would have been in trouble with her had my mental state, my collapse from the effort of removing my childhood from the Ogre's, not been so grievous.

It would be suitably dramatic to say that that night I received the first alarming signs of my womanhood, but it happened in reality a few nights after, and leaning over my bed at dawn, consoling me, my mother said, "Now you must start to behave like a woman, and less like a child."

She seemed close to being amused. My attempt to push the imperial party down the steps had by then become more a story along the lines of "What a wild thing our Betsy is!" rather than the scandal it had been on the night. My father also visited me and could be heard discussing my condition in mutters, and reached down to feel my brow with an ineffectual dry hand. My sister Jane brought me a plate of arrowroot, which I did not eat.

On the second morning, when I lay mute and desolate, by now despairing at my inability to expire, General Gourgaud apparently visited our door with a letter for me from the Emperor.

"I don't want to hear it," I protested.

I stopped my ears as Jane read, but of course I heard as well, because I wanted to hear. It was not beyond him to have included the formula to make survival tolerable. "My dearest Betzi," Jane said. "He spells it B-E-T-Z-I!"

My mother laughed hopefully in the background as if this eccentric spelling might coax me out of my state.

Jane read, "'My dearest Betzi, I have gone too far and treated you as if you are a child and not a young woman. When I play with children I become flippant, because I did not have much chance of childhood myself—it was all serious, my father so solemn about Corsican independence and the great Pasquale Paoli, and I not being permitted to do anything but agree with my noble father. But enough of that! I am desolated that I have offended you, and thus hurt your kind parents too, who—with you—have given the exile a more generous home than many would have desired him to have. I ask you to forgive your friend, who has treated you too recklessly and will not make that mistake again. Young Las Cases apologizes fluently for pushing you. This letter comes to you with my thanks, esteem and gratitude.'"

Jane studied me in an educative way, as if I were to learn something from her responsive face rather than she from mine. I turned my head, refusing her the illusion.

"It is signed," I heard her say, "with a large N."

My mother said, "He apologizes to no king, Betsy, but he apologizes to you."

I was aware that nothing of ease or certainty had come from my playfulness with the Emperor, so I did not seek reconciliation and tolerance. Thus I accused Jane, of course, of caring more about the Ogre than about me. But this was just more of the business of childish retaliation. There were, it seemed suddenly obvious, hopes of adult equality in that sentence "I ask you to forgive your friend . . ."

"If you want to make a reply," suggested Jane, "I can transcribe it."

And though I had left my infancy, I had not left behind my bluntness, and I dictated to Jane a reply that read, "Though indisposed at the moment, Miss Elizabeth Balcombe acknowledges the correspondence she has received and accepts it as a full requital of any pain inflicted on her, and extends her concern for any offense she might have given, but does not choose any further to involve herself at the infantile level that seems to be the one her friend considers suitable for her, but which she does not!"

"Do you really want to say that?" asked Jane.

"Yes," I howled at her.

"But he writes a number of gentle sentences and you give him back a few blunt ones."

"He can write ornately," I said. "It doesn't mean I have to."

Jane shook her head but then won me over by smiling, with a kind of gratitude, because I had in a way just proved that I had returned to my normal being. In that second I loved her and more than half-hoped that she would add some further softening sentiment in her own hand, which was very much like mine.

I had achieved the status of one of the women towards whom he was regretful, and I knew it was time I gave up baiting him and let him get on with writing his account. And once more I put forward his letter as a sign that, being amenable to me, he was following his nature and could not possibly seek any advantage. He could not have, because I had no advantage to extend to him. If he would be simply a man to my woman, that would be enough and all would be well.

*C*ount Bertrand, in uniform and with a sculpted face, and the Count de Montholon, often in darker, statesmanly clothes, were frequently at the Pavilion. I was pleased to see them walking on the lawn mournfully discussing matters of the renovations of Longwood with the Ogre. So concerned did they seem that there appeared a chance the Ogre might never have to leave The Briars, an outcome which, despite the contest in which we were joined, and because of it, I would have welcomed. I dreamed that we would nobly vacate our home and be given quarters in town, and that he would stay and be fixed in place by gratitude, avoiding forever the rebuilt and repainted farmhouse at goat- and rat-ridden Longwood.

In that time, we also had more visits from Fanny and Albine. On arrival they would first pay their respects to the Emperor in the grape arbor or, if it were raining, in the Pavilion. The Countess Bertrand always finished chatting to the Emperor first, and the Countess de Montholon, now a little more visibly with child, stayed at the Pavilion or the arbor longer.

Madame Bertrand did not seem to mind that she was let go first. Of the French party she seemed the least enchanted, the most at a remove, of all of them. But my mother became more reluctant to have Jane and me at the tea table with the two Frenchwomen, claiming she could not take us away from our French translation.

My mother asked Fanny Bertrand on one such occasion, "Shall we be fortunate enough to see the Countess de Montholon today?"

Or Madame Bertrand would give a little blowing of the lips and say, in an accent still flavored by her Irish childhood, "God only knows when we'll enjoy the ultimate honor of Albine's company."

Our soundless desire for elucidation filled the vacant air.

"She lingers with the Emperor, doesn't she?" said Fanny Bertrand, in that way of saying more than the exact words. "Since she is with child, there is little risk, one would think, of an impropriety. But I would still like to see all parties spared the low gossip of the town. The servants visit women down below in the port and spread all manner of nonsense. Marchand is in love with one of those English girls down there, and visits her. I don't condemn Marchand. He's one of the more reliable. But there are plenty of others as well."

My mother seemed to be getting a taste for what was said in these taut, crisp, breathy sentences, and I had at such times the painful experience, new to me, of finding her not a goddess but a mere woman at sport amongst women. Yet in a way I loved the example laid before me by Madame Bertrand, because she said what she wanted to say with such openness, her jaw raised and not stifled in a handkerchief.

"Men are crazy about Albine," she reflected. The reasons could not be readily discerned by me. We knew old Admiral Cockburn liked to spend time in her company in the parlor at Mr. Porteous's boardinghouse establishment, where they were all crowded in together.

"Of course," she said, with candid archness, "it's the way you present yourself, is it not?"

I glimpsed through her how crowded life must be down in the cramped rooms of the Portions—Fanny Bertrand and Albine de Montholon on the one sofa, their children confined in the rooms, the husbands at their allotted duties of supervision at Longwood, of dealing with my father, of correspondence with France and within the island, while contemplating the chance that in these narrow walls their alliance might fracture because of the different kinds of men they were, and the different kinds of women they were married to.

I had taken a deliberate resolve in my new adult life to let the Emperor have, without any mockery from me, his friendship with Madame de Montholon. It was impossible for me to say why their friendship bloomed, but, overlaid with the flavor of the improper, it seemed far easier to tolerate than the frolics he directed my way. I had decided to be solitary now, and broadly tolerant even of the Las

Cases, who would notice my new gravity as a woman wise beyond years in her judgment of others, though ever capable of lamenting their limits in a neat sentence.

One afternoon the Emperor suggested we visit the farming family to which little Miss Robinson belonged. Jane and I were ready for the ride across to Prosperous Plain, looking forward to a diagonal over rough ground, as we both liked. I was to ride plain old Tom, whereas Jane was permitted to ride our mother's bay mare, which had been brought in by ship. The Emperor's Arab horse, Mameluke, brown with white markings, had been led down to the carriage gate by Ernest. It was a stallion, even though stallions were considered far too flighty for the island's more precipitous tracks, and generally they were used for breeding. Last of all was the English escort Captain Poppleton's gray.

But before the two slave boys could help us into the saddle, the Emperor stopped at the tea table under the trees to see what Madame Bertrand was showing my mother. It happened to be a locket with a miniature painting of her cousin, the dead Empress, the paragon to whom he had with undue weight compared my mother. Old Huff emerged from one of his intermittent lessons with my brothers and, in his tattered suit, fell to his knees before the Emperor.

The Emperor took his hat off to him and called with more concern than amusement, "Oh, not again, dear Huff. Not again." But he was not easily distracted from the miniature, from the transactions of memory and longing, mourning and justification. The vanished Josephine, the divorced one. She had got a cold one evening while showing the lilacs and the roses at her house at Malmaison to the Russian emperor, while the Ogre was in Elba. But she was not dead as ordinary women died. She was immortal. How could she be compared, and how comprehended?

So he ignored Huff for a while and murmured to Madame Bertrand, "Fanny, do you see a chance that you would let me keep this?"

I could see she was reluctant to surrender the object yet also felt she should, and before she left that day she would hand the miniature into the Emperor's possession, and he would hang it by its black ribbon from a nail above the mantelpiece in the Pavilion, a point to which he would often direct visitors' attention.

"Please rise up, Mr. Huff. The Emperor does not like such displays," I meantime called, as the transaction proceeded between Fanny and the Emperor. It was still some seconds before the Ogre actually kissed Madame Bertrand's hand as a sign that he had accepted the little treasure from her, and gazed on it and closed it and raised his eyes and saw that, indeed, Huff was kneeling still, leaning into a breeze, trembling.

The Emperor rose from his chair and walked towards the old tutor. "Sir," he said, with a gentle breathiness, and in French, which Huff understood. "I believe you have been a student in one of the great universities."

"At Cambridge, my Emperor," Huff answered, in a brisk but reverent French.

"Ah. And you enjoyed reading the English radicals? John Wilkes and others?"

"And Tom Paine," said Huff. "A great Englishman, an immortal American, and a friend of France."

"And you must know from Tom Paine that an enlightened man does not kneel to any other of his kind."

Huff protested, in perhaps too loud a voice, "But to an incarnation, sir! One kneels to an incarnation."

"You are clearly mistaken in that, my dear friend, for I am an incarnation of nothing but myself. Besides that, your government does not want you to kneel to me, and might consider it a crime on your part and a further reason for punishment of me!"

"Let them consider it such!" Huff affirmed in a cracked, throaty voice. "I have had revealed to me a divine intention that I should be your liberator. You must be spirited from this garden of exile. That is the judgment of the gods. For this is an island of murderous airs."

"For God's sake, no, Mr. Huff," the Emperor murmured. "You make things hard for me by such utterances. The revelation you tell me of is not reliable. Austria and France and England have not concluded terms yet and may well be my liberators themselves, and thus you need not fuss. Then you and I might well live together in your homeland, as gentlemen, under English heavens."

"English heavens are not kind," Huff asserted. "They are pitiless." He shook his head emphatically. "I am not permitted to return. I was considered to be intemperate in the past. Nor do I see that you will be permitted either. Hence, you must be rescued, and the Lord, the Master of the Universe, the God of all Reason, has appointed the matter to me. This is the meaning of my life, of my being caged here all these years. It is why I was permitted in my youth to disgrace myself. This was a divine mechanism to bring me to your presence. To ensure, indeed, that I was in position to rescue you."

The Emperor had grasped Huff's hands and was trying to raise him before Poppleton and the guards who stalked the edge of the property saw this excessive veneration.

"I think that is not the case, Mr. Huff," said the Ogre. "And we are all a disgrace in our youths. It is our fault. It is not a divine plan."

"No, no!" said Huff. "It is all of divinity! For not all of us consume Italy in our youths. Only you!" He lowered his voice and brought some frayed pages from his breast pocket. "I have already studied the arrival and departure of commercial ships."

Next he pulled from the other side pocket a paper on which a map had been clearly drawn. "I have made a note of lookouts and batteries, including the one above the waterfall. They expect us to leave by Sandy Bay, but I am pondering unexpected points of escape. I must say, it is all a great weariness to my mind, but it is demanded of me even though far beyond my strength."

"Please, no, sir," said the Emperor, pushing the map and the pages back into Old Huff's coat. "You see that Miss Betsy has over-heard this, and Miss Jane, as has Madame Bertrand. The Balcombes are honest English girls and would be forced by duty to inform the admiral and the government of Britain of what they have heard. And young Captain Poppleton may overhear you too. So, you must understand, your plans are uncalled-for and cannot succeed."

As if by summons, a red-faced young Poppleton appeared on the verandah then. "Yes, yes, Captain Poppleton," the Emperor called to him. "I know you must report these manifestations. Don't feel awkward about that. But report my refusal to accept Mr. Huff's veneration as well. And leave him untouched, as any man of decent sense would, for he is well-meaning and he is . . ."

The Emperor made a waving gesture with his hand. Then he tugged Huff upright, and Huff rose in a sort of obedience, waved his head about, put it close to the Emperor's ear and whispered something, something he clearly believed would act as a revelation. After that, he grabbed the Emperor's hand and landed a kiss on its dimpled plumpness. At last he left, reached the gate, turned back, and raised just one finger to wave it solemnly back and forward like a conjuror, something meant to be of significance to the Emperor alone. Then he opened the gate and sloped off down the shadowy carriageway.

The Emperor turned back to Poppleton. "You must do what you can to ensure they treat him lightly or not at all."

Poppleton saluted the Emperor. "Do you intend we should ride, General?" he asked.

And so we rode south, Gourgaud with us too, past the foothills of Diana's Peak, flags fluttering atop it to signal the Emperor's expedition to the chief posts of the island. We passed through green country and a ravine into a land of stone fences and cacti. Finally we came to the stony farm of Mr. Robinson, its fields occupied at this hour of the day only by a scarecrow. A mastiff sat before the daub-and-wattle farmhouse, under its shingle roof. Poppleton knocked on the door, and Mr. Robinson emerged, tall and barefoot and dressed in canvas.

"There be the rail, Your Gentles, for tetherin' your horses," he genially called. "You are right welcome to come into the house if the honor of your enterin' be mine!"

He knew who was visiting him. He was trying his best to be urbane. Somewhere in the farmhouse or outbuildings were Mrs. Robinson, the handsome mulatto, and her daughters. Mr. Robinson nodded us inside to a spacious dark area in which stood a table, with a sand-soaped smell as if Mrs. Robinson were a very particular woman. The man of the house suggested that the Emperor and his party each should take a seat and offered them wine.

"You have wine?" the Emperor asked him.

"Not the finest, Your Worship. But from the Cape."

The Emperor said to me, "If we are not depriving him of it, Betsy, tell him we would like a glass of the Cape wine."

I told Mr. Robinson, and that Jane and I would abstain. He fetched a bottle from a dresser and pulled the cork and poured a claret into three tin cups, which he handed, one each, to the Emperor, Captain Poppleton, and General Gourgaud. The Emperor gave his cup the honor of a serious sniff and looked around the room with his usual curiosity. This was why men had loved him, I understood: his curiosity was undiscriminating; he brought it to every human, and every habitation.

The Emperor asked me to request of Mr. Robinson whether he had a wife. I did so, though I knew the answer.

"Yes, and may it please you, Sir Emperor."

"And I met your little girl," said the Emperor. "She was alarmed at first and I was reduced to reassuring her."

"My daughter said you were jolly, sir."

The word "jolly" confused him because of its clash with "*joli*." "I don't think *joli*," said the Emperor, with a mock frown and that harsh laugh of his, and Mr. Robinson did not try to pursue the subject.

"How much land do you have?" asked the Emperor then, leaning forward. Again he was interested in such facts.

"A hundred acres."

"All of good farming?"

"Sir Emperor, not one half of it, but things are on an improvement."

Now Anna, the girl the Emperor had terrified in our garden, emerged through a door, and she led by the hand her mother, who was somewhat hollowed and much wrinkled by the labors she shared with her husband. The little girl brought the farmwife straight up to the Emperor, who stood and bowed.

"Madame," he said, "I am question this husband yours. And now I go beyond English. Miss Balcombe, give me help."

I saw that the girl, a worldling now by comparison with her parents, beamed up at him, and he said, "Young mademoiselle, in case of terror, this gift I brought."

He reached inside his green chasseur's coat and withdrew a napkin tied into a bundle, which he now undid on the table to reveal four sugarplums. "I fear I did not bring six," he told her.

Like my brothers, who had frequently been treated to sugarplums, Miss Robinson was captivated for life. The Emperor had a chair drawn up by Gourgaud, and the Robinson girl sat on it by his side. Jane and I again took the translation of the questions he had for Mr. Robinson, as if his dynasty was to be recorded in a gazetteer. The Emperor wanted to know, did the land bring Mr. Robinson much profit, if it was not half-arable?

"Why, Sir Emperor, you know we cannot grow corn on this island, what with the soil and the goats, and it is hard enough to grow vegetables. But that we do, and before you came, our vegetables would have a ready market only now and then."

"Now," murmured Mrs. Robinson, nodding, "and then."

Her little girl kept smiling up at the Emperor and looked like someone else's child, for Mrs. Robinson kept her children dressed well, if roughly, by her own needlework. I had heard she poured much of the profit of the farm into her ambitions for them. Even the girl's calico skirt had a grace to it.

Mr. Robinson continued, "Generally we had to wait and pray for the coming of a ship or blessedly a convoy before the vegetables rotted. They would often all spoil before the ships arrived. But now! Now, Sir General, we sell our goods every time we want to. This is what you have brought us!"

There was nothing like improved vegetable prices to make an Englishman into a true admirer of the French republican imperial system. (Boney, as my father with tender whimsy said, had become Emperor merely to save the republic.)

The Ogre turned to Jane and me. "Tell him I am delighted to have been a boon to the economy, and to that extent I am gratified. But ask him where his other children are."

When we did, Mr. Robinson declared, "Dang it and please you,

Sir Emperor." He was getting used to discoursing, and his quick intake of wine had made him less stiff. "Two of the boys have gone for sailors, but for the rest, I believe they have all run out and hid on us. Except the little 'un, who knows you."

"Send for them," said the Emperor, through Jane, "and let me be introduced. Pray, have you some good water to go with the wine? And shouldn't you fill your own cup again?"

But first Mr. Robinson had to continue to praise the Emperor for making things so good.

"So good, so good," repeated Mrs. Robinson, nodding. She forced the words through her remaining teeth.

Jane earnestly said, "Your Majesty, I wanted to point out to Mr. Robinson that our father was an honest fellow, but he could only buy from farmers when ships arrived and said what they needed. And so no one ever looked out more anxiously for a ship of any kind—slave, store, navy—as did he."

"Indeed," said both the Robinsons, nodding in chorus. "Honest fellow. Yes, honest fellow."

I wondered when Mrs. Robinson had resembled her daughter, but the one who had not yet been sighted and who was a great beauty of the island.

At last little Anna was sent to find this fabled daughter in one of the farm's outhouses, and eventually led her back, a glorious young auburn-haired woman, as I knew her to be and took a pride in, wearing a plain dress of calico. She was green-eyed and there was a wondrous luster to her hair.

The Emperor, Gourgaud, and Poppleton stood up as she entered. The longing and infantile desire of Gourgaud was in the air of the kitchen, almost like an unpleasant aroma, the smell of spoiled fruit. The Emperor too was stunned with a somehow more honest brand of longing, having—or at least I believed this—something more of substance and persistence and respect than Gourgaud's avid canine hunger. But like all girls of my age, I still had my education in the fickleness of male attention ahead of me. I knew that Captain Edwards, the young master of a cargo vessel named *Chloe*, had sat at our table six months before, praising Florence Robinson at length. By the time he left the island—aboard his ship trading with the Cape—there was thought to be some form of understanding between himself and the Robinsons. But how could the captain of a merchant vessel stand up against the radiance of a world-changing man?

I would later interpret what charmed the Emperor that afternoon. The French, for all their stress on *ton* and fashion, were demented also about the unspoiled pastoral girl, untouched by the blemish of the city or by the paint of the salon, the one with the rustic glow of honest suns in her face, whose teeth gleamed with enough vigor to make up for the toothlessness of her parents. If the Emperor had a picture framed in his head with the title *Bucolic Beauty*, the goddess of Thermidor, Florence Robinson, stepped in to fill it with her glory.

That glow of suns is what Miss Robinson possessed, and the Emperor said in French, as if for our party's attention, "*Cette femme— c'est vraiment La Nymphe.*" This is truly the Nymph! *The* Nymph like *The* Briars.

She made a little bob of the knee, but it struck me that it was a more knowing one than a sprite of the landscape should be up to. She had an instinct for how she had affected these celibate men. "Does Mademoiselle Robinson work with her father and mother in the fields?" the Emperor asked, through the plain Balcombe girls. The idea of her as a barefooted goddess with a basket of harvested fruits on her hip no doubt appealed to him, though the effect was a little spoiled by the fact that she had a sort of shoe, made of canvas uppers and a leather sole.

"She is a seamstress, Sir General," said her father, beaming. "She makes the dresses for weddings and parties. Things have turned better for her now too."

"Admiral Cockburn is having a ball for you, sir," said Miss Robinson with a soft directness. "At Plantation House."

"I am afraid I shall not be attending," said the Emperor in French, "since Admiral Cockburn will not address me in the proper manner. But I hope that does not influence your trade in dresses, so let us keep my intentions a secret."

He smiled while Jane translated for him. The Emperor raised one of his plump fingers. With that soft instrument he had directed corps and armies, and was also willing to contract a seamstress.

"Ask Miss Robinson, would you, Mademoiselle Jane, whether she would make a ball dress for young Betsy here? Betsy will need something more elegant than pantaloons, for she has achieved a height that brings her to the level of my ear."

Jane was about to ask the question, but I told the Emperor in French, "I have not been invited to the gala. And my father has told me in any case I cannot take up such invitations until I am a year older."

"I shall speak to your father," the Emperor told me, but he was very quick to turn back to his goddess of the day and lay his ardent eyes on her. "Ask Miss Robinson this: If I or the Countess Bertrand bring her the material, could she make our Betsy something that will arrest the eyes? For she is a beautiful girl."

Being fifteen, Jane already possessed a ball gown, and was in any case not an envious girl. She had no hesitation in translating. Then she murmured to the Emperor, "I don't know if my father will relent."

But she was amused and far from appalled by the course the Emperor was taking. To her it was all great entertainment and she saw no traps in it.

The Emperor said, "If he listens to anyone on the question of our Betsy, he will listen to me."

"Am I back to being spoken of as a child?" I asked them in French. "In my own presence?"

All four Robinsons in the room were greatly impressed by our conversation but were beginning to seem lost.

"Oh, dear Betsy," exclaimed the Emperor. "I am spoken of in the third person all the time. Do not take it as an offense.

"You wish going to ball?" he then asked in English. "It is not?"

I spent time on the proposition, and suddenly he laughed and said to Jane in French, "Yes, our Betsy wants to go to the ball."

And thus I was the pretext for the Ogre to confer with *La Nymphe*,

Florence Robinson, who was contracted to make me a dress. I knew I was a convenient dupe and yet for once it generally pleased me.

The next day the Ogre lunched with my father and other gentlemen, and my father called me in and told me in front of the Emperor that, due to the intercession of my great patron, I could attend the Plantation House ball.

Blurred by port, he told me, "The dress will be long."

"Am I to have a true gown?" I asked the Emperor. "I would like something high-waisted and white. A woman's ball dress, with red roses at the bodice and on the skirt."

"Ah," said the Emperor, and his laugh seemed level, with no malice in it, no barb. "I shall have Madame Bertrand assemble the elements and we shall deliver them to the Nymph."

So the Ogre and Madame Bertrand would ride out there with Gourgaud and Poppleton, and leave the gentlemen waiting outside as he and Fanny Bertrand discussed my dress with Miss Robinson, Fanny Bertrand being the translator.

On their return, Fanny told my mother and the rest of us, "The girl is more knowing, I think, than the Emperor would prefer her to be. Believe me, she has the means to be more than a rustic."

My mother could tell that I did not necessarily like to have the Emperor's gesture serve as his reason to visit the shrine of *La Nymphe* in Prosperous Plain. But she pointed out that I had my chief wishes on all counts. Through a grand intermediary, who had already insisted he would pay for my first ball gown, a woman's gown and not that of a juvenile.

I still did not quite trust him not to make some prank of it all.

In the meantime, my brothers were still drawn to their Boney by unalloyed play. It turned out the young *lampiste* Rousseau could make toys too—carving pieces out of wood. So he made my brothers a little articulated carriage, with axles and four wheels, and to it he tethered four mice he had managed to trap.

The Ogre invited the boys to see it one evening, and they crowded into the Pavilion, past the mattresses of Marchand and St. Denis, who slept in front of the Pavilion door every night, guarding entry. I followed, but as observer. The Balcombes' hot boy breath and wondering eyes fell on the vermin, the minuscule steeds, and their minuscule carriage.

"*Avanti!*" the Emperor cried, but the mice were stunned by the presence of such a fervent audience.

The Emperor reached down and began to ravel and squeeze the tails of the front mice with the fingers of his left hand, and they took off across the teak table as if they meant to hurl themselves off the other end. But, amazingly, they turned, like a real coach—too sharply, though, since the cart went over on its side and the harnesses tangled. Laughing, Rousseau and the Emperor recaptured the mice in a cage and untangled the harnesses. And, yet again, this was private amusement. It sought no one to chronicle it, or to expound upon it, or to build it into a claim or an apologia.

Some days before the ball Florence Robinson rode to our place on a coarse-haired mount, carrying a dress folded before her in a tin box. Invited in, she clumped up the hall in her agricultural boots and opened the box in our drawing room, and took out the dress, as if it were a newborn child of uncertain health.

I gasped at what I saw. It was a perfect thing in island terms. Immediately I forgave Miss Robinson her splendor and declared, "Oh, Miss Robinson, this is a wonder you've made."

I tried it on and sought my reflection in each of the two mirrors, and my mother and Jane exclaimed. I was utterly captured by its elegance. The gown delivered me from all contradictory feeling. I wanted more moments like this.

"How do you know to make such a fine dress?" asked my mother, with a renewed admiration for the girl who had until now seemed merely to be a rose amongst the cacti. "You have not been an apprentice to a dressmaker surely."

"I get the fashion plates from the ladies who come here by ship," said the Nymph. "If they cannot spare them, I make drawings. That is how it is done."

I felt so sisterly towards her for her industry and earnestness that all at once her passive flirting with the Emperor seemed a harmless thing. I was shallowly won over by this elegant gift. On impulse I kissed her flawless, downy cheek. It smelt of milk.

I had achieved the mountain. I felt Olympian.

*B*efore the ball, and without my being present, my brothers' play with the Emperor turned noxious.

The admiral had given them a box of bonbons, and they wanted to offer some to the Ogre. Alex was permitted to taste one bonbon that evening, and the next morning waited to offer the Emperor one from the near-pristine box near the grape arbor, under orders from all of us not to enter, as the Emperor dictated to Las Cases and the others. When the dictation was over, Alex regretted that the box was nearly half-empty and tottered to my parents' room, where he found a packet of senna pods my father had been using and filled out the missing bonbons with these. The box of bonbons adequately reinforced, it was presented to the Emperor at the door of the marquee by young Alex. Looking at the available sweetmeats, the Ogre chose one of my father's canary-colored pellets. Overcome by that strange powerlessness to warn him, and hoping as children always do that he would not notice, Alex watched the Universal Demon as he theatrically placed it in his mouth.

"Take two, Boney!" Alex urged. "Take two!"

The Emperor did take two, and the smile with which he began the process of consuming them was replaced in ten seconds with an expression of broad horror. His face reddened and he held his throat.

"Have they sent a child to do it?" he cried to the surrounding air. He stumbled away towards the marquee, my mother following and calling for Gourgaud, who for once was not close behind him, and for Cipriani and Marchand.

Alex began to wail too, and to plead, "It's only pills. It's only pills."

My mother called to Sarah to fetch tea for the Emperor. The Emperor was vomiting into a basin held by Marchand by the time Sarah, Alice, and my mother took the tea in to him.

"Your Majesty," my mother said, a term unfamiliar to her lips and brought on by desperate concern. "My son has given you harmless senna. I am appalled that he knows where to look for medicines that imitate the *confiseur*'s art. But it is a harmless mixture!"

We managed to get this message through the deafness of his panic, and he began to gasp like a man retrieving his living breath. From dire expectation of being strangled by toxins, the Emperor passed in five minutes to utter hilarity.

"Madame," he said, barely panting, "your son has nearly succeeded in doing what the Chouan agents of Britain could not manage. And he did not receive even a twenty-franc napoleon for frightening me nearly to my grave."

But within a day the Ogre began coughing and suffered congestion, and my mother, guilty for what she thought might be the long-running effect of the senna pods, nursed him, was frequently in the marquee, and came and went with vapor inhalations, insisting on carrying basins of camphor in boiling water herself.

The Emperor proved a difficult patient and had Marchand take away the first basin she brought, but after a few days asked for more to be provided—without fuss, he specified. He could not stand the ado people made about the temporarily afflicted.

O'Meara rode up from Jamestown and found that the Emperor would permit himself to take a little mercury chloride, but would not be blistered—as O'Meara had suggested—to draw out the afflicting humors. My mother told us at dinner, "Our Emperor believes that blistering is quackery."

"Well," murmured my father, "he did grow up on Corsica."

"Corsica" was code for a primitive society.

"Escape," or any other word
of that same meaning . . .

My view of time was all to do with the coming ball in late No-
vember. My attention was distracted, though, when Old Huff
failed to arrive to give his lessons, and Poppleton confessed to my
father at breakfast that, against Poppleton's own recommendations,
Huff had been summoned to Plantation House for a terse conversation with Admiral Cockburn. He had been escorted there from town
by soldiers, though according to rumor they spoke to him calmly and
did not threaten him with either the lash or a prison cell. The admiral
explained to him that he was not to kneel to the General anymore or
mention the word "escape," or any other word of that same meaning.

This interview came at a stage when we were seeing more soldiers at the crossroads and at the signal station atop High Knoll.
It was as if they were closing upon the exile; and there was a new
encampment near Hutt's Gate on the way to Longwood whose presence made the Emperor unwilling to ride in that direction.

The Emperor, rather pleased that he was blameless in the Huff
matter, remarked to my father that, alas, only mad Englishmen
seemed interested in freeing him. It was primary proof that the British Cabinet, he said, though far from admirable men, were not mad.

A letter arrived from the admiral's residence at the Castle advising my father that Cockburn expected him to employ Huff no more.
The admiral was aware that this would affect Huff's income, but he
intended to make funds available for Huff's modest upkeep.

My father informed the Ogre of this letter and the Ogre asked him whether Huff would starve. My father had heard that Huff received a remittance from his family in England and tried to reassure our guest on that point.

On Monday morning my father set out for Jamestown in his trap, but while we were working on French translation he returned—he had obviously not reached Jamestown or anywhere near it—and dismounted, advancing on the shade of our tree, frowning and flushed in the face. He called for my mother and Sarah, and he muttered whatever news he had to them both. Sarah's eyes grew wide; it seemed her irises shrank amidst the white of her eyeballs. My father collected Toby and Ernest from the orchard and ventured out of the gate on foot to the carriageway again. He called to us, "Jane, Betsy, keep the children in the house. Please stay here yourselves."

The men advanced a little way, and my father and Toby went on further still while Ernest returned to harness up the dray, as if freight would be involved. As soon as the dray had gone up the carriageway, I went to the gate and began to squint down that tunnel of pomegranate trees.

Far off, a considerable way down the track, beyond the avenues of trees, I saw what looked like a large black comma suspended in the thin shade of an isolated gumwood, the tree of the island, crooked with ugly pale leaves. There were two or three soldiers standing by and my father and Toby approaching it. It was as if an emanation from that shape immediately passed through my body. I returned, frightened, to my sister.

"What is it, Betsy?" she asked.

I told her I didn't know, but the truth was I dared not know yet, and soon I returned to the gate again.

My father and Toby had arrived by then at the spot where the soldiers stood. The sentries at the crossroads beyond were facing the solitary gumwood, but could not leave their post.

Toby and Ernest took a stepladder from the back of the dray and erected it by the black punctuation mark. Ernest was sent up the stepladder and sawed at the air above the thing. I knew the party had not had time to hang a man, and lacked the authority to do so, and thus a man must have hanged himself there.

My mother appeared behind me, exasperated.

"Didn't your father tell you to sit down?"

When I went to join Jane, I whispered to her, "There is a man, hanged."

"Who is it?"

I could not say. My mother stayed at the gate and placed a hand to her mouth. My father was returning to us by foot. When he reached the gates, he cried to my mother loudly, "Have we destroyed the poor man by rejecting him?"

So it was the man he was worried about, the man with the escape plans. Huff.

Robert and Roger, our house servants, now grown men, came out howling onto the verandah, as if they had had a vision of what had happened, and began to chant and shudder. Alice stood with large eyes full of a blazing alarm. I knew that in the song the twins had set up there was a desire to diffuse and allay the evil spirit let loose in our carriageway.

My mother cried, "Then it *is* Huff. That's who it is. It is Huff."

I felt trapped. The track to the crossroads, which we needed to use in all our arrivals at and departures from the house, was now a tunnel stopped up by Huff's terrible plan, and by limbs stretched out to us not just from the vegetable but from the spectral world.

The Emperor had emerged from the marquee in shirtsleeves, and approached us across the lawn, looking bewildered.

My mother told him, "Sire, it is Huff. It is Mad Huff."

"But what?" asked the Emperor. They spoke like old neighbors.

"Hanged himself, it seems," said my mother.

The Emperor peered down the arched trees of the carriageway. "My God," he murmured, and turned to Jane and me. "Did poor Huff hang himself because I refused his ravings of escape?"

"No," I said, as if talking sense to a family member, "you would have been hanged had you listened to him."

I wondered what would become of Huff's body now—would the thing be brought to our door? But in fact Toby and Ernest had been told to take it down to the coroner in Jamestown, and a sentry was allocated by Captain Poppleton to travel with them.

The fact that the body was gone from the road did not seem to allay the terrors of Sarah or the stupefaction of Alice, Roger, and Robert. We moved into the house, since the normal world of order could be encountered only indoors. My brothers ran about asking us, "Did Old Huff hang himself? Jane? Betsy? With rope? How'd he tie the knot?"

"Dead, is he?" asked William.

"Not dead," said Alex. "He was just arsing around." And everyone worked at being normally offended at the imp's crudity.

"*Aleph, beth, gamel, daleth,*" said Thomas as a sort of eulogy.

I was in terror of the night. Darkness fell hazy, like smoke. We were told that evening by my father when he arrived back that he had gone with the town officials to Huff's shack. There, he and Major Hodson found a locked box within a chest under Old Huff's bed. My father broke the box open and found 250 sovereigns in a bag. The belief that Huff had hanged himself because he had lost all sources of income was thus allayed.

My father and Hodson took the box and a journal to Plantation House, for he still trusted Governor Wilks to behave with discretion over the matter. On the last page of the erratic diary was written, "It is too great a weight for a fallen child—I mean the contrivance that is demanded of me by the God of Reason."

It was as if Huff had chosen sentiments to exonerate us. Even I felt less subject to his baleful ghost. For we all knew by evening that it was the weight of his delusion, not of his true situation, that had sent Huff up the tree, and the weight of delusion had pulled on him fiercer than his own weight when he had descended from the branch, and the weight of delusion had squeezed the spirit from him. It had not been any rejection by my father, the admiral, or the Ogre.

My mother said to us, "Why should the Emperor feel such a burden from Huff's foolishness? I mean to say, in terms of robustness of soul, he left a whole army behind in Egypt."

"Perhaps it's easier to leave a whole army," I suggested earnestly, "than one madman."

This caused my father to laugh. It was still the case that when I proposed what I thought of as a transparent truth, my elders laughed.

A few uneasy days and fitful nights followed Huff's suicide. It was taken by all levels of society with great seriousness, and after a quick inquest it was deemed that Huff should be buried at the crossroads nearest the site of his self-destruction, where the road from The Briars to Jamestown crossed the road to Longwood.

No one attended the funeral except the Chinese gravediggers and two slaves. It was in our secret thoughts and amongst the servants that the stricken imaginings ran. The carriageway was now a haunted place, leading to the last residence of an unhappy spirit. If our servants wished to meet at the freed slaves' camp above Jamestown, they would be for years inhibited by the crossroads through which they must pass. And so was I.

But the Emperor came to feel perhaps too exonerated, and that was shown by his actions on a summer night soon after Huff had been buried. That night he had the lights put out early in the Pavilion and the marquee and sent the Las Cases to bed, and we presumed that he too had retired early. I could feel Huff's ghost settling as a frigid insomniac shadow over me.

The Emperor had secretly recruited Sarah's two nephews to collaborate with him in a joke, designed to relieve their steely terror of Huff. He had persuaded them to sneak down the carriageway, each wearing a white sheet, and to intrude, clad in that way, into our garden. It sounds like a primitive trick that should not have impressed us. But we were simple people, and it did. The light, what was left of it, was an amalgam of the darkness that precedes a new-risen full moon, but it was precisely right to make an ordinary bedsheet gleam with a faint blue emanation of a persistent presence.

The Emperor's relief at being innocent of causing the suicide's death still allowed him in nights thereafter, when crossing the lawn at evening from our house to the Pavilion, to utter in a *faux* ominous voice, "Old Huff! Old Huff!" But he would ruin the affright he was trying to induce by bursting into the sort of laughter that embraced itself in undue self-congratulation, the sort of laughter a puckish child might emit having performed a trick.

My mother was of course always forgiving of him. She would go to the door and call, "Good evening, Your Majesty."

She laughed and shook her head, and I wondered if she would have been as forgiving of Robert and Roger had they done such a thing, on their own initiative. But it was clear that the Emperor was supremely forgivable. It was endearing of him to concentrate, even in jest, on one lost wretch.

*A*ccording to ghost-struck Alice, a fear of the evil spirit of the man he had handled caused Ernest to vanish from The Briars that night of the Emperor's first Huff trick. She and Toby both solemnly reported at dawn that he was missing. My father in turn reported the matter to Major Hodson, and the constables were sent to the camp of the freed blacks above Jamestown, fairly sure that he must have sought to place himself on the safe and uncursed side of the crossroads there and could be easily retrieved.

But he was not at the camp. Military patrols were ordered to keep watch for him, but, as days passed, none of them sighted him. It began to be muttered that he had hidden on a ship, or had drowned trying to reach one, or else had fallen from a cliff or thrown himself from it.

I heard for the first time my parents and other adults who visited them for dinner mention the suicide season. Was this a proposition Old Huff had introduced? Because I did not know until then that the island had such a season. But there was a theory now that humidity and heat and the fuggy air of summer through which illimitable sea could be glimpsed might confirm people in the idea of their paltriness and suggest they were candidates for self-destruction. On one of our late-afternoon rides towards Diana's Peak and the heights around it, we saw a patch of white on a cone of rock. When we drew closer, we saw beneath the peak to the apex of a large boulder what looked like a white linen bag, a bundle of laundry, pungent, stinking of disease—at least as I thought of it.

The party reined in perhaps twenty paces from this soiled whiteness, and a black decayed face lying cheek by jowl with the rock at first justified the idea that we had found Ernest. But it was apparent that this version of Ernest wore military pants with a stripe, and one military boot dangled from a leg. The fact was that a soldier had vanished a little time before, something unremarkable amongst soldiers, one or other of whom occasionally went unaccounted for, blown off the cliff-side artillery placements, it was said, like rag dolls.

The Emperor solemnly ordered Gourgaud to ride to Deadwood camp and report the discovery to the colonel. Jane was retching behind one of the tumbled great stones. I wished to join her, but I would not permit myself to do so in the Ogre's presence.

Gourgaud, as it turned out, did not go far before he met one of the patrols who were still out looking for Ernest. The guards ascended the height above the stone on which the soldier had been more or less impaled and found no boot marks that would have indicated an involuntary fall. Again, the suicide season was invoked, and apparently the poor fellow had been rejected by a yamstock farmer's daughter so had perhaps yielded to his resultant melancholy.

"Did you notice," Jane asked me after our return, "Our Friend was not afraid? He has seen so many soldiers fallen, so he is not afraid of the dead."

We were both quaking, again, in anticipation of the night. I feared Ernest's returning by dark and appearing like an impersonation of the dead soldier's putrefied black face at my window or, worse, as a specter in his own right.

As the news of the self-destroyed soldier made its way around the island, I was reminded of the Ogre's earlier story of his sachet of poison carried round the neck against capture by Cossacks. Had he, so practiced in thoughts of self-harm, summoned up this supposed suicide season? His grief at Old Huff's death seemed to do him credit, however, and I had no appetite for accusing him of creating the general ailment.

The next day I asked Alice whether she was afraid of Old Huff. With a deep breath she drew her fine-featured face to sharp definition. "We're afeared of Old Huff surely," she told me. "But not of that man Ernest."

"Why not Ernest?"

"Ernest is gone," she told me, "flung into the sea by his own will, just to escape the spirit of Old Huff. The spirit cannot go through water." Thus Ernest was not yet a ghost, but a being of the tides and profound currents.

It would have been fashionable for me to be patronizing towards this belief about water, but I had sufficient English superstition of my own to cause me to feel dread.

"Why did Ernest run away, though? Everyone's scared of Old Huff, but we don't run away."

"Old Huff one day tells him," said Alice, "to get out of here. Ernest find Old Huff stealing the fruit one day and chase him off, and Old Huff turn and say, 'You I curse! You, Ernest, I curse.' And then he point at him and speaks in all these tongues, with the voices of dead people, Ernest says. So when Old Huff hang himself, Ernest has nothing else left but run from that thing."

Mr. Lett the farmer and Mr. Robinson visited my father at his office and said they would go to Major Hodson to report stolen chickens—not taken by foxes and found as a rummage of feathers and bones, but utterly gone. People were talking about encountering sprinkles of blood, votive or prohibitory, by roadsides. It was believed the African and other slaves had stolen the chickens to perform ceremonies of slaughter that might allay the island's less tranquil spirits. Or else, I wondered, could it be a living Ernest, dining out?

Now I had begun to talk to Alice about the ghost, she became freer in discussing the subject with me. She told me that she and Sarah and the twin boys, returning one night from the camp on the slope above Jamestown where they'd attended some gathering or ceremony, saw Old Huff's white ghost flitting at some speed, more lithe than Old Huff had been in life, beyond the crossroads. The farmer Miss Mason who, lacking horses, rode cows, reported vegetables had been dug up from a garden worked by slaves of hers near Deadwood camp.

Town Major Hodson, who by his title was the military keeper of good order on the island, had spoken to a freed African who had a grievance against Ernest, a man who had lost a beloved woman to him, and the hunt was renewed one morning by a squadron of East India Company hussars who had now joined the 53rd, and by my father, simply for recreation, and for similar reasons by Generals Bertrand and Gourgaud. The Emperor, however, found he could not avoid continuing the dictation of his history that morning. Or perhaps, having captured kingdoms, he had no taste for the cruel capture of a single slave.

The aggrieved freed slave led the party up over a stony ridge and into the great bowl in the rock into which the water fell in a thread from the heights. On the side of the slope, unseeable from Jamestown or Deadwood or The Briars, they found a cave, a low lintel of rock shielded by other boulders. The soldiers crowded in towards its entrance.

An officer of the hussars ordered Ernest to emerge or suffer a fusillade of musketry. There was no answer. The infantry fired into the black hole and my father later declared he was sorry he'd come when he heard Ernest scream. But then chicken theft and vegetable theft were despicable things, and slavery was still the order of the world. We had the freedom to choose paths of folly or wisdom, piety or impiousness, departure or remaining. It was a misfortune that the slave did not, one that the East India Company believed must be endured.

Of course I saw nothing of this and heard only my father's report, but once again there was white on the mountain, the blood-blotted linen in which wounded Ernest was wrapped and, praying in his Malay tongue, taken down to the Castle Terrace at Jamestown to be nursed and punished. If one believed in curses, Huff's curse at being prevented the plunder of mangos had operated very powerfully upon Ernest.

The afternoon of Ernest's capture and removal, the Emperor all at once wanted to ride out and inspect the cave. The idea of a cave in which a man could escape detection at least for a time attracted him. These days I believe the truth of him was that he was a fluid personage, given to depression at one hour, exuberance at another, interested in one soul for an afternoon, indifferent to the destiny of thousands for a day. It was later declared, as I have read, that he kept his populace exhilarated and distracted by this fluidity, and it had not ceased at The Briars. For he was on the lawn calling, "Betsy and Mademoiselle Jeanne!"

We had our horses saddled, and off I went, as ever, on Tom, an animal conveyance pitched somewhere between the Emperor's Arab, Mameluke, and Miss Mason's cow. Gourgaud knew the cave we were bound for, and when we neared the ridge that fell away into the crater of the waterfall, we dismounted and he led us down on a stony track to the well-hidden cave. We ducked under the narrow stone lintel. There was a whiff of coolness but also of faint rot.

Enough light entered to let us see how Ernest had heaped clothing together for a bed. There was a can of water still standing in the cave, and along the edges of the wall the bones of every animal Ernest had caught or stolen or devoured were laid out like a message, like a precaution, in lines. This script of bones, arranged in order like incisors in the mouth of a phantom brute, would protect Ernest and drive off the ghost of Old Huff. I imagined poor Ernest placing them with care and fear. Having been myself driven by my night fear down the corridor to Jane's room after Huff's death, I found an answering trepidation from her. Now, seeing this frantic artifact of fear, I felt a rage sweep up my body with such force that I was tilted forward and in the Emperor's direction.

"I blame you for the whole of this," I told him. "All your playing around with sheets. What may be play to you, sir, is a serious business with the slaves. But as soon as you found you hadn't killed Huff you couldn't wait to play hoaxes. And now you want to look at these bones as if they were a curiosity and not of your making. And the blood on the cave floor, the same. You've made blood flow on this island like you did in the big world! And you think it's all funny."

Gourgaud stepped up towards me. I could smell his souring perfume and his licorice breath. "Mademoiselle Balcombe, you cannot speak to the Emperor in that way. We have overlooked sins of protocol on your part before, allowing for your having lived since childhood on a barbarous island. But this is too far." And he extended a small, bridle-harshened hand as if he were going to remove me from the cave.

The Ogre murmured, "You are very cruel, Betsy, very cruel. Would you like to hear your father say this manner of thing to a visitor?" This time there was no humor in him at all. He asked, "Would you like my enemies or jailers to hear this of me? That I have some magic to make slaves escape? That is what you are as good as saying."

He and Gourgaud took to their horses and we rode back, Jane turning towards me with an annoyingly benign inquiry of the kind that suggested I shouldn't have spoken, or else that *their* solemnity mystified her.

It seemed that to canvass my accusations against the Emperor, Gourgaud spoke to Count Bertrand about them, and about their potential danger, and Bertrand thought it necessary to walk down to the seafront at Jamestown from the Portions to the Company warehouse where my father's port office stood.

Having heard Bertrand's complaint about what I had said to the Emperor, my father rode home in one of his rare ill tempers. He listened willingly to the French: their complaints were infrequent but held a special authority for him. When, red-faced, he rode into the yard, I could see signs that he would direct at me one of his rare spasms of severity. From the table under the trees, I saw his horse taken away. He asked me to leave my book and to come into the house.

In the drawing room he shook me by the shoulders as my mother and Jane entered the room and watched in melancholy. During the shaking, I did not discriminate one of his words from another, any more than one does individual hailstones when a torrent of them hits bare flesh.

"This girl will not be content until she has driven Our Friend away from here into the hands of his bloody enemies," he yelled to the ceiling.

Jane began weeping, and this almost instantly sucked half the fury out of him. Once his rage was pricked, it began to deflate very quickly, and he let go of me, paleness and sweat replacing the ruby hue of his face. My eyes ached with tears, but I still retained the power not to yield them up. I would thus always be deprived, by temperament or habit, of the power and sway that weeping represented as an essential item in women's threadbare arsenal.

"I don't believe you understand that he could have been impossibly contemptuous towards us," he said, as he calmed. "That he could have dismissed us! After all the *gloire* he has known, who are we? An insignificant English family. But he's indulged you, and when he takes a little sport, you insolently accuse him of the greatest malice."

I raised a small flag of protest and argued that "malice" was too big a word for what I had accused him of. But that only needled my father again. He saw that I could not surrender even when I was wrong—and especially when I was wrong.

Jane meantime was rereleasing the flow of tears that should have been mine, and they, and the obvious bronchitic harshness of her breathing, washed away the flimsy knoll of certitude on which he stood. Now he fell into self-reproach, which was normal with him as his anger declined.

"But," he said, with a cooler reason, "what was simple impudence when we were just island-dwellers can become a matter of State now that we have *this* guest—*this* Phenomenon! *This* Friend! Imagine if your accusations *did* reach a British newspaper. God forfend they should, but suppose they did? What would the friends of the Emperor, those good Whigs of England—such as the mythic Lady Holland, Elizabeth Fox, who visited him in the peace of the year when you were born, Betsy, and became a champion of his—say then in his defense? What would the Prince Regent make of the accusation? And from a Balcombe!"

He reflected on these distant possible reverberations, and his thoughts caused a small shudder to move through him and rattle his shoulders.

"I must impress that on you," he mused. "Beyond all argument, therefore, I am sending you to the cellar."

I gave a gasp, a nontheatrical one. I hated the place. I had been put in there once before, with a chamber pot and water bottle, but only for a day, when the rats were not so active and Old Huff not abroad.

"You will have sewing, a book, a palliasse, and pillow. And other comforts. Alice will bring your meals."

"For how many days must this happen?" howled Jane. Better it was she who asked.

"You know the answer to that. Until the lesson appears to penetrate."

I abominated the idea of sitting down there sewing and waiting for my enemies to appear from hidden places.

"The cellar belongs to rats," I told him, trying to adopt a reasonable tone.

"Alice will give you a cudgel," my father told me.

I emitted in his direction the purest hate. For the modest chiding of a guest, no, a household tenant, for a venial crime of insult, I was to be punished like a person condemned for a crime of state.

"I am to be the Duke d'Enghien then?" I challenged him. "Abducted and thrown into a cellar for indefinite spite."

"Don't be absurd," he told me.

Jane assured me, "There will be no firing squad."

My mother looked pale and stricken and yet seemed to believe that forces beyond her impelled her to consent.

"So I will go *now*," I said, determined to choose the hour myself.

My father became uncertain, but then regathered his resources of resolution.

"Yes," he said. "Yes, you are to go now."

I fetched the needlework I was working on from the drawing room, and the book I was reading—thank heavens, Henry Summersett's fantastical *The Wizard and the Sword*—and went to the door of the cellar with lacerating dignity. I waited there for Alice to bring a mallet for me to whack rats with. Alice gave him one stare—was she an ally?—before lowering her gaze. She left. And so he unlocked the cellar door onto the musk of rat droppings, aging port, and mold. We descended the stairs, and he pointed to a small table and a stool beyond it.

"There is a chair for you. Now I must do this." Then he turned on his heel and, as fast as he could, rushed up the stairs, unimpeded by gout. I heard the door lock. I was in a space hemmed on one side by racks of port and sherry and claret, beyond the first of which I would not venture to go, and the three walls of the cellar in which sat the draped shapes of unloved or unrepaired furniture. The half window high in the wall behind me would be my chief daytime illumination. I noticed that a ventilator pipe rose from the corner, up through the house and no doubt ultimately through the roof, to dispel the cellar's miasmas.

Alone now, without antagonists and left purely with the fear of rodents, I began to weep and felt a panicked constriction of the throat. At last I swallowed. It took a time for me to assess from the pallid light through the half window that there were not many rats visible at the moment and they probably preferred night. I began to work desultorily with my needle, and to ration out the famous Summersett book. Perhaps, if I finished it, there was another one down here, warping with mold in some corner, but I had a fear of treading on living rat fur and I did not dare go looking. I stayed in that clear space where I had elbow room for the mallet in case of attack.

I noticed that when in the afternoon my father came to his small office and library, I could hear all his movements, his laying down of papers, his sitting in a chair, his cough, and the clunk and slide of his boots, all clearly transmitted through the ventilating tube. I held to a hope that my mother might join him and I would again learn something of how parents talked in the absence of their children. It would be delightful if they fought about me. But it did not happen. Soon enough my father left and did not enter the room again that day and evening.

By now I had come to believe penitently that my father's punishment did have its reason, that his intentions were not fatuous, and that I must be careful. For towards the plump man with the dimpled knuckles living in the Pavilion and its associated marquee, the simplest gestures of sportiveness or irritation could race across oceans and echo in spectacular rooms with gold-leaf moldings glinting above the heads of mighty creatures. My actions were no longer dependably obscure from attention. And yet still I was not ready to tell my father I had come to this realization.

To face the coming evening I had a lamp and two candles, and a pillow and palliasse and blanket to place on top of the table, where I would rest—or not—for the night. I was determined not to be frightened of Old Huff. If I had shown fears, it would have been a sort of surrender to my punishment. But rats were of the temporal world, and dread of them dominated me.

Alice brought dinner.

"I suppose you think my father is kind because he doesn't starve me," I challenged her.

"Miss, he is kind," she said, engaging the use of her startling broad eyes. I had seen her pray in the manner of the Mussulmen, on a mat outside the kitchen, facing northeast across the Atlantic, penetrating Africa diagonally with her supplications, which struck home at last in Arabia.

"You feel you must say that," I called after her.

I burned one candle to extinction while reading and saved the other in case the lamp ran out of oil and I possessed just the one taper by which to see. In my nest on top of the table I fell asleep earlier than I expected and, mallet handle in hand, must have slept for some hours. The night was full of rat-tread when I woke by dwindling lamplight and saw that my table was an island in a trade road of furred vermin. I could see them busy below me, twitching with that ratty inquisition of objects, that perpetual nosing for small verminous advantage. I gripped the mallet and threw it into their midst. There was certainly a squeal, but reinforced by one from me, since the mallet head fell off the handle in flight and disappeared under the wine racks. I was now in a fury. They had given me not only an absurd weapon against the little beasts but one that failed at first use!

This rage was of assistance. It impelled me to jump to the floor, my feet surrounded by pestilential squealers, my bare flesh meeting the unspeakable pelts as I broke the siege and reached the wine rack, where I set myself lustily to demonstrate to my father that I would not be left in dim places infested by living demons with negligent weapons. So I hauled his wine bottles, one after another, from the racks and hurled them at the floor where they shattered and drenched the rats in vintages and sherry. The noise would have filled my father's small library upstairs but, sadly, would not penetrate to other rooms. I must have thrown a dozen or more before the furor of glass-splintered and claret- or port-sodden creatures died, and heavy, part-sweet, part-tannin air pleasantly filled the room. I trod tenderly, suffering only small cuts to my feet, back to the table and my bed-clothes. I wiped my bloodied, sticky feet with a towel, and, elated but spent from my warfare, and my awe at the damage I'd done, I lay down. I dreamed of achieving grandeur through spurned fatherly tenderness and discipline.

I woke in pinkish dawn from the cellar half window. The rats were quiescent. Sarah entered and began at once to repair the condition of the floor in silence. She brought everything she needed for cleaning, and a new dress for me. I had wanted her to rush out a report to my father of the destruction of bottles. But she did not want him to know, and cleared up as I harangued her. I saw her push three dead rats into a corner. "Go and tell him, Sarah, go and tell him!"

She fetched me new stockings and shoes, bathed the cuts in my feet, emptied and returned my chamber pot, and brought me a new mallet, which she tested against the surface of the table. She took away the lamp to fill it with oil.

I sat at the table with a sense that I had cowed the rats, returned to my book and reveled in it, enforced in confidence by my survival of the night. It was midmorning when I looked up with a shock to see the Ogre's visage, bent sideways, looking in from the cellar win-dow. He must have been on his hands and knees, or even flat to the ground beyond the window, and there were briars around his face, though he did not seem to have been scratched.

"Bet-see!" he called, so that I could hear him through the glass. I left my book on the chair, arranged my needlework—he need not think me anxious to rush to him—and strolled towards the half win-dow, looking up to it.

"Why do you hide in the cellar?" he called.

"I don't hide. I was placed here. Because I endangered you."

"Endangered me? You?"

He seemed oblivious to the possibilities my father had made so much of.

"I thought you wanted this. Your General Gourgaud certainly did."

"*Do* we want a pretty girl locked in a cellar? I think not."

For some reason the stubborn tears arrived now and the flood began, and I despised myself.

"I am a prisoner," he called. "And now you are a prisoner. That's why we are a pair, Betsy! Now, don't cry!"

"But you have cried. I've seen you."

"I have cried—that is true. But you are sure to escape and I am not."

As I remember him lying sideways amongst the briars, beside The Briars, let me from my distance of time yet again pour scorn on those who thought all he did was to extend witnessed charm as a plan to procure freedom. There were no witnesses to where he then lay gaping in at me, a fat little man with large, volatile eyes.

"Betsy, I see your needlework. Very nice. But I do not think you are a needlework girl."

"I don't pretend to be," I confessed.

"I must see your good father. A more decent and temperate fellow there cannot be! But with you he does too much on my behalf. I will go and speak to him."

"Brush yourself down first," I ordered him.

And now he struggled upwards, and I could see by the window how he had soiled his silk hose, and the knees of his breeches, while lying on the ground to talk to me. That's his concern, I thought.

With such an eminent advocate, I sat enjoying the grimmest sense of self-justification and sewed away, plunging the needle with a fury. Within an hour he was back, kneeling again at the half window.

"I tried to persuade him, Betsy," he roared in through the glass panes. "And I think he will yield. But he argued that *his* welfare is at risk too. He may pursue this affair for another little while, but he is a tenderhearted man . . ."

"Everyone says it. But I'm the proof he's not!"

I saw that doleful face and those remarkable Italian eyes, which had gazed into men's souls and infused them with some unutterable concept more important than their blood and their lives and their own offspring.

"I don't care if I have to stay here forever," I told him, totally dry-eyed now.

"My brave creature," he said. "But it will not be required. Your father is of a soul to let all people go."

My father remained contrary to his soul, however, all that day. At dusk the lamp and the dinner arrived, and as I ate, thinking of myself in appropriately pathetic terms, I assured myself that this would be my habitation, amongst the abounding rats, forever, and the rats and my family would both pay. My kin would beg me to come up to their level of the house, and I would spurn them. I would break and devastate my father's bottles before he could empty them. I would become an island legend, the pale girl in the cellar. People would deal vengefully with my heartless father.

He opened the cellar door and came down the stairs as I finished dinner. He stood before me. The smell of his slaughtered wine had not disappeared from the space around, but he did not choose to notice. He adopted sage and severe airs.

"Do you know to be careful now, miss?" he asked.

"I am willing to spend more time down here to discover it more fully," I told him. "And to smash bottles of your wine on the heads of the rats whenever the beasts attack me."

"You see," he complained, "you always exact a price. You never bend your stiff neck. Do you think God is amused by your style of obduracy? Where does it come from? It is not a thing of our family!"

"It is a thing of me," I boasted. "But I know how to be careful. The Emperor is a man, you are a man. I do not want to harm either of you unless forced beyond toleration."

"Forced beyond . . . ? My Holy Christ. You're rich, Betsy!" He took thought. "I suppose such a statement from you is, after all, a small miracle!" said my father, his eyes widening. "And it is not only the Emperor and I who must be treated well. You must live too. You must live for many, many years. You must live in the shadow of this great thing that has befallen us. You must live on when Our Great Friend is vanished, when I am vanished, when the island is behind you. But these events will never leave you!"

I stood with a level determination, which he read as consent—and a form of consent it certainly was. On balance now I decided that there were conveniences associated with being reconciled rather than locked away. There was as well pus in one of my cuts, and I wanted my mother to see and be reproached by it. And it was apparent that my father both knew of the ruin of wine and had chosen not to pursue it.

"Come upstairs and see your mother and Jane and the boys."

And so I emerged free and changed, chastised and intractable.

*A*nd back now to the full status of riding with the Emperor to visit the lovely yamstock Miss Robinson, *La Nymphe*. On our next journey there we encountered on the road Miss Polly Mason, less well mounted than us but in her way a grandee of the island. She lived beyond Prosperous Plain, in a good and elegant house her loving father had begun to build, and which, when she was orphaned, while still a young woman capable of intimidating island carpenters, she had finished.

There grew in her quarter of the island lovely groves of ferns, and avenues of pines, and clumps of gumwoods, and it had lately been rumored that she had offered her house to the admiral as a place for the Emperor, and it might indeed have been a better place than the proposed Longwood. Though she had few visitors, those who had seen inside her house, including Mr. Solomon the merchant from Jamestown, said it was full of sturdy furniture, Dutch-styled from the Cape. But her stable of horses had died off and she had not replenished it, so in a faded and unpretentious calico dress and canvas shoes she rode one of her dairy cattle across the island without a saddle. Astride her cow, her short legs, as modestly skirted as the posture permitted, stuck out comically from the cow's saggy flanks.

Encountered on the road by the Emperor, she too was interrogated about her farming. Jane and I watched the plump yet august contours of the mounted Emperor as he gazed down at Polly on her cow, and the slim, grave Gourgaud waiting, reined in, by his side.

"How much acreage does Miss Mason have?" the Emperor wanted me to ask her.

I was rather astounded to know that she owned 350 acres—I had not presumed she was such an affluent woman.

"I am, Yer Highness, growing vegetables for the garrison at Deadwood, on my very Deadwood acreage," she said.

The Emperor was interested in all this, and watching him, I thought, It is all supply—the making of a war is all the passage of food and fodder and cannon shells.

Polly said to the Emperor, "My father was a gentleman, and he would not like the fact that I have let myself go. But it is the way that I am, and it cannot be denied, and I am quite happy to ride to Deadwood on a cow. I might use a mount if it were necessary to get down to Jamestown, but that place is a den of thieves, and best to be avoided."

This encounter, Polly and the Ogre, resembled a parley between an august man at the height of his energies, a man who could roll the earth downhill like a boulder, and Polly, who was as confident as the Tsar of all the Russias, her legs poking out heroically and without apology.

I still believed as a woman of thirteen that my elders, elders such as Polly, for example, were set like stars or mountains, and had been immutable before my birth and would remain immutable for an untold period. I did not think they were creatures of flux as I was. Only later, when I no longer saw her so regularly, did I speculate whether as little as twenty-five years earlier Polly had ridden as a fresh girl on good horses with other women to balls at the Castle Terrace or at Plantation House, and danced with the neat officers of the navy, and with the garrison of the East India Company, and charmed them, and rendered them lovesick. And that she was in their company all the night, since it was too perilous and long a track back to her father's house.

And thus I saw her as a sort of warning, not as a raw yamstock but an Englishwoman born in soft airs. The island had, however, by now made her one of its own. Unlike me, the Ogre knew better than anyone that people were not born as they became. The Corsican child, speaking Italian, looking to Genoa as the great city, had become the Emperor of France, and now the great bull contained raging within a palisade of cliffs. Nothing was fixed, and the woman riding her cow was a manifestation of a more startling history of shifts and accidents than the woman on an unexceptional horse.

The Emperor therefore wanted Jane to ask Miss Mason her origins.

"My father was an Ulsterman," she said. "He was a younger son, and joined the navy, and while visiting the island on a ship had ridden its length and width and so had chosen the reach beyond Prosperous Plain. My mother died when I was too young to acquire memory of her. My father had his weakness, Sir Emperor. Took to our slave housekeeper, and I assure you that I have half brothers and sisters in the freed slave quarters. And you will see the resemblance. There is no filament between me and them. I am an exhibit for the fraternity of all men and the sorority of all women."

"You are speaking of one of the ills of slavery," the Emperor opined.

"Perhaps. But men will mock any certainties to have a bit of company and a caress. I must get to Deadwood now."

As she kicked her cow's flanks and urged it on towards her vegetable gardens at Deadwood, I had the impression that she was riding away from a treaty-making, pondering the terms of existence offered her by the Great Ogre.

There was an island consensus that something within Polly, some fortress of proprieties, had once tumbled. A now deceased male slave was in some way obscurely connected to this fall of hers.

Was it a Man of Reason
or a clown . . . ?

One clear and balmy spring evening (the island being in the southern half of the world and thus reversing the accustomed seasons), my parents had gone out by cart to dine, over near the great column of rock named Lot's Wife at Horse Pasture Farm. The house belonged to the gentleman farmer Knipe, uncle of yet another beautiful young woman, Miss Knipe, whom the French had named *Le Bouton de Rose*.

Because I had made a tolerant accommodation of all the Emperor's vagaries of soul, including those involving *Le Bouton de Rose, La Nymphe,* and Madame de Montholon, I thought somehow that he might have made the same equivalent arrangements in his attitude as well. I had thought that, since he had given me a ball gown paid for from his own resources, I was now conclusively beyond the restless frolicking he brought to his play with children. So I was calm at the idea that the Ogre and his attendants were to entertain us in my parents' absence. The Ogre came up to the house attended by Marchand, and with his card softener, Las Cases senior, his son as a phantom at his elbow, and the eternal Gourgaud, to play whist. I was confident that our earlier disasters at cards would not be repeated. Whist was my favorite game of all, beautifully simple, understandable by children but challenging to adult intelligence. I loved to draw the lowest card and come to triumph playing in partnership with the other lower drawer.

We got the two card packs from the hands of the chamberlain, and I became Gourgaud's partner, since he and I drew the two higher cards.

There is something in me that cherishes the rules of games. They are an authority higher than human, or so I like to believe. It turned out that the Ogre, however, saw this evening as a continuation of an earlier farcical game we had played. He talked to Jane, his partner, about his supposedly poor hand, he played false trumps, refusing to follow suit. He seemed to fail a compact of respect owed to me.

I will not deal with all the silliness of which he was guilty, except to say that Emmanuel frowned, as if he could foresee the danger, but callow Gourgaud laughed at any trick of his master and increased the pressure I felt within me. At last I asked, "Do you think this is the way for a Man of Reason to play games?"

Las Cases the elder raised his eyes in mute shock, but the son lowered his.

"Who created the Code Napoleon?" I asked. "Was it a Man of Reason or a clown?"

The Ogre said, "Ah, my Betsy, is whist a game that's suitable for a Man of Reason? That is the true question."

"God help a Man of Reason who cannot follow the game of whist!" I was on my feet now, leaning over him. I could hear Las Cases making small squeaks with his lips, which were meant to counsel me to be more measured.

By a fathomable but unlucky chance, the ball gown crafted by La Nymphe lay on the settle at the far corner of the room, a display piece at the heart of The Briars for the admiration of visitors. He had bought me this woman's dress, but his behavior proclaimed me unfit for it. He rose to his feet now, and an instant later so did Gourgaud, hand on sword hilt, once more grotesquely ready to defend his Emperor as he had against the aggression of the Holstein cow. Las Cases's parchment skin exuded a gloss of sweat and was sourly bunched at the lips.

"Come, Betsy," said the Ogre, in a voice pitched between adult reproof and amusement, "making laws for an empire is a happy experience compared to playing whist with some young women."

With his customary nimbleness he advanced to the settle and hauled up my ball gown.

"In exoneration, I demand my gown back," he said, with annoyance but also playfulness, the worst of combinations, the one most offensive to me. He walked out of the drawing room with it over his elbow and down the hallway towards our door, and I leaped up and called after him as he passed out into the darkness of the garden. "Bring it back!" I roared.

For I seemed to be losing everything, my new agreed-upon being, my serious advance towards the grown-up world, my claim on my own years and stature, derived from the vivid blood that now flowed more or less monthly from me. I was ready to follow him and launch myself at him and fell the little top-heavy man. At the same time a despair set in, a knowledge that I could not be the first on the island to deliver punches to the Emperor, and that if I were, it would embed me further in childhood and ignominy. So it seemed, unimpeded, the Emperor was gone from the house with the patent of my womanhood over his elbow.

Gourgaud had followed him, and now Las Cases and his son stood, nodded curtly, and left. Emmanuel stared bleakly at me over his shoulder, and I did not know what the bleakness meant, disapproval or sympathy.

Jane came up to my side. "He's joking," she assured me. "My heaven, you did get far too upset with him, Betsy! But he'll give it back in the morning. And I think you should wait until then, until his temper, or whatever it is, recedes."

She understood nothing. I felt exhausted from my continual struggle at self-certainty. It was the Ogre who kept shifting the terms on me.

The next morning, I got up leadenly from a profound sleep and appeared at the breakfast table wan, and through shameful tears I begged my father to go and intercede for me.

"I will not," he told me, with that gratuitous firmness of his, a rigidity generally missing from him. Because his severity was so intermittent and irrational, it sounded pompous when he adopted it, like a man wearing another's grander clothes.

"Your sister says you were very abusive to the Emperor. I cannot have that, either in terms of his dignity or of my being his provedore."

"My sister is not right in what she says," I claimed. "She cannot understand why a person would feel outrage."

Jane bore, of course, a burning face and furiously wished to help me now. "I did not interpret it as abuse, Father," she said. "I told you only that she said a man who had made the Code Napoleon could certainly understand the laws of whist, and that is very close to being a just statement."

What did she truly think, amidst the sweetness of her temperament, about Gourgaud? Had she lost all breath and reason for him?

"No, not just," said my father. "Far too hot indeed, considering his sins were so venial and you were playing for sugarplums and not for fortunes." He turned to me. "You must do your own pleading, miss."

That put paid to any lachrymosity of mine. I turned at once and set out to go to the Pavilion. The purpose with which I moved was to impress my father. Secretly I decided that the first aim was to win back my gown by any means, and thus I was ready to be contrite. I was fearful in case the Ogre had crushed the gown, or vengefully stripped the roses from it.

As I came to the Pavilion, I was met from behind by Gourgaud, and Las Cases appeared on the doorstep and told me that the Emperor was not to be disturbed. I did not have gravity or judgment enough to tell him I would wait for an audience, and so I withdrew to the verandah of The Briars.

I waited for an hour and a half, eating nothing, taking some tepid tea Sarah brought, and then I saw the Emperor, Gourgaud, and both Las Cases descend to the garden and enter the grape arbor. Coming down into the garden myself, I glanced into the entrance of that grotto of vines and could dimly see the Emperor pacing in his peculiar cock-sparrow manner, hands behind his back, vaporing on about some battlefield performance of his which must surely have risen above the level of childishness he imposed on me.

I opened the gate and entered the arbor. I called softly in the vegetable dimness. "I've come for my gown."

There was silence, and the Count de Las Cases emerged and told me drily the Emperor could not see me.

"Tell him," I said, "that he is killing me as he killed the Duke d'Enghien."

The little chamberlain reached back his hand and struck me across the cheek. It stung a considerable swathe of skin, bigger than his hand, but the sting was irrelevant. I looked him full in the face. He hissed, "The Duke d'Enghien was a traitor. Do you not execute traitors in England? In my time there you executed people who were not even traitors. You should please go now."

And he turned his back and walked back into the deep shade of the arbor.

I called in a level voice for the Emperor's edification, "He has struck me, your chamberlain. He strikes me in *my* house."

I heard the Emperor muttering, "Did you strike her?"

"She accused you of murder," said the chamberlain, as if the entire career of the Emperor had been bloodless and an imputation of any spillage was an outright insult.

"Next time I shall bring a pistol," I called. And then there were a few seconds of private tears as I stood there, after which I called out with a cruelty I decided was in measure with the damage Las Cases had done me. "I feel happy that you are persecuting me instead of your son, the King of Rome, as you would if you were with him."

Could it be suppressed laughter I heard then? Not from Las Cases anyhow. I was sure he didn't have any talent for sustained laughter. And so I withdrew before I was sure about the laughter, because if it were confirmed, that would be intolerable. I had an assassin's pistol to fetch as well, though I was unsure whether I would use it on Las Cases or the Universal Demon.

I returned to the house in a stupefied state. I knew I could not enlist my father to punch Las Cases in return, or to call him out for a duel; there was little gain in a parental revenge inflicted at a distance from me. I needed to devise revenge for my own hand.

I did not seek a pistol. Not even I could sustain a killing mania.

My father, seeing how I was, let me off my French translation for the day. By midafternoon my natural obduracy had reached a high state. I went to my mother and called in Sarah and Alice and asked them to tuck in the waist of one of my mother's gowns for me. I would not shine at Plantation House, but I *would* be present.

Sick and sullen, I was with Jane and my mother as we packed our dresses and combs and powder and rouge and all other requirements for the ball in tin boxes. They were carried out by Robert and Roger to the carriage the Ogre had lent us for the journey to Plantation House. The barouche stood there, and the two brothers, the Archambaults, stood by the team of horses.

The Archambaults were ready to mount the horses in front and the tin boxes had been loaded into the barouche when we saw the Emperor running across the lawn, up the slope to our house with my gown over his arm. My father, already in the barouche with us, kept his face neutral.

"You are leaving without your dress, Mademoiselle Betsy," the Ogre cried. He had it draped across his arms. "I hope you are a penitent girl now," he said, offering the gown to me, and I took it and felt its unsullied satin and intact roses. "I hope that you are not going to tell those who are having a jolly time with you that they are somehow cheats." He lowered his voice. "I have spoken severely to Las Cases for his ill-placed zeal." He resumed in a normal voice, "You will like the ball, and you will shine in this dress, but you have to dance with Gourgaud here."

General Gourgaud climbed aboard the barouche with us, since he was permitted to attend the levee, "General" being the correct designation for him. I only partly listened to his halting conversation with my father. The now forgiven seducer of my sister! I was still inspecting the dress, enchanted by it, revived by its roses. The Emperor saw this.

"I had them removed by Ali in case they were crushed, and he re-attached them today. You always knew I would give it back. Farewell, eminent Mr. Balcombe. Splendid Balcombe women, madame, and mesdemoiselles, rejoice! General, sir. Off, Archambaults!"

We rattled forth in the half dark, but with the Emperor still striding at the stirrup of the older Archambault, who prevented the horses from speeding away even though he had a repute for recklessness. The Ogre kept pace with us all the way down the carriageway, where two soldiers of the regiment presented arms to him, their eyes flittering over him as they always did, trying to puzzle him out, memorizing all they could of that half-lit visage to relay to those who had never seen it close. Now the Emperor had seen the lights of a house about a mile away. He delayed my father to ask him, *"La maison? Là-bas?"*

My father understood as much French as that. He told him it was Major Hodson's.

"Not invite to ball?" asked the Emperor.

I tried to imagine the tall Major Hodson dancing. In any case, he was of the East India Company garrison and not quite of the same status or novelty as the officers of the 53rd.

My father said, "I don't think he is of a temper, Your Majesty, to go to balls."

"You must go now, all of you," the Emperor told us. "And remember that a ball is a rapid form of destiny. Consider that you might meet your husband tonight, mesdemoiselles!"

Thus, while we were at the ball the Ogre of Europe, accompanied by the Count de Las Cases, rode across to that lit house, hungry as ever for company, and bringing with him that avidity to know about the childless Hodsons, husband and wife.

The squat Emperor and the towering Hodson, as it happened, got on quite well, because after the ball it became apparent he had awarded him a nickname, Hercules, as he did for all people he admired.

We, in the meantime, were driven on up the ridge behind The Briars and by pleasant country lanes, though some traversed steep ridges. Tonight even the crossroads seemed exempt from the influence of demented Huff. Along a track to the east we reached the plain that led to Plantation House and so debouched into the grounds, where I glanced at Jane and we exchanged tight smiles, anxious at the challenge, eager for it to happen as well. In the last of the light, we could see in the broad green garden the land tortoises, moving just fast enough not to be mistaken for rocks, and an occasional peacock, beak down, tail furled, and lights in all the windows of the white rectangular frame of the house. Colonel Wilks, his gentle wife, and beauteous daughter Laura reigned here, he as governor for the East India Company, cooperating gently in Admiral Cockburn's management of the Colossus.

Long before we came to the house, we could hear a hubbub of voices, and found the ensigns and lieutenants were hauling a farm dray up towards the main entrance. It was a substantial vehicle, and as we rolled closer they swept their hats off and told us that they intended to drag the wagon in front of the portico once all the ladies had arrived and so keep them captive till dawn. The idea was heady, and carried an innocent whiff of abduction.

So we rode past them laughing breathily, and the barouche was taken, and we were handed down by slave servants dressed in livery and led by a black serving woman inside the door of the house and to a parlor set aside as a dressing room for the ladies of the ball.

I felt that for the first time in my life I had arrived at last at a destination. In the dressing room I took off my traveling clothes and was helped by the Wilks servant to put on my dress of satin and calico roses, and I was a woman amongst women, in a musk of perfume and fabric and excited wives and daughters and slaves, many of them beautiful enough to look with longing at what I wore.

Knowing that I was an initiate, that this was a rite of womanhood for me, various ladies, including Mrs. Solomon and Mrs. Captain Younghusband, came up to compliment me. Mrs. Younghusband was a woman of the same age as Madame de Montholon and Fanny Bertrand, her husband a very fresh-faced captain, seven years younger than her. She possessed, beneath her brown curls, large, shifting, limpid eyes, and as she spoke I wondered if her gestures had been influenced by Fanny Bertrand's. Her broad arms were spread wide at the end of her imparting any modest piece of information. At tea at our place she had complained about the fleas that infested the whole Deadwood site where the camp was being built, and where she lived in a tent with her eight-year-old daughter Emily, a sweet English child rather overborne by her mother. After taking a walk on the grass, Catherine Younghusband was quick to tell us all, she would come home totally infested with fleas and have to enter the tent and throw her clothes out of the flap to be boiled up and deloused. So she was trying to persuade her husband to build her a more permanent habitation. Her husband was besotted and had the vigorous intention to save her from parasites.

At The Briars once, Bonaparte had seen her from the grape arbor or the marquee and came out calling, "Who is this lady?"

Speaking first in French and then in Italian, in both of which Mrs. Younghusband was fluent, he had ushered her into our house to give her a chance to present a recital of Italian airs on our piano in the style *grandissimo*, and play an Italian duet with little Emily. Emily was clearly a gifted child, but Mrs. Younghusband herself brought from the Emperor an extraordinary compliment. "Ah! There is a woman of spirit."

She had told him, as she often did with others as a conversational gambit, that she had descended from Oliver Cromwell, that enemy of the dance. But here she was, determined to be celebrated at the Plantation House ball.

Mrs. Nagle, wife of a lieutenant, was also very kind, and Miss *Rosebud* Knipe. I had been admitted by them, and I exulted. I was meanly pleased that *La Nymphe*, Miss Robinson, was not invited; nor many of the yamstocks.

At a supreme moment, Madame de Montholon, her compact belly leading, crossed the floor to compliment me. It was her approval that excited me most since it seemed to come from a woman more deeply emplaced in the mystery of womanhood than anyone else, including Fanny Bertrand. Madame de Montholon's voice had a small and silken quality, yet at the same time was forceful. She said simply, "Oh, dear Betsy, how I envy your dress! Is it true the Emperor had it made?"

In the ballroom on the ground floor, frowning on my joy, hung the portraits of members of the Council of the East India Company, distant gray men of a seniority that yielded precedence only to the long dead. By contrast the room glittered with light, and loops of fabric canopies had been erected along its length to give it an appropriate feeling of licensed pleasure.

Fanny Bertrand had already entered from the dressing room, and we found her in the garlanded ballroom, high-waisted and glowing-shouldered in fabrics of powdery blue, and around her neck and shoulders a grand, structural necklace once worn in salons superior to this one. So we chose our seats about her, having, as women are doomed to do, located our father and assessed his happiness as he chattered beside Mr. Ibbetson, his fellow professional, commissary for the military, a man my father dealt with almost daily. Cups of punch were delivered to us by a number of young officers. The pretension of their uniforms seemed far removed from mud and blood, and I always wondered, and do to this day, why men wore such splendor to go to die or be maimed. My mother forbade Jane and me to drink what was brought, and more innocent concoctions were fetched from the bowl the few children present drank from. My dress did not qualify me for intoxicants.

There were two officers, two very different men indeed, one mature, one young, on that night, which I remember as the highest night of the island, before our steep decline. One of them was the lean, leather-faced major Oliver Fehrzen ageless, possibly younger than my father, in a uniform that had been turned according to need and that had been used in other stations than this. It had become pink from campaigning. He was a little narrow in the face, but his features were those of a reliable human. He assuredly had the seasoned look of one who had campaigned in the war in Spain against my Grand Playmate from The Briars.

He asked me in a direct, decisive voice whether I would permit him to mark my card as a dance partner.

"I'm not good at quadrilles, Major," I warned him, "and I hear they'll be dancing quadrilles."

He laughed benignly. He had amiable eyes whose gravity elevated my words pleasantly.

"I have not been much exposed to them myself," he confessed. And he wrote his name in a space in my card and moved on to bow to other ladies and to seek dancing partners, but without anxiety, a man merely fulfilling his pleasant duty.

Then I saw Lieutenant Croad, as did everyone. For he was the young man, a little beak-nosed but with eyes abrim with enthusiasm, who was said to be set on introducing quadrilles into the program, no matter how much they tested the skills of an island girl. Mrs.

Nagle told us Croad had been training the officers and their spouses in the movements required for the dance, but he had not spread this benevolence beyond the camp. I recognized Croad as one of the courtly officers who had bowed to us in a Gallic manner on the day the Ogre arrived at the dock. His uniform was a great variation from the workman's uniform of Major Fehrzen. The epaulettes trailed gold thread down his shoulders. Everything on his clothing that could be frogged with gold was. His breeches were a dazzling white, and below the knee ended in gaiters.

His bows were, as earlier, most profound, and involved not just his body from the waist upwards but a genuflection of the knee, with an appropriate near kneeling of the other leg, while his gold-handled sword and golden jewel-chased scabbard stuck up in the air so that other members of the party had to make a circuit around their point to accommodate his gallantry.

He had already greeted the Frenchwomen, Mesdames Bertrand and de Montholon, with an even more extreme stretch of his limbs and more reverent smoothing of his lips against their white knuckles, and Madame de Montholon's eyes glowed when she saw him. In that she was honest. She liked, more than Fanny Bertrand, to be flattered by men. Then Croad moved on to my mother, about whom he enthused, as a number of men did too much. He charmed Jane and finally me.

"I must say, Miss Balcombe, I have not seen in my campaigns as apt a dress as yours," he palavered on, yet with a saving enthusiasm behind what he said. "Sufficiently rustic for the island, sufficiently elegant to remind us of nature but also of ceremony. I offer no promises that I will live to be an eighty-year-old general, but if I do I shall celebrate each rare future encounter with such a dress." And then, a further twist to the oratory. "I do not plan to have, Miss Balcombe, the memory of your splendid equipage eroded by any future encounters, however exalted."

I could merely gape at him, uncertain as to whether to beam or not, and lower my head.

"Thank you," I said at last, in an ungainly voice.

It had been a wonderful encomium to my dress—at least I think that's what it was, as I could not absorb the words discretely—and I could neither answer him nor escape the suspicion either that he might be putting me in my place as a girl stuck in the mid-Atlantic.

I danced first with the rather distracted surgeon of one of the ships of the squadron, a friend of O'Meara's. The Irish surgeon was also there, laughing in a corner near my father, and being eloquent and red-cheeked. The man who held me was pleasant but too clearly saw himself as being engaged, perhaps at O'Meara's instruction, in patronizing me.

The dance I looked forward to, and the one for which Major Fehrzen had signed his name, was a country reel. I knew the steps and it seemed to suit Major Fehrzen's unpretentious nature. I felt very small in his hands, hardened by unimaginable tasks in the war against the Ogre, and could feel his calluses, yet decided to be calm, since women around me were being similarly quil in the hands of other men.

"I have been up to your place, Miss Balcombe," he told me. "I was visiting the Emperor. Like everybody else, such crowds of people try to go there and have a sight of him."

"Are you supposed to call him the Emperor?" I asked. "I thought that soldiers were required to call him General."

"Sometimes our tongue betrays us," he said. "He was a great mischief-maker, indeed the mischief-maker of my lifetime. But one looks at all that—the canvas marquee and the summerhouse, an absolutely charming one, of course, but . . . I think you would admit it's not Fontainebleau. How remarkable it would have been if he'd come tonight."

"He would have come if the admiral had called him what you called him."

"Well," said Major Fehrzen, quietly and with a smile, "we have gone from a war of cannon to a war of words."

I said, rather proud of myself when I got it out, "There is always war where words come in."

And now this mature man looked at me appraisingly. It was somehow wonderful and unutterably awkward. Yet he was looking at the face from which my opinions emerged. I was like an equal in discourse.

"You are very serene, Miss Balcombe—for a young woman who has *the General* at the bottom of her garden."

"He doesn't act up to the level of his repute. If this island were the world, he would still be interested, and be its ultimate authority on population and vegetable gardening and goats."

He smiled and nodded emphatically. I found myself quite taken with the experience of being held by this large, weathered frame. In spite of the inequality of strength, there was an equality of conversation and, I suppose, of will.

"May I ask you blunt questions?" I asked, as we danced. I was playing with the limits of my social gifts, but it was a very hot night, and there was something in us all that did not mind uttering bold sentiments in pursuit of the real.

"What manner of blunt things do you have in mind, Miss Balcombe?" he asked.

"I wonder, were you wounded? Were you wounded by the servants of the mischief-maker? Or near to being wounded? And where did that happen?"

"I had a scratch, I admit," said Major Fehrzen. "An age ago."

"What does a scratch mean?"

"I suppose it means a glancing wound from a fragment of ball. A fortunate wound."

"And where did this take place?"

"Have you heard of Salamanca?"

"Of course," I said, though I was uncertain of its location. "And if it was a scratch, then you did not need to undergo treatment from a surgeon?"

"Perhaps for a few weeks. It was combined with a touch of fever."

"So you soldiers suffer from scratches and touches. It's a wonder so many of you manage to get killed."

He laughed at this. "I was adjutant of my regiment at Salamanca," he told me, "so I was protected by the line. The colonel, seeing my wound in the upper thigh, poured brandy on it from a flask he carried. He believed that was essential treatment for all wounds."

The regimental band at the end of the ballroom, after demanding a crescendo of whirling from us, now paused. I was exhausted not only by the dance but by the experience of being even more a new person than I had been an hour before, so Captain Fehrzen returned me to my seat.

"If I come to The Briars again," said Fehrzen, returning to his long, leather-faced solemnity, "I shall come and see you, Miss Balcombe, and your sister and delightful mother."

I feared my coming encounter with Lieutenant Croad. It was hard to imagine such a lustrous, smooth-faced young man living under canvas at Deadwood, amongst the fleas Mrs. Younghusband had complained of, and, further, dancing with a rancorous little girl like me. The dance he had put down his name for was certainly a quadrille, and I barely knew what that was. I was grateful to revert to girlhood and go to my mother.

"Could you please tell Lieutenant Croad that I cannot fulfil my obligation to him?"

My mother raised her eyebrows. Her face was flushed, though she had had only the one dance, and that with General Bertrand, and I could tell she too felt that she was not quite up to the level. Just the same, she asked me why.

"Tell him I have faintness, fatigue, and a fever."

"That's a lot to have," said my mother.

The quietly spoken Madame de Montholon sitting nearby had overheard my pleadings. She reached out and took my hand.

"Oh, it is nothing," she said. "It is a cotillion, but of shorter duration. If you can dance the cotillion, dear friend, you can dance a quadrille."

"Explain that I'm more comfortable with the country dances and the Scottish reel," I pleaded with my mother.

Madame Bertrand now turned. She and Madame de Montholon both laughed as if it were endearingly typical of the young me and the ancient island, and its entire population. To these people, I knew, we were probably all yamstocks.

Madame Bertrand told me, "You will be in the hands of the dance master himself, and he will be tolerant and a good guide. He might not qualify as a dance teacher in Paris, but he's adequate for St. Hélène."

And so Lieutenant Croad presented himself, smiling pleasantly, and I stood, feeling sick. He took my hand delicately but firmly as we strode out onto the floor and offered our compliments and bows to the opposing couple, the Younghusbands.

There was not a chance for long conversations in a quadrille, but Lieutenant Croad did have time to say to me, in his voice as crisp as a wafer, "I had heard of your father before I landed on this island. The sailors told us about him."

Sailors *did* have stories about my father, and I wondered what their derivation was. I knew my father to be a considerable worthy of the island, but had never expected him to have a repute that stretched in all directions across the encircling ocean.

Croad said, "I have already expressed my compliments to him this evening and hope to visit him at The Briars. Is the General himself a good dancer?"

"I have never seen him dance," I confessed. "I'd say he doesn't have the figure for it except that he is agile."

"Madame Bertrand is an excellent dancer," Croad told me when I next saw him, passed to him by Captain Younghusband. "And I've observed General Gourgaud."

Croad had an extraordinary gift for keeping his breath in the rigors of the dance. They weren't rigors to him. "They have the *ton* that seems to come naturally to the French. It is a relief that we can say such things about the French now without being chastised by some patriotic yahoo. How they can dance! Without the jerking and rabbit-hopping and plunging of our country dances."

It was the jerking, rabbit-hopping, and plunging for which I had any assured gift. Croad, I meanwhile noted, had a narrow, pretty face, and I found I had a weakness, not previously revealed to me, for that type of boy. I liked a great deal of brightness in wide eyes, a well-formed nose, less like a statement of will than that of Admiral Cockburn. And the Cupid's-bow lips Croad had. I realized I had developed a vague interest, and thought it would be worth spending more time in his company, unless he withdrew it after this dance.

The dance ended, and I appreciated his offer to fetch me an ice, for the exercise had evoked a level of competence in me that had dried me out. Croad went off to find refreshments for me and Madame de Montholon, who was feeling the warm night.

When Croad came back I said to him, "These sailors, what did they say about my father?"

"Oh," he said, suddenly evasive, because he could see a certain bewilderment in me, "as the purveyor to the ships and the company he is well known."

"There is no nobler man," I agreed, "but I still can't imagine why he's so broadly known."

"You . . . you've heard no intimations from your family?" He could see I hadn't and seemed to blush. "Please, Miss Balcombe," he said, "I was talking off the top of my head rather than as an intelligent fellow. And as you know, on a ship everything you hear gets said, however minor and unreliable it is, to fill out all those sluggish hours. I heard his nickname, Prince, that's all. Now, enough of that. If I came to The Briars, I would be delighted to accompany you and your sister on a *tour naturaliste* around Diana's Peak."

And then, to override our conversation to this point, he rushed to ask, "Do you think the General would consent to talk to me a little? I fancy I am a great student of his Egyptian campaign."

"He seems to be writing on exactly that matter right now. But if you want to please him, as I told Major Fehrzen, call him *Emperor* when you see him. He objects to the appellation General."

I took an abstract pleasure as the night went on in having been asked permission to be visited by two officers, Fehrzen and Croad. I had not any overmastering desire to see them specifically, but now as a young woman I was delighted by the idea of having visitors. I had become a fisher of men.

More ices were brought. Some women went and slept a few hours in a parlor. My mother was one, but not Jane or I. When not dancing, I sat self-sufficient in my gown, and that was for me the central joy of the night.

And, amazingly, all at once we heard the dawn gun fired from the top of Ladder Hill. The music ceased. One of the silken banners had fallen. The scale of our exhaustion became apparent to us. We found the Countess de Montholon already asleep on the settle in the women's dressing room as servants helped us take off our dresses and pack them in our tin boxes.

They were transmuted now, these robes, a different and somehow used-up fabric. So in a sense were we. Fabrics had been reduced by motion and gravity, and my roses drooped and would require a tender reopening by hand before I wore the dress again. Powder had clotted in the warm sockets of the body, perfumes had soured, inevitable and indelicate sweat had eroded the night. The wagon was rolled away from the gate by a party of soldiers—the young men who had put it there were slumped on camp cots amongst the trees or off in the Deadwood lines or on duty to contain the Ogre. My father was sleepy and a little irritable. It was not the time to ask him why sailors knew him and why his nickname was Prince.

As we rode home, Jane seemed uncomplicatedly tranquil and sleepy. She could accommodate a world in which men said fantastical things and not have them leave her feverish. I had two males to think about, which seemed to me to be another token of new stature, certainly, but also a spur to uneasiness. The pretty face of Lieutenant Croad was clear in my head as we left the high road and took the track towards The Briars. But since I was still practicing at womanhood, Croad remained a kind of roadside phantom, a teasing chimera rather than some sort of destination for the affections. By his suicide tree Huff was at that hour definitely dead.

When I rose in the afternoon and found Jane and my mother drinking tea in the drawing room, they seemed to be sitting in a strange light, the altered light of a day in which one has slept long and unnaturally and without refreshment. I was sullen and dislocated. The question that abided from the night before was that talk of Croad's about knowing my father, a remark that chimed in crucially with other mysterious pronouncements of sundry visitors and even that of the Emperor.

"Boney sends his compliments," said Jane, brightly amused, "and wanted to know if you had brought home an affection for some officer. He asked had you met someone who would supplant what you feel for our friend the young Emmanuel de Las Cases?"

"A tired joke, that one," I said, slumping down.

I knew that if I asked my mother a question she would not lie before Jane. Jane was a hard presence to lie in front of. The opportunity existed now, with the three of us in housecoats, and outside the trade wind making its daily combing of the upper air and nudging vigorously at the windowsills.

My hand dangling loose as if I were not asking a great question, I said, "Strangers are always saying they knew of Father before they met him. Even the Emperor. Lieutenant Croad said he heard him mentioned on ships at sea. Why do so many of those who come here seem to know him already? And why do I hear people call him Prince?"

My mother looked away an instant, a sign it was a complex question, and then looked back at me with her hazel eyes, which, I realize now, later became mine.

"Oh, you shouldn't worry—there are rumors but that's all," said my mother. "I've told you, your grandfather was in a cutter off the Isle of Dogs when the young Prince of Wales was aboard the royal yacht. The yacht collided with the cutter and your grandfather drowned. Your father might have told this story as a dark joke when in his cups, not realizing how it would get around and be misunderstood. Sir Thomas Tyrwhitt visited the boys and their mother, and offered to fund their education and position on the Prince's behalf. So the gossip about the Prince's interest in your father got started. These are the sorts of stories people love to tell. And on the strength of it all they call your father 'Prince.'"

"Why doesn't Father tell people it's not true?"

My mother stared a little and said in a whisper, "I think it's the kind of rumor human beings like to set going about themselves. Otherwise, they are just who they are. And on an island like this, that's barely enough."

She smiled and nodded. The idea that my father embraced his nickname had not occurred to me.

"That was how he got that particular pet name, which you notice I never choose to call him by."

I studied Jane. I could not judge if she had already known all this. For now I was satisfied and thought I had received the truth entire.

Marchand was at the door. As ever he was elegantly dressed, more so than Las Cases, his neckcloths and shirt immaculate. His English was better than his master's too.

"The Sèvres china has arrived," he told us. "The Emperor has invited you to see it."

This was a welcome distraction, and we pleaded for half an hour to dress properly.

"Cipriani is relieved," Marchand told us of the Emperor's maître d'hôtel. "He never liked that Nanking crockery we've been eating from."

As I prepared myself, the evening seemed to fill with new color after that reduced fretful day of sleep, as if the pigments from the Sèvres had overflowed the plates and enriched the whole evening.

In the marquee, we found the Emperor dressed in his green coat and his vest and wearing his orders. It was clear he was delighted by the arrival of china, as if it restored something he had nearly forgotten yet nonetheless needed.

He cried, "Young ladies! You will see that the painters have given me a history of my life to watch, even as I dine."

Two-handedly, he passed us plates on which his Italian and Egyptian adventures were depicted, and I saw a younger, thinner Emperor stepping amongst the Pyramids. He could tell I was taken with this and declared, "Never think of going to Egypt, Betsy. It is the country of the blind."

The next plate showed him young and bareheaded and grim in an Alpine pass, with a shattered cannon beside him but his will intact. Then an older Emperor listening to reports, his staff around him, and again a shattered cannon, to indicate how regularly he courted catastrophe that destroyed things of iron and wood but not his flesh. At the head of each plate, atop delicately painted wreaths, gold on blue, stood an "N."

I remembered that at the ball beautiful Laura Wilks had asked me whether we, the family, had ever seen the Emperor pray. She was full of frank interest, though more interested in rumor than in theology. "Does he pray like a child of Mohammed, on a mat, facing the east?" she asked. "I believe he has been a Child of the Prophet since he was in Egypt."

I had heard this too, and it had been said to my mother by people in town that he had betrayed Christendom and, to no advantage, become a Turk. I held the plate of the Pyramids as this rumor recurred to me.

"Did you become a Mohammedan in Egypt?" I asked him.

I heard Jane and my mother groan and could not quite understand why they did so. For if a man lays out the Pyramids before you, it is a fair thing to ask him had he taken the religion as he had sought to take the country.

"Ah," he said, though not too obviously offended, "that English canard again! And from the lips of my Betsy."

"Who else would dare ask?" said Jane, and the Emperor was fully appeased by her and became rueful.

"It might shock good Protestant girls like you if I said that my religion is that of the country in which I am serving. Even here, Betsy, had you impaled me with my sword that night, I would have been happy to be buried by the man that replaced Jones, the Reverend Mr. Boys."

"That would be a very dull funeral," I said.

"Indeed, I would have been chastised from the pulpit for my life and for my death."

"So in Egypt, the religion of the Turks is as good as ours?"

"If you were a young Turkish or Egyptian girl, you would say it was, and better."

The Emperor now walked up to my mother. He stood close to her and looked at what she was holding. "Oh, that! I sit astride a horse on a hill, don't I? But that's a plate I will choose not to eat from because I remember that day, and had a fever and did not leave my carriage. . . . He who would eat from that plate would eat half-truths."

His lips were quite close to her ear. "Would you like it, Madame Balcombe?" he asked. "For it's of small comfort to me."

"You don't mean it," said my mother, and though she was excited by the offer of this wonderful piece of clay and porcelain and art, she had the fiber to refuse it.

The Emperor picked up one of the plates himself. "Perhaps you should take this one," he said. "That one you hold is a mild lie. This one is a calamity. Leipzig. Perhaps in a state of irony I may eat from the other, but never from this one."

He turned round and called for his maître d'hôtel.

"Cipriani, take note. These two plates can be set before the innocents but not before me. One of them, this of myself mounted and a grand equestrian, when in fact I was a coach traveler. But perhaps Mrs. Balcombe will not take the Leipzig plate. Would you take it as a favor to a friend? The people at the factory have not understood how fierce a blow this Leipzig business was in a catalogue of the events of my life."

I was rendered uneasy by the way his hand suddenly touched her shoulder and the closeness of his suggestions to her ear.

"No, General," said my mother, shaking her head with some severity. "I could not consider taking either."

We said goodbye and walked back to the house. It was as if the failure to pass off the Leipzig plate on my mother had shortened the visit.

That evening O'Meara came to dinner, but the Emperor preferred to stay in his marquee and eat off his beloved Sèvres. There was something in O'Meara's pleasant, jocular face and bright eyes and humorous delivery I had begun to be concerned about. Before dinner I asked my mother, "Is Surgeon O'Meara sent to spy on the Emperor?"

"Perhaps," said my mother. "It may be his duty. For God's sake, don't ask him." And she laughed in my direction, as if she could foresee what a sensation it would be if I did.

I decided I would ask him one day, privately. I did not want him passing on to the admiral details such as the Emperor's breath against my mother's ear.

She said, "He is a decent fellow, O'Meara. You can be assured of that."

At dinner, O'Meara was still amused by the Emperor's being a medical skeptic. He was worried about the sudden prevalence of jaundice in the fleet.

"And I think in the Countess de Montholon," my mother remarked. Apparently, without my noticing it, Albine had the yellow coloration.

"Indeed," said O'Meara. "To be deplored in a woman in her condition! And there is nothing to be done except hot ferments and bleeding, and the rest must be waited out."

Jane told my father and O'Meara about the dinner plates the Emperor disowned. "Betsy asked him if he was a Mohammedan," she said with a kind of admiration.

"Oh, he's all things," said the Irishman. "Believe me. One day he is a Deist, another a Catholic, another an atheist, another a Mohammedan, and the next a predestinarian Calvinist. He talks himself into a different religious situation each day; the Almighty cannot keep up with the fellow at all."

Jane now took up the matter of the wounded on the Sèvres plate. It had struck her that the Emperor carried them in his memory with some composure. "Has he spoken about the wounded to you, Surgeon O'Meara? Wouldn't it be natural for him to speak of the wounded to his surgeon? His wounded at Gaza, about whom stories are told, just for an example."

"I can't stop him talking," admitted O'Meara. "He raises the wounded of Jaffa quicker than any enemy could. He raises all that there is against him quicker than malice can manage." O'Meara, as so often, turned to me to make me the object of his answer.

"Yes, Betsy. His wounded in Jaffa, have you heard of them? Well, according to Our Great Friend, his army was forced to withdraw from Jaffa, and we know that as a fact, and there were wounded to be left. What should be done with the poor fellows, further from home than any Frenchman who died in all those years, far away in Palestine? So he suggested to the surgeons that the sickest be given a merciful dose of laudanum. He knew they would be terribly treated, says he, if they fell into the Turks' hands. He declares that had he been in their situation, he would have welcomed the option of laudanum. Our man invited me then, Betsy, to put myself in the situation of one of those fellows. If it had been his own son, he said, he would ask the surgeon to apply that remedy."

O'Meara paused to be sure of the weight of this tale upon me.

"Now, his chief surgeon presented the concept to his corps of surgeons, who to their credit took the Hippocratic view that it was their duty to cure and not to kill. And so the rumor that he poisoned them is utterly a fiction, an evil rumor. Truth be told, he left a rear guard to protect them. He would like to think that the rear guard did not withdraw until his wounded were all dead, but certainly they did not until most of them were."

"War is complex," murmured peaceable Billy Balcombe. "It takes away choosing between good and bad and leaves men with choosing between bad and less bad."

O'Meara said, "Our Friend's enemies say Jaffa became a poisoning en masse. But had he been a man to poison soldiers secretly, or to commit such savageries as driving his carriage over the bleeding and smashed bodies of the wounded, do you think his troops would have fought under him with that zest and love they uniformly displayed? For so long and to our great Britannic discomfiture? If he had been such a man as some of his naysayers would have it, he would have been long ago shot by his own people. What you think, Betsy Balcombe? I think that is an argument of some sinew."

"But I will never eat off that dish with the Pyramids," I told him.

For some reason, not entirely flattering, he laughed.

Consider the burden . . .

*M*rs. *Stuart, the surgeon's wife* who had taught me French on my voyage back to the island some years before, or had somehow ratified my capacity to speak it, was now on her way home from India with her daughters, and her ship put into Jamestown Roads as so many did. My mother insisted that she and her two young daughters should stay at The Briars. The two little girls I had played with were changed and had become waspish—my mother said it was exactly what happened in India to such people, being surrounded by opulence over which they had no composure through ownership. Mrs. Stuart was unchanged; however, there was no doubt that in staying at The Briars one of her chief motives was to sight the Great Ogre, and being of French-speaking stock herself, the desire to do so must have been intense.

By sitting in the garden with my mother, she would see him pass into the marquee or the grape arbor, emerging from the latter with all the exuberance of a released schoolboy. But his greetings in our direction were curt though genial. Mrs. Stuart saw him, but did not really *see* him.

My mother rode out one afternoon to show the beautiful Mrs. Stuart our island. Having given birth to three sons here, she had become something of a St. Helena patriot, and commonly made the point to visitors that, however forbidding the outer crags—the awesome coast studded with artillery—within those walls, one found the inner valleys and hills of delight.

The two women—I have this tale from my mother—were returning to The Briars and came to the intersection with the road that led to Longwood. There they had the fortune to meet the Emperor, riding his Arab, Mameluke, and escorted by "poor Poppleton" (as we now called him, given that he had the ceaseless task of being a witness) and Gourgaud. The Emperor reined in, itself an act of urbane horsemanship involving more grace than the normal stern tugs, which were the equestrian style of most island folk, subtleties of pressure that enabled his horse to obey in its own balletic manner and show off the contours of its head and neck. The Emperor thus did great homage to the man he always boasted of as his movement tutor, François-Joseph Talma, the famed French actor.

Also passing down this road towards the building at Longwood was a line of Chinese and Malay laborers, bearing every imaginable necessity for a large house—from mortar and bricks to window frames and wallpaper—and in the distance behind them two wagons were groaning under the weight of a pianoforte and what would prove to be a dismantled billiard table shrouded in dustcovers.

The Emperor had demanded a billiard table for his future home, and this was still a season in which his requests were listened to. But he took little notice of its perilous journey from Jamestown. It was, my mother noticed, Mrs. Stuart who had arrested him, and she was amused to see him halting so elegantly by the visitor. She had by now long recovered from being compared to Josephine, and knew, as all we Balcombes did, how intense but fleeting his affections for women were.

We believed at that stage too that the Emperor had been warned, perhaps by Las Cases, that he should make fewer visits to Miss Robinson, that each one became common knowledge on the island and in the garrison and squadron, and thus a news item likely to reach England and Europe through the hand of some scribbler. Indeed, her parents were said to be thinking of sending her to Cape Town under the care of an older woman to await the arrival of Captain Edwards of the East Indiaman *Chloe*. Miss Robinson, of whom I had been so jealous, was not a woman who could have an open association with OGF. Her own parents knew she was no Josephine and no Countess Walewska—it was all too improbable and mismatched, except in the Ogre's fervent mind.

As I had observed with Miss Robinson, the Emperor was enchanted by a revolutionary archetype of rustic vigor rather than by the breathing young woman herself. In the same spirit he was now willing to be enchanted by this young, ruddy woman, Mrs. Stuart, whose hair ran in streams of vivid chestnut down her shoulders and who, as my mother told him, was returning on a ship only one month ahead of the troop transport on which her surgeon husband would return. There, near Huff's lethal crossroads, the Ogre began to interview Mrs. Stuart, just as he interviewed all comers, a man intrigued by the history of obscure Britons (French-speaking as they might be) as of so many other matters. For him interrogation seemed to be a form of enticement.

He was deep in discourse about Canada, and Canadian French, and Mrs. Stuart's husband's home in Forfar, and what acreage her father-in-law owned there, as the line of burden bearers neared the crossroads to turn east to Longwood. My mother eased her horse away from the conversation and made a gesture to the slaves to swing wide of the track and leave the Emperor undisturbed. They began to obey, but the Emperor's wide-set eyes noticed the untoward movement about him. He abandoned for now his interest in Mrs. Stuart's family's Highland sheep and protested to my mother. "Madame Jane," he told her, "consider the burden on their shoulders!"

By further artful maneuvers he edged his horse to the verge of the road with such elegance the others followed. My mother told me later she was angry, wanting to chide him with being no champion of slaves, having crushed the slave revolt in Dominica. "You did not worry about the burden of the slave leader Toussaint l'Overture," she itched for a moment to say—as indeed I had once said.

He was posturing before Mrs. Stuart, she decided in irritation, but she was by no way certain. The French-Canadian woman's brown eyes glinted to see his fraternal concern for this train of mute bearers, whom he now directed back onto the road.

Then my mother counseled herself that she must simply accept him as an unarguable whole, his vanities, his impulses for showing humanity as well as those for making mischief, as the one manifestation, in the way that weather is one and diverse and, above all, changeable by its own inimitable will. If she did not do this, she saw, she would be teased beyond tolerance by his multiplicity of faces.

It was a resolve that would influence our lives. Forever.

*D*ecember began, and the Emperor, breathing better after suffering a cold, thought it was time to visit Longwood and to have Jane and me accompany him. He had already decided not to like Longwood, and perhaps the attitudes of islanders towards it, a tendency to sneer at its unsuitability, had contributed. He did not enjoy riding there, and the garrison on Deadwood, whose rows of tents could be seen as we rose up out of Devil's Glen to the Longwood plateau, might have made him too aware of the severe brake they represented on any idea of getting away.

By the time we approached the house and saw the many workers and slaves hurrying to finish it, Our Friend's pessimism had intensified.

"They think they are being kind to me," he suggested bitterly, taking in the long villa and inhaling the smell of butchered and planed wood, the sight of the tar-paper roofing being placed over the rear apartments, the quarters of his dependants and servants. It gave off an insinuating smell and bespoke cheapness. He looked at the great stone block of the Barn, the mountain just to the east, which had the effect of reducing the view of the ocean and helped confuse the advancing trade winds, so that they often dropped their moisture and their vapor around Longwood in particular. "That evil block," he said, that day and always. "It will be a gag across our mouths and our eyes." He made grumbling noises with his throat. Then he turned his horse and rode away, back towards The Briars.

Some few days later, handsome General Bertrand arrived in our garden, having done an inspection of the new house. We knew that the move could not be far away, and the anticipation of loss began to afflict the Balcombes. We found out later that Bertrand had come to report on the smell of paint in Longwood and to tell his master it was still powerful. The Emperor apparently claimed to have a phobia of that smell, and the unchallenged idea was that he would not move until the oppressive odor had dispelled itself. He asked Las Cases to go to Longwood the next day to reassess its offensiveness. We heard by way of Marchand that Gourgaud, whom Marchand himself did not like, had tossed his head when Las Cases was sent, wondering why he could not be the monitor of paint odor.

There was a deliberate purpose to delay in all this, and the Emperor was pleased when Las Cases was able to report to the admiral that the smell had not sufficiently evaporated, that it still cloyed and would be a threat to the Emperor's health. Soon Admiral Cockburn and Colonel Bingham of the regiment were seen crossing our lawn to the marquee and the Pavilion, where a new mood seemed to attend their conferences with OGF and his staff.

On the Monday morning at the start of the third week of Advent, the Emperor declared he had decided to look forward to the new existence on Longwood plateau. It was as if it represented the real life of the island, and he had been under a spell, a lotus-eater, amongst the Balcombes. Fanny Bertrand came up to see us and murmured that Admiral Cockburn had helped along Our Friend's sanguine attitude by asking whether he would need to be escorted to Longwood by troops. The Briars had been now exalted massively in our eyes by his preference for it; that we, the Balcombes, even at the risk of senna bonbons, were inhabitants of the Emperor's only tolerable place. Longwood was barely two miles to the east, but until now one thought it a far more extreme exile.

It was probably best he went when he did or else our family would never have recovered from the way the Emperor flattered us by trying to stay with us. There were more conferences with the admiral, and the Emperor told us at dinner, "I am going tomorrow. It is settled. The paint is no longer such as to strangulate a person."

We woke to find the Chinese laborers all over the yard, carrying his possessions. His camp bed and the green curtains, boxes of books and Sèvres porcelain, his miniatures and his ornamental alarm clock were disappearing out of our carriageway. Soon the Pavilion would be empty of all its interest—the locket of Josephine, the manuscripts, his silver commode and washstand.

I saw Marchand and Cipriani set out by horse for Longwood to intercept the goods as they arrived there. The Emperor's whole party came up from the Portions to The Briars that morning, and I saw the ever more pregnant Countess de Montholon get down with her husband from the barouche to go and greet the Emperor as he emerged for the last time from the Pavilion. It was clear that the Bertrands, already conversing with my mother, had no reason to think of Longwood plateau as a place of worse exile than Porteous's boardinghouse had already been for them. To them a change from the narrow town to the broad plateau was a form of liberation. On an island not ten miles across, a journey such as was under way here, from humid sea level to a place high on the broken plateau—somewhere at least notionally freer in atmosphere than the precipice-enclosed port—was, I supposed, like traveling from Brussels to Paris.

My brothers ran around the garden with the Bertrand boys and with little Hortense, a girl after my own heart, out-boying the boys, and the wistful de Montholon child, Tristan. They had not often seen each other during the time the French had lived in Jamestown. They looked healthier after time ashore, and they spoke the same language as my brothers, the language of childhood, amongst the myrtles and the trunks of the gumwoods. Through mutual incomprehension they came to the same intents as regarded climbing, falling, and using sticks as mimic swords.

I vividly recall the French still, as they lined up in honor of their Emperor. Bertrand, dark-eyed and with half-smiling long lips and an engaging dark stubble on his face, stiff-collared in his blue marshal's jacket, curly haired and, despite all, bearing the worried, hungry eyes of a child. In that I now see he was a bit like my father. And then the august Fanny Bertrand, larger in frame than her husband, a luxuriant woman in a white dress of the empire. To call a dress "empire" was not forbidden. But to call an emperor "Emperor" was.

*B*ertrand, who knew Longwood, must have understood how limited a relief it would be for the Emperor. We knew that at Fanny's insistence the Bertrands meant to live at a remove from Longwood farm itself, at a house named Hutt's Gate. Longwood would still, however, be the place to which the count went each day to serve his master, and Fanny would need to have recourse there on a frequent basis, perhaps especially now, after many weeks of intimate existence in the company of Madame de Montholon. Fanny surely too wanted to keep her heart free from the voracious competition for the Emperor's favor that would mark Longwood.

Before OGF emerged from the Pavilion, Gourgaud came to stand with the others, and then Las Cases and Emmanuel appeared. I saw Gourgaud glance at Jane.

Admiral Cockburn and the colonel of the regiment arrived with their escorts. Now the Emperor emerged, and it was not like his casual emergence but a manifestation, as on the first day. Once again he wore the green coat with facings, the sash of the Order, and the face not whimsical but militant. The drums sounded from the sergeant's guard on the lawn, salutes were exchanged, weapons solemnly presented—ceremonies appropriate to a journey of hundreds of miles. We Balcombes stood on the verandah steps absorbing the moment, boys silent, women in tears, patriarch very solemn.

He greeted everyone, kissed Albine's and Fanny's hands, and thanked the admiral as if it were not that big shaggy man's duty to see him to Longwood.

He kissed my mother's hands and, against all resolve, she began to weep. He kissed Jane's two cheeks and she blazed with the compliment of it. And then he came to me and grasped my hand.

"Betsy, we are going just a little way. It seems more, doesn't it?"

"Yes, it does."

"But it is at most two English miles. Your father will bring you, since he is my provedore and has an unchallengeable right to come there."

He had pressed gifts into our hands—for my mother a golden snuffbox, for Jane and me each an enameled bonbonnière. His supply of these decorative boxes, all dazzling in themselves, faïence and enamel, seemed limitless, and we were slowly acquiring a trove of them.

The admiral had bought him a new horse, a sable Arab, whose name was the Vizier, though the General was welcome to change it, he said. It seemed a well-meaning bribe to get the Ogre to move.

The Emperor mounted, and so did the British officials and the French generals. Nursemaids hunted the Bertrand and de Montholon children to make them join their mothers in the barouche. The drums sounded again, with an enforced emphasis, military boots thudded, and muskets were once more presented, and the greatest cavalcade ever to leave The Briars began to move, preceded all the way to Hutt's Gate by pipes and drums both, with young Emmanuel de Las Cases on a gray pony at the end of this pathetic equipage.

During the day the admiral's sailors arrived and dismantled the marquee, the signs of our shared familiarity, as if the powers of Great Britain and the world wanted his habitation at the Pavilion forgotten. Their voices seemed to echo in a great absence. But as the marquee came down, we became aware that it had all been a test of our nerves, an effort of deportment, a struggle to maintain grace that all the Balcombes had probably passed except me.

I knew there would never be blind man's buff again.

More solidly caged there . . .

It was only a few days before we rode out to see Madame Bertrand in her house at Hutt's Gate. She was entertaining some of the officers of the garrison, and they graciously left as we arrived, as if to make room for us. Hutt's Gate was like a two-storey English country house in disrepair, though it too had been painted and furnished, largely with chests and chairs and tables provided by the admiral. The Bertrands did not have as many items of their own as the Emperor, and the combination of furniture was clumsy, English and Cape and island, at odds with their Gallic natures and their experience of courts.

When my father himself came back from his first interview at Longwood, he said at dinner, "Our Friend told me he feels not freer but more solidly caged there." The Emperor had taken my father out for a short walk and shown him the bare ground around, studded with gumwoods and goat droppings, and spoken of a garden he meant to grow and to use as a refuge. But he pointed out above all that there were sentries on Flagstaff Hill and even on the goat tracks either side of the Barn, from which heights they could see all his movements in case he went on the African side of his house for a few minutes, and became not as visible to the garrison as on the Diana's Peak side.

The garden was a plan of his in part to defeat this continuous visibility, and to ensure shade beyond the gaze of men.

"They are honest enough fellows," he told my father about his sentries, "but have been placed there to harass me."

I think of us, innocent about the table, unaware that more stringent things were coming, and so the Emperor's situation struck us as uniquely poignant, and he had done us the compliment of telling my father on that open plateau that he felt hedged in by the gaze of others in a way that had not been the case amongst the Balcombes at The Briars.

*L*ongwood, much bigger than the Pavilion, seemed to me always cramped; an unfortunate sense of density hung over the house. It had an air the Emperor by instinct feared, an atmosphere congealing there, and yet—outside—the trade winds blew relentlessly, clarifying nothing, heaping humidity on Deadwood and Longwood both.

"Now that I have my court together, I must live accordingly, Betsy," he told me one day. And it was as well that I was approaching womanhood and a mature cast of mind, since Longwood was never a venue for childishness. There was from the beginning a serious-minded attempt to treat Longwood as a genuine court, to try to deny its mere manor-house dimensions. Las Cases played at it, Gourgaud welcomed it, Bertrand and de Montholon pursued it as appropriate. It was clearly going to be fantastically harder here to be ceremonious and attentive than it had been in France, but they were determined to try it.

When my parents, Jane, and I first went to Longwood, we entered by way of five steps and across a little porch into a salon, quite a good size by island standards, but not imperial ones, its walls painted pale green, two windows looking out to the Barn, three to Diana's Peak and the outline of the fortress on High Knoll. Novarrez, the young Swiss, now official porter, conducted us through this room. He was a sturdy youth and had been specially chosen for his willingness to tell pretentious people they must not enter.

Late in the Emperor's day at the Pavilion, Marchand had begun to tell me stories about Novarrez, and their time with the Emperor in earlier exile on Elba, and how when their master had them all leave with him and follow him back to France, and they landed, on faith, on a shore that had turned against him, in a town in the south named Orgon, a violent mob rushed to open the door of the carriage in which the Emperor was traveling. Novarrez had pulled his pistol and saber and jumped onto the step of the coach and defied the whole crowd. Like so many of the servants, he had his tale of militant devotion; he was a man fit to guard a door.

We progressed from this entryway with Novarrez into the drawing room or salon, where maps had been hung, and bookcases and card tables erected by the windows, and so into a living room and then, in the crossbeam of the cruciform house, the dining room. It had lost its windows, if it had ever had any. The Emperor was not permitted to eat and see the outer world at the same time. The chamber was dim even before sunset, when the *lampiste* lit the candles early. It would always grow hot too easily, even as Marchand and others, under Cipriani's supervision, laid out the table.

That first time we were bidden to dinner, the entire suite and the Balcombes sat in this dim, compressed, dispiriting place. By the time the soup had been eaten, it was already stifling and I felt a rivulet of sweat descend the line of my neck and lose itself somewhere in the fabrics at my chest. Everyone wore his uniforms and orders, though, in defiance of the clotted island air.

The Bertrands had come in from their house at Hutt's Gate, and Fanny's conversation was fluting away in the space and outshining the melodic undertones of Albine de Montholon. The chatter was merry enough at table, but when there was a lull one could hear rats at work behind the walls and beneath the floor.

"Our friends the rodents," said the Count de Las Cases drily. Already there was a plate of tin nailed over the corner of the floor by the side table—a sign that a gang of the beasts had eaten their way through the floor.

As we enjoyed the beef prepared in an excellent sauce, the matter of Christmas and year's end arose. In our heads was a surmise that the Emperor might be pleased to say farewell to this year by celebrating some sort of Gallic Hogmanay. Discussion of the supposedly safe subject was instigated by my mother, but

Albine de Montholon seemed to have little enthusiasm for it. Tristan would place his shoes out on 6 December, she said, as she had done where she grew up, so that candies and small wooden toys made by Pierron could be placed in them. She was clearly a good revolutionary and knew there was no Christmas for the God of Reason.

It turned out too that people from different areas of France had different Christmases. The Emperor had unified the French but not their Noël. Hortense and the Bertrand boys, or their robust mama, knew when Christmas was, however, and Fanny's boys were expecting gifts to be placed in their shoes on the normal date, some eighteen days after Tristan de Montholon expected his.

*A*nd so at The Briars on a sweating and hazy Christmas Day, we held the normal revels on our own, aware that there was no echoing festivity at Longwood. Admiral Cockburn, who had visited Longwood on Christmas morning, reported that the Emperor, who was working on his history as on a normal day, seemed well, but complained that he lacked the full set of the *Bulletins de la Grande Armée*.

But then, O'Meara suggested, himself indulging at our place a more traditional taste for the festival, every day was a determined sort of Christmas at Longwood, with that solemn windowless room illuminated and—within the resources of the cook—a banquet made. The ceremoniousness of the meals was not, however, reflected by the accommodations the members of the suite endured. "I have the honor at the moment to share a large tent with Poppleton and Gourgaud," O'Meara told us as if relating a mock tragedy. "And I can assure you of the reality that Poppleton's more scrupulous with his small linen than Gaspard is! Gaspard is on a perpetual campaign and has no time for the humbler comforts. The fellow's costive to boot!"

Young Emmanuel and his father, I heard with some interest and even concern, occupied a small room near the kitchen, and the lingering heat from next door made the place sweltering. In the end Our Friend would have them moved into a room off his library.

On Christmas Eve Captain Younghusband and the lively Mrs. Catherine Younghusband had ridden with their young daughter across from Plantation House and stayed in the Pavilion. The experience of occupying a previously imperial space seemed to excite Mrs. Younghusband. She was exuberant since her husband had been posted to Plantation House and the family was living in its grounds, far from Deadwood Camp and its fleas.

On Christmas Day at The Briars, though my parents had invited a range of people, the Ogre remained the great absentee, and his significant absence grew amongst us almost as did the presence of the man. But Mrs. Younghusband was still engaged on the fleas of Deadwood.

"The camp," Captain Younghusband suggested with a mild loyalty to the army, "was surely not as bad as that, my dear."

"Deadwood itself is such an unprepossessing name," she told him. "You, my dear, are used to bivouacs in Spain, and your expectations are simple. But a woman notices if a camp is so infested with biting creatures and ground rodents that it could with truth be named Fleawood or Ratwood."

"No," he persisted bravely, as if trying to reconcile her to the island for her own good. "Deadwood was chosen by our engineers after consulting the surgeons. It was adjudged a very healthy place."

She seemed to be amused by him, yet could not let his innocence stand.

"Perhaps the engineers," said Mrs. Younghusband, "should now return and inspect the soldiers' teeth, listen to their chests, and report on the color of their skin, which is turning yellow."

With Captain Younghusband bested, O'Meara was moved himself to defend Deadwood's ills.

"There is an endemic malaise that began with the fleet and has moved to the garrison," he said. "And it *has* now infected the soldiers broadly. But I think you will find, madam, that it is not the fault of the location. The illness arose from the unventilated depths of some negligently run ship. Longwood itself is, I can tell you, a more unhealthy place, for there are morning fogs and bullying winds. If the British Cabinet had sent an agent to discover the least savory location on this island, he would have come back and said, 'Longwood! Put the man you want to oppress there!' And when I ride out from that place to visit the Balcombes, there is an instant improvement in the weather and the clarity of the air as I pass the mountains above Hutt's Gate and skirt Deadwood."

The surprising Lieutenant Croad had by now arrived and joined the table, his expressive eyes swimming towards me. Why had my father invited him, I wondered—for the sake of Jane and me or because he considered him a good fellow? Like a peacemaker Croad asked, "But have you noticed that there is no thunder and lightning on this island? The Emperor need never mistake thunder with his memory of cannonades."

And there was a rare flash of irritation in Jane, who thought Croad was overdoing things. "Nor need you," she said. Her outburst might have been caused by the fact we had heard much from that young officer on the subject of the island's unique flora and beasts. They were, appropriately, all small beasts. There was another possible reason for her answer—she had forsworn a true artillerist or at least a provider of artillery, Gourgaud. She had been chastened out of him and now had to bear with the limited Croad.

But Croad took it so well. "Oh, miss," he said, "you do me too much military honor. I came to the Iberian campaign late in the day and have not had enough experience of cannonades to mistake them with the voice of the heavens."

"Why then is there no lightning or thunder here?" asked Captain Younghusband as if he had found a positive attribute of the island to appease his wife with.

"It is my belief," said Croad, "that the galvanic fluid of electricity from the sky is attracted by Diana's Peak and the more sharply conical hills about here, and so conducted through the ground and thus into the seabed without ever concerning God's humble servants at the lower levels of the island."

"Then why does this same immunity to lightning not operate in the mountains of Italy?" asked O'Meara, reasonably.

"For geologic and conductive reasons," Croad told us authoritatively.

A number of people agreed that it must be so, that it made sense, since the great rocks of the island were of such regular shape and could carry away the electricity of lightning very smoothly. Having been successful in the matter of lightning, Croad rashly addressed himself to that other fiery element, Mrs. Younghusband.

"Perhaps," he declared to her, "many a suffering woman, the life partner of a soldier, tells similar tales, madam. The man has chosen soldiering whereas the woman chooses the man. The military is by nature a test of endurance not only for the soldier but for his loyal followers."

Mrs. Younghusband's eyes coruscated. "Do you think you have sufficient knowledge of encampments and marriage to sermonize on the matter, Mr. Croad?"

Croad, too used perhaps to applause, held his hands up and bowed to the lady as if willing to absorb her chastisement. But Mrs. Younghusband's anger was not appeased.

"Only another woman who has lived in encampments could, or indeed *should*, make any significant comment on the suffering of military wives. Soldiers are the least qualified of all to do so, since they are already half-enamored of the squalor of it all."

I turned to O'Meara and whispered my plan to make Mrs. Younghusband's quarrelsomeness a nothing. "I will ride to Longwood and demand he come."

I had been looking for a pretext to summon Our Friend.

"Today of all days you must avoid doing that very thing," murmured O'Meara. "The man *wants* to be left with his ghosts and his absences. Besides, should the Emperor come, the admiral will not address him with his proper title. So it's as impossible as the ball."

Our conversation was gradually becoming public and overtaking the acrimony between Croad and Mrs. Younghusband.

"But he will do it for me," I asserted.

The Irishman smiled his soft ironic smile. "No, he won't do it, even for you, Betsy. It is your festival but not his."

Mrs. Younghusband forced a smile at me across the table, but there was a warning in it, something I did not appreciate in my own home, a suggestion that she disliked whispering—given that she was never guilty of it.

The arrival of the Bertrands in the midafternoon improved the uneasy balance of the day. Fanny Bertrand, despite her passion for gossip, also had power to draw people in the direction of their more spacious feelings. That is, she overwhelmed the squalling Mrs. Younghusband.

*A*fter the Plantation House ball, Lieutenant Croad and Major Fehrzen had come regularly to The Briars. One of the reasons I liked Croad better than my sister did was this perhaps excessive but unfeigned enthusiasm he had for the natural habitat of the island. If we went out walking or riding with him, trying to sight animals, I would watch his lips moving in Latinate definitions, fresh and replete with the blood of a boy on the edge of what it is to become a young man. There was both prettiness and cleverness in Croad, but it was clear he was not flippant or shallow.

Oliver Fehrzen had more solidity and less color. He would sit and converse with my father with an air of workaday sagacity and of having been tried in the furnace. We could tell he was a man made—by merit but not by fortune—for greater rank.

"I would suggest," Lieutenant Croad told us, as on horseback we patrolled the rocky, eroded edge of Devil's Glen, the young officer leaning over in his saddle to inspect the leaves of black cabbage trees and ferns, "that your little island here is exciting in two respects. One finds many invertebrates, of which, had I visited the place fifty years past, I might have had the honor of first discovery."

He decided to dismount to inspect a complex of rocks, and after doing so, with easy, undistracted grace, helped Jane and me down from our ladies' saddles. On days of slack vigilance I had sometimes ridden astride Tom with a saddle of burlap, and enjoyed the liberty of it. Now we dismounted from our polite saddles with a gentle, audible slide of fabric.

"For example, look here!" Croad cried.

On a ledge of moist rock, a high-kneed spider, reddish and vigilant, could be seen. The golden sail spider, Croad told us, *Argyrodes mellissii,* found nowhere else on the globe! It *did* look plausibly golden, enough to justify the poetic name. It could have been *Argyrodes croadii,* had Lieutenant Croad reached the island just five decades past. (He was oblivious of the fact he had not even been born fifty years ago.) A wire bird alighted in the glen and stalked around a fern on its fragile little legs. "The cousin of the plover," sang Croad. And then there was the St. Helena petrel and hoopoe, he declared, looking into the air as if in the hope of conjuring them up.

All this authentic learning was at the same time uttered with such circularities of hand gesture and solemnity that Jane and I were driven to hilarities. And yet if you had asked me, I would have said in my ignorance that I felt a marked affection for him. It was like reverence, and it increased as he spoke of the *Labidura herculeana,* the St. Helena giant earwig, which lived in the gumwood trees and was believed to obliterate everything in its shadow except other earwigs and the sticky flies that savored the gumwood fruit.

"The earwig was identified by a Dane named Fabricius only seventeen years ago," Croad lamented. "The giant of earwigs, you know—three inches long."

"I don't like them," said Jane, shivering. They had malicious-looking pincers behind them. I had thought to say that it was strange that the island's claim to the gigantic extended only to an insect. I was sure that was a symbol of something. But Jane again jumped in and commiserated with him that the Dane had forestalled him. And behind his epaulettes and gestures I saw a serious man of ferocious, diverse ambition. The Emperor, I was sure, would like him. For the longer I spent with him, the more I doubted if at any deep level I could match his spaciousness and his passion and his intellect.

I also doubted his fitness for soldiering. I could not imagine him commanding hardheaded British soldiers of the kind we passed on the way to Longwood. And I was uncertain yet whether he was with us to court me or to court Jane or the earwig. Like every loud girl, I doubted my capacity to interest men; it was only later in life that I discovered that loud girls had an advantage, however momentary, with some types.

"Is there anywhere left on earth where you can go to find a creature that you can attach your name to?" I asked, since his desire to do so was clearly so fervent.

"There is Australia," he said. "It is in botany and zoology a terra incognita. There are the cores of Africa and Amazonia. There is the coast of the Russian colonies, in Siberia and Alaska, fertile with unclassified insects and with minute flowers to which the Indians of the region could lead one. But, alas, a soldier is limited in his discoveries to the places where he is sent."

"If the Indians have already found them, are you entitled to put your name to them?"

Croad considered this question.

"Well, there is no denying the Aborigines have known these plants from aeons past. But in terms of Latin classifications, they do not yet belong to the European system, and it is in the European system we plant-sniffers seek our fame. In the meantime, the indigenes are free to carry on with their traditional names, and are unlikely to be distressed if far away, in some institute, some rarely encountered bird or Arctic midge is labeled *croadii*."

My mother rode out with us on one of our excursions and, giving Croad tea later, asked, "If the natives lead you to a species, will you leave their dances unchanged?"

She was teasing him about his missionary fervor for the quadrille.

"The quadrille exists because we are admirers of all things French, Mrs. Balcombe. I don't think this is true of the native Esquimaux or of the savages at Africa's center or of the Aborigines of America and Australia."

Jane reacted by asking him a sudden question.

"Do you think the man who lives at the center of Africa will become an Englishman in time? Or a Frenchman?"

Some serious weighing up went on beneath Croad's extravagant epaulettes.

"I think he would be better off," he said at last, "as an English constitutional Protestant than as a French Jacobin or as a member of the Roman Church. For he has already in his existence been seriously enough damaged by demonism and superstition."

"That is a good answer, Lieutenant," said my sister, who was certainly finding her voice in his presence.

Croad looked at her with dewy, slightly moist eyes. He did not feel patronized at all, which was in his favor.

When we went into the house for tea, my mother drew me to one side. A hazy blueness invaded from the day outside.

"You should know, Betsy," she told me, "Croad comes here to court you, not Jane. The reverse is true with that fool Gourgaud. I thought it would be useful to you if I made that clear."

"And what of Major Fehrzen?" I asked her. I felt a strange pleasure and shock at her clarifying of Croad's purposes.

"You are the girl who interests Major Fehrzen too. He is a decent fellow and will play a waiting game, and will not require any gesture from you until you are some years older."

Yet my meetings with Major Fehrzen were purposefully educational by contrast to those with Croad. The major included me in complex conversations of European politics. On those occasions when his references to statesmen rose above my level of learning, my mother always took up the necessary duties of intellection, of response and comment and question. Fehrzen was a man so earnest that he seemed to carry his own share of the burden of England, and the question of its perfecting through reform. He excited us by asking us whether the Allied powers and their Congress might not give the General the chance to live somewhere that did not smack as strongly of exile as did our island.

"You see, he speaks so much of his desire to be an English gentleman," said Fehrzen.

My mother was now irreverent enough towards the Ogre to say, "It is a pity it's a course he did not choose twenty-five years past."

"Ah," said Fehrzen, smiling, "but he had ambitions then. Now he will never rise again—it would be fanciful to believe he could. He was an exile a hundred days on Elba, but there he had not a thousand troops to guard him but a thousand troops of his own, and it was a business well within his powers of planning to take them to the south of France and commence his restoration. That is the act of ingratitude which may so drive our ministers to sternness. So, here he has merely maps and pins, and Bertrand and de Montholon, Las Cases and Gourgaud. Yet I think it would be a better concept altogether to permit him to live in our kingdom than to have him settle in America, where his brother Joseph lives, and the Americans themselves, tempting him to some new aggression against Britannia."

Though it was mere common sense, I was quite dispirited to hear it confirmed by an admirable soldier that I would never see a risen Emperor.

Fehrzen's hungry mind extended itself also, when he came to dinner, to the matter of slaves. My father, in his practical and unpoetic way, was quite driven by this subject and, though he had been provedore to companies whose slave ships reprovisioned at the island, insisted that he had no taste for slaving. "We are told," my father discoursed, "that Jehovah described Job as 'perfect, upright, fearing God and eschewing evil.' Yet Job was a slaveholder, say the slave traders, often a rare recourse on their part to the Bible. 'Your male and female slaves are to come from the nations around you; from them you may buy slaves,' says the Book of Leviticus. And there are other passages of Leviticus I do not want to cite before the ladies."

Fehrzen declared in agreement, "Slavery was one of the unquestioned terms of trade in biblical times. But it is not the reason for calling people godly."

Would I ever be able to sit at a table and converse so earnestly, so neatly, with a man who wanted to be considered godly?

My father said, "Some say that for the conscientious master, slavery offers more challenges for the exercise of virtue—that we must mind them as we mind our children. And that this is not as true of the owner of the mine with his miners, or the man who owns a mechanical loom shop and his weavers."

They sat together in fraternal Whiggish agreement, two good citizens letting their ideas settle around them.

Suddenly my father asked Major Fehrzen, "Do you think that, when they are alone in Longwood, the French speak of escape?"

"I think there must be at least a daydream of escape," said the major, and his eyes flicked a moment in my direction and he smiled in a manner I could not interpret. "But the means available have been limited."

"I can think of undignified means a lesser man than the Emperor would take," my father declared. "If I were in his place I might try to hide myself in an empty barrel and be carried down to a transport. But I am an undistinguished man, and that is the sort of comic escape ordinary men attempt. Our Friend could never countenance the indignity of being discovered in a barrel. It would become the symbol of his life, and all who hated him could depict him forever as a monkey-like creature bobbing amidst the staves. It is easy to think of escape. But harder to think of an escape worthy of him."

Fehrzen remarked pensively, "America is full of escape plots, but then no one there has seen this island—a rock designed as if God had a hatred of beaches. If we had one broad strand, some sort of rescue might be possible even though our fast cruisers would be on patrol."

"We have our consuls in America, though, and they must hear these things."

"But then there is Brazil, of course, Miss Balcombe," he addressed me, or more accurately, my father through me. "They daydream of having the General as their leader."

My mother commented that Fanny Bertrand was sure the Emperor would not go to Brazil without Madame de Montholon. Major Fehrzen nodded. "While your friend's brother lives in America, then there is always a chance of mischief. . . . We could not, however, have more troops on this island without, I think, sinking it."

Such were the colloquia to which I was supposed participant but more witness, as Major Fehrzen tried to win the approval of my parents, and my father attempted to gain the respect of Major Fehrzen. They did not employ such efforts on Lieutenant Croad.

*B*efore me on the wall of Longwood hung a vast map of Saxony, and in his white dressing gown and a red turban on his head, Our Friend was instructing me where to place the colored pins on the map. Gourgaud stood by him. Now that he had to share the house with all of them, with the de Montholons and the Bertrands so often to dinner, he seemed to have even less the style of an adult than he had had at The Briars.

None of these thoughts deflected me from my task, since the place names were printed in Gothic script and I had to be alert. As the Emperor directed me, I ran about placing black pins to represent Prussia, following instructions as to where the red French pins should go in relation to Erfurt and Eisenbach and Jena, and the blue Austrian ones with Bamberg at the center. Each pin represented a corps, which I advanced as ordered. I had got the idea by now, and moved Lannes's corps up on the right to Auerstadt. Even had I not already known the Ogre had won dazzlingly, I would have guessed it from the dispositions. So I got into an almost meditative state of exaltation, and for some reason my father and Fehrzen's dialogue returned to me, so that I said suddenly, as if I were a year younger, "Before you escape from us, will you say goodbye to me?"

"Before I *escape*? How can I escape from here, Betsy?"

"I don't know, but the world has plans to come for you, and when we add in your own plans . . . surely . . ."

"Surely we have confusion," he told me. "It is all absurd, Betsy."

"But you would say that."

He took me by the shoulders and stared into me with his large dark eyes, limpid and intense at the same time. "No, it is all absurd, and you do not help me by pretending it is not." He went and sat by the window and moved some of the papers there.

"The admiral, as an example, gave me an English paper with a story by a man I have never met declaring that I had told him I would escape to Africa in a basket hung from a balloon. It is a good idea if I could find a balloon gondolier, or have one secreted in by ship, and if that balloon would kindly travel twelve thousand miles in the teeth of the trade winds. Then, this fellow says I claimed I would civilize the Negroes of Africa, recruit an army, and form an empire there, and call in my supporters and my family to help me be pharaoh—the Charlemagne of Africa's hip!"

He shook his head. Gourgaud remained po-faced, and I felt he was indifferent to the conversation, to the hopes the Emperor at least pretended to mock.

"This is the standard of escape plan suggested to me and attributed to me!" OGF said, pawing at a page of transcription. "If one has never left the English counties, a journey from St. Helena to Africa seems a small thing. But when you are located on this island . . . then you know the world's dimensions."

He put a hand on mine and continued, "Place two blue pins by the crossroads west of the River Saale. Not there. No, a little to your right. There. Jean Lannes's Fifth Corps. That's right. Yes, both sides of that road."

"But there is only one pin to a corps unless a cavalry division is involved," I told him, quoting back his own rules.

"But two together means a corps spread-eagling a road. All right, put it on the north side of the road to Apolda. Yes, you would be a splendid lieutenant, Betsy. Come. Don't worry with the pins anymore. We'll win Jena tomorrow."

He was restless. He stood up and gazed out of the window to the west. Gourgaud stalked him. The Emperor opened the shutters and pointed out over the low trees beyond the fringes of the plateau on which Longwood stood. Along its edge a line of Chinese could be seen, half a dozen men, carrying the vegetable peelings, the bottles, the discarded paper, cheese rinds, and night waste of Longwood to a nearby gully.

"It has been proposed to me, not by any of my suite but by well-meaning outsiders, that I could disguise myself as one of those refuse-carrying Chinese. If I will not go to Plantation House because the admiral will not honor me with my proper title, why would I pretend to take on the appearance of someone other than I am, and wear a conical hat and slink under a pail of rubbish down into the gully and to Jamestown? There are, you see, a thousand chances, broad and narrow. The question is, should they be entertained?"

"This is exactly what my father says," I confessed. "That your escape must honor your past."

He made a gesture with his hand at the outer day and the far sea.

"And how do I know that any agent of rescue is not an assassin in disguise? How do I know that three or four leagues from the shore they will not throw me into the sea?"

Still, I could not believe that behind the regular rehearsals of battles past, schemes of escape did not plague each hour.

"You can use two pins if you like." He groaned. "For Augereau's Seventh Corps."

*A*s I left that day I could see, as well as soldiers of the 53rd marching forward from across the natural causeway to the east to relieve the guard, some of the Chinese working on breaking up garden beds in the arid and disordered skirts of Longwood. The Emperor said he liked the Chinese and believed they would introduce an Oriental flair into his garden. From the shade of a gumwood tree at the side of the house Emmanuel emerged. There was a strange hunger and discontent on his face.

"Mademoiselle Balcombe," he called as one of the French grooms appeared from the back of the house with my horse. "Where is your sister?"

"She is not well today," I told him briskly. He raised his jaw sideways to me, in a sort of challenge, an onset of hostility.

I wondered whether for a kind word he might change his demeanor. But I could not find that word to say.

I said to him, "Monsieur de Las Cases," as if to remind him to try to behave well, and went to pass him by.

He said, "You believe you can travel through life artlessly. Yet there is a price to be paid for all that mischief and impudence of yours."

It was the sort of accusation that made me set my face and step forward in defiance, in spite of the accuracy of what he had said.

"It is easier to be blunt with some people than with others," I told him.

He lowered his voice. "You and your sister were discussed at dinner. They talked as if I were not there, or as if I were not one of them. They entered upon a discussion as to which of you was the more charming. Your sister was described as 'sweet,' and you were called 'alluring.' Do you wish to be called 'alluring'? Your sister was declared 'enchanting' by General Gourgaud, but you possessed, said one I shall not name, '*une allure vertigineuse*.'"

In desperation to make him stop, I found the kind word that had eluded me previously.

"They should have had more care than to talk like that in front of you."

"But they talked like that just the same. To them you are meat. And one of the men at the table declared—and I leave you to guess which one—'If I wanted to marry a slave, I would choose the taller sister, but if I wished to become a slave myself, I would approach Betsy.' And the same person then said, 'I suspect that His Majesty has the same feeling as mine.' And there was laughter at the table, but the Emperor did not protest. So they think of you as just a woman, do you understand? They think of you as a woman."

For a second it seemed as if he might begin to cry. I had my own confusion to conceal from him. I knew that St. Denis, the one the Emperor called Ali, and Novarrez stood behind OGF's chair at dinner and would have heard all this, and I wondered if the women had been there, Madame de Montholon and Madame Bertrand. Surely not Madame Bertrand. For she would tell me such things. Unless her sense of delicacy intervened.

My mind had flickered about the idea of being desired, but now my sense of outrage submerged that sinister ambition. For I never wanted to be desired in a way that was reflected to me by the little Count de Las Cases.

"You are a poisonous child," I hissed at him, but I was fearful that he seemed to know, from the flush and gleam and misery of his face, that he had altered me. I could not think of the Emperor in the same way as I had when placing the pins that morning. How could he ever be approached again, on his own or in the company of others?

I went and took my horse and rode home in confusion behind one of the twins, who was riding bareback ahead. Remaining tatters of pride prevented me from turning back and questioning him and trying to dissolve my discomfort—which seemed broader than my very body—in tears.

I was still overburdened by this encounter with the young Las Cases when Madame Bertrand next visited my mother at The Briars. I was sent for to join them at the table, and I grunted at Sarah and remained where I was, determinedly reading in the parlor, until Alice was back with a note, and said to me, "You better come now, miss, or your mama get over-cross with you."

"Over-cross" was Alice's excellent term for fury.

I waited in the hallway before I entered the drawing room, clenching all my muscles for the entry I must make. I went in, insubstantial as a ghost but also feeling, as I had since I had been confronted by Emmanuel, vaster than the island, bloated with his inferred weight of the desire of the French. I was relieved to hear that Madame Bertrand and my mother were talking about other things, about abrasive Mrs. Younghusband, who had become unpopular with the garrison by her quarrel with the Nagles.

Lieutenant Michael Nagle had fought in Spain from the age of sixteen, and had suffered a number of wounds in the next three years. He was still barely older than twenty, and his wife was the daughter of a clergyman, though of a lively character, and thus, it was thought, not only a threat to Mrs. Younghusband's preeminence but a culpable ten years younger than her. She had now been accused by Mrs. Younghusband of trying to advance her husband by flirtations with senior officers—and worse, of course. Mick Nagle had challenged Captain Bobby Younghusband to a trial of honor, an exchange of pistol shots. This being a delicate thing to arrange, it nonetheless hung over poor Captain Younghusband like a raised sword, for he would be fighting for his wife's right to be waspish, whereas Mr. Nagle would be fighting for a larger thing, his wife's entire honor.

In the self-importance of my shame I had imagined that all conversation would end when I walked in, that Madame Bertrand's discourse would have been utterly on me, as if I were the only woman who had discovered she had been weighed and balanced in that particular way by the Emperor and his suite.

"Hello, Betsy," she said in her English, an English that had traveled far and from which the brogue that one heard from the mouths of some of the sentries of the 53rd had been squeezed by the pressure of events, by the speaking of French, by the attendance at an imperial court, by the weight of politics and war. "You have not been so well, my dear girl . . . ?"

Severe anguish is often cured or at least lessened by accidental things, and so Fanny's casualness, nothing to remark on in absolute terms, seemed to reduce my shock and dismay to the size of a mundane burden. For Fanny was still what she had been, somewhere between an earthy younger aunt and elder sister. Since she had not been changed, perhaps I had not been altered as much as I presumed I had. For I saw at once that to have one's merits and demerits as a woman weighed at the Emperor's table and to have the garbled details passed on to me by a strange, malicious boy was not such a large thing in her universe, and perhaps should not be in mine. These women were used to this sort of commentary. My mother had survived comparison with Josephine. This was not considered a crime, a reason for forswearing the world, by Fanny Bertrand, and probably not even by my mother.

Once again, I was back to being Betsy. Whatever that was.

NAME
AND NATURE

Built to return things in kind . . .

On a day in April 1816, English and native yamstocks, slaves and freed slaves squinted at a newcomer, Sir Hudson Lowe, who landed from the *Phaeton* with his handsome wife and stepdaughters, and Sir Hudson, built to return things in kind, squinted back.

He was a new kind of governor. The Crown now considered the island so significant that it had taken it from the East India Company. In a way that had never occurred in its history, Sir Hudson landed with vice-regal power, not simply the power of the Company. The Tory Cabinet of Great Britain had endowed him with a profounder authority than anything dear Colonel Wilks had dreamed of. So he landed, and he poisoned the earth with his tread.

It was later that I reflected that the gumwood, giving out its sugary juice that attracted no one except the large blue-bodied flies, which sucked its sap and then flew on to plague us all, thus replicated in botany the sort of man Sir Hudson would let himself become, with a crooked purpose and a fraudulent sweetness of manner likely to attract the wrong creatures.

Jane and I were heedlessly working on our French translation when, the morning of the day following Lowe's arrival, the merely rumored Sir Hudson was installed as governor at Plantation House, attended by our father and other merchants and worthies. Letters Patent were read by a plump young aide named Sir Thomas Reade, his inquisitor and chief of police, and so was the governor's commission, which dealt above all with keeping the Ogre secure.

241

During Sir Thomas's reading, the island became a property the Tory Cabinet in England would hold close to its heart, no longer a rock at arm's length from the Crown, but an intimate possession of the British Sovereign. It must be so to keep the Demon in place.

Father reported Sir Hudson to be a man of reddish hair and pale, sun-bleached eyelashes with a permanent band of dark skin on one cheek. He might prove a pleasant fellow, you couldn't tell, but he did not at first impression pass my father's easy tests in that regard. His wife was very pretty and barely older than my mother.

A brief message—more an edict, said O'Meara—was sent to Longwood that the new governor would visit Bonaparte at nine o'clock the following morning. There was a rare torrent of rain that morning, and an Atlantic gale was blowing around the Barn, scouring Deadwood Camp and Longwood, but Sir Hudson put on his mess uniform and orders and cape and set out with his adjutant, Major Gorrequer (again, not a bad fellow by nature, very British despite his French Huguenot name, as my lenient father said), and Sir Thomas Reade. Dear old Admiral Cockburn, who was rumored to have become smitten by Albine de Montholon, now close to childbirth, also rode out to Longwood, together with a range of smart officers, under humid great puddings of cloud. The governor and the others dismounted, and, with the admiral advising a cautious and polite approach, Gorrequer knocked on the front door. Our stately young friend Novarrez met them. General Bertrand had been waiting with Novarrez and came forward to greet Gorrequer. He had also dressed to the height of his station, in the splendid blue uniform of a French general with golden facings that were his answer to the red- and navy-coated gentlemen waiting for entry in the downpour.

Bertrand was a man in whose soul truculence was not the usual sentiment. To him, it did not seem wise to make enemies of the jailers. But the message Bertrand's master, who must have waited in his bedroom, full of glee and contempt, and unable to sit, had told the marshal to give the visitors was not a conciliatory one. He had been instructed to say that this was an hour at which the Emperor did not receive any person. And apart from that, the Emperor (as Bertrand insisted on calling him) was indisposed—which happened to be, at least to an extent, the truth.

Gorrequer brought the message to Sir Hudson.

"When he's like this," grumbled the admiral, "you can't force yourself on him."

"But you can besiege him," Sir Hudson suggested.

"You'll need endless resources of stubbornness for that," the admiral told him.

Lowe insisted on dismounting and pacing up and down before the windows of the drawing room for a few minutes, and then requested to see Bertrand to make an appointment with his prisoner on the following day. Poor Bertrand must have known that whatever hour was chosen the Emperor would accept it with rage. Two o'clock was fixed upon for the interview.

Sir Hudson went back to his steaming, streaming horse, and the party rode away under the low clouds. It had been a triumph for the Ogre. Hadn't it? At that time no one understood, except Sir Hudson himself, the frenzy in his soul to hold on to his prize Corsican. Yet that day he had been unable to find out, by direct observation, whether the Emperor was retained or not.

At two o'clock the next day—a bright one, the gale having abated—we saw from our verandah the entire gubernatorial force set out again across Deadwood Plain. Sir Hudson had prepared for the meeting precisely, and so had Talma's theatrical disciple, the Ogre. What do I know of what happened? Well, the instant gossip, from the lightning fork of O'Meara's tongue, and many other of the island's speedy lips, including those of soldiers in the governor's group, gave us some concept.

The party was at first ushered into the waiting room, behind which was the billiard salon, where they were to be received. Cockburn suggested to Sir Hudson Lowe that he, the admiral, who had something of the Ogre's confidence, would introduce Sir Hudson. Lowe agreed, and they waited for the Ogre to emerge.

At the door to the salon, Novarrez appeared again. As soon as he heard himself announced, Sir Hudson stood up and rushed forward, entering the salon before the admiral could accompany him. Novar-rez closed the door to the admiral and told him calmly the Emperor had not called him.

The admiral raged out to his horse and rode away. He would be departing soon, leaving his flirtation with Albine and the querulous Exile himself.

*S*ir Thomas Reade sent a letter to my father saying that Sir Hudson wanted to talk to him. It was the fourth day since the landing of that potent man.

After my father got home from that meeting, he sought straight-away the solitary comfort of brandy. I heard him muttering to my mother. "There's something disordered . . . incomplete in the man," and "the man" of whom he spoke could only have been Sir Hudson.

To us my father's job was the musty business of supplying kegs and bags and panniers and boxes of comestibles. It was a trade that, as encountered at the warehouse, had an unappealing if not unpleas-ant odor of burlap, even when it was spiced by a supply of cloves or cinnamon or mixed with the treacly aroma of brandy-soaked kegs. And it seemed the least likely of occupations to furnish a quarrel between Sir Hudson and my father.

On the fifth day after the arrival, my father was again summoned to be quizzed over the items supplied to Longwood, from wine to soap to pork. Sir Hudson claimed to have orders to cut down on the expenses of the population of Longwood. But these budgetary arguments were not all that worried my father: it was that the man was very pleased to be as punitive as he could with the expenses of Our Friend's ménage.

During these meetings Major Gorrequer made notes of what was said by both Sir Hudson and my father, and my father found this of-fensive, as if he were being advised to weigh, measure, and trim his words. It also implied that, later on, if he were to utter something to contradict what he had already said, his mistake would be revealed to him by quoting from the record of these interviews. Gorrequer was not going to side with him, my father said, as pleasant a fellow as the major might seem. He would not lend comfort to anyone except Sir Hudson.

On the sixth day, when my father had been grilled about all items available for the French household, he was told that the £12,000 per annum previously allocated to Longwood must be cut down to £8,000.

Did Sir Hudson not know, asked my father, that nearly all human amenities had to be shipped long and expensive distances, either from Britain or the Continent or from Africa? My father reminded the governor that he, William Balcombe, was bound by his contract with the East India Company to include these costs in the price of goods he purveyed on the island. If the two thousand men of the garrison, no less than the presence of the flagship and its flotilla, had driven prices up, it was no fault of his, and it necessitated him to employ new clerks and warehousemen.

But the edict was ineluctable. Sir Hudson was calm and close-lipped in declaring that the cut was decreed by forces that transcended the island, transcended any one nation, transcended the cherubim and seraphim.

It could only be done, my father knew, by grossly cheapening the quality of what he supplied to Longwood. For the fifty-five persons of Bonaparte's suite, said Sir Hudson, twenty pounds in total a day, the new level of expenditure to be followed, could be considered an indulgence. Much could be cut, he said blithely. For example, the household should receive from now only half a dozen fowls a day—the very Longwood servants had been eating fowl, Sir Hudson claimed. Butter should be five pounds only. Salad oil—surely no more than three pints. Coffee, two pounds of it, but restricted to the suite and O'Meara. Thirty eggs a day were permitted. Given the French appetite for eggs, this was not a generous amount. Eight pounds of candles was, after weighty conferences with my father, settled on as the weekly maximum and would at first blush also seem generous. Yet the Emperor possessed candelabra and liked a well-lit house. Vinegar was a mere quart, flour just five pounds, and

fruit restricted to ten shillings a day, even though all the time produce rose in cost, as my father yet again warned Sir Hudson, now
that a new regiment and three European commissioners had arrived
on the island. Sir Hudson told my father, "The Emperor had better
become an orchardist and a gardener if those French want more." Sir
Hudson declared that the farmers, such as Polly Mason, should be
encouraged to temper their prices, and if they didn't he would seek
the power from Cabinet to curb them.

It was the delicate paring that offended my father, the brain for
small measurements that His Excellency Sir Hudson Lowe had
brought to the exercise—the niggardly glee, for example, with which
he decided that two hams a fortnight should be all that were offered
the house and that these should not exceed fourteen pounds each.
Fish for the same period should not be more than four pounds. Sir
Hudson's sword similarly fell on salt, mustard, pepper, capers, and
preserves, all combined not to exceed seven pounds. My father had
no idea how Sir Hudson decided it was specifically seven pounds
that provided a rational limit of these enhancers of the French table.

Champagne was to be considerably rationed but Cape wine
could be supplied in its stead.

"After all," Sir Hudson told my father, his eyes askew and rancorous, his mouth pitched somewhere between a grimace and a smile,
"prisoners cannot afford to be fussy."

My father came home quite clearly harried by questions to do
with provisions. "Sank Bootay," Alexander or William might yell as
they saw him open early his first bottle of evening port. This most
amenable soul was now utterly alienated from Plantation House. It
had taken Sir Hudson such a short time to achieve.

*P*ersonages who would once have seemed astounding on our
island also landed from the same squadron that had delivered Sir Hudson and had brought three other unpredictable and
grandly entitled presences—commissioners from the Great Powers,
from Russia, Austria, and France. Given all the inroads made upon

us by Sir Hudson, and his growing contest with the terms of the Ogre's detention, we barely had attention to give them, but we did have time to weigh them and decide there was nothing special about them.

To keep an eye on the management of the Emperor on the island and to report on how he was guarded, the Russian Tsar had sent a small man, wiry, though, and of quick movement. His name was Count Alexander Antonovich Balmain. He was perhaps my father's age, still on the lower side of forty years, and he walked like a calm and measured man. Though he was Russian, his ancestors had been Scottish, as he liked to tell people and would emphasize to us at dinner, and this accounted for his un-Russian name.

The man sent by the restored King of France was much older, nearly sixty and corpulent and named the Marquis de Montchenu. Apparently, on his arrival on the warship *Oronte*, he had begun telling Major Hodson in the main street that he must see the Emperor urgently. "I have known this person, Bonaparte," he shouted. To show he believed in the wonderful and sanctified old days before the Revolution, he wore a long queue, about the length of the tail of an average-sized dog, and seemed thus to come from an earlier time. "I commanded his regiment when he was a child! He knows me, and my king requires me to interview and assess him. Please ensure this is possible this very day! Where are you all? Where is the governor?"

Even as de Montchenu raged, a rider was on his way to Longwood, and came back reporting that the Emperor would not receive de Montchenu or any commissioner appointed by kings or emperors—those he had once addressed as equals and by name, had liked and exchanged pleasantries with, or, in the case of the restored Bourbon King of France, despised as a charmless inheritor of a poisonous bloodline.

The third of the triumvirate Sir Hudson had to greet was the Austrian Baron von Stürmer. He was an ancestral nobleman with a beautiful young French wife, of no more rank than the Balcombes, who liked to tell people that Las Cases had tutored her brother while they had all been in London hiding from the Terror in France.

I managed to grasp the idea that these three new officials were largely immune from Sir Hudson's edicts, though their servants were not. Sir Hudson had the power to insist that when the commissioners were with the Emperor, he would be present too. Immediately the three men met somewhere in Jamestown, considered Sir Hudson's decree an intrusion, and swore they would not try to visit the Emperor until Sir Hudson relented on that matter. So they settled into the life of the island. Once they would have seemed gods, the most exotic novelties. But now that we had the ultimate standard of mankind resident amongst us, and he refused to see them, they became, at least for now, no more than other householders.

O'Meara had to make a medical report on the Emperor to Plantation House at least every two days, and he told us of an extraordinary incident he had heard about from Sir Hudson's clerk, a man named Janisch. Sir Hudson, a few nights past, had woken from a nightmare that the Emperor had vanished from the island. "He is always having nightmares, this commander of bandits and thieves," O'Meara asserted. "So he rouses his policeman, Sir Tom, and they gallop across the plain and come to Longwood and hammer on the door. They are met by Novarrez, who sleeps in the corridor. The governor's eyes were darting and wanted to be assured OGF was in place, so I woke Captain Poppleton, who rushed from our fresh-finished quarters at the rear of the house and assured the governor that he had seen the Emperor."

In the meantime Reade had ranted round the house, opening doors and calling, "Come out, Bonaparte. We want Napoleon Bonaparte!"

The next day OGF murmured to O'Meara, as O'Meara palpated the Emperor's side to find the cause of pain there, that if he had known that his voice would give Sir Hudson any comfort, he would have kept quieter, but he had cried out to let the governor know he was in residence.

On the strength of this story, Jane and I rode across with my father to commiserate with OGF and de Montholon, now firmly in charge of the household, to Gourgaud's occasional chagrin, over the governor's night visit and Sir Thomas Reade's crass banging about the house.

"And he was mad enough to have done that, this Sir Thomas," said OGF with his eyes beginning to start forth. "Just as his master is mad enough to have nightmares. May they worsen! It is not the case that I detest Lowe on principle, because I have received visits from his stepdaughter, Miss Charlotte Johnson, a woman of whom the Countess Bertrand approves without any qualification—a rare distinction when it comes to our dear Fanny."

Then he rushed off towards his bedroom calling over his shoulder, "Do you know why I'm so happy?" He turned again for a second but was impatient to be going. "So sanguine? So willing to bear the manias of Sir Hudson the bandit chief, the jackal? It is because I have received the hair of my son in a letter from Marchand's mother, who nurses my boy."

And he went to get it.

But we found out, after he had brought it, opened it, and displayed the wisp of child-silk, that even this had come to him by difficulty and via a Sir Hudson imbroglio.

*F*ollowing the arrival of Sir Hudson and around the middle of the year, there were stories that our friends of the 53rd would leave for India soon enough, for we saw that a new contingent of men wearing 66 on their facings had already landed to swell Deadwood and all the other camps to a great size, yet had arrived without the influence of good humor such as Cockburn had brought ashore. Other omens of beginnings and endings included the birth of Madame de Montholon's baby, begotten at sea and born at Longwood at the island's heart. It was reported to be a girl and very healthy, and her parents gave her the name Napoléone. Of all exiles, she was one of the more piteous, an involuntarily detained child who, in the end, as I had once done, would need to face the shock of the larger world when the Emperor was pardoned, liberated, forgiven, and transmuted into an English squire.

Lieutenant Croad, meanwhile, was certainly spending a lot of time with us, as if uncertain he would find decent company in Bengal. I must confess I find it hard to remember what my expectations were of Lieutenant Croad. I do remember that at some level of fantasy he was a potential husband, and I dreaded he would give a sign that he had a similar flavor of an idea, yet was anxious that he would leave without confirming his regard in some way.

One day Jane, Croad, and I decided we would walk to Plantation House, where I assumed we would be welcome to Lady Lowe, who everyone said was pleasanter than her husband. It was not a long walk, but my plan was to go westwards by the heart-shaped waterfall and over a peaked hill not far from The Briars, a tor scattered with volcanic scree and thus unsuitable for horses. I had many times suggested it as the most direct route to Plantation House, and now I was of an age to assert my opinion, and when I urged Lieutenant Croad to it, he was all in favor.

The only aspect of the tramp to give us pause as we set out was Croad's welcoming the suggestion of the route I had in mind because it was the one most likely to yield a sight of the island's sole venomous animal, the scorpion *Isometrus maculatus*.

"If the shale moves, you should merely be conscious of where you put your hand," he cheerily advised us.

Thus we set out to traverse the higher ground, which would then bring us down into that fertile eastern basin on which Plantation House stood. Despite the lack of anything but lichen, the hillside was populated by goats—they seemed to cherish the heights, and I hoped their hoofs had been an adequate terror to the *Isometrus*. Our scrabbling hands feared the scorpion, but instead they often found sharp stone and goat droppings. The sun, which was more merciful everywhere else on the island, found us there, and burned my shoulders through the light fabric of my dress, and blinded and bullied us along. One of our two young servants followed carrying a canteen, a silver cup attached by a chain. I called on the mercy of that cool water twice before we reached the high crest and began the descent, arriving amongst the trees and finding the Plantation House road. Croad had barely picked up a stain on his uniform during the scramble, and his epaulettes bore no dust on their gold thread. He went on talking to Jane and me about the difficulty of finding that St. Helena earwig he had looked for on an earlier excursion. He bemoaned the fact its carapace was no protection at all against the rats. The rats and the goats were destroying the primeval species, he lamented even as the loose stones shifted beneath his feet.

It surprised us that Laura and Mrs. Wilks were in the drawing room when we got to Plantation House—their ship had not yet sailed—and we found them sharing one of their last afternoons on the island with Lady Lowe and her two daughters. Laura Wilks stood up to greet us.

"Major Fehrzen will be jealous," she warned me *privately*, and as ever I did not know how reliable such observations were or even if I wanted to hear them. Nor did Miss Wilks herself, so assured in her polished good looks, in her lustrous self-possession, seem to think it was in any way to be deplored that these two men with whom I could not conceive sharing a drawing room, let alone anything more, seemed to want my company.

Lady Lowe had not come as readily to her feet. A woman of sweet features but a certain undisguisable acerbity around the mouth, she was the possessor of brown, piled hair, only a little frowzy. She let Croad approach her and treat her to one of his exaggerated bows, which made her daughters titter.

My first meeting with the Lowe women suffered from an intervening yellow membrane of nausea from our walk, and since I felt the sun had bludgeoned me, I excused myself and went down the corridor looking for a door into the garden so that I could be sick. I bent by hydrangeas and let loose the sour contents and stood unresisting and stunned by weakness as a slave gardener moved in with a shovel and erased my shame with a layer of dark soil. Recovered, I stood upright and walked inside, trying to make a figure to whom frailty was unimaginable.

When I came back, Lady Lowe smiled remotely at me. There

seemed to be a person submerged in her who was sending messages to the surface of her skin, signaling when to be approving or congenial. Since my father, Sank Bootay, was a drinker who concentrated that vice into the span of a few hours a day, I did not recognize the signs in Lady Lowe. Hers was exactly the remoteness of the chronic tippler always absent through calming dosages of—as would come to be said—all-day sherry.

I did not suspect that at the time because of her undeniable prettiness, the amplitude of her olive cheeks. What teased my mind was the puzzle of how her beauty consorted with the russet patchiness of Sir Hudson's features, and the unimaginable idea of her sharing a bed with him.

She liked Croad, I could see. She took the trouble to study his face.

Her daughters had no disdain but seemed very much engrossed in each other's company and not ready yet to take warmly to Jane and me. The elder, Miss Charlotte Johnson (she carried the name of her father, Lady Lowe's first husband, an officer in the Canadian garrison), who might have been sixteen, lent an ear to Croad's account of our expedition, from which he graciously left out all references to my heatstroke.

"It was Betsy's expedition," he said, with a sort of whimsical gallantry. "She marshaled us and directed us onward."

Charlotte suddenly composed her mouth in a certain way, in what could have been a moue of friendship or a pout of contempt. I had often rebuffed and chastised genuine friendship, but could not quite understand what to do with dislike, and with an idea that my reputation—of which these women may have heard, as a friend and persecutor of OGF—might have colored their opinion of me.

It felt essential that when we went to a late luncheon I try to eat. With Charlotte's pretty eyes on me—or I thought they were, and could not look often enough to check—I ate the turtle soup, which I knew should be delightful but instantly brought out my arms and throat in a cold sweat.

Lady Lowe watched the slave-waiter pour white wine for her and said, with more assertiveness than she had brought to any matter until now, "I must meet your mother, Miss Balcombe, and take an assessment of her beauty, since my husband much admires her."

My husband much admires her? I felt an acidic skepticism. On what basis would this admiration by Sir Hudson stand?

Then some flounder was served, and I strove to treat it with respect, but found myself dreading the second half of our expedition—the proposed journey from Plantation House across the island to Mr. William Doveton's house at Mount Pleasant. Mr. Doveton's family had lived on the island as farmers for generations, yet he had been educated in England and no one dared to call him a yamstock.

Afterwards we were offered a carriage ride home, and I hoped Croad and my sister would decide that they should take me back to The Briars. They both turned to me, but I stupidly assured them they need not take account of me, that I would continue the journey with them. The path was easier, and the Doveton house had the distinction of not harboring a woman desired by the Emperor or Gourgaud or even Sir Hudson Lowe.

Oh, how the Balcombe girls were hardy! I had little doubt that I was more hardy because I was less feminine than Jane. But I sickened all the way there, and Jane did not, and after we arrived at his hillside house, Mr. Doveton had me lie down in a cool dark room to recover, instead of taking in the view and exclaiming, as did the lieutenant. I emerged after a humiliating hour to declare there was no need for a carriage. "I'm fully improved, sir," I assured Mr. Doveton. We could *definitely* walk again. I was so insistent, and I realized that I wanted in part to defy my mother with pain and, through becoming reproachfully sicker still, to punish her for insisting on being desirable to outsiders.

On the way back Croad and Jane talked merrily as if they did not notice that I had dropped out of their conversation. They became solicitous when, a mile from home, with shadows growing long and my head like a ball of heat, I embarrassed myself again by being ill.

Mr. Croad did not sight his earwig or the scorpion, and this illness meant I did not visit the Emperor for some time.

I sulked and writhed in my room. The whole amalgam of human-kind—Sir Hudson, OGF, my mother, Lady Lowe, young Emmanuel, the mysterious intentions of Croad and Fehrzen—had me in a disgruntled fever. I realize now I was suffering a chronic condition of bewilderment, and slight shifts in normal conversation could plunge me into it. In fact, this story is in large part a tale of its comings and goings. I hoped that this time a revelation or simply a chance event would shake me out of it.

Ultimately it was a highly colored event that did so. Admiral Cockburn had finally left the island. The barouche of Pulteney Malcolm, the new admiral, arose out of the Jamestown saddle, crossed the upland without turning to Deadwood, and came past Huff's haunted crossroads. Jane told me it was coming and had already guessed from the spectrum of colors within that it carried Lady Clementina Malcolm, the new admiral's wife.

Jane then broke to me the news that, dressed in vibrant swathes of cloth, her hair like a flame above the fabric, Lady Malcolm was in the drawing room and was asking for me. I went to the drawing room, and there she was, her face blazing not so much with freckles (though it did) but with raucous and eccentric goodwill.

"I wrote to Countess Bertrand from Jamestown," she said, "and she told me to bring both Miss Balcombes and their pretty mother."

From her lips "pretty" was fine, in a way it was not from Lady Lowe's.

"So I've called in, and your mama has been kind, and we're all going first to the Bertrands and then on to the Emperor!"

She had said "the Emperor." That itself was an omen to feel better. I thought this woman was wonderful, a Fanny Bertrand without a taint of acid.

We got into her cart, driven by a sailor, and as we settled she cried, "Off we go, my brave tar, eastwards into the day!"

The sailor drove carefully, which suited my fear of carriages. We made a safe transit of the jolting dip into and out of Devil's Glen and reached the Bertrands' house at Hutt's Gate, where Archambault, the postilion rider, and his younger brother were with the Emperor's carriage, to which we were now to transfer, both of them leaning against the horses taking mouthfuls from a silver flask.

"Oh, that is no doubt spirits," claimed Lady Malcolm. It concerned me because Archambault was said to be a reckless driver. He had been fine on the way to the ball, but the path to Longwood lay through some breakneck ravines. Yet we gave up our cart and climbed into the barouche, where we were joined by Fanny Bertrand, placing herself in the forward-facing seats, her features benignly composed.

As we thundered over a ridge, I thought with some fear of the ravine between us and Longwood, and of how that would be negotiated by the Archambaults, each on his horse bent like a jockey and urging it on as if there were a prize for arriving immediately at the house. Indeed, those who have not been to the island cannot realize how vertical it all is, how precipitous.

All the way, at every jolt, Fanny Bertrand was on her favorite subject, willing to include the newcomer in what she might imagine was an island-wide coterie of Madame de Montholon's critics. She remarked, "You will see that the new child resembles Montholon—she has his eyes. His Majesty was very worried while his wife was in labor. But that *is* his nature. He has expressed the same delicacies to me." She had never a shadow of blame for the Emperor himself for his flirtations with Madame de Montholon. Albine and her husband were the culprits in Fanny Bertrand's map of the world.

The more Fanny talked, the more we could see the impact of the island and the unchosen restrictions upon her. Lady Malcolm made a mouth at me as if she had perhaps had more information on Madame de Montholon than she actually needed. According to Fanny, Albine played deliberately rousing tunes like "Marlborough" and "Vive Henri Quatre" on the pianoforte, or practiced scales and reversed the pedals if the Emperor did not pay sufficient attention, all the time smiling like a nun. In the meantime, Fanny was suffering from the fact that she could not travel to town and expect to be greeted on the street. Only the most defiant military officers now visited her, she said, and were being asked by Reade to report back anything of importance that they might hear. I had already heard myself that Major Fehrzen had decided he would not submit himself to this restriction.

Fanny Bertrand told us in jolly vein as we rolled along that she had listened to Gourgaud complain to the Emperor one evening, after the de Montholons had gone: "She is always scratching her neck and spitting her food into her plate. I never thought Your Majesty would like her for that, but she goes around telling everyone that you do like her."

"Of course," said Fanny Bertrand in the barouche—and she was careful not to exonerate Madame de Montholon even while condemning Gourgaud—"this is the whole thing of internal jealousy in that house. Gourgaud is quite mad, or if he is not, he is saved from being so by the arrival of the Russian, Count Balmain, who seems a pleasant enough man and has made a fuss of him. Oh, Lady Malcolm, I am grateful nonetheless I live elsewhere, what with Las Cases drying up into a walnut before our eyes and mummifying his son with a glance, that lost boy, and the de Montholons and, on top of it all, Gourgaud."

I looked at my mother and, like friends, we both raised our eyebrows.

"Oh, my heavens," said Lady Malcolm, but it was because Archambault's horses dragged us askew on two wheels, down into the defile and up again with all the brio of artillery being hurried into place. Artillery it was, when you counted the high caliber of Madame Bertrand.

Lady Malcolm said, recovering, "It is not our intention to cause misery at Longwood."

"No," said Madame Bertrand, kindly. "But exile is exile and a desert island is a desert island. As Madame de Montholon says, 'One ages rapidly in St. Helena.' That is true of men and women. You see, Lady Malcolm, the Emperor is very wearied by this place. He feels he is beyond life."

Lady Malcolm was abashed and plucked at the fabric about her shoulders. "Oh dear, I regret that."

"But I do not say it that you should feel uneasy. You have been a friend to him. And remember that what he has lost, *he* has lost. No one can make that up to him. Though there are those who could behave towards him better, of course!"

I was not certain how Lady Malcolm was "a friend to him," but I was sure I would find out. Admitted at Longwood by Novarrez, we all sat down in the salon, which had windows opening to the west, and the Emperor had not ordered the shutters drawn on the view today.

When OGF entered, he was in uniform and he embraced Lady Malcolm by the shoulders. She bobbed her face for him to kiss and began to speak in French. An immediate, enchanting energy rose in the room, and the Emperor himself seemed revivified.

He would tell my mother that Lady Malcolm was the first plain woman he had ever admired, and that he could see why the admiral remained in her thrall. Fanny told me that the books I had one day seen OGF unload from crates had been a gift from her.

Now the Emperor talked with Lady Malcolm about her brother, Colonel Elphinstone, who had commanded a regiment of foot at Waterloo, and whom the Emperor had, during that day, seen lying on the ground. Brandy and surgical care had been summoned immediately, and her brother could hear through a haze of pain and damage that the Ogre was taking a personal interest in his welfare. Possibly, as Miss Robinson had filled the role of bucolic beauty, Lady Malcolm's brother had thus presented himself as an archetype of the fallen soldier. Still, it was clear Lady Malcolm credited OGF with saving his life.

She said chirpily, "When he was recovered, he was made a Companion of the Bath and received Dutch and Russian honors as well. But every great man who honored him asked him about you, Sire, and your famed rescue of him."

This information sparkled in the room, and the Emperor said, with a full smile, "Some men rise and some men fall, and all in an afternoon. We live for years. But at every turn, from our conception to the end, our life swings on twenty minutes, if not twenty seconds."

This grim reflection seemed to cheer him a great deal. Lady Malcolm, however, appeared to feel that she had unduly boasted of her brother as a survivor of battle. She declared, "After all, it was the Duke of Wellington's own regiment he commanded, so his valor was inevitably visible." She turned to the rest of us. "Pulteney and I were in Brussels on the eve of the battle, when the city was a ballroom, and then the following night when it was a vast hospital."

The Emperor weighed Lady Malcolm's neat contrast with the *tristesse* it deserved. He began to discuss his famous friends who were also friends of Lady Malcolm's, Lady Holland and her husband—names that hung over us like biblical names, remote and benign and unquestioned, mythic rather than plain friends of OGF. "Had Henry Fox's politics prevailed," said the Emperor piously, "the history of Europe and my history might have been altered for the better."

"Would he have stopped you invading Russia?" I asked.

I heard Jane's breath, taken in quickly. The Emperor stared at me ruefully and without reproach. My mother gave a brief shake of her head in my direction, as if mine had not been an utterly reasonable question.

"Have you heard from your son?" Lady Malcolm suddenly asked the Emperor.

The memory swallowed all thought, all regret, and his face lightened.

"If I said something hurtful . . . ," I doubtfully proposed, in a little access of wisdom.

"No," he declared, holding up his hand. "I cannot have you doubting your words. For that would not be Betsy, would it? But I can show our friends what I have of my son." He made a wide gesture. "Please, ladies, follow."

He led us through the room and past the dining room, to one side, and on the other side—the door into his bedroom. Through one further door in this compartment we saw Marchand's truckle bed in a dressing room. Marchand remained on call all night, it would turn out, always a victim of his master's insomnia.

The bedroom was an unimpressive space in which the green-curtained bed looked almost like that of a monk. A mat, we would later be told, had been bought from a lieutenant at Deadwood to dimly adorn the floor. The walls were covered with dark burgundy wallpaper, and there were long gauze curtains on two windows, which looked out in the direction of Deadwood. I noticed the silver washstand, which had been the glory of his furniture at the Pavilion. It seemed dulled by the gloom. White walls might at least have suggested greater spaces; walls covered with nankeen bespoke heaviness and containment. Here was the shrine of the house, and he took us to the mantelpiece and enumerated the relics: pictures of Marie Louise, to us an unimaginable spouse living in an unimaginable home in Vienna, and a miniature of the King of Rome, his son, bearer of a lost title, and of course the Josephine cameo that he had extorted from Madame Bertrand. At one end of that mantelpiece was the ornate alarm clock, which, he told us, had been Frederick the Great's. As at the Pavilion, it seemed too complex and grand an apparatus for the plain wooden shelf, and shone earnestly in a way that led me to believe it felt some insensate superiority to its surroundings. From a nail hammered into the wall at the other end was his own Consular watch, hung from a plait of hair of Marie Louise. Its lid was marked with the huge letter "B" picked out in diamonds. We Balcombe women had seen this piece before—it had been similarly displayed in the Pavilion at The Briars—and we knew how he always fondled the plait as he showed the watch to anyone, and how this gesture had such power that somehow when you saw him do it he was forgiven all. And at that moment it seemed the most barbarous thing in history that Marie Louise was not permitted by her imperial house of Austria to join him on our island. She was instead a hostage of her own family in her own household, stuck, said O'Meara, in a parallel island to his, the island of an imperial court.

OGF took up an envelope off the shelf and exhibited more hair still, soft and thin of filament and fair. "This lustrous strand," he told us, "is the hair of my son. You have seen it already, I believe, Betsy and Jane."

"Lucky girls," said my mother.

We had by now heard how the package of hair had reached him, but it would seem that he was too delicate to mention the noxious details to Lady Malcolm. O'Meara had been fast to town to see the Allied commissioners patrolling Jamestown's streets, trying to interpret the cliffs of volcanic rocks hopefully. He had introduced himself—being the physician to the Ogre gave him something like an equality of status to them. Husky Baron von Stürmer told him confidentially there was a newly come Austrian botanist, staying at a house in the town, who had a package it might be in Longwood's interest to collect. The Emperor, hearing this from O'Meara, sent Marchand to retrieve it, and the valet did everything as required by ordinance. Not having been to town since he stopped living in the Portions, Marchand asked Poppleton to give him a soldier as escort, and Poppleton gave him a subaltern.

Marchand rode to town, called at the botanist's lodgings, received from him a letter written by Marchand's own mother, who was nursemaid to the King of Rome in the castle at Schoenbrunn. Inside it was a further letter from Napoleon's mother, and in it the skein of hair. Marchand, leaving town with this treasure, saw Sir Hudson and a party of horsemen (including Tom Reade, no doubt, and Major Gorrequer) going to town to find this Austrian botanist, who had been in the Austrian commissioner's party, to expel him. Who had told Sir Hudson? He had many spies, of course, and then there was simple gossip. The botanist had wanted to visit OGF to tell him about the good health of Marie Louise, and the tendency of the King of Rome to lead the whole court along the rooms of Schoenbrunn naming objects—doors, clocks, pictures. But instead he was detained in the Castle until a ship was ready to remove him from his botanical investigations on the island.

While the other women exclaimed over the locks, I slowly paced out the bedroom, but in a way that made my meanderings look normal. Seven paces long and four wide. Even to me, who had never lived on the same terms as Our Great Friend had, in the Elysée Palace or the Tuileries, it seemed a hutch. Fanny Bertrand saw what I was doing and smiled at me, approving and mournful.

At that second two soldiers, one from the 53rd and one from the newcomers of the 66th, approached the window outside. We could hear one saying to the other, "He nair closes shutters in this yer room. He nair does." An island veteran taking the newcomer on a tour of the Ogre in its cage. The Emperor raced to the window.

"I am been here, infants," he yelled at them in exasperated English. "Now get away all far please!"

Novarrez rushed in and pulled the curtains closed. OGF turned back to us and addressed not us but, it seemed, some other presence. "Why can't the governor place his pickets around the outer rim of the island, close to the sea cliffs? He already has parties and horsemen on the hills to see where I walk. Why does he have to cram them in against the house? If an adequate soldier, he could place his dispositions without letting me know about it. Can he not do this without obliging me to tell Poppleton, if I travel forth, that I want to go for a walk and want a way clear before me?"

He obviously did not intend this outcry to be reported to the governor by Lady Malcolm, who was pale and whose freckles had emerged like reluctant stars. It was a *cri de coeur*, not a *cri politique*. The Emperor muttered then, "Not that I have an objection to Poppleton. I always loved a good soldier and Poppleton is one, though I fear he is about to be replaced—for being too amiable!"

It was a torrent of complaint and qualification, and yet in the corner of my soul, a strange remaining Britishness still held me back for the moment from joining him in the fullest condemnation of Sir Hudson, whom my father had already turned against but who had not fully turned against me. (It would not take long, of course.)

He said to Lady Malcolm, "I have to ride seven or eight leagues a day, my good friend. For my health."

Fanny Bertrand echoed him. "Seven or eight leagues—perhaps twenty miles. That would keep a man in honest trim. You should seize them daily, Your Majesty, whatever hindrance they put in your way."

But we could still hear the soldiers clumping about the garden, trying to gawp in through other windows. He sent for Marchand now and told him to order the soldiers off the flower beds, and asked him to take the ladies into the new garden to see the roses growing there.

"I have become a digger of the soil," the Emperor told us. "But Marchand is the grower of roses. Betsy, will you stay a moment with me? You and I will follow soon."

My mother frowned at me and then at Fanny Bertrand, though not perhaps at the Emperor himself. She did not like this arrangement.

"Dear Jane," said the Emperor to my mother, sensing her unease, "I am your friend, and Betsy's friend." His earnestness convinced her, and the women went out with Marchand.

The Emperor's benign smile turned into a thunderous frown as they left.

"What is this I hear of you becoming ill from the heat? That ridiculous long expedition of yours—what were you thinking? The roads on this island are bad enough. But to take a route via the mountains . . ."

I did not know what his intense concern meant and felt he was somehow not entitled to it.

"You have never made an unwise choice?" I challenged him.

"Yes, and you take the chance to point them out to me. But I wish you were more aware how important you are to your mother."

This sounded paternal of him, or at least uncle-some. It was not the normal mode. And did he tell Miss Robinson, *La Nymphe*, that she must avoid sunstroke for her family's sake?

"Please," he said, "there is a dangerous state of nullity in you. To choose death out of spite. You must resist it. You are like a conscript who, to show me how wrong I am in throwing him into battle, places his chest against the mouth of an enemy cannon."

This overwrought imagery amused me. I laughed, but forgivingly. I had no idea where leniency came from. I was fairly pleased to be aware that it was arising in me.

He placed a hand very delicately on my upper arm. That was all it was. A hand.

"You are my friend and you are not to get sick," he told me. "I want no more recklessness from you."

I did not quite know what any of this meant but found myself consenting to be cautioned. We heard my mother calling from the garden. Her voice seemed to me to have a number of strands—that of an anxious mother, but that of a jealous friend as well.

"Your Majesty, are you going to delay Betsy much longer?"

"We will go," he said, "but you must not harm yourself, Betsy. There is a restless beast in you, looking around for some way to harm you. You must not yield."

Novarrez seemed to hear and came in to put the Emperor's normal bicorn hat on his head, but OGF had already seized up a straw gardener's hat, so he ushered us out to where the rosebushes had been planted in a long line between his house and the edge of the Longwood plateau, almost as far as where it fell away towards Deadwood.

As an aunt watching
a heedless nephew . . .

My father decided he would make one more attempt to win over
Sir Thomas Reade and thus, at a remove, Sir Hudson Lowe.
He had a self-conceit, my father, that he could make any reasonable
fellow a friend between soup and pudding. I was myself as dubious
as an aunt watching a heedless nephew, and I wanted to throw my
arms around him and tell him that even I knew now the world was
no longer as innocent as that.

Sir Thomas did come to dinner and seemed harmless, a man
younger than Fehrzen, florid, jowly like a sleek parson, but with features that looked deceptively given to casualness and dreams, a certain sleepiness about the eyes. It was easy to believe there was no
real flint within.

My father warned me to be nice to him and play the piano. Like
Madame de Montholon to Our Great Friend, I thought.

Also at table that night with Sir Thomas was one of my father's
old regulars—the captain of the storeship *Tortoise*, Philip Cook, at
least fifteen if not twenty years older than Sir Thomas. But they got
on well enough, even if Cook had said in genial complaint early in
the evening, "Your searchers put my ship through a thorough combing, Sir Thomas."

For Sir Hudson and Sir Thomas were determined that nothing
would come in and nothing leave but what they had assessed and
judged harmless.

The conversation during the meal changed from policy to more urbane things, such as the poetry of Ossian, the ancient Celtic poet. "Ossian's work has been by my bunk these twenty years," asserted Cook.

"I believe the General at Longwood is much enamored of Ossian too," Sir Thomas Reade told him.

Captain Cook, gliding naturally from Ossian to the Ogre, said, "So, this general can't be too bad if he likes your Scottish poetry. I heard they were hard up for variety at Longwood, so I sent up three English hams and a keg of American biscuits—American biscuit is superior to ours. I thought that a fraternal thing to do, a gesture to wayfarers. But now I know he likes the Scots, I am doubly glad."

"Sir Hudson and I thought that rather a large reward for appreciation of things Pictish," Sir Thomas Reade declared, with an apparently dreamy smile.

"Well," said the old captain of the *Tortoise*, "it was a plain sort of tribute from my side. When you consider the lives those people at Longwood must have led when they had all of Europe by the coattails . . . ham and biscuit seem like a mere introduction to plain taste."

"Um," said Sir Thomas, and I saw behind his soft features another being of flint.

"I was going to say too, Colonel Reade," the captain continued, "I have had a letter from one Comte Bertrand inviting me to visit His Majesty."

"Bertrand's Majesty perhaps. Surely not *Your* Majesty, Mr. Cook."

"Maybe not mine," agreed the storeship captain, "but this fellow, think of him what you may, is a feature of the world, a breathing sphinx. It is surely normal, Sir Thomas, for all parties to wish to see him and balance him on whatever poor scales we happen to possess. But I believe one cannot approach the place when challenged without the countersign. I wonder, could you, as a kindness, Sir Thomas, supply me with tomorrow's countersign, so that I might get close?"

"I shall write it on a piece of paper, sir," said Hudson Lowe's Sejanus, "if Mr. Balcombe will supply one."

My father had Sarah bring pen and paper, and Sir Thomas wrote out the countersign, blew on it until it was dry, folded it, and gave it to Captain Cook. And then my father, beaming at all, said that his charming daughter Betsy had agreed to entertain the party on the piano.

I went to the instrument and sat on the stool. I decided that the Scots tunes were safest for me and for the entire dinner party—"Ye Banks and Braes," my safe wager.

I contemplated the keys, and the mistrust that had been building in me even as it was diminishing in my father asserted itself. I embarked on *"Vive Henri Quatre,"* and did not care if Sir Thomas knew it was the Emperor's favorite tune. I was ignorant of the fact that as much as OGF liked it, the French royalists liked it even more, and what I hoped Sir Thomas could tell was that it was martial, but that it was not martial in an English sort of way. I thumped it out, for it was a tune for thumping out. Its forceful rhythm implied threats just beyond the border, just beyond the sea, and I punished the keys to emphasize these threats.

I was disappointed when Sir Thomas clapped as enthusiastically as Captain Cook and my mother.

My father found his way home the next afternoon, in the midst of a fog that totally obscured the heights of the island, and he was flushed with rage. He had discovered that Cook had ridden up from Jamestown in the murk and approached the sentries at Longwood, and when he was challenged, he uttered the countersign as written down by Sir Thomas. This caused him to be surrounded by a harsh set of challenges in the mist, and the men of the 53rd and 66th regiments both moved up and solidified around him, cursing him, having been warned that conspirators might be abroad under cover of the weather. My father had encountered Captain Cook in the fog on the saddle, with a surly military escort of four soldiers, banished to the port, not to be trusted on the heights and headed for a night in the guardhouse of the Castle Terrace.

So poor Cook, having blundered up the dangerous track on horseback and uttered the wrong password, deliberately fed him in apparent vengeance for his gift of superior American biscuit, had been betrayed and humiliated by evil counsel given at his, Sank Bootay's, Prince's, Billy's table!

To my father, sharing a dinner was like making a compact with the other diners. He recounted to us the argument he had had with the lieutenant in charge of the escort. My father had been so angered that he had then followed the misty road to Plantation House and confronted Sir Thomas in his office.

Sir Thomas sympathized and said that there must have been a mistake with the countersign and it was to be regretted. But when my father proved not at all easily soothed, more sensitive to an insult against a friend than against himself, Sir Thomas spoke more frankly. He told my father, "The enemies of Britain should not be comforted with hams. All such gifts are meant to go to Longwood with the governor's permission. This wasn't mentioned by your damned captain. He will be more aware of the formalities for next time."

"You contrived that foul arrangement at an equable board you'd been invited to."

It seemed Sir Thomas was not sentimental about shared meals.

My father knew that he had wasted his port and lamb upon Reade. If hams were to be proscribed by the policeman and his master, then he knew finally and beyond argument that he *would* be required indefinitely to provide the very cheapest purchases to Longwood—the prison basics.

Some would say my father's anger was self-interested, his income diminished by the diminished rations he supplied to Longwood, but it is not so, since he did handsomely enough, or the East India Company did, out of the garrison, about whose expenditures there were fewer quibbles, and out of the naval squadron, who did not constitute the main cause of the governor's fretful anger or Sir Thomas Reade's scrutiny.

Thus it was, given the shrinkage of supplies to OGF and perhaps more significantly to the smaller Bertrands and de Montholons, that the governor came to be referred to in our house as the Fiend. My mother speculated that Sir Thomas Reade might try to cramp our own table, but was delighted to find that he did not have the power. O'Meara visited us in that season of fogs and helped calm my father down by telling him of the Emperor's witticisms about said Fiend.

O'Meara said, "Of course, the Fiend wishes to use me as a spy on OGF. I told them at Longwood that some remarks would be required of me—a daily health bulletin in general terms, no medical secrets given away, some harmless intelligence on the household. And there's one great thing about that Fiend fellow. He tends to be satisfied as long as you give him plenty of details. He's more interested in knowing not so much whether the Emperor ate boiled eggs for breakfast than whether they are soft- or hard-boiled, as if their condition is somehow an omen for him. And, by the way, we can't call the man the Fiend indefinitely. We need a code, as for OGF."

I declared, "Name and Nature."

"What is that?" asked the men.

"Lowe by Name and Lowe by Nature."

O'Meara cast up his hands to the ceiling. Then he knelt before me.

"You, lovely Betsy, have achieved it. *Lowe by name and nature!* This is the code of codes."

My father beamed and kissed my cheek.

I meanwhile wondered, was O'Meara right or somehow salving his conscience for having to collaborate with a governor he did not like? Or was it even possible he liked him more than he said? It was as if the Fiend had put multiple meanings into previously simple acts.

It would come to be argued in some quarters that the Emperor was as narrow-minded as Sir Hudson Lowe. But he did not have power to impose his conditions upon Sir Hudson, and the small man was making the great man dance to his tune, and a very poor and rough and niggardly tune it increasingly became.

And so our house was full of plaints from my father and other visitors—that the servants from Longwood who carried the Bertrands' share of the provisions across to the little house at Hutt's Gate were stopped by the very sentinels who taught the young Bertrands their profanities. At last a sergeant allowed the provisions to be passed over the fence of Hutt's Gate to the servants, but in silence. Such was the panic of severity in which Sir Hudson Fiend had the soldiers.

O'Meara went there to attend to one of the Bertrands' servants, a Frenchman who had caught hepatitis, the disease that had come on the ships and which appeared to flourish particularly here, like the blue flies that gathered on the gumwoods. It seemed that one in every three islanders carried on their face that unhealthy bronzed look. O'Meara was told he could not go inside the house to see the patient, however, and wrote instructions in French so that the dosage could be taken indoors to be administered. Though the sergeant of the guard could not read it and thus destroyed it, O'Meara's entry was barred still.

This was the sort of daily absurdity that was recounted and complained of in our home, and my father laughed bitterly now over every instance of the abominable and inane restriction. And so no doubt did the soldiers, for one had been relieved of his duty and sent to be tried by court-martial for having allowed a passing slave to go into the Bertrands' courtyard to drink water. The man could have been carrying a missive! Someone else begging water might later carry a message not authorized by the august Name and Nature, and that thought now had the capacity to put unnecessary starch into those who guarded the Bertrands, as into those who guarded Longwood itself.

The governor, Admiral Malcolm at his side—this was told to us by O'Meara, who was present—went to Longwood to argue with de Montholon about the amount of refined basket salt used, proclaiming, "We don't use half as much at Plantation House. I want you to use gray salt for the servants in their cooking."

"But, Your Excellency," said de Montholon, "gray salt clots in the humidity."

It has to be said that a better disposed witness than our friend O'Meara might have seen this as a reasonable enough economy. *Sel gris*, gray salt, not whitened by drainage through baskets, even when clotted would not kill the servants. But such an instance of the rational was consumed by the irrational. Good sense was lost amidst absurdity.

Sir Hudson could not prevent the admiral from entering Longwood and being welcomed, and indeed need not do so, for the admiral could reassure him that the Emperor was there, in his salon sitting at a table experimenting with a Leslie pneumatic machine for making ice, which an admirer in England had sent him and which had been allowed to be delivered to Longwood the day before.

This was the machine that we Balcombe women visited. We rode across there as by right and were exempt from Sir Hudson's normal requirements that visitors to Longwood should receive a ticket at Plantation House, to be returned to that source of authority on completion of the visit. We did not inquire into the privilege that operated with us, which seemed to me to derive from our having been hosts to OGF in the early part of his island career. We came to Longwood and found the new wonder of the machine had clearly enlarged the Emperor's day, as he sat there telling us how ethyl bromide worked in a vacuum inside the machine to turn water at room temperature to ice. "We are far, far from the fields of ice to the south," he said. "This chemical wonder denies geography."

Was it, in defying geography, a comforting mechanism of escape?

He had got permission through Captain Poppleton to let some of the yamstock farmers, the Letts and the Robinsons, including *La Nymphe*, Florence Robinson, and Polly Mason and others, visit Longwood to see the machine grind, fizz, and groan as it produced a chip of ice in the tray below. Mr. Lett, a lump of ice deposited in his hand by the Emperor, was astonished at this devil's work; he had never seen ice before, having lived all his life within the narrow limits of St. Helena's temperatures. He held it and exclaimed, amazed, as it began to melt in his hands.

Could OGF melt through the fingers of Sir Hudson in this same way?

More confrontations, more strictures, reported to us by O'Meara, and I became increasingly uneasy about some of them, the extreme of feeling invested in them. To the point of oddity, if not madness. Once again anxious from not sighting his captive, Sir Hudson arrived at Longwood one day while OGF was walking around the garden with Bertrand, de Montholon, and the Las Cases. And here is the meat of my captive, Sir Hudson must have thought, seeing the Ogre's pale wrists beneath the sleeves of his white suit— the one he had taken to wearing in the garden. He sent Major Gorrequer a few steps ahead to ask whether the General would tolerate an interview, but Sir Thomas opined loudly at His Excellency's side that it should not be a matter of the Ogre's permission. So Sir Hudson and Admiral Malcolm stood a little distance from the French group, conferring, then moved in and saluted OGF. Sir Hudson told OGF that he had come from Plantation House to Longwood three times already to discuss the reduction of the budget with him and was told each time that the General was in his bath.

"I was not," the Emperor declared, "but I had one poured especially each time so as not to be able to see you."

Sir Hudson declared in French, "You are a dishonest man, sir." He turned on his heels and walked up to Poppleton and O'Meara and said, po-faced, "The General has been very abusive to me. I ask you gentlemen to observe as much."

The exchange between the Great Ogre and the Fiend, which O'Meara rightly or wrongly admired, was rightly or wrongly admired in turn by us. We had not reached the stage of asking if it was wise of the Emperor to speak this way to Sir Hudson, or if it was unavoidable that the Emperor would react to being governed by him exactly as he did. And standing by at Sir Hudson's shoulder, Sir Thomas, whistling a bitter tune between plump lips, suggested in a low undertone that £8,000 per annum was an obscene indulgence, a cell being too good for the fallen General.

"Slit my throat, sir," called the Emperor. "Then you don't need to feed me."

"You do not know my true nature," Sir Hudson asserted.

"Know your nature, sir," replied OGF. "Could I know you? People in my world make themselves known by commanding in the field. You never had such command, and if you did it was to lead Corsican brigands and deserters. I know the name of every English general who has distinguished himself in battle and I have never heard of you but as a clerk to the Prussian general Blücher, and a briber of German princes to jump the fence in England's direction."

"I have only done my duty," Sir Hudson was heard protesting by O'Meara, to which the Emperor answered, "So does the hangman."

Bravo, we cried in our souls. The Emperor had won resonantly. But do resonations count against power?

And with that, his career dismissed, Sir Hudson's red patches glowed and his lips tightened and he mounted his horse and so did a head-shaking Sir Thomas Reade, who probably thought the Emperor should have been shot, and, after waiting for the admiral hanging behind to make a melancholy bow towards the Ogre before joining Sir Hudson's cavalcade, they rode away.

*N*ow Sir Hudson decided to trim the household too. Three of the French servants were to be sent back to France. One was Archambault, stylish groom and postilion rider. The other was Santini, a man we children found forbidding. He had served in a Corsican regiment in the service of OGF and was a dark man with emphatic features and ancestral grievances, many of them directed at the families of those Corsicans who, for similar grudges, had decided to serve England. He was a rifleman, and had a hunting rifle provided him. Now he began to mutter to other servants that vengeance against the debasing of his master was a divine prerogative, which sometimes entrusted itself to the hands of a Corsican with good aim—himself as an instance.

It was a classic Corsican ambush Santini planned for Sir Hudson: atop the eastern end of the saddle to Jamestown, taking the governor as he descended to the port. Or he could fire from the rocky defiles near Hutt's Gate or the geologic debris south of Devil's Glen. Santini, concealed amidst rocks or trees, would blow Sir Hudson out of his saddle. As we heard from Fanny Bertrand in her narration of the aftermath of the dismissal of Santini, the news that he would be leaving in a ship within a day and a half convinced him that he must carry out his assassination. Seeing him oil the bore of his musket, Cipriani, fellow Italian speaker, warned the Emperor, who was appalled to hear of his fellow Corsican's intentions. It was obvious to the Emperor, of course, that if one of his servants killed the British governor there could be no hope for his ambition to be admitted to the British Isles and live there a free, easy, and cultivated life.

Santini was therefore called, and OGF told him that he was not to consider such a gesture of vengeance and honor. Much later still I would hear that he had won Santini's obedience by giving him an alternate and somewhat less lethal task. De Montholon—again, the devotion in this cannot be gainsaid—had stayed up all night writing on silk an account of the harshness of Sir Hudson's policy. Santini was to wear it in his nether garments and, should he be searched by Sir Thomas Reade, who did not stop at the outer layers of a man, and should it be discovered, was to say that he had been bullied into it.

From The Briars we saw a little procession come across the Deadwood Plain and descend down the mountain the next day, and Santini and young Archambault in a trap driven by Marchand. They reached the saddle above the cliffs that led to Jamestown and vanished altogether, out of the vision and knowledge of The Briars. My mother went to her room to, as she phrased it, "have a little swoon" before riding over to commiserate with her friend Fanny.

Novarrez told my father, when he was next at Longwood, "They will strip us one by one like leaves from this dead tree. The Great Soul will be left alone."

It was not the first time my father had evidence of how profound was the affection between OGF and his servants. Of course, if a master or mistress is ill or has died, servants tend to tears under the weight of the solemnity. But with Novarrez and Marchand it was a far less occasional and a more unrehearsed thing. Novarrez loved OGF, even though he knew what the Emperor was in his nakedness, in his nightmares and insomnia, indigestion and costiveness, and in all other demonstrations of his imperfection.

My father, more confident at French after his regular exposure to it, was led to the salon with the billiard table in it, where the Emperor was striding about in his turban and dressing gown, and Las Cases and Emmanuel, with their pens poised, sat at the *écritoire* waiting wanly for the Emperor's next sentence. OGF always seemed delighted to be distracted by outsiders. In some ways it was as if he had repented of his history and kept working at it for the good of the souls of the Las Cases and to keep Gourgaud out of trouble or appeased.

"Guglielmo," he cried, as usual when seeing my father.

The earnest Las Cases, father and son, looked up with infinite patience at their unruly master. OGF raised his hand to my father's shoulder and drew him into an embrace and told him that both de Montholon and Bertrand had assured him the household could not get by on the allocated sum. Proposing for the sake of simplicity that servants and the suite ate precisely the same food, it brought the weekly budget for each person to five pounds. "This means a soldier as excellent as Bertrand," said the Emperor, "and a woman as delicate as the Countess de Montholon—these people who have known the most sumptuous quarters and the most elevated European luxuries—will now eat as well as the drummer boys of the 53rd or 66th regiments!"

It was about then, I think, though I cannot be sure, that the Emperor for the first time gave my father a money bill drawn on certain resources in France, written out by Las Cases and signed by the Emperor himself, a bill to be transported, without any intrusion from the governor, to a broker in England, a friend of O'Meara, and so on to relatives of the Emperor in Paris—a bill for negotiation between the English broker and the French bank, the sum settled on after commissions to be returned to the household at Longwood.

In later years, in his distracted final time in a penal city on another continent, my father would tell me that when he was first given a bill drawn up on the Emperor's behalf, Las Cases had told him to extract a fee for himself from the overall sum when the discounted amount was returned by way of the coffers of Fowler, Cole, and Balcombe. My father always claimed, almost as a self-condemnation for naïveté, that he refused to do it for any such commission, but he knew he might have to pay an agent, a storeship captain perhaps, to carry the bill away from the island. (A fellow, for example like Captain Cook, might have been amenable after the treatment he got at the hands of Sir Tom Reade and Name and Nature's troops.)

The Emperor's household trusted my father with these affairs, when he might have made himself safe in his stature on the island by betraying the dealings to Sir Hudson Lowe.

That's what I sing in the silence of the bush: that he kept the faith, that congenial poor old plump wine-bibber. He had honor and played a simple game when he could and should have played the new serpentine ones. Of course, Name and Nature had demanded to be the clearinghouse for all bills and all correspondence, and my father, out of the plainest sympathy and friendship, subverted that, but to eternal cost.

My father secreted the note to be smuggled. OGF dolefully rubbed his hands. "The other thing," he announced, "is that I need to sell my plate, and I want you to handle the sale."

Selling the silver plate is considered an evil omen in most families, and, I believe, even in French ones, and my father stared at the Emperor.

"Yes, I want you to handle the sale, my dear *Cinq Bouteilles*. God knows, there must be merchants who'd see a good thing in it, or officers in the squadron or the garrison who might like to have a piece as a memento of their delightful times in this little acre. I trust it will go at an outrageous price, like the fruit and vegetables on this island."

My father began to argue with him. He should not sell anything as precious and see it dispersed from this geologic phenomenon of a midoceanic rock to every obscure latitude.

The Emperor told him, "Come, *Cinq Bouteilles,* there is no reason to possess a plate when there's nothing to eat off it."

This, of course, was a dramatic statement of the truth, and perhaps the Emperor was seized by a desire to exhibit to the world the extent by which the British and Sir Hudson had reduced him.

And so the plan was made that the silverware of the Emperor's household would be carried down to Jamestown on the shoulders of slaves and Chinese and advertised for sale in Mr. Solomon's newspaper and on a handbill produced in his printery.

My father rode away utterly depressed. He knew that having refused to take a margin on the money bill he was carrying in his breast pocket, he would also need, as a consistent admirer and friend of OGF, to undercharge his commission on the sale of the silver plate.

The possessor of the bust of . . .

$\mathcal{A}$fter *another jolly Christmas at* The Briars, from an officer from the English vessel *Baring*, it became known that a Mr. Radwick, a gentleman sailor, had brought a bust of the King of Rome to St. Helena. When he had landed and inquired innocently of members of the garrison how to get it to the Emperor, Sir Thomas Reade found out in no time and at once visited Radwick's ship. By evening Sir Hudson Lowe was the possessor of the bust of the son of OGF, and was said to have mused aloud that perhaps he should break it up, for the British Cabinet had not approved its arrival.

Lady Holland had sent books and other items by the *Baring*: these had also been seized and retained at Plantation House. And O'Meara had learned all this by doing what he liked best: conversing at length and sometimes drinking in that same dimension. When he told the Emperor, OGF became agitated, indeed beyond comfort.

The bust of Bonaparte's son was in Name and Nature's possession for two weeks. We weren't the only ones who knew it; the freed slaves *and* the slaves knew it too. He was hanging on to it at Plantation House until he had communicated with Lord Bathurst in London about whether to give a man an image of his son, something that might have been allowed to the most common of common criminals.

It was now that at The Briars our feelings against Name and Nature really began to mount. We understood nothing of his fear and his monomania. We understood that he was prepared to be inhuman and saw denial as a duty. Only at this distance of time and place do I feel almost sorry for the anguish these possessions evoked in Name and Nature, the way they rankled and bespoke the bigger world's unwillingness to bring down severity upon the Ogre. But Sir Thomas Reade—so I believe even now—had no inhibitions about prohibiting comforts to OGF. His was a vileness unsullied by mania and thus more to be deplored.

At last Reade, though not known for his moderation, pointed out that the bust was made of marble through and through, there could be no secret traps to it, and that it could be safely forwarded to Longwood. The governor called on Count Bertrand and said that although the bust had come in a very suspect manner, it seemed to be no reason to separate the breathing father from the marbled child, except for one thing—that the sculptor expected £125 for it, which Sir Hudson suggested it was not worth. The statue arrived at Longwood, and the entire household gathered to see it. It was placed on the mantelpiece of Bonaparte's small and strange study, and the Emperor sat down and stared at the features for at least half an hour before he said anything.

I would later see this bust of the young Napoleon, the King of Rome, François, the simulacrum of the infant Emperor himself, in OGF's rooms, and his demeanor towards it was intense even by the standards of those times. You have to remember that in those days men dwelt upon carvings and cameos as one now dwells upon photographs, so he gazed on the statue of his son, and the lovely boy smiled back, miraculously in his own features. OGF did not have complicated features, merely complicated lines to his face, and yet the Italian sculptor had somehow managed to delineate his son in a way that flattered and delighted the father.

The weeks Name and Nature had detained the bust, depriving OGF of the sight of his child's countenance, made us discuss whether Lord Bathurst, had he been here on St. Helena, would have been more accommodating than Sir Hudson and permitted all manner of things Sir Hudson would not. We wondered between us if this island was unable to accommodate great men, wider souls.

Yet it was the only place I would choose to be, and from which I have ever afterwards been an exile.

*I*t was almost in a desire to relieve the expenses of the table at Longwood that my father would invite either the Count and Countess de Montholon or Madame and General Bertrand to The Briars for dinner. He wanted to ask the Las Cases men, but I am ashamed to tell you that I had pleaded with him not to. "The boy hit me fair in the face here, in our own garden," I told my father, and I demanded that if he ever asked the Las Cases he must allow me not to attend the table. I was frightened not of the boy as an assailant, though. I was frightened by his ardor, and its messiness, and by his delicate feelings that had been violated at the table in Longwood.

I saw that Madame de Montholon was pregnant again, a tribute to de Montholon's virility, yet she was at that same time losing weight, the column of her neck becoming stringy, and there was a gloss of fatigue on her broad forehead. I was still fascinated by her having been married three times. It was a grave and eternal matter to marry once, and since I had become aware of the bewildering news of Major Fehrzen's supposed interest in me, I was engaged by the idea that Albine had first married an old man when she was just two years older than me—my source in these matters was as ever Madame Bertrand.

Admiral Malcolm and his wife liked to attend when we had the French at the table. We would find that the admiral too had smuggled goods to Longwood from his own store at the Castle, but in the end did not permit himself to show disloyalty to Sir Hudson, the commander by land. This tiny clump of dense rock outweighed in authority, it seemed, the vastness of Admiral Malcolm's Atlantic when it came to managing the prisoner.

Lady Malcolm had become quieter of late, as if at the advice of her husband, uneasily caught in such a delicate position. She still came in her swathes of color, or in exorbitant turbans of many hues, which echoed her general air of jolliness and enthusiasm. But she was more subdued, and the corners of her mouth would tuck themselves away in reflectiveness. It seemed clear she did not like the over-punctilious reign of Name and Nature over the island. It oppressed her too, though she could not say so.

The Count de Montholon, a guest at The Briars with Albine, closed his mouth firmly and made his eyes blank as Major Gorrequer arrived one evening. My father had given up attempting friendship with Name and Nature and Sir Thomas, but not Gorrequer, who he felt could be a moderate influence on his master. However, de Montholon and Bertrand considered Gorrequer more vicious than he pretended to be, a less than reluctant bearer of impositions, *un finaud*, as de Montholon said—a sly one. So de Montholon was not won over when Gorrequer greeted everyone with apologies and with a proper round of acknowledgments and titles, extending them even to Jane and me. Indeed Gorrequer's tentative and regretful demeanor made us anticipate some edict he carried from Sir Hudson, and so instead of convincing us of his sympathy, by his very presence he sucked the joy out of the room and made the French anxious.

Gorrequer observed and inquired, "So I believe, since I've seen a caravan hoisting it down to Jamestown, that the General wishes to sell his plate."

My father said that the Emperor considered it necessary.

"And you are to be the agent for the sale of this plate?"

My father agreed that he was honored to be so entrusted. Gorrequer conceded, "The governor believes it's within the General's right to do so."

"Well, I should think it would be in his right," said my father. "It's his plate."

Later, as Gorrequer was leaving, he buttonholed my father in the hallway.

"His Excellency has ordered that these items of silver not become relics to a supposed man of destiny. I told you he has permitted the sale . . ."

"Of course," said my father. "He must."

"The silver as silver has a value, and Sir Hudson believes it is at that value the General is entitled to sell it. But he is not entitled to sell it as mementos of his lost power, and have it reach distant places with the symbols of his past ambitions. The plate's ornamentations lie under the same prohibition as would advertisements in newspapers for the General's return as Emperor of France."

"Oh, my heavens," said my father, totally undone. "What does he mean we should do?"

"The plate is to be melted down," Gorrequer said. "That's what His Excellency the Governor requires. Imperial insignia, whether the humble bee or the eagle or any other motifs—shields, swords—are to be removed from the plate and melted down with the rest in the Jamestown forge. The government has fixed a fair price of five shillings an ounce for the silver."

"But that's a barbarity," complained my father. "These are fine pieces, well wrought, work crafted from the lofty imagination of humankind."

Gorrequer said, "I know, my dear fellow. I know. But the fair price of five shillings an ounce compares well with the price of silver on the London market as quoted in the last edition of *The Times* to reach us."

My father made guttural noises. He said, "In that case I shall advise the Emperor to keep his plate and spite your master. And the porters can bring it all back from Jamestown again."

"Well, there you see," said Gorrequer, "it's already settled. . . . The governor has foreseen such an attitude on your part, which he knows does you some honor, and tells me that since the decision has been made to sell the plate, the proposed sale will stand and the purpose will not be altered."

There was a silence, and then my father said, "What sort of man bent on torment would come up with such an order as that? I mean to say, you've seen some of the decent fellows on this island—open-hearted fellows. Hodson, Ibbetson, Doveton . . . We do things honestly and face each other frankly. What in God's name is wrong with your man?"

"It is not within my power to speculate," Gorrequer said piously.

"My God, Gorrequer, what sort of man is not disgraced to deliver such an order?"

"I cannot say, dear Balcombe, I cannot say."

"But you were a brave fellow in Spain, used to shot and the detonations of artillery. Cannot you be brave in this matter?"

"It is entirely different," said Gorrequer.

My mother seemed to spend much time with Lady Name and Nature. The summonses to Plantation House were regular, and my mother would say, "Lady Lowe needs to speak to me, and I may do some good." Lady Lowe had taken a liking to my mother's company, perhaps, in contradistinction to the animosity between the husbands. This did not seem a totally strange business. They were both Englishwomen of about the same age, and of some similar experience.

One of the matters my mother said she must take up with Name and Nature was that Madame Bertrand had written a letter to Mr. Solomon, a normal letter of trade, which was intercepted on the tiers above the port and sent to Sir Hudson by his watchers. He returned it to her with a note that it had been written without his permission. He added an observation that if the restrictions imposed on the Emperor's party seemed too hard, they could relieve themselves from them by simply leaving the island.

Nonetheless, it was a time OGF briefly gave those who knew him a sense that his world was ample. He had the bust of his son. He had books from Lord and Lady Holland and from French friends, and even Sir Hudson's delaying of the crates that contained them did not spoil the pleasure the prisoner of Longwood took in receiving them. Jane and I rode over to attend the happy opening of the boxes. The Emperor had dressed formally in uniform and set to opening them himself with hammer and chisel. He was ecstatic to find bound volumes of *Le Moniteur Universel*—the paper he had founded and which still prevailed under freedom of the press—and gave up any attempt at dictation to stay up at night reading them.

"What a pleasure I've enjoyed," he told us. "So far, only the dear French titles. For I can read forty pages of French in the time it takes me to read two of English."

Even the mist that blew past Longwood, like squadrons of stoop-shouldered sullen horsemen, or sat down on the roof and on the lungs, did not ruin his spirit for some days.

"Surgeon O'Meara is limited in his cures," O'Meara reported OGF as saying. "*Le Moniteur Universel* is far more accomplished in his effects."

Letters from France, however, soured things. They turned up by way of Sir Hudson's office, where they had been opened and scoured, and Name and Nature had written on them his reason for delaying them—which was that before being posted from Europe they had not been passed through the office of the secretary of state in Whitehall.

Delayed letters, and the fact they had been violated, cast the Emperor down again—my father saw it on his daily visit to Longwood. The delay in correspondence and the rats in the wainscot, raiding for crumbs in darker corners, sitting on sideboards, imitating his bicorn hat and tempting him into the absurdity of trying to don it with them still slithering from it, impinged more upon him, and the nankeen-clad walls crept in in dim alliance with them.

*W*e next visited OGF for his birthday on 15 August. He was forty-eight years. There was a supper of all the French, and Bertrand and de Montholon proposed toasts. The Emperor came to me, eyes gleaming, and said, "I went for a ride today."

"That's good for you," I told him.

"Do you know the valley beyond?" He hitched his head in a southerly direction. "The one with the spring and all the ferns?"

"Geranium Valley," I said.

"If the Fiend has his way and I perish here," said the Emperor quite cheerily, "that is the place for burial, don't you think? It's the only pretty place. We could transform it from Geranium Valley into the Valley of the Tomb. And geraniums . . . there are worse weeds to lie amidst."

"The world will have set you free by then," I asserted. "You will lie somewhere better than that little notch."

He thanked me for my assurance and kissed my hand. I barely saw him for the rest of that night, though I noticed him speaking to my mother with brotherly animation.

I was not as aware as I might have been of how the reports of events overtaking his family elevated and cast down the spirits of Our Great Friend, even as he made a little room for our visits. He felt betrayed by Marshal Murat, married to his own sister Caroline. He had elevated the couple to the stature of king and queen of Naples, and Caroline had sought to retain that stature by renouncing Bonaparte. It had been a comfort to OGF that Madame *Mère,* his mother, a shadowy goddess to us, had denounced her daughter. He was nonetheless upset that Murat had been executed by firing squad by the restored French monarchy. Yet all we heard of his distress was what O'Meara told my father during a drinking session. Apparently OGF considered the execution (an echo, I felt, of the fabled d'Enghien's) an infraction of the rules of public decorum: a king (the talentless French restored king) had caused another king, acknowledged by all the others, to be shot. But through pure graciousness, he did not impose grief about the collapse of his great world upon us in his shrunken one.

When we were leaving Longwood, I saw the young Las Cases amongst the barren trees in the garden, striking the trunks idly with a dropped branch, uttering an occasional word to himself. All around him the French house mourned—doubly because of Murat's double-dealing, a man lost by both betrayal and death. And there had been a terrible pathos in his brave cry at the end, facing his firing squad clear-eyed and calling, "Straight to the heart but spare the face. Fire!"

I was consumed by thoughts of Murat. What impact must his fate have had on Emmanuel, whose hair had no doubt been ruffled by that cavalryman and king? And then what acid from Vienna splashed down on him from the treaty signed by grand men in that city, men whom the Emperor had once dominated? And what reflected vitriol came down to him from the intention of the minister of state, the dreaded Castlereagh, to declare OGF not a fallen Emperor but a usurper?

Emmanuel saw me and stopped and tried to direct his gaze at me. But he did not quite have the spirit for it today and hung his head. I saw Gourgaud emerge from the side door of Longwood, as if on his way to the stables or to visit his bête noire, de Montholon. He was dressed in the uniform of a general of the ordnance, and when he saw the boy, he came striding towards him, though Emmanuel was not conscious of it and stayed on his dawdling tangent. Gourgaud had gloves in his hand and, drawing level, turned the boy by the shoulders and began striking him with them. This was very French, but it also looked worse than a blow from the hand itself, and seemed as if young Emmanuel had not merited flesh upon flesh. The boy suffered it with lowered head, taking only one step backwards, enduring. I ran from where I was and cried, "General Gourgaud, what are you doing?"

There was no doubting Gourgaud was discomforted to see me, but not enough to cease. He got in three more swipes before I reached them, and only then stood back.

"This is something you do not know about," he said in French.

"He is mad," said Emmanuel in English. "One day I shall take a whip to him."

Gourgaud walked away five paces, rather like a duelist, turned, and declared, "His father presumes to be the Emperor's especial familiar and to exclude me from the presence, and this brat sits smirking! But where were the Las Cases when we were crossing the Berezina, this toad of a chamberlain and his abnormal son?"

"He is more normal than you," I told Gourgaud. "Are you going to hit me?"

For I could tell he was tempted, and that it would destroy him somehow with the Emperor.

"Does the Emperor know you're treating Emmanuel in this way?" I asked.

I could see a most uncomplicated, unworldly gratitude in Emmanuel's eyes, and I did not want that, for it presumed too much.

"His family is a family of thieves. He has stolen the Emperor from me without the Emperor's having made an attempt to recompense me for monies I have outlaid. My mother . . . my mother is sick in France. My fortune has been spent by the Emperor, and this child's father says no one can repay me. I left the meeting with a sense that I would strike the father, but I met the son and struck him. And God knows, miss, that's normal enough."

"Look," I said. "Your knuckle clipped the corner of his lip. The boy is bleeding." For some reason it seemed to me the most pathetic blood of all time.

Gourgaud turned to Emmanuel. "You are the child of a plunderer. Give me back my money." And then he trudged away, his boots emphatic on the barren ground of Longwood.

"What a brute," I said to Emmanuel. "Doesn't he find it adequate to hate Sir Hudson?"

"He hates me more than he hates Sir Hudson."

"But why?"

Emmanuel's eyes rolled. "On the retreat across France, we needed francs and the Emperor borrowed them from Gourgaud. Now Gourgaud has a letter from his relatives saying that his mother is in need of money. He asked my father and de Montholon for his money back, but how can we get a hundred thousand francs in a lump from Europe? And so he hits me to match the damage done to his mother." Emmanuel shrugged. "Perhaps there is a justice in it."

I cannot define what impulse led me to touch the bloodied corner of his mouth. I could see with horror that all at once he was contemplating attacking my mouth with his, but my alarm caused him to drop his head and cover my hand with kisses.

"That's enough," I said. "I'm sorry you were hurt. Well, goodbye!"

And with that I mounted old Tom and galloped off.

Against the killing drafts of salt . . .

On a clear morning in this period, when the vise of Sir Hudson's administration was beginning to straiten the souls and indeed the bodies of the French at Longwood, the Emperor woke feeling fresh and went around knocking on the doors of each of the exiles and demanding their presence at breakfast in the garden at Longwood. Bertrand was already in the house, having come from Hutt's Gate, and so was quickly alerted. Only Madame Bertrand was missing, and a servant was sent, and she arrived during the breakfast.

The first roses were trying to grow in that hard soil of Longwood, struggling against the killing drafts of salt that came off the sea on the southeast trade. The table was placed in the scattered shade of a few pines and of a sail Admiral Malcolm had had the sailors erect, and amidst the contorted gumwoods coffee was taken in the clear air, and everyone was invigorated by this amalgam of conditions, including the condition of the Emperor's will in bringing them together. When the conversation began with the predictable complaints against Plantation House, OGF held up his hand and told them, "None of that. For when you are restored to the world one day, you have to think of yourselves as brothers, on my account."

But the Emperor was not talking about his death. The good news had come in the British newspapers that Lord Holland and the Duke of Sussex had moved a remonstrance in the House of Lords against what they called the illegal imprisonment of Bonaparte. The Lords would not in the end vote to accept it, but OGF did not know that. It had for now been eloquently argued with plentiful accusations of ill will against Castlereagh and Bathurst, men who had sent troops to shoot down protesters in England and had also set them to cramp the soul of OGF.

De Montholon looked at Las Cases, whose prissiness he hated, whose air of being the Emperor's confidant, said Fanny, irked him. Las Cases simply gazed back at him with transparent eyes and bowed his head in the simplest goodwill, and de Montholon was won over. Bertrand, seeing it, smiled and held out his hand to de Montholon, and Gourgaud sat in his place, rocking his head back and forth, as if saying, "Very well. But have you assessed all the elements? And what about the money I loaned you?"

"Help each other?" Fanny asked us later. "They are nearer to murdering each other. And the Emperor himself thinks he is the sun and shines equally on all, and wonders why I'm careful about exposing myself to his rays.

"He has got feeble again, turning back from walks, and of all things eating his dinner in the bath from that device that straddles it, with a small table placed by the side for Las Cases to eat from. Which means that Gourgaud is moping all the more at the table in the dining room and has—if you can believe it—challenged de Montholon to a duel. To a duel! How Sir Hudson would enjoy that. Two Frenchmen killing each other and saving him the trouble."

The Emperor had observed to Madame de Montholon and Fanny Bertrand at dinner—as Fanny Bertrand said wryly, "just to win us over"—that their garments would soon resemble those of the old misers who buy their wardrobes in secondhand clothes. "For once," said Fanny, "Albine de Montholon looked at me with a wan face, as if we were sisters in our misery. And we were. I must say she dotes on her little girl, Napoléone, and wonders if she will live. Though the child's so healthy, a true little barbarian—and I think there's another in progress. Lately Albine's been worried about looking old—she believes the island ages us at twice the rate—so now her misery is deeper. I told him, 'We take all the care we can, Sire.' And he said,

'But your clothes no longer show the freshness of Leroi or Despeaux or Herbault.' Imagine how dowdy we all felt."

Moved by an impulse to succor the big, square-shouldered woman, I said, "I think he was teasing you, Fanny." I wanted to push that gracious lie. "You are still," I insisted, "the most sumptuous and comely of women within thousands of square miles."

"No, Betsy, my darling. He criticized his own hunting coat, and now they have thrown Santini off the island he has lost his most skilled repairer." Santini, the assassin, had been the expert at maintaining uniforms, reversing cloth, and producing a new suit from an old gray frock coat. He had made the Emperor a pair of shoes from the leather of old boots, and could always make something plausible out of the irreparable.

To help accommodate Gourgaud's valid desire for money for his mother, and perhaps to avoid a duel with him, Count de Montholon had made an earnest submission to Plantation House. It said that the Emperor was ready to pay all the expenses of the establishment if any mercantile or banking house in St. Helena, London, or Paris, chosen by the British government, could serve as an intermediary through which the Emperor could send sealed letters, and receive sealed answers. The Emperor would pledge his honor that the letters should relate solely to pecuniary matters. De Montholon explained his reasonable proposition to my father. The secret, smuggled money bills were not working so well. Bankers in France did not know whether they were forgeries, for example.

Two mornings later, Sir Thomas was delighted to announce to de Montholon that no sealed letters were permitted to leave Longwood.

*B*almain had told O'Meara that his own instructions were not to trouble OGF but simply to report to his master the Tsar on how he was held. So Balmain was content with island life and the gathering of sightings of the Emperor from Poppleton and other officers at Longwood to include in his elegant reports. But the French commissioner de Montchenu in particular, and even the Austrian von Stürmer, believed regular sightings of the Emperor were part of their instructions. And being prevented from seeing him by restrictions placed by Sir Hudson and by OGF himself, they lived in a sort of frustrated nullity.

It was later discovered that Las Cases secretly and regularly wrote to the Frenchwoman Madame von Stürmer, him having when young been a tutor to her brothers, but it was said her husband, who was a fairly straight and narrow Austrian diplomat, forbade her to answer. This young lady came one afternoon, somberly dressed, to The Briars and introduced herself to us. Jane and I loved visitors to whom we could show off our passable French, and we strolled with her as she made her solemn circuit of the garden and the Pavilion.

She asked gravely, looking pale, "Was he inconsolable while living here?"

"No," Jane said. "It suited him. He seemed lively."

And we told her the family stories—the carriage with the mouse, the occasional impudence, the bonbon poisoning, and all the rest, the tales that would recur throughout our family's existence, and that even now I tell virtually to myself.

After inspecting the empty Pavilion, Madame von Stürmer stalked our garden, where the trace of the crown the Emperor's servants had drawn in the lawn was still vaguely visible, not by way of the scoring of the ground but in the grass. I wondered if she was snooping for her husband, but it was with an authentic teary-cheeked reverence that she walked the crown outline with us. Was she mourning her own surrender to the Austrians, or OGF's? For her to fail to meet the Emperor was a great loss, and yet she was also terrified of such a confrontation.

Count Balmain and the von Stürmers were sharing Rosemary Hall, a rambling two-storey house inland. With the help of ship's carpenters and many porters they had made it habitable. My father dealt there with the commissioners over their household supplies and the unsatisfactory warrants with which they paid for their requirements, warrants issued in the name of far-off treasuries in Vienna, Paris, and Moscow. All three of the commissioners were exercised by the cost of living on the island; all three of them were writing to their masters saying, "You must not let your delegate be embarrassed by the ample resources of the other commissioners."

One day at The Briars I saw a paper addressed to Count Balmain and written in my father's hand. It said, "Beef 22 pence per pound, pork 30 pence per pound, stock of the smallest kind 40–60 shillings, duck or chicken 10–15 shillings each, turkey 40–60 shillings." These prices impressed even me. The silver at Longwood had by now been melted down and sold as Sir Thomas had ordered, *en bloc* without imperial insignia, and what it had earned for the Emperor was being consumed by turkeys worth their weight in gold.

It was O'Meara's mode to be quite whimsical and open in recounting what he said to OGF. "Don't think I'm a spy for Sir Hudson. I'm not permitted to be. I'm a spy for my friend Finlaison at the Admiralty," O'Meara told OGF one day. And the Emperor laughed and said, with a strange kind of complacency, "Well, of course. You're a sailor under orders. And I don't mind the Admiralty. Honest men, by and large. But what do you report to that appalling Reade and to the Fiend himself?"

O'Meara replied, with Hippocratic purity, "I am here as your surgeon, and to attend upon you and your suite. I have received no other orders than to make reports on your health, but I do so in general terms except in the case of your being taken seriously ill, when I need to receive promptly the advice and assistance of other physicians."

"First obtaining my consent to call in those accursed others, is that not so?"

O'Meara agreed, perhaps more glibly than he should have. OGF said, with sudden lack of humor, "If you are appointed as a surgeon to a prison and to report my conversations to the governor, I want never to see you again."

Then perhaps even for OGF this axe of a sentence seemed too extreme for the conversation in progress. "Do not suppose that I take you for a spy," he rushed to tell the Irishman. "On the contrary

I have never had the least occasion to find fault with you, and I have a friendship for you on this *isola maledetta*, without which I would be poorer, and an esteem for your character, a greater proof of which I could not give you than asking you candidly your own opinion on your situation."

But this was another sign that suspicion pervaded all. It became known, as things did on the island, that Name and Nature had sent an order to the shopkeepers of the town that they were not to give any credit to the French, or to sell them any article, unless for ready money, under pain of not only losing the amount of the sum credited but of suffering such punishment as being turned off the island.

Many of the 53rd officers who were in the habit of calling to see Madame Bertrand at Hutt's Gate received hints from Sir Thomas and Major Gorrequer that their visits were not pleasing to the authorities. The officer of the Hutt's Gate guard was ordered to report the names of all persons entering the Bertrands' house. Several of the officers of the 53rd went to Hutt's Gate to say goodbye to Countess Bertrand. They explained to her that since they would be ordered to make a report of any conversations they had with her to the governor or to Sir Thomas Reade, they could not as men of honor allow themselves to comply with that regulation.

"Sir Name and Nature," O'Meara narrated, "intends to have a ditch dug around the house, to prevent cattle from trespassing into the Emperor's garden. So he walks it out with me, this notional ditch of his, and we come to a rare low-branched tree with foliage near to the ground. 'This has to go!' he cries, and he asks me to send one of the servants down to the port for Mr. Porteous, who, it turns out amongst other glorious honors, is the superintendent of the Company's gardens. And I have to wait with him making conversation until Porteous is back, none too happy at being dragged up there from his establishment. And Name and Nature orders him to send some men instantly and have the tree grubbed out. It blotted the terrain and introduced the chance of intolerable subterfuge, you see!"

When O'Meara left, my mother asked my father, "Do you think O'Meara protests too much?"

"In what sense?" asked my bibulous father, with a soft hiccough.

"In the sense that he may be closer to Name and Nature than he says," said my mother, with a new kind of speculation in her voice.

"Why would he be so mischievous?" my father asked, and tears appeared at his soft lids.

"This is what the Fiend has done to our circle of friends," my mother admitted, close to tears herself. She kissed him tenderly. It was the kind of kiss you give an unknowing child.

And all continued to close in. Longwood was surrounded at six hundred paces by a string of subaltern guards, while at nine o'clock in the evening, when Sir Hudson had decreed no one but the garrison should be abroad in the open air, the sentinels were stationed within voice of each other, strangling the outskirts so that no person could come in or go out without being examined by them. At the entrance of the house double sentinels were placed, and the patrols continually passed backwards and forwards in the garden, hampering its growth. After that fated hour of nine, the Emperor could leave the house only in company of a British field officer.

Our father told us that every landing place on the island, and indeed every rocky cove that offered half a chance of one, was furnished with a picket of patrolling victors of Toulon, and sentinels were even placed at night upon every goat path leading to the sea, though it was hard to imagine the Emperor trying to struggle his way down them.

Name and Nature's mania lacked a cause. All of us knew ships could be seen at twenty-four leagues' distance when approaching the island, and I know now through inquiry what I then did not—that two ships of war continually cruised, one to the windward and the other to the leeward, to whom signals were made as soon as any vessel was discovered by the patrols on shore. No ship except a British naval vessel was permitted to sail down to the Jamestown Roads unless accompanied by one of the cruisers, which remained with her until she was either permitted to anchor or sail away. All these precautions, all the time, around our island. All the fishing boats belonging to the island were numbered and anchored every evening under the control of a lieutenant in the navy, and no boats, excepting guard boats from the ships of war, which rowed around the island each night on patrol, were allowed to be put into the shore after sunset. Every human precaution to prevent escape, short of actually sealing OGF in a cell or enchaining him, was adopted. Yet apparently, and I realize this now more than I did then, in Name and Nature's fevered mind, the Ogre had already slipped forth.

There were admittedly rumors enough to disturb Sir Hudson's and thus Lady Lowe's sleep. Texans were said to be plotting the Emperor's deliverance from the island, and in Louisiana they had already built a palace for him to occupy. And yet during the day British passengers traveling through from India and China requested an audience with Bonaparte (even at the cost of making a report), who rarely disappointed them unless he was sick. He was like an actor whose repute was attached to the one theater: Longwood. As O'Meara told us, many ladies and gentlemen who had ridden up to the house at inconvenient times waited in his room long after the fore-topsail of the ship that was to take them to England was loosed, just on the chance of seeing through O'Meara's window the Emperor's appearance at the windows of his apartments.

*A*t dinner at our house, the Marquis de Montchenu seemed to me the duffer O'Meara had depicted him and peered at us like a pink-eyed mouse. Anxious about where to sit and what to say and what might be served, he clung to his aide, a young French officer named de Gors. When soup was served, de Montchenu required Captain de Gors to produce from his jacket an emetic and place it by his master's soup bowl in case the liquid was poisoned. Captain de Gors explained in an embarrassed tone that the henchmen of the French Revolution had once, twenty-five years past, tried to poison his master. De Montchenu's long queue tied with ribbon bobbed up and down, and he was absorbed in the drama of his eating, for each un-envenomed mouthful was an exciting gift from the gods.

He was shortsighted, clearly, and it turned out that he loved cauliflower, of which there were two dishes on our table with boats of white sauce. He, for all his peering, had not seen them, but noticed them at once as the twins arrived to take them away. As the vegetables passed him, he turned on poor Captain de Gors and yelled, in French, "Imbecile! Why didn't you know that in this awful place there was cauliflower?"

All around the table there was choked laughter. Half of us ate cauliflower out of a dietary duty to avoid boils, but here was a pallid man who liked this pallid vegetable, his *chou-fleur*. I nicknamed him Munch Enough. Someone else more wittily, *Montez-Chez-Nous*. Altogether we were pleased he had escaped the guillotine so that he could come here to wear his queue and pretend that he was so important he was in peril of death by poisoning.

Everyone thought he was harmless enough, though, and we were willing to tolerate him. That is, until copies of the *Chronicle* arrived on a ship and reached our table, and other tables on the island. In it, translated into English from a French newspaper, was an article by de Montchenu, detailing in a garbled way some of the games the Emperor and the Balcombe children had played together during the residency in the Pavilion. I had, in fact, told him these stories, though there was no recognition of me as the source in the article. He described the blindman's bluff, my drawing the sword and seeming to threaten the Emperor, the hide-and-seek with my brothers, and spoke of me as "a wild girl" and "a particular familiar" of the Emperor. He did not mention in the article that he had never clapped eyes on the Emperor himself.

According to O'Meara—our map of Longwood was mediated to us by O'Meara and Fanny Bertrand as ever—de Montchenu had approached Name and Nature with the crazed proposition that the commissioners could easily force their way into Longwood with a company of British troops. Name and Nature was wise enough to know that this could be a debacle, that the Ogre would resist, that someone would be killed, perhaps even the Emperor, who would thus achieve an apotheosis in the view of his followers in Europe, a martyr who cried out for the mean souls of Earls Liverpool, Bathurst, and Castlereagh. And now, after that absurd suggestion, another—

the imputation that I was a "familiar," a term I did not understand, or at least did not understand why it so exercised my father, and that I was "a wild girl," which some would have thought a fair description!

The article had first been shown to my father by one of the store-ship captains who had arrived with a cargo. My father had immediately gone half-striding, half-hobbling (under gout's influence) from his warehouse up the road to the Portions. None of the servants knew where the Marquis de Montchenu was, but they suggested Plantation House. His day's work ruined, my father rode home and called my mother to the drawing room and showed her the piece. He planned, he said, to call de Montchenu out, demand honor, and fight a duel.

"If a man can't see damn cauliflower from ten yards," my father ranted, rendered unsporting by fury, "he has no chance of hitting me."

He declared an intention to go to Plantation House and hunt the little weasel from under the shadow of Sir Hudson. But rage is tiring, and I felt my father collapse, and my mother urge him to rest upon it for an hour or two, and perhaps write a letter of protest to the old French count. He wrote to the count certainly, but asked him to receive a visit from Mr. Balcombe at six that evening, or at an alternative hour Munch Enough nominated.

Passing to his room, he saw me through the open door of the library, where I was extracting a book with every display of literate intentions. He came to me and embraced me, and I smelt snuff and brandy and a perfume. He had shaved for the murder of de Montchenu, or the outside chance of his own death. He had used clouds of a delicate powder that brought up his childlike and soft complexion.

"My dear child," he said, pulling my head close to his chest and kissing the part in my hair. "You must worry about nothing. You are a wonderful and honorable girl."

I was delighted, and clung to him, and then he stumbled off.

My mother had been behind him and came up to where I still stood, astonished.

"Eavesdropping again," she remarked, with a smile, as if that were not the main issue. Her face was one of weary delusion. "I will get the horses saddled. We must go and find Count Balmain. He'll be spending time with the Lowe women at Plantation House. He's always there for tea these days."

I realized my mother would know this from her frequent visits to Lady Lowe.

We had our horses saddled. We followed the road, with the waterfall to the side running well from the rains of the midyear of 1817, and behind and above us, in a separate patch of paler, hazier light, Longwood. We made good progress on the surface mud of the firm road to Plantation House and passed its old tortoise, unhurried by any care on its lawns, and we reined in and were met by a groom from the East India Company of hussars.

We were led into the drawing room, which still seemed naked now that all the Wilkses' refined paintings were gone and had been replaced by dull oils of dead pheasants and unnameable and meaningless battles. Lady Lowe and her daughters sat beneath them with Count Balmain, who rose to greet us as the women kept their seats. He declared in French that the balance of women had now swung too strongly against him, and as delighted to see the Balcombes as he was, he felt he should leave and allow appropriate conversation to occur without the inhibition of his presence. It was a typical flow of courtly palaver on his part.

As he kissed hands, including ours, he muttered French phrases over them. He lingered over the hand of Miss Charlotte Johnson, the elder daughter of Lady Lowe.

"Before you go," my mother said, when he reached her hand and was opulently gesturing over it. "Lady Lowe, I wish I could have a word with Count Balmain."

Lady Lowe looked up with a strange contemptuous benignity.

"Conduct the count and Mrs. Balcombe to the smaller parlor," she ordered a servant immediately.

I stood up to follow my mother, but she made a "stay there" gesture and said, "Lady Lowe, you don't mind if Betsy remains here?"

I was disappointed I would not behold the urgency of my mother's appeal to Count Balmain, her plea to intercede and prevent a slaughter.

Lady Lowe nodded in her normal distrait manner, negligent, one would have thought, as if my mother had not been her occasional confidante. So I sat.

Charlotte Johnson surveyed me with that edge, the look of a woman who was secure in her control of men. "Has Major Fehrzen visited your family recently?"

She exchanged a significant look with her younger sister.

"I see very little of him," I said, more stiffly than I would have liked. It emerged almost as a plea.

A secret amusement crackled between them, a shiver, deniable and not nakedly vicious. Their appetite to see me shift in discomfort seemed strange, as if they did not understand I had convinced myself, on one level of my soul, that it was all the same to me if Fehrzen and Croad stayed or went. It was, wasn't it? I liked to think I did not play the sort of game they did, but then I had almost forgotten my treatment of poor Emmanuel. And remembering him now, I thought, They are causing me pain from some instinct of the kind that provokes me to cause young Las Cases pain.

I could hear my mother's voice raised somewhat in another room and the honeyed voice of Count Balmain playing a minor part. At last my mother returned. I could tell from the way her face had reddened that she had persuaded Count Balmain to intervene.

She said, "Betsy, we must not inconvenience dear Lady Lowe and her daughters any further."

Lady Lowe rose now and I did too, and my mother thanked her again for allowing this intrusion. They sounded like strangers to each other. Because of the enmity between their husbands, had they become enemies too?

"Count Balmain left," said my mother, "but wanted me to say that the reason he would not return was that he did not want to incommode the company."

"What a flight by our friends," commented Charlotte. "What a confabulation you must have had with the count to make you wish to escape us simultaneously with him."

"As you wish, dear Mrs. Balcombe," murmured pretty Lady Lowe, with a tiny belch.

We stood in front of the door as our horses arrived.

"I believe we should ride to town," said my mother.

"Yes," I said, "in case Father has gone after Munch Enough with a pistol."

The contest of honor, which we knew could become a contest of mayhem and tragedy, was about to either take place or be prevented.

But our journey down into Jamestown was abortive: as my father had left for that port himself, he was intercepted by two fortunate arrivals. One was Captain de Gors riding up from the Portions with a propitiating letter in French. My father agreed to go to The Briars to receive the letter formally there. At home, he took it to his library office, asking Jane to come with him and help with translation, while the young French aide waited fretfully yet humbly for him in the drawing room. My father deliberately kept de Gors waiting, as if he were still looking to impose such a large retributory slight that old Munch Enough would fight him anyhow.

De Montchenu's letter turned out to be an exhaustive apology, claiming both that the term "wild girl' would have been more properly translated as "spirited girl," and that the term "familiar" had been mistranslated from the French *jeune amie*. He offered to show my father his manuscript copy and also accused de Gors, the deliverer of his own letter, for having made the final polish to the piece, and said it was de Gors, not him, who had entered the names of the Balcombes.

My father returned to the drawing room.

"You should leave that old man's service," he told de Gors. "He is a liar and a coward."

De Gors maintained his blank discretion and politeness, and handed my father an enclosure for me expressing Marquis de Montchenu's profoundest apologies. I never quite accepted them.

*A*mongst all the pent-up suspicions, there were still times for shows of amity. The commissary to the military, Denzil Ibbetson, my father's friend, organized one for us. He had arrived with the regiment and the naval squadron at the same time as the Emperor, and had got to know my father well since he managed the government stores that fed the garrison and the servants of the small protectorate, and bought goods when necessary from Fowler, Cole, and Balcombe. When the Bertrands moved into a new-built cottage closer to Longwood, Mr. Ibbetson in turn moved into Hutt's Gate.

Denzil Ibbetson was a great painter of views and watercolors rather than a student of stores and inventories. Many of his works were hung proudly at Hutt's Gate, and he had even been allowed by Sir Hudson to go to Longwood and sketch the Emperor, in a general, rustic context, however—a garden or drawing room—not in a martial one.

He declared that on an afternoon in September he was to hold a picnic at his home, which he had renamed Little Pasture. He had no wife, and my mother attributed his absorption in commissary work supplying the army in the Iberian Peninsula to that apparent oddity. I had heard Sarah and Alice talk of his interest in a Tamil slave woman.

On the afternoon of the picnic, Mr. Ibbetson had tables set out in his garden, and a young male slave in white gloves and exotic striped green-and-white livery poured punch for the adults and lemonade for the children, and brought around sugarplums and ices, puddings and pastries—not quite of the delicacy Pierron the *confiseur* used to create at the Pavilion, but adequate for solid tastes. And no child was told to restrain himself. I saw my three small brothers attacking buns, and wished that Madame Bertrand's children and young Tristan de Montholon had been there. But they were now prohibited by Name and Nature from joining our general company at these events for fear that people would give them advice on how the Emperor might escape down the groin of the hill that led to Sandy Bay, and how to hide behind the Doveton wall to await rescue.

Madame Bertrand was still then in a situation on that island for which I have not forgiven Name and Nature to this day. Her allies in the town were people biblically accustomed to exile, the Jewish family the Solomons. Even so, if Madame Bertrand wished to purchase anything in Jamestown, the Solomons had been warned by Sir

Thomas Reade, she had first to submit a form to Sir Hudson, even for clothing she was buying on her own account. Rouge and powder, dental whitener and fabrics all fell under Sir Hudson's proscription and could not be bought except with vice-regal assent.

Once the permission to shop was received, she would have to ride down from Longwood with an officer of the guard, who was required to make a record of everything she said to any other party. Often these were urbane men—Major Fehrzen once told us he had accompanied her, for he was characteristically fascinated by the connection between the Irish Wild Geese, men like her father, who had chosen to serve France rather than stay in a British Ireland.

After she reached town, the Solomons let Fanny use the trying-on room of their store to change out of her riding habit into something more elegant, since she refused to be dowdy in front of the cowed locals. Some greeted her on the street—my father, and, by his orders, the Company clerks. She would also accept greetings from any of the commissioners who might have been progressing through Jamestown, and from the warder of the prison at the Castle. But many still evaded her gaze and hustled past. Madame von Stürmer seemed to enjoy her company and put herself in the way to meet her, but she was a shy woman and did not have the confidence for a full friendship.

So, no Bertrands at Mr. Ibbetson's party. Some officers called in, including Major Fehrzen, who came over and presented himself to Jane and me. He leaned earnestly, and when Jane turned away, he said, "What do you think of India, Betsy? Does it have any prominence in your imagination?"

It was a fair question, or appeared to be so. I considered it.

"It exists as one great brown clot of earth," I told him.

He smiled. "Do you imagine it habitable?"

I considered this. I thought of Mrs. Stuart and her daughters.

"I believe it can spoil people's fiber. The rest, it seems to inflict fevers on."

He smiled again, in a way that said he found the conversation disarming rather than informative.

"And no one comes back whole?" he asked.

"Some don't come back at all," I said.

I had no idea, in the face of his towering allure, why I wanted to depict India so darkly. My sister now turned her full attention back to us.

"We must talk about this further, Betsy," he said. "You clearly cannot see yourself ever living there, then?"

"I could if my father was sent there," I said, willfully playing the child instead of the woman.

He saw through that. "I meant, when you are a woman under your own direction."

"I shall consider it when the time comes," I told him.

He laughed in a kind of surrender. "You should," he assured me. "There are fables and religions and images there that have never crossed the minds of people in Europe."

And he went. I have to say in admiration of him that he seemed to understand exactly my stance as a stubborn and wary girl-woman.

The vice-regal party arrived, as it was required to, and included Charlotte and her younger sister Susannah. Lady Lowe and her husband stayed long enough for her to drink a quotient of sherry, for which performance she had by now become notable on the island. We had heard the rumor that Sir Hudson went to the Lantern Tavern each night to get away from the rather pointed lamentations of his wife, who had predicted that this appointment would create stress to little personal benefit and who could now say as often as she liked that it had. When Name and Nature had ridden up with the Prussians, late in the day of Waterloo but crucially for the chances of Wellington, he might have expected a better post than to be guard to a vast ex-potency on a small island.

Mr. Ibbetson had provided donkeys for children to ride on, and there were races and conversation, and Sir Hudson and his women vanished early in their fug of vague discontent. Major Fehrzen bowed to us and said he would return to Deadwood to undertake some obscure military duty. For all my supposed independence and wildness, I kept close to my sister Jane as he was departing. I did not want to be questioned further about India. Jane was my anchor in the indeterminate waters of supposed courtship or—I could not tell the difference—conversation.

No one, in visiting the picnic, neither Major Fehrzen nor more significantly Sir Hudson, had mentioned the curfew, towards a violation of which the party in its very spirit seemed to be aimed. I cannot remember all the conversations that occurred that day, since they were effervescent and fumed up into the sky. It was one of those seductive subtropical afternoons when the light seems eternal, itself a lingering guest at the party. Florence Robinson strode proudly but without arrogance through the people, accompanied by her new husband. *La Nymphe* had recently married Captain Edwards of the *Chloe* and had acquired leather shoes. She was about to sail in them to England with her husband, and might well accompany him back and forth between England, Cape Town, Calcutta, and the island. She had survived the Emperor's desire and come to a safe harbor, even though, contradictorily, it was a harbor at sea.

Darkness came suddenly. There had been a sort of communal forgetfulness over the greensward in front of Mr. Ibbettson's place. The air was then remotely jolted by the curfew gun sounding from Ladder Hill above Jamestown, a sufficiently far-off shudder in the air to convince us that we lived in another sphere altogether from it and had latitude to go on playing. But it was only at this profound though distant sound that the more serious of the party suggested we should break up, and farmers and their wives, who would not have to pass too many patrols, looked for their horses and drays. Those who lived in Jamestown were offered accommodation by Mr. Ibbetson, and the Solomons wisely accepted it. For the coarser members of the garrison would have enjoyed too fulsomely encountering a Jewish family by evening light.

One of the men of our company called out, almost as a joke, "Do we know the countersign if we run into pickets?"

But all the soldiers who had attended the party were long gone home and would not have told us in any case what the password was.

My father assured my mother, nonetheless, and Jane and myself, that he knew the garrison well. He declared this in that expansive and not necessarily reliable way, his trust in humanity perhaps superseding the stringent orders humanity had from above. But in any case we all got on our horses and set out and expected to be lucky for two miles on an already bright night even before moonrise, in which we would be able to travel without fear of the gaps that had a way of appearing either side of roads on the island.

The Reverend Mr. Boys was with us, and an old fellow called Colonel Smith, who lived in the northwest of the island and would need simply to sneak by Plantation House. So did the Knipe family, who lived in the nearby Half Moon House and whose niece the French so loved and had dubbed *Le Bouton de Rose*. Sometimes I would develop an ambition to have a name implying beauty applied to me by the French, but most of the time I was relieved, knowing that I carried a sufficient burden for the repute I had as the Emperor's fellow buffoon and *jeune amie*.

As we traveled on horseback, the stars came out. There was nowhere in the world, said the Reverend Mr. Boys, where stars could be seen with such lucidity should the conditions be right. I remember that there was some discussion about the Cassiopeia constellation, but everyone was on sure ground in identifying Venus. The Reverend Mr. Boys then set himself to discourse on Cassiopeia, the god of rainbows. A distance existed between Mr. Boys and the other men. They let his words fall like brief showers of sparks, confident that the dark could be relied on to extinguish them. They liked him and thought he was an honest enough fellow, but he was getting to be one of those overbearing parsons. There had been complaints about some of his sermons, which were said to speak of the sinners of the island, particularly the males, in terms that were too easily transparent. I knew that he had named the white fathers of slave children who were christened in the church. Over the baptismal bowl, he did not let either parent, the slave woman or the owner, escape chastisement, and it was clear, so it seemed from what I had overheard, that he considered the owner more reprehensible.

There were things I had not known a year past but were now

somehow apparent, though I could not understand how this new knowledge had arrived in me, and certainly could not remember my mother explicitly imparting it to me.

The men of this island therefore obviously thought that Mr. Boys was taking religion too far, to the point of fanaticism, and that he would be better to preach reformation rather than denounce and advertise the sinners. The good man had been appalled at the time of the funeral of a slave to find his high altar decorated with myrtle leaves, some of them soaked in a form of blood, a chicken's or a man's. This violation of the sanctuary, like the violation of slave women, caused him to fulminate in a way that people thought was beyond his correct realm, but which I thought surely someone must do.

So the formal politeness between the other men and Mr. Boys flowed densely amongst the company. The men changed the subject, and it was characteristic in such an equestrian group that men conversed easily and women responded with the laughter of votaries. Altogether, though, we had talked ourselves into being pleased for the bright night, even if the conversation had been interrupted when our horses began to slip on the edges of a track, which by starlight was hard to make out.

We were perhaps half a mile before the moonlit junction of the road to The Briars and Longwood on one side, where Old Huff was buried, and to Plantation House on the other, when we saw that a party of soldiers was stationed exactly there and their watch fire was echoing the watch fire on top of High Knoll.

"Attention!" called the old Colonel Smith, sighting the fire, in a staged imitation of an officer, ironically, not like a former military man at all.

"Here we are then," said Mr. Knipe, the uncle of Rosebud. "They're good lads, though. Good lads at base."

We British believed this of our soldiers. Indeed, my father reflected aloud that some of them had fought the French throughout Spain, and were under the most severe orders to cage a person who might present them with further battles, as unlikely as that was.

A sentry stepped forward from the circle of firelight and asked who went there. He had his weapon leveled, and his bayonet on the end.

"Who else but a friend?" said my father reasonably. "Is there any other species on this island?"

The young man might once have laughed but was now under severer threats and could not afford whimsy. He declared without humor, "Advance, friend, and give the countersign."

He sounded as urgent as I imagined a bivouac in Spain three years before to have been.

"You know we have no countersign, young man," said Mr. Knipe. He sounded terse and wanted to get this nonsense over.

My father told the pickets, "There are no French folk amongst us, except the dear Baroness von Stürmer, whose husband is vowed to contain the French." He pointed back down the line to where her white features shone with a faintly blue luminescence in the night. "The rest of us have not a single barrel with us to install Boney in and send him wallowing off to America."

Another officer had appeared, and these verbal forays of my father produced no smiles. For Sir Hudson had killed laughter and they had the most definite orders not to smile.

The officer said, "You are all under arrest, ladies and gentlemen. I must require you to dismount."

There were satiric groans from the men of the company and cries of incredulity from the women. But then we were surrounded by soldiers who ordered us off our horses. After many complaints we dismounted and, our horses confiscated for now, were ordered by guards to march towards the lights of Deadwood.

"I could show you every face in this company," my father told the officer accompanying us, "and you would know it, sir, you would know it."

"I regret, sir," said the officer, "it is not the known faces but the question of whether they know the countersign."

As Colonel Smith, Mr. Knipe, the Reverend Mr. Boys, and my father further pronounced that all this was ridiculous and the governor would receive blasts from them, we were led across to the edge of

Deadwood and crowded into a long hut. We were numerous enough that by the time everyone was inside we could stand only, and the officers sincerely conferred with older women such as Mrs. Boys about the proprieties regarding calls of nature that might occur, but warned against frivolous claims.

When the door was closed, my father and Mr. Knipe arranged things so that the women were able to sit either on the camp cots at each side of the hut or, if they were young enough, on the floor. My mother stood raging, saying she would seek a chance to cut Sir Hudson for his vile policies. I insisted on standing too. If it went to prove Name and Nature wrong, my patience was limitless.

It was a mild night. Older women went to the door in the care of younger ones, and returned from the outer night unmolested. But the fleas that had plagued Mrs. Younghusband in the past were at work amongst us, ecstatic for such a feast, while through the slats of the window mosquitoes from the few swamps on the Jamestown coast found us.

"A commissioner's wife is here, for God's sake!" said my father.

A young officer was called. We propelled the beautiful Baroness von Stürmer in front of us.

"It is very unfortunate what you do," she told a captain. A more senior officer who knew all the commissioners was summoned and validated that it was her.

"Aren't you embarrassed?" called my father gleefully to the officer outside. And then, "How wise were the Solomons? To stay as guests of Ibbetson. If you let Madame von Stürmer loose, why not liberate the other women? They were guilty of nothing except the act of accompanying their husbands."

But such a voice of reason had no place on Sir Hudson's island. The Reverend Mr. Boys told us we must endure our penance when it overcame us, and here it had overcome us suddenly at the end of a golden day.

In the early hours of the evening there was a contest about what music should occupy us. Mr. Boys had opened up by suggesting that we sing together, "All People That on Earth Do Dwell." It was obvious the men did not go along with this, though a number of women did, and it was sung, with everyone striving to make up for the reverend's tunelessness. He had become less popular in the hut than he had been on the road.

"Does penance have to come with fleas?" asked my mother.

Le Bouton de Rose had her face tucked into her aunt's shoulder and was dozing and reconciled, or, perhaps like Jane and me, almost enjoying this, seeing in it the future anecdote. Jane had been conversing with Florence Robinson, asking how she had taken to the open ocean after a childhood on her father's farm. The army of Britain had locked up yet another of the Emperor's admired women. Florence said she had found the life of a captain's wife a congenial experience, since being an islander she had always had to look at the horizon, which in the case of a seafarer was the advised method of progressing across oceans without harm or malaise. She had learned to walk with the roll of the ship, she assured us. She was on the island visiting her parents while her husband took his ship *Chloe* to Cape Town, and then on his return she would say goodbye to her mother, and go to an England she had never seen, and so be transformed into a new person and escape the condition of yamstock-hood. Meanwhile, locked in here with her mother and father, she endured well. They were plain people, and few of the railings emitted concerning Name and Nature came from their mouths.

In any case there was enough interest and sufficient questions contained in that hut to keep me awake for quite a time and then, exhausting me with their own stimulation, to cause me to sleep in the small hours, leaning against my mother, waking often clammy and sore, and hearing other women complain of fleas. Miss Knipe now sang a little from *Love in the Village* and Jane sang "The Padlock," and I was encouraged to sing "The Waterman," and Florence Robinson had the culminating success with "The Comic Mirror."

Suddenly we were having a memorable night, with the bonus that we would take away from this hovel, all of us, an immutable contempt for Sir Hudson, the contempt we had always been trying to achieve, but which we had now been fully provoked into.

We were released at first light. Many of the men harangued the officers of the guard about our imprisonment, but it was clearly not their substantial fault. In morning clarity we saw army grooms leading our detained horses in our direction.

Not a curative environment . . .

The startling news O'Meara brought with an almost jubilant suddenness was that Name and Nature had ordered the Count de Las Cases and his son arrested and detained in that same flea-bitten hut at Deadwood we had all become acquainted with on the night we failed the test of the countersign. The surgeon was worried about heart palpitations he had detected in the boy, and thought detention in the hut on Deadwood Plain not a curative environment for them. My mother rode to the camp with a hamper for the father and son.

At the time of the arrest Las Cases had been conferring with OGF when a servant arrived to say that a party of horsemen, including Name and Nature, were searching the rooms occupied by Las Cases and Emmanuel. "I'll go and see to it," Las Cases promised, and OGF had said plaintively, "Hurry back." But Name and Nature and his servants had found a report of the treatment of OGF further to the one earlier given to Santini, and again inked on silk, in the hands of a servant of Las Cases about to board ship for England.

Within a day they were imprisoned down on the Castle Terrace. They were to be evicted from the island.

My mother asked, "Do you think the Count de Las Cases put himself in this position to save his son and take him to doctors in Europe?"

My father said, "But he is so devoted to OGF."

Yet the question remained; life, which had been direct and readable before Name and Nature, was no longer so.

When we rode down to see them in the naked stone grandeur of the Castle Terrace, Major Gorrequer was sent from Plantation House to accompany the visiting Balcombes. My parents were close-lipped with Gorrequer. He took us into a chamber not too ominous or oppressive by the Castle's standards. The Count, hair combed forward, properly dressed—"shirtsleeves" not being part of his mental vocabulary, and that fact now seeming pitiful—stood. His son was in one of the two beds. I went straight up to the boy. He had a pallor screening his jaundice and a clamminess of fever.

"I am very sorry that I find you like this," I said in a small voice, then adding, "Emmanuel."

He said croakily, "I am very sorry in return that I beat you that night in the garden." I had never noted until now how good his English was. I had been busy trying to prevent myself giving him credit.

"Well, I should not have tripped the Emperor. I wouldn't do it now. Not these days."

"And I wouldn't beat you these days. Or say other ridiculous things."

I could smell that his breath was foul from his sickness.

"I beat you because you were very beautiful," he told me quietly. "I didn't know how to state the idea then."

He closed his eyes.

I told him, "They are sending you to the Cape, I hear." That at least would avert the peril of further praise, and it would end his uncertainty too. "But in the end they will send you to England or France and you can go to an academy and meet other boys your own age."

I realized this implied a deficit in him. There was a deficit in him, as there was in me, and he was as confused by his behavior as I was by mine. I sounded anyhow like an insincere aunt and as if he were a companionable, harum-scarum boy.

"Please, when you're better, could you write to me at The Briars and tell me how you are?"

"Yes," he said. "It is a pity we could not have spoken more normally here. But the circumstances didn't permit it, did they? And I am to blame, of course."

I now found myself protesting it wasn't so with the same energy I had earlier put into blaming him for existing. Captain Fehrzen entered my mind. How would I be able to talk to him when I couldn't even talk to a male more than half his age?

"Would you like me to cut you up a mango?" I asked, with a sudden inspiration, for we had brought mangos from the orchard. I thanked God that he said yes, and asked my father for his knife and began to peel and slice the succulent mango on a plate, its smooth flesh yielding to the blade easily. Then I fed it to him with a spoon. His eyes concentrated on the fruit but not on me, and he savored it.

Gorrequer said it was time to go and I asked Emmanuel if he wanted a book. I felt a sense of loss. I had deprived myself of an ally, a companion, a friend, and some sort of indefinable accomplice.

OGF wanted the Count de Las Cases to be brought to Longwood to say goodbye before he went, and all without requiring a third person to be present. That was, of course, refused. OGF sent Bertrand down with an officer to see Las Cases, which the Emperor himself refused to do unless, again, there was no escort present. OGF complained, "Lowe must think that Europe is a mine of gunpowder and Las Cases the spark that would blow it up on a word from me."

Gourgaud, who had once wanted to fight de Montholon *and* Las Cases in duels, had somehow found a new contentment and ease of soul. Las Cases was a sort of martyr, who had to be revered like most martyrs when they ascended to Heaven or to Cape Town. O'Meara told me Gourgaud asked Las Cases to look into the reimbursing of his hundred thousand francs, and into the health of his mother.

Young Emmanuel—it had been decided—was fit for the sea voyage. Yet when they arrived in Cape Town after eighteen days, they found that, on the basis of a letter written by Sir Hudson Lowe, they were imprisoned as before, albeit in a house, and it would be seven months before they were sent to England, where Las Cases had been an émigré himself and written his famous atlas. But still, as it turned out, the malice of Sir Hudson preceded them there. They would be arrested by order of the British ministry, prohibited from landing, sent on board another ship, and after a few days at Dover spent under guard in an inn, they were placed on another ship, which took them to Ostend, where their persecution did not end.

For in Ostend they were both arrested again, placed in a carriage between two police officers, and passed from town to town, from police station to police station, across the entire kingdom of Holland. When they arrived at the frontiers of Prussia, the count was placed in the hands of the Prussian police, and on arriving in Cologne, Emmanuel and his father were so ill that they could not be forced any further, and were allowed twenty-four hours' rest.

Here the Countess de Las Cases caught up with her husband and son after having been for many days in energetic pursuit, and consumed by fierce concern for them, following them and always one rumor behind until now.

Las Cases took the chance to write to all the relatives of the Emperor, and then to the British Cabinet and to the Prince Regent, and to the King of Prussia and the emperors of Austria and Russia, explaining the circumstances of the Emperor on the island. Receiving Las Cases's letters, OGF's brother Lucien, a man of independent mind who had not liked the Ogre becoming emperor, and their mother, Madame *Mère*, asked Lord Bathurst if they could be permitted to go to St. Helena to bear the exile with the Emperor. Lucien proved particularly insistent, being willing to stay there for two years, with or without his wife and children, and promising not to occasion any increase in expense, while guaranteeing beforehand, and with a full heart, to obey all restrictions placed upon him.

I never saw Emmanuel again, and he would return not to the Emperor's history but to that of Sir Hudson and be a better vengeance than any of us—apart perhaps from Surgeon O'Meara himself.

*I*n the days of strange grieving after the Las Cases left, my mind turned despite itself, flippantly and like a compass needle to the true north of the coming Deadwood races. They were a new event for the island, the creation of the horse-mad Captain Henry Rous of the navy flotilla. All the fuzzed outline of my life, the question of whether I was a woman, the likelihood I was still a child, the question of why Major Fehrzen spent such an effort to impress me, if that was what he was doing, all this was drawn to a point, and the point seemed to be the Deadwood races.

I was aware of my rough and ruthless horsewomanship. I knew I was flexible in the waist and inflexible in the will to victory. I could ride in a manner even in a sidesaddle that other women might consider uncouth. I could outstrip the field, one leg hitched, the other, under the hem of my skirt, thumping the flanks of Gargoyle, the family gelding I had decided my father would allocate me for the races.

I would make myself apparent in a new way through that race. I would be one thing, the victorious girl, not all the many confusing things I presently was. The girl bent at the waist with eagerness, not leaning back on the saddle with hauteur or a desire for comfort, but aimed as forward as a woman could be.

I had no small regard for myself as a horsewoman—even on Tom, long in honesty, energy, and pliability as his name was short. When out with others I tested the limits of my daring sitting on a sidesaddle, and believed I was up to the ladies' race at Deadwood and that I would do well enough in the men's, if it were permitted.

I was unlucky that the races coincided with one of those intermittent periods when my father felt a passion for education and would quiz me on Latin and give me passages from Montaigne to translate. I protested as I had in the days of the cellar punishment: I was a speaker, not a translator. Drop me down in France, and I was sure I could order bread, meat, water, and fire. But the exercises of translation seemed willfully removed from those obvious requirements. Since I had enough French to converse with OGF, translating Montaigne seemed a meaningless exercise and provoked a fury in me. I both could and would not try.

I could not help also but adopt a desultory air when my father sometimes, forgetting he was indulgent, came striding into the parlor to see my progress. Then he became enraged as in past spasms, in part at guilt for his own educational neglect to this point, wishing to make up with today's severity the indifference and lack of application to the matter he considered himself culpable of. It was as if he believed that if ever I were to be admitted to any polite company, I would be first asked to do a passable translation from Montaigne or La Fontaine's fables.

"All right," said my father, on the evening before the races. "Lieutenant Howard of the *Vigo* asked me if I had a horse, and I told him no. But I now find I do have a horse to spare, since you will not be needing it."

And in this same rare bout of grimness, he wrote out a note for one of the slaves to take down to Jamestown for transmission to Howard. The lieutenant would now have Gargoyle, even if he were inevitably inferior to some of the shipped-in Thoroughbreds of the Plantation House stable. I saw Howard arrive on foot that afternoon and ride Gargoyle down the carriageway without apparent happiness—a dismal moment amongst many. So I sullenly told my father and mother later that morning that I was not going to Deadwood if I couldn't ride, and my father's quick, erratic anger mounted again, and he told me that, very well, I was not obligated to attend the races and could suit myself.

Surgeon O'Meara came down the track from the Longwood plateau just before my parents, Jane, and William were leaving, William riding on my father's horse, encased within the arms that held the reins.

I could see O'Meara discussing the day with my parents near the corner. At one stage my father nodded to where I sulked on the verandah. Then the Balcombe party set forth largely unrepentant about me, except for Jane, who looked back dolefully. I was manufacturing the purest bile but was interrupted when O'Meara cantered up to the carriageway. He leaned down and opened the gate without dismounting and rode in with whimsy aflame in his face. I stood up from my chair and was about level with his head as he advanced on his bay.

"I am an ambassador from your father, Betsy," he told me. "He is reconsidering the terms of your punishment."

"It's like him that he does," I said. "Angry one moment, and then the next, well . . . equable."

"By far the best sort of father to have, wouldn't you say? A man has to get irritable now and again and has to look as if he's legislating for his bairns. And there are some who are like it all the time. And then there's my good friend Billy Balcombe, who's kind to everyone and so must have almost by force of nature a mere occasional outburst. You should be better to him, Betsy. You should go to pains not to grieve the poor fellow."

It sounded a reasonable proposition, but I knew it was like a well-meaning bird telling a rabbit how to fly. The principles were solid. It was the gulf of nature that did not work.

"If he must be occasionally irked," I told him, "then I must be occasionally awkward. Actually, I am awkward most of the time, as you know."

"No, no," he said. "You are lively, something much admired where I come from. Who would want a girl to be supine? Not I, Miss Balcombe, not I!"

We looked at each other and a new form of alliance-making passed between us.

"Betsy, like your mother, you are uncommonly handsome and agile. Jane too, but with that florid breadth your father has—amiable features, Jane and your father. You and your mother are beautiful. You would not consider giving an old Irishman a kiss?"

I was halfway persuaded to, because it did not seem to carry the normal male weight, this suggestion. It was a fancy of his.

"What if I tell the father you admire so much what you suggested?"

"Then I shall ask his permission in writing before I make such a suggestion to you again, Miss Balcombe. But I am always open to your acceptance, should you change your mind. The question is indeed whether I deserve that little oscillatory pleasure. Because your father told me this: that if I can find a spare mount, you can go to the races, but not immediately. You'll miss the fun and games of the first two hours, the sack races and buffoonery and all the rest of it, and so will I. It's a small price. Meanwhile, I'm willing to pay it too.

I can get you a horse—I want to get you a horse. I want to get you a horse for this reason: up at Longwood a friend of ours has made a notch in the shutters of Longwood through which he can watch the races, and he would be very disappointed not to see Betsy putting them all in place in the ladies' race. I am off to get you a horse from the Longwood stables." He held up a preventive hand while his bay stepped around and shifted its stance. "Too late for you to show me a gesture of gratitude. I'd better go and do it. Meanwhile, young woman, French translation if you please."

And he waved his arm in a heroic gesture and made to the gate, and I saw him galloping up the track, ultimately disappearing up the hill to the east in the direction of Hutt's Gate and Longwood, where the Emperor waited with his spyglass.

I went into the parlor, got the Montaigne passage, and, enlivened, began working on it to the limit of my wits. The exercise did not take long, given the motivation I had, and so I went to wait on the verandah and could see O'Meara returning on his bay with a mounted groom behind him leading a magnificent gray beast. It was one I knew from the Longwood stables, Mameluke, the Arab, an echo of the long-ago Egyptian endeavors of OGF against the Mameluke Turks.

I seized my straw hat and ribboned it up and went tearing down the carriageway to meet him at the crossroads. I dashed past the burial place of Huff, and for once his spirit failed to oppress me.

"Madame Bertrand has offered you the use of her saddle," O'Meara called. "They are all watching at Longwood."

Indeed Madame Bertrand's two-pommeled saddle was lustrous astride Mameluke, and beneath it lay a saddlecloth of crimson velvet and heavy gold embroidery within one corner of which stood the golden bee, OGF's own symbol.

I told O'Meara gratefully that I had ridden Mameluke once before, on a visit there, that Archambault had let me, and that I found him as pleasant temperamentally as dear old Tom. The groom now tried to help me to the saddle, but my alacrity beat him.

"In the name of God," said O'Meara, "I have never seen a woman ascend a horse as quick as that." He nodded to the groom to follow, and we cantered off towards Deadwood. On the way O'Meara told me that Napoleon had instructed the Comte de Montholon to run a betting book on the races, and that in this book my odds were very short indeed.

"You see how much harmless joy the Emperor would have been deprived of if you hadn't raced," said O'Meara.

We dismounted, and the groom attended to the horses and tethered them to a rail, and I thought it was my duty to go and thank my father. I found him at a table in the luncheon pavilion with my mother, drinking a tumbler of punch, something that much improved his humor.

I told him in an appropriately soft, maidenly voice that I'd done my Montaigne. But his urgency for my education had been totally appeased by the punch. He leaned towards me and I heard his hot spirituous breath in my ear.

"O'Meara persuaded us OGF wants to see you ride. That trumps all, don't you think?"

A table was set with dishes prepared by the regimental cooks, and at a side table a perpetual supply of ices was brought forth from some cool place to be devoured by the garrison and islanders. I drank a far too syrupy orgeat to quench my thirst, and waited for Captain Rous to mount his rostrum outside and declare the racing under way. Meanwhile my parents and Jane talked with those illustrious yamstocks the Dovetons, and William, at nine, ran wild outside with the Bertrand boys and young Tristan de Montholon, who had all been especially invited as an indulgence.

An officer called for entrants in the sundry races to report themselves to the clerk's tables to record their names and the names of their mounts. I did so, in the line especially for the ladies' race. I stood holding hands with Jane, who was not by temperament a racer but cosier in a line of women.

At the head of the line as of right were Sir Hudson's two stepdaughters, Charlotte chatting with the Count Balmain—the Russian ambassador seemed determined to court her and take her to Russia as his prize from the island. Captain Rous could be suddenly heard, a voice that could surmount storms at sea, roaring for attention and for the obedience of riders. "Let us honor," he shouted, "the Arabian stallions from which our horses are sprung—indeed, even the horses of this island. Let us honor the Godolphin Barb, the Byerley Turk, and the Darley Arabian, the three founding stallions whose blood is represented here today. Let us honor the great Jockey Club, and the humble jockey club of this island, sending its greetings over the waves to more esteemed ones located in our beloved British Isles. And let us honor Newmarket Heath and the laws that govern the sport."

It was a curiously showy introduction to a race of six furlongs, which was the length of the course for the opening race, the one for boys. I could hear my brother William exhorting our father to let him join such a race in future.

The ladies' race was midprogram, two miles, twice around the course as measured out by the military surveyors. It would come after the mile-and-a-half for mares, the mile-and-a-half for colts, and, of course, the aforesaid boys' race.

We poured forth from the marquees again when the racing trumpet was sounded and each race time came. Sir Hudson and his wife and various officials left their tent and mounted the vice-regal stand beside that of the judges. I saw the two Lowe daughters and Adela Porteous there chatting by the base of the scaffolding. They were looking at me? Really? Yes, looking at me, the daughter of Lady Lowe's friend Mrs. Jane Balcombe.

In any case, I would reveal myself in the equestrian mode. I watched the boys' race, and a yamstock won it from a drummer of the new regiment. I saw my mother and Jane speaking to people, yet managed no more than pleasantries myself as the other races were run. Lieutenant Croad approached us with a gloss of fever on his face. "We have not seen you lately," said Jane, in a merely social reproof, and he apologized and declared that he was too indisposed to race in the regimental handicap, and that he was thinking of retiring to his sickbed. I watched Jane, beneath her parasol, receiving compliments from odious de Montchenu, despite his and Father's earlier threats of a duel. De Montchenu's company was balanced on the other side by the far more welcome presence of a surgeon named Stokoe from one of the squadron's ships. But she treated Stokoe with the same carefulness as the ridiculous old Munch Enough.

My problems began in the saddling yard, after Captain Rous had stentoriously called us. Lady Lowe had accompanied her daughters to see them mount their Thoroughbred geldings. She seemed to take a practical care by testing the girth straps with her strong little hands. When an army groom helped me onto my horse and my elegant saddle, the vice-regal woman showed me immediate notice.

"By your saddlecloth, Miss Balcombe," said Lady Lowe, "one would think that to be General Bonaparte's horse."

"Yes, one would," I said, dissembling. "I have Madame Bertrand to thank for this comfortable saddle."

"I wonder, are French horses and French saddles appropriate to this meeting?" she said, as if it were a suitable subject for a debate by savants. So she liked my mother but, it seemed, showed exasperation at me. It struck me that she wanted this race for her daughters, and they had looked like good things for it—except this unexpected Thoroughbred had arrived.

I realized that my father, in his keenness that I should ride to please OGF, might have no idea I had the Emperor's own fine gray stallion. He had every reason to think O'Meara had brought me one of the surgeon's own horses.

Lady Lowe returned to inquiring about her daughters' comfort and further testing the horses' girths. If Lady Lowe, generally a much calmer person than her husband, was annoyed with me, her husband, who made a speciality of being irked, would not react in a lesser way.

It had become apparent to me now that this was to be a contest between the imperial bee of OGF and the Crown of Great Britain—a petty sporting matter, you would say, but everything was serious on this island of ground risen so sparsely and from such a depth of ocean that small wonders became marvels, and small insults took on a scale they would not on more spacious ground.

I saw the younger Miss Johnson, Susannah, stroll her horse round the saddling yard, pointing out my error of taste to other women, including Miss Knipe, who did not seem to be changed one way or another by the news of my saddlecloth and the heroic horse it identified. But I could see others nod, happy to be drawn into a conspiracy, or more accurately to be made allies of, avid to pursue the normal girls' sport of ostracism.

I partly envied one of the Miss Letts, who rode with a standard saddle, astride, but only because nothing better was expected of her.

The trump sounded. So we went out one by one onto the track. Was there an extra flurry of comment when Mameluke and I went by the fence? So I fancied. The Johnsons and their mother, whom I presumed too easily to be in alliance, had made me self-conscious and filled the air with a sense of imminence I would have preferred was not there.

I longed to be able to bestride Mameluke like a yamstock and send the world to Hell. I felt that either way my brash success or dutifully chosen failure could be better addressed that way. As it was, the very ornateness of the pommel restricted me to the use of only one leg to give direction. It was not even athletically possible to ride astride with Fanny's saddle.

I hoped Mameluke had had lots of use from the much heavier Madame Bertrand and so was accustomed to responding to women riders. My left heel was loose in the stirrup to guide him. I decided that I would not be intimidated into sitting slovenly on this horse. I would sit straight-backed, heels down. Our grooms lined us up at the start, and if not our grooms, various gallant gentlemen smelling of spirits stepped in to do it, yelling such things as, "Whoa, Dolly!" The Count Balmain had hold of the elder Lowe stepdaughter's bridle.

When the judge, an officer of the 66th, brought his flag down, each groom stepped back and slapped our mounts on the hindquarters, as all the women shook their reins, sometimes—comically—with no effect. Mameluke ambled forth, and I saw ten women ahead of me, and Miss Porteous whacking her mount with a whip, since he too, though an imported Thoroughbred, seemed more impressed by the sociability rather than the urgency of the event.

Mameluke lunged all at once and was on his way, and I could feel through my body that the realization of contest had arisen in him. But after a hundred yards he seemed to settle companionably amidst the other horses. There were most unfeminine grunts from riders when their horses' shoulders or haunches collided with those of others. These young women became combative. I saw the afore-said Miss Porteous raise her stirrup and push an offending opponent off, and judged her even though I was doing precisely the same to the horse of a surprised Miss Knipe, who did not have her soul as invested in this tournament of vanities as did Miss Porteous and I. Mameluke ran fraternally and for some time on the shoulder of Susannah Johnson's horse. There was some jostling between Mameluke and her mount, which I would have liked to blame on her, for she came up on my right and, I chose to think, aimed a kick at Mameluke and tried to push us wide on the course. I responded by turning Mameluke's massive shoulder against her and tried to ram her left leg to an extent that had I succeeded she would have woken next morning with a deep blue bruise from the knee downwards.

My aggression was justified. I knew its origins in nature and motivation. And I had greater motives than hers. I was watched through shutters, and that awareness revived all the more strongly in me once Mameluke began really to move.

I am pleased to say that I did not cause the younger Miss Johnson the damage I was willing to. I passed her and her sister and Miss Lett, and felt a dizzying exaltation grow, even as a captain's young wife was keen to assert leadership on the back straight and into the bend and so to the end of the first mile. Mameluke's breath sounded like laughter, a celebration of boundless energies yet to be deployed. I could hear much of the garrison, and the soldiers in the infield, yelling at us, seeing Mameluke bear me along and interpreting me purely as a sporting woman, not a vindicator of a lost empire.

The second mile was the purest amalgam, the unity of simple intention between Mameluke and me. We were on the shoulder of the young wife's mount, and she turned to me with the simplest smile of permission, an acknowledgment that she expected to be passed and had been lonely at the front of the field. This surrender was delicious, yet I did not at once avail myself of it until we were emerging from the home bend. I went a little wide on the turn into the straight, but this was merely to give myself room for singular triumph. The garrison and yamstocks whistled and hoorayed Mameluke on, but I was most aware of the eye at the spyglass aimed at me.

I crossed the line five lengths ahead of everybody, and Susannah ran in second. But Miss Knipe and one of the captain's wives, without knowing they were doing it, cast a mocking light on the contentiousness of Miss Johnson and me by deciding they were so far behind that, laughing, they trotted their horses over the finish line in perfect indolent unison, honest triers who were there only for sociability's sake.

As we milled beyond the finish line, girls and women came to congratulate me with flushed and open faces. Some, who belonged to the other party on the island and had laid their bets on Plantation House, might be brisk in their greetings but were fair enough to make them. Susannah Johnson went as far as to half-smile and say sportingly, "I tried to drive you off the course, Miss Balcombe, but you wouldn't be driven. Fair play to you!"

Charlotte declared, "I admire your horsemanship, Miss Balcombe." She leaned over and said in a half whisper, "I would love to see what would happen if you rode astride. You'd beat half these officers." But then she leaned back. "I find it hard to applaud your discretion, though. However, that's your business."

I was cheered back to the saddling yard. Was Captain Fehrzen there? I had not seen him. Somehow I hoped he was on duty somewhere. In front of the refreshment pavilion men were clapping my father's shoulders. Sir Hudson was very upright on his dais, gazing without apparent interest in what had happened, and without discernible pique, even if on that ambiguous red face pique was hard to differentiate from his normal expression. It would of course have been unworthy and un-English of him to believe that his stepdaughters must triumph by reason of mere vice-regal relationship. But one could not be certain.

My mother and Jane were there to greet me, and their faces were flushed with plainest family pride. "You fought it out like two roughnecks, you and Susannah Johnson," said Jane, approvingly.

I leaned over and whispered to them, as Charlotte had whispered to me, "I have OGF's horse. See the bee on the saddlecloth? The saddle is Fanny Bertrand's. The Emperor was watching it all—I rode for him. That's the reason Susannah Johnson could not be permitted to succeed."

My mother and sister were awed as they took in the imperial saddlecloth and the bulk of this Thoroughbred. I said, "Lady Lowe noticed it before the race and thought it was improper."

My mother swallowed, aware now of the potential machinery for ill will that I had set going. She said, "Lady Lowe doesn't hold spleen long. She is not like her husband." And again a lowered voice: "But her tipsiness . . ." Its weight in any animosity could not be predicted.

Jane argued that I should not concern myself but let the groom take the horse home. "We can watch the rest of the races, and as long as O'Meara doesn't get bosky with liquor himself, he will be able to lead Father home. You will have Gargoyle back, for Lieutenant Howard, who did dismally in the officers' plate on the poor old thing, is very disillusioned in him."

I saw that at the mouth of a marquee O'Meara stood and raised a bumper of port and solemnly, though with his feline Celtic smile, toasted my win. Officers innocent of the meaning of this victory approached, bowed, offered their congratulations, and went off to ride in the last races of Captain Rous's great festival of the horse.

As the afternoon went on, the news that I had ridden the Emperor's horse got round. Some gentlemen laughed at the idea, the sauce of it, the style. Others shrugged and cast their arms wide, as if asking why Balcombe had allowed his daughter to do it. I could feel blood in my face as I ate a last ice for the day and savored my pride, my gift to OGF, while wondering whether I was an outcast.

Finally, in ambiguous air, all we Balcombes went home, accompanied by O'Meara and the groom. In my hand I clasped the small silver cup that Captain Rous had presented, with my little brother looking on in astonishment. Then O'Meara and Mameluke and the groom went off into the night, O'Meara singing the disreputable words of "Lilliburlero."

"My thing is my own and I keep it so still,
All the young lasses may do as they will . . ."

I wanted to cry out to him to ride back with news of the Emperor's joy and approval, even though O'Meara might only have the capacity left in him to find his own bed.

*T*he next morning my father, a little tremulous from the riot of the previous day, arrived at Plantation House to go through the orders for Longwood from the Count de Montholon. Sir Thomas Reade was in Name and Nature's library, and in his presence Lowe declared, "I saw your daughter's remarkable ride yesterday. She contested it strenuously, wouldn't you say? The racetrack isn't for ninnies, so it is not that she was victorious that I complain of." And here, without a doubt, his lips took on that pursed solemnity and his red-splotched forehead a slight frown. "But I must ask you how your family thought it correct to use a horse from the General's stable without my permission? The Crown stands mocked, Balcombe. Isn't it subversion that, either consciously or unconsciously, you permitted this mockery of authority and violation of discipline to occur?"

My father pleaded the fact that he had not known prior to the event what horse I was using and that I reacted as any child of spirit might when offered the loan of an unspecified horse. It was a succession of accidents and not a stratagem.

Sir Hudson held up his hand. It was symptomatic, he asserted, of the undue closeness between the Balcombes and Longwood. "I am forced to look again at your serving the French as provedore at Longwood."

My father would have paled at this. He did not mention O'Meara's part in providing Mameluke because O'Meara claimed to have his own problems with Name and Nature, yet my father was secretly angry with the surgeon for putting me in that situation.

He was clearly shaken when he arrived home and inveighed against O'Meara and even OGF for using me as a dupe. My mother soothed him, declaring O'Meara thoughtless but not vile.

After he had recounted the interview with Name and Nature, my mother declared that Sir Hudson *did* resent my win and the small silver cup that now sat in the drawing room of The Briars. My father composed himself with port and settled into his chair and was soon restored to his sense of security, with my mother, Jane, and I defending O'Meara, though I felt more dubious about him than my mother and sister seemed to. "I think," my father sighed, "that you are right, my dear woman. Everyone on the island *is* playing their own game and even two games at once."

I went to bed uneasy. Sir Hudson, who was said to be a frantic letter writer, might, at this hour of the night, be complaining by dispatch to the home secretary of my father's connivance in the Ogre's trick, a trick that I had been more than willing to perform. I did an impeccable translation the next morning as an offering of propitiation to the merciless cogs of the world and left it in my father's study as a tribute. Then I went to the stable, saddled Tom without calling on any groom, and rode out to Plantation House.

When they took my horse at the side door, I told a sentry that I must have an appointment with Sir Hudson. He saluted me, winked, and said, "Well ridden, miss."

Major Gorrequer arrived, that small, precise man, and led me down the hallway through the vacant ballroom. I could hear Name and Nature's voice from a room at the far end, directing his dire grammar to his clerk, Mr. Janisch.

Gorrequer indicated where I was to stay and went into the room, and I heard the magisterial dictation cease. The major reappeared and ushered me in. The room smelt of ink and of official paper, and the slight sweet, vegetable smell of cooling sealing wax. Sir Hudson was dressed soberly today, in a gray morning suit—no military excursions planned. Janisch retired to the corner and adopted a hear-nothing, see-nothing posture and expression.

Sir Hudson did not invite me to sit but ordered me to, on a plain chair in the corner.

"Is Sir Thomas in his office?" he asked Gorrequer, and Gorrequer said yes.

"Have him come," said Sir Hudson, not taking his watery, pinpoint eyes off me. I realize now they were the eyes of a frightened and in some ways overwhelmed man. That morning, however, I considered him engaged in the pure sport of power, and for my father's sake I had to be submissive. He gazed at me, that strange unevenness of color on his face. I crossed my hands like a supplicant.

"Your Excellency," I ventured, having never used the term previously. "I have come to make an explanation of my behavior yesterday."

I knew that I was being greeted with unwarranted seriousness. Major Gorrequer was back in the room, obviously to stay, and Name and Nature attempted to impale me to the chair with his red-lidded eyes. Still waiting for Sir Thomas, he went through his papers on the desk until he had found a passage to read, which, by its pure gravity, caused him to lean forward to reassess it. He raised the document and pointed it in Gorrequer's direction, indicating a particular one with his index finger.

The imputation—or so I thought—was that the passage was both far above my understanding yet at the same time reflected damnation on me or my father. After a time, accumulated like a weight inside my chest, we heard Sir Thomas's boots in the ballroom, and he entered.

"Miss Balcombe wanted to regale us with her understanding of what happened yesterday," said Sir Hudson, immediately.

Sir Thomas nodded twice, then bowed to me and sat in an easy chair. Major Gorrequer remained stranded with the highly significant paper still in hand. All three men leaned forward a little, as if the room were so capacious they might not hear unless they paid proximate attention.

So I began, fearing that I appeared at the one time pompous, deceitful, and childish. My father had not known, I argued; the Emperor's groom had offered me the horse after my family had already left for Deadwood.

"Ah," said Sir Hudson, raising a finger. "But who . . . I ask you who . . . gave the groom the authority to do so? Do grooms normally have control of the General's stable?"

"I am uncertain who told him, sir," I said. For how could I betray O'Meara without betraying my father?

"Did you not consider it a sufficient matter that I should be approached?" His voice rose. "Shouldn't I or Sir Thomas, in whom my trust is absolute, have been acquainted with this transaction?"

I said that I did not know it was a matter of such significance. But, I said, I had ridden rather clumsily and in an island manner during the ladies' race, and if I had in any way hurt Miss Susannah Johnson, I was very sorry for my enthusiasm.

"No, it is not the race," he told me, waving that consideration away. "I've told you—it was not the race itself or its result that affronts us here at Plantation House. No! It was the slyness—the slyness of that man at Longwood, whose tool you allowed yourself to become. And even at your age, could you not have seen that you were being used as an implement of insult? My family do not care who won a silly race. My daughters were more amused than perhaps they should have been by the entire incident. If you do not understand that it was a matter of much more significance than that, then it confirms what I have heard of you—that you are a vacuous, frivolous girl."

I said, "I believe it was Madame Bertrand's saddle the groom kindly loaned me. But she would not have known."

"What that woman knows . . . what she knows . . . is volumes. *Volumes!*"

Sir Thomas asked me, "Did you not think that that great criminal at Longwood would take some joy to see his horse engaged in a race in the middle of a British military camp?"

I said, "No, sir."

"Well, I hope you see it now, young woman," he said. "Because you have done your family great harm, and everyone must think twice now before they rashly receive gifts. I am interested in what you can do to make amends."

Sir Hudson intervened. "No, no, Major. Her intelligence is not advanced enough for her to be a reliable agent." He waved his hand even more broadly. "Do you really think we could trust her to tell the truth in any case?"

I saw with some relief that I had narrowly escaped being appointed a spy and that my father's career on the island might have depended upon my being willing to be one. But Sir Hudson was right. I would have lied. Just to tease his taut imagination, I would have reported American sloops off Sandy Cove, or repeated some similar rumor that would burrow into his brain like a worm.

"You would be a beautiful liar, would you not, Miss Balcombe?" Sir Hudson asked me. "A beautiful liar. A sweet face and a venomous soul. Yes, I principally see the General and his servants behind this, and you as a mere used thing. Do you like to be a used thing?"

I said indeed I did not.

"Then be *warned*, just as I have already warned your father."

To be warned by Sir Hudson was a frightening experience. Color shifted across his face as if there were, behind his features, some bloody flicker of the power of the state. And after more predictable chiding, he ordered Sir Thomas to take me out. The pink-cheeked Sir Thomas led me back through the ballroom and downstairs to the side door. I saw through the window the ancient tortoise grazing the lawn.

"The governor is very lenient on you Balcombes," he told me cheerily. "If he listened to my counsels, the General would not dare try any of these pretty little ruses. Nor would those who were party to them escape imprisonment. You should therefore be grateful."

The sentry assisted me up onto the inferior and agricultural-looking Tom as Sir Thomas observed the entire process.

"May I go, sir?" I asked, like a cowed, obedient girl—once again for my father's sake, and for O'Meara's. I could taste furious words now, a shame at my own supineness, but if I exercised them I would humble Sir Thomas before this soldier, and the news of that verbal storm would travel round the regiment, and he, whenever he was absent, would be mocked by soldiers. It was an indulgence I must not take.

"You may go," he said, as if it were in his power to delay me.

By the time I got to Huff's crossroads, I grew happier. I did not dare think I had saved my father, but it was possible that I had.

The next day I asserted my contempt for Name and Nature and his creatures by riding across to Longwood. The garrison still let our family through the sentry lines around Longwood, while others required a pass. Today, it seemed, I was let through on the grounds of my notoriety as such a spirited rider. The garrison had not yet been instructed, at least at the level of privates and corporals, to disapprove of me.

The sergeant of the guard, by the ditch Sir Hudson had ordered dug, declared, "You showed them the tiger, miss. They saw the tiger as soon as you prodded the stallion." I did not mind this mixture of animal images at all. It indicated what pleasant fellows the men of the 53rd and 66th could be if severity of mind and manner were not demanded of them. This sergeant, ageless and leathered, would have roared a challenge had strangers presented themselves there, for fear of Sir Hudson and of a distant government whose will the sergeant believed to be incarnate in Name and Nature.

Marchand met me at the door—in a frenzied household, he was still the center of calm ceremony. It was known that he was the lover of Elizabeth Vesey, the daughter of a sergeant in the East India Company and an African woman, and that Elizabeth was now pregnant. It was in this season, of picnics and drinking, that I began to hear these things, couched in argot or insinuation, and to understand them. I began to hear rumors that Alice was pregnant too.

Marchand led me past the salon with the billiard table, which was now a book table holding volumes newly arrived by permission of Plantation House, and into the drawing room. There, OGF, wearing a turban and a white dressing gown over white pants and shoes, sat on a contraption called a seesaw, made for him by the Chinese workers who had become loyal to him. On this, O'Meara hoped, the Emperor would have exercise while being able to converse with his partner on the other end, and his partner at the moment was the Count de Montholon.

"Our Caenis, daughter of Elatis, has come," cried OGF to Gourgaud, who sat palely by the window and showed enough interest to rise and bow. I knew the Emperor was referring to some horsewoman of antiquity. I did not know then that the maiden Caenis pleaded with the god Nestor to be turned into a man. And was. Our deity, the Emperor, signaled to de Montholon to abandon his end of the apparatus, which he slowly did to ease the Emperor's end down and allow him to dismount.

"It was a delight to see you, Betsy," cried OGF, "conquering the Fiend's daughters, and the daughters and wives of all! The servants bet for and against you, and enough were doubtful about your capacity to handle Mameluke that those who put their investment in you were well rewarded. Gourgaud, poor fellow, went so far as to put his small resources upon Sir Hudson's daughter Charlotte—not out of any sentimentality for her, you understand . . . ," and here he winked because Gourgaud had been going to Plantation House for some time, was not inhibited to go there, ". . . but because he was uncertain about your horsewomanship. Yet I told him, didn't I, Gourgaud?"

Gourgaud stood there, still pale from the liquors of two days before and not enjoying himself. But if he had an interest in Plantation House, I believe now that it was because OGF suggested to him that he might become a familiar and thus a spy there. My spy, the Emperor would have said, which would have inflamed Gourgaud with a desire to be the spy superlative there.

"I told him," OGF continued, "that you were afraid of carriages— not a bad fear to have, given the incidence of harm they cause—but that you were a splendid, rough rider, and the surface of Deadwood was rough, and that you were both rough and elegant enough—and I hope you do not object to my using the term 'rustic'—to win. And I knew you would do it for me."

"So I was a tool for your pleasure?" I said, in my own old abrupt way. It was not pure insolence that drove me on. It was the pain my father had had over the matter. And yet I decided I did not want to tell OGF about that; I did not want to destroy his good cheer, his plain, boyish jollity.

Indeed, he cried, "Oh, please don't be so severe on your friend's small enjoyment." He pointed to himself as he said "friend." "There is surely little enough permitted me."

It was true. I pulled out of a pocket in my skirts the silver trophy they had given me for my triumph.

"Since you gave me your horse," I declared, "I must give you this. If you do not choose to accept it, then I'm sure Madame Bertrand would take it as payment for the use of her excellent saddle."

The Emperor clapped his hands and reached out and took the cup. He let his fingers explore its roundnesses and flanges and handles. How could he, who had consumed Prussia, and exalted and devoured Poland at the same time, let his eyes glimmer, his smile come so easily at such a trifle? I was close to embarrassment at his gratitude and said, "You have given the Balcombes many gifts."

Including, of course, though I did not say it, grief.

"General Gourgaud," said the Emperor, "would you be so kind as to put this on the mantelpiece in my bedroom?"

Was this pretense? The mantelpiece was where Josephine and the King of Rome sat, and Marie Louise, the wife he did not seem bitterly to miss.

Gourgaud brightened at being given this small errand. He stepped forward and received it, and bowed to the Emperor and to me before leaving. The Emperor invited me to get on the other end of the seesaw, and we bounced up and down as he happily, and almost without a falter, read to me for forty-five minutes from Corneille, one of his favorites.

Gourgaud came back and, as he sat, nodded and smiled in a particular way at me while I rose and fell. My dear God, I thought. He has noticed me. I did not know whether to be pleased or to flee.

Some huge ugly insect
at the heart of Africa . . .

*W*here is Croad these days?" asked my sister Jane one day. "I see him nowhere I go."

"Yes," Fanny Bertrand agreed. "He made a brave point of continuing to visit me, but I haven't seen him for weeks."

"I don't think he would have repented of his bravery," said my mother. "He is not that sort of man."

It was not now easy to find out by approaching an officer at one of the guard posts, since they had been primed to see conspiracy in the mildest question, so we resolved to set O'Meara the task of looking into Lieutenant Croad's present activities and an explanation of his absence. It didn't take him long to find that Croad had hepatitis and its associated fever badly—he was in the army's hospital at Deadwood.

Jane and I thus rode with our mother to see him. The wind blew strong across Deadwood, but Croad was sitting on a protected verandah, in a bath chair, half-in, half-out of the light, wearing a white linen dressing gown over canvas trousers and slippers, and by him on a table sat Bancroft's book *Natural History of Guiana*.

"Oh, oh," he declared with full lips, an "oh" worthy of a thespian, as he tried to rise from his reclined position to greet us. We protested and told him to stay where he was, and he surprised us by bursting into tears. My mother placed a hand gently on his shoulder. "So you see me," he intoned as if we had caught him at a crime, "in this fallen state."

We made our sympathetic noises, and he sent an orderly to search for extra seats. Soon we were seated around him and he was composed again.

"You must forgive me," he pleaded. "You know quite well what a person of show I am. I am thus humiliated by my lethargy and fever. I reach for a gesture and lassitude intervenes, and all my pride of conversation is rendered hollow."

I had heard people say this: that the fever brought melancholy.

"You'll be back teaching the quadrille at Plantation House very soon," Jane assured him.

"Oh," murmured Croad, "Plantation House is no longer. But Nature awaits me. Your daughters, Mrs. Balcombe, have done me the honor of asking me where. I said Africa. I said perhaps Brazil and Australia. In that I should now make myself an honest man and go. But, oh dear, how lacking I am in the necessary force."

"Well, of course you don't feel up to it at the moment," I told him. "But there's some huge ugly insect at the heart of Africa ready to receive your name."

My mother's eyes widened, until she realized that this was a botanical promise and not an adolescent insult.

"But the world has become too great for my few ounces of energy," Croad complained.

"Well, as Betsy says," my mother persisted, "you'll get your energy back."

"I've barely seen battle, you know. I encountered the French when they were already in disorder. And having barely seen battle, I am already ingloriously felled."

The statement would have been laughable had he not been so convinced of his own spiritual and physical distress.

"His Excellency," he said, "has a team of officers who convene at Plantation House to read and report on the letters of the French, those that come in to them, those that go out. It is not a very gallant activity. None of us enjoys it. That's what Plantation House has become: a sieve, a clearinghouse. I read a letter from Las Cases to his wife. Oh, says Sir Tom Reade, don't be deceived by any poignant sentiments they include. For every one missive they submit to us they may be smuggling out a half-dozen subversive items! Watch for slyness, says Sir Tom, and yet a letter of Comte de Las Cases, dry old insect as he may be, was potent, and without any pretension, in his concern for two beings, the Universal Demon and his own son, Emmanuel. I thought that, of all the military things I could have done, reading that brave letter was the most futile, the one most vacant of valor."

And he shed further real tears, authentic and very soft.

My mother placed her hand on his shoulder again. "Come, you will have much better spheres of activity in your future."

When we rode home from the hospital, my mother said, "It seems that the Fiend at Plantation House poisons everything. Even honest fevers."

We returned to see Croad a few more times and noticed that his exhaustion became more profound. I did not enjoy these visits. One day I received a letter from him. The handwriting lacked the scientific sharpness it must once have possessed. He had written, "Come, please, dear Betsy, and bring your dear mother. But, if you would be so kind, not this time your sister."

We rode over to Deadwood and found him on the same verandah, being fed broth by an orderly. He seemed weaker still to me, and I remembered that there was a military graveyard, ill-visited, that accommodated the victims of this fever. I could not commence on the cheerful talk that instinct told me the sick detest, so I left it to my mother.

He said suddenly, "Do you know there are Englishmen of my era buried all across the earth? No desolation of Canada or India is innocent of their presence. Fever and shell bursts seek them out to baptize barbarous places with their young men's blood. You must all know that, you have seen the stones. 'Sacred to the memory of Lieutenant . . . of Captain . . . Erected by his Fellow Officers . . . Did his supreme duty in the engagement at . . .' I don't think I can claim to have earned the enthusiasm of my fellow officers to that extent."

My mother declared, "I am certain it will be a long time before anyone composes your stone, Mr. Croad."

I added, "O'Meara believes you will live to be a great age."

Croad shook his head. "There are murmurs of the heart associated with this disease."

"O'Meara says you don't have them." I rushed in to lie to him.

"I don't want to be one of those," Croad pleaded. "I don't want to display those predictable dates in stone—1797–1817. But it seems that I must be marked after all with such banal mathematics, and it strikes me that if you would marry me, Betsy, young as you are, I could bear a stone that would describe me as 'Grievously missed by his young widow.' Hence the question, will you marry me on my sickbed, Betsy?"

I was of course rendered stupid by the weight of such an offer. This was the great commerce between men and women, the great arrangement! And the arrangement proposed here was such a strange one—that he would give me his hand and then his death, and I would bring my grief to the party and all that would be merrily recorded in stone.

My mother said, knowing I would not be able to speak, "I think you may be overimaginative, Lieutenant Croad. Of course Betsy is fifteen, but that is not the point. The point is that you should wait until recovery has given you a more even mind."

I had already decided that I must flee, but that I must also say something decisive. "You will get better, Lieutenant Croad," I declared. "You won't need me to grieve for you. And what if we were to marry and we hated each other for half a hundred years. Consider that. Be sensible. Be moderate. I must go."

The next time we saw O'Meara my mother wanted to know if Lieutenant Croad would benefit from being shipped back to England if he were judged fit for it. "Getting away from this island would improve anyone's health," said O'Meara.

Not mine, I thought.

Sunk in herculean matter . . .

Another Christmas was celebrated at The Briars with O'Meara, but once again without OGF or Fanny. With Sir Hudson weighing and measuring all our tables, it was not the ample time it had once been.

Months past, the *Conqueror* had brought out a new admiral to replace Pulteney Malcolm, whom the navy had recalled, as if careful not to allow any sailor too long an acquaintance with the Emperor. We saw the vivid, wire-haired Lady Malcolm off with some sorrow: her going diminished the island's pool of amity.

The new admiral, Plampin, had lush gray locks and a long, tanned face. It had created something of a scandal on the island that this man had hove to off the Isle of Wight to welcome a cutter carrying a woman who was not his wife yet would share the cabin with him, and about whom the prurient on the island now gossiped hard. We remotely knew the woman, since Plampin had asked us before Christmas if he could stay in the Pavilion for a while, and the lady, Miss Daphne Bilham, was sometimes there too, the admiral's naval status overriding the moral question even for my parents. As well as that, Plampin might prove an enemy of Name and Nature's and an ally of ours.

A New Year's picnic—a fête for the island's young—was to be held aboard the *Conqueror* out on the Jamestown Roads. For the occasion of the maritime celebration, the shrouds of the ships were bedecked with uniformed and welcoming tars in ribboned hats. The young men and women of the island arrived at the docks in late afternoon to be greeted by a naval lieutenant and two midshipmen, who handed down the ladies into the cutters. The gallantry with which this was done was extreme.

I could not get over the sense that cliques were predominant, and the further uneasiness that my part in the race had given impetus to these groupings. First to board a cutter were the stepdaughters of Sir Hudson, with little Miss Porteous and her brick-colored hair and complexion still determined to act as admiring companion and thus to touch a more elevated world. She could have had greater advantages by cultivating the French at Longwood, except that she was not, like us, a flouter of mean authority. She was one of those who rather preferred it when conditions were such that the puny had authority and the paltry thus dominated the august.

Jane was by now seventeen—certain, I was sure, to have secrets; watchful and occasionally stricken by congestive chest complaints, which she bore with characteristic forbearance. She and I rode forth in the second cutter and felt the implicit force of the sea moving beneath us and the briny smell that had thoroughly claimed the timbers of the cutter, and the rowers who themselves had a deeply kippered odor. There was a sense I'd always had about the oceans, even about the business of mooring a cutter by the steps and flanks of a ship of any sort. Things seemed always barely managed at sea, barely safely brought to a conclusion. Calamity on the earth was at a polar remove from safety, but at sea the two were just a hair's breadth from each other. Even during my return from the academy in England I would wake in my bunk, or that of one of the Stuart girls I had sought for company, with a suspicion that I was being scarcely allowed my survival in fragile timbers sunk in herculean matter.

We came to the *Conqueror's* side. The cutter kept bumping itself against the landing stage, but we vaulted onto the latter. When we ascended the ship, we found at the top of the stairs a cordon of saluting officers. The air was full of jovial music, as the regimental band, borrowed from ashore, played on benches by the quarterdeck. The tars in the rigging waved to us and to the distant town, and ships' servants circulated with cooling drinks and ices.

All the signal flags were flying near the quarterdeck, and Plampin was there, with an air not so much of greeting us but almost of shyly assessing us as recruits. The Johnson girls were already seated with their coterie of female friends amidships. We sat at a diagonal from them with Miss Knipe, whose conversation was unpretentious and without malignity—not, however, without gossip. She murmured, "Did you hear the new admiral secretly had a woman not his wife come aboard at Ascension, who had traveled there by her own means?"

I said as politely as I could manage, "I believe she actually came aboard earlier, at the Isle of Wight."

My mother, reasonably safe from the town's judgment—rules became a little looser as one came to the interior of the island—had invited Miss Bilham to tea one afternoon some days before, and had chatted with her amiably, taking perhaps too much trouble to show a certain tenderness towards the sinner as, after all, the Gospels argued we should. Miss Bilham was very pretty and small-boned—in that regard like the admiral himself. She had been a milliner, an elegant one, and our family of course did not have any prejudices against making one's way by trade or the handling of fabrics or supplies.

There was already talk of her expulsion from St. Helena, and the Reverend Mr. Boys had denounced from the pulpit one he called "a man of considerable rank," who had come to live on the island with his concubine against the dictates of Christ.

My mother had taken to explaining to us that women would suffer exile for a man, often a very plain man, if they perceived wit in him. They would endure all the disgrace, their own and the man's. But it was a hard price, and not to be recommended morally or socially, for people *relished* shunning you—it repaid them for their own miseries. Such women, my mother instructed us, suffered in this world. People presumed, even when they most condemned such an alliance, that there was some extra luster to an illicit union. But it was not so. It was just another marriage but with a different kind of price to be met.

That was what she had said. *Just* another marriage. Surely this modifier didn't attach to her marriage to William Balcombe, and I took some trouble, internally, to persuade myself that she was speaking of the usual run of alliances, not hers with my father.

The band ceased and we were served the promised plates, a harsh picnic but considered amusing because it mimicked the food—lobscouse and hardtack—that sailors ate. Miss Knipe ate with a healthy and uncritical appetite. I thought that it was as well she was engaged and safe from the Emperor, because she was not serpentine enough to deal with him.

After the heavy plates had been sampled but in most cases not finished, a sailor with a pipe and another with a fiddle began to play, and sailors invited us to do hornpipes. As we danced around the deck, one hand above our head, then another, trying to be light of foot, Miss Porteous swung close to me.

"Where is your mama today?" she asked, with a smile intended to be knowing. For whatever reason, the question entered me like a pointed object.

"Lady Lowe is here," she said, "my mama, Mrs. Solomon, but not your mama."

There was a snide air of knowingness about her, as if she had more intelligence on my mother's movements than I ever would. She swirled away. She had made a point.

I wanted to say, "My mother is perfectly happy at home." But that sounded to me like too childish a defense. My mother had told us she was not sure that she had been invited, and that perhaps for an hour she would ride across to Madame Bertrand's and try her luck with the guards to visit that worthy woman. What was there in this to cause Miss Porteous, proud of her Plantation House connections, to belittle us?

All she had to do on her next circuit near me was to smile in a terse, canny way, scarifying my soul because I could not imagine what, possibly very plain, thing it was that my mother was doing. "I'll show you motherhood!" I wanted to yell after her. I meant that I desired to do some vengeance that would make nothing of her mother's being on the boat without mine.

I saw Major Fehrzen come aboard—he would have been welcome earlier, his augustness serving as a protection for Balcombe dignity against Miss Porteous's girlish presumption. But now I barely glanced at him. I had been brought down so easily to Adela Porteous's schoolgirl level, I did not want sane company.

Lady Lowe had been instructed where the privies were for the sake of young women on board. They were aft, down a large oaken corridor beneath the quarterdeck. To mark them for our sole use, a triangle of white paper had been pinned to each door.

My conversations had renewed with Miss Solomon, and even with the Johnson girls, whom I approached and who were gracious enough not to mention any quarrel we had had at the Deadwood races. They were again in the company of Count Balmain, whose eye was still on Charlotte. She had the flushed cheeks of a young woman who knows she is yearned for.

In the period when everyone was telling me that Major Fehrzen and Lieutenant Croad might, one or the other, propose marriage to me, a prospect that reality had overtaken, I felt at fullest force the nullity of this picnic on deck.

Late in the afternoon, I went by nature's desire down the aisle towards the captain's cabin and saw Miss Porteous enter one of the chambers marked with a white triangle. There was no other presence there. I was at once at a cusp. I could be a mean girl or an urbane woman. I chose in an instant to be a mean girl. These chambers were of course capable of being locked on the outside to secure them between use in storms. I shut Miss Porteous away with the commode.

Having locked the privy, I went full of a strange excitement and confusion to rejoin Jane, who was conversing with a midshipman of about our age, but a sage one who had been tempered, according to Jane, by action in the West Indies at a young age. Instead of being rendered uneasy by the contrast between my childishness and this young man's careful politeness, I felt confirmed in my perverse delight to have confined Miss Porteous, that utterer of insinuations too hard for me to interpret. Coffined in oak, in her malodorous closet, she could mutter her insinuations to the stinking air.

I decided to hold my ground and confess nothing when the dipping of the sun above the crags to the west set people to gathering themselves for the ride back ashore. It was then that Mrs. Lowe and her daughters and various others went looking for Miss Porteous. "She could not surely have slipped over the side," was a breathy statement I began to hear from various mouths. The Count Balmain, speaking his glottal English, was calling for her all the more energetically to impress the elder Miss Johnson.

There are only so many places a person can hide or be involuntarily hidden on a ship, so I would like to tell you that members of the party ran around, tears on the brims of their eyes, frantic, and still speculating that Miss Porteous had gone overboard into the deep roads. A young lieutenant found her by tentatively shaking the door of the closet marked with the triangle of white paper, and hearing her cry from within, going to Lady Lowe to allow, according to propriety, Miss Porteous to be liberated.

Lady Lowe walked determinedly out across the deck to Jane and her midshipman—for hers was normally the conquest—and to me also tarrying there, sitting one leg tucked beneath me, one dangling, a posture much criticized by my mother. I was disappointed at once to see she was not furious. It seemed my little ruse had not deserved fury.

"Stand up, Miss Balcombe," she said.

I did, but it took me a time as I maneuvered my tucked leg from beneath me. As a human I could have done it very quickly. As a young woman with a reputation to uphold, I played it to its limit of time. Then she slapped me across the face, and it was the calm authority of the gesture that most produced pain and encouraged the tears, which arose but which I did not let flow. My sister was upright straightaway.

"Lady Lowe," she declared, "you can't strike my sister."

"Your sister is the sole girl here who would persecute my daughters' friends. The *sole one*!" Her conviction was terrible and accurate. "Your sister is a nuisance to the public life of this island. A playful impishness one could forgive. But Betsy is in all respects disordered. She brings the General's horseflesh to our notice and pushes it under our noses. We know she habitually sneaks past the garrison to visit the General and the French as a group. When not engaged in subversion she is sullen. As now . . ."

Lady Lowe pointed at me to prove her argument.

"A slap in the face will make a girl sullen," I told her.

"Go back ashore by the first cutter and ride home," said Lady Lowe.

"But she is not to be hit," Jane insisted.

"If you wish to make complaints, refer them through your parents," said Lady Lowe. "You, Jane Balcombe, you . . . deserve a better sister."

Lady Lowe nodded and turned, and Jane called after her, "I'm content with what I have, Lady Lowe."

But to me it sounded a hollow boast, the best Jane could think of in such a confrontation.

Unexpectedly, Major Fehrzen appeared at her shoulder. I imagined a large cabin in which he and other officers spoke earnestly on matters of the world while the heedless picnic progressed outside.

"Please, dear Lady Lowe," he said, urbane but authoritative as well, "don't agitate yourself."

Her head jolted around like that of a much older woman as she searched for a number of expressions of dissatisfaction, only to be defeated.

Major Fehrzen said further, "It sounds as though this was a standard girls' quarrel, and not worth your anguish."

A standard girls' quarrel? How did he know that? And what was a standard girls' quarrel? But I supposed he was right. I did not want to be thought of under that light.

Lady Lowe had discovered what to say. "The Balcombes, Major Fehrzen. You have had your adequate aggravations from them too. Good day." And she turned away.

"So what do you say to me, Betsy?" asked Major Fehrzen, turning to me in her wake and not hostile but of course not in the mode of man to woman. In the mode of uncle to child.

"I say to you that you should send Lieutenant Croad back to England as soon as you can. Because he can live there or die here and he is far too gifted to be buried here."

"I don't have the authority, Miss Balcombe," he said, though he took the suggestion without condescension and with scarcely a trace of annoyance.

"I know you have the influence, though. If he stays here, he wishes to marry me so he has the comfort of a widow to miss him."

Fehrzen's eyes widened.

"If you take him to India, he'll die," I asserted. "We all know that. You must excuse me."

*J*ane and I descended into the cutter. Other wide-eyed women sat around us.

"I give it to you," murmured Jane as the sailors began to row. "You do not cry."

It had been noted by my parents that dry lids were my religion, and indeed I would not cry now, and bit my inner lip to keep the hot blood out of my face, and to give the other women in the boat nothing to stare at, which caused them to turn their eyes away. As we reached the dock, mutely we climbed the steps, and Jane and I walked to the stables at Solomon's and mounted. It was not until we were ascending the tiers towards The Briars that Jane brought her barrel-chested mare level with Tom and me on the narrow, perilous path.

"Why do you make it so hard for us all?" she asked, and I could see an unexpected and accumulated fury in her. "You rake us all back to your level, and we're paid out in your coin. Do you think that's fair? Do you know what they call me? 'The one with the difficult sister.'"

I did not know what to say to this. The weight of it was equal to all the occasional approbations the Balcombes received, added together.

"How often do people say that to me?" Jane hissed, and hissing wasn't part of her daily performance. "How often do I have to smile as it's said?"

This was too much. I had brought my sister's grievance to a head; I had alienated Plantation House to the limits; and destroyed two potential marriages in a mere hour. But in that second I saw myself as the despised person I *knew* myself to be. I was in that frightful condition of naked worthlessness we are usually able to avoid seeing. If we see it for too long, it kills us.

"Do you think Major Fehrzen finds your behavior sane?" called Jane.

Thus convinced (and I cannot deny there was a little self-indulgence left in me), I knew the only company for me were those officially despised, the French, who had never taken my pranks as a reason for denying me their fraternity. I began to spur away in the direction of Longwood, not making for the road junction, and—in shame and self-pity—welcoming the idea that even amiable Tom might pitch me into a ravine and rescue me from the packed-in contempt of the island.

Tom did his best to hold his footing on broken and boulder-scattered ground, and I dimly heard Jane calling after me, her voice fluting in urgency. If she followed me, I knew she had only the horsewomanship to go by the road, and that would do no good in catching up with me.

Soon I encountered a curious sight—all the Emperor's servants were sitting picnicking on the slope of a hill to the south, their fête coinciding with ours aboard the *Conqueror*. It was as if, separated from their masters, they seemed more real, and Marchand had his arm around the waist of the English servant, Elizabeth, who was to be his wife. There was something so unconstrained about it all, bodices loose or unbuttoned to admit cooling air, jesters unabashed, that I both despised and envied them, and yearned for some of their freedoms.

I saw Novarrez break from the party and come hobbling down the hill as if to meet me. Soon thereafter Pierron, the pastry cook, followed, and was quicker. I did not want to speak to them and be delayed, and despite the difficulty, I hitched my skirts and swung my right leg over the saddle and rode astride, my left thigh being hammered up against the second pommel, and taking a bruise on my upper thigh, which was of no importance to a rider driven by such gales as I. Glancing back, I saw even the fleet Pierron give up the chase and stand, hands on hips, mystified. So there would be no servants to open the Longwood door, Marchand and Novarrez, the two normally given that duty, now left behind.

I saw the sentries ahead, by the ditch, the great daily boredom of their task, dramatic as stated, grinding as fulfilled, upon them. I was level with some of them before they noticed.

I heard a sergeant call, "Miss, not today!"

But I had crossed the ditch by a little earth causeway and, reining in Tom, dismounted like a circus rider, whacking my left thigh a last time as I vacated the inappropriate saddle, and landing unevenly but without falling over. I righted myself and strode, skirts held up, past the rose garden and right into the house, opening the front door beyond which sentries could not intrude, and continuing through the vestibule and library and into the salon.

Before I opened that door, I felt human presences and the question that possessed me was whether to weep before the Emperor. And what to weep about? His exile was deeper than mine. My rant must be sympathetic to the depth of his entrapment. Yet he had had a life already, and I had had none. He had been praised, and I had been sometimes excused but regularly condemned. And now, for the first time, by my sister, my upholder, who had managed to champion me in front of Sir Hudson's wife, but could not manage the trick for the length of our ride home.

I broke into the salon and I encountered a scene so undue, so crowded with people who had burst the limits of my knowledge of them that I did believe this was death and instant Hell.

The Emperor, wearing a splendid green dress with décolletage that I remembered from observing Madame de Montholon's repertoire of dresses, had his arm companionably around a naked Surgeon O'Meara. That part of a man's body of which I had but heard rumors of its existence in normal life and its properties in the abnormal business of what I had thought of as marriage was red and straight.

On his farther side sat my mother, whom he was kissing. My mother's breasts were bare and her lower body veiled only by some half-cast-off muslin garment. Her breast interested OGF, who gently kneaded with his tapered fingers. Looking on from a straight-backed chair, legs apart, a very pelt of dark hair marking her groin, was the utterly naked Madame de Montholon, who had just three months past given birth to another girl whom she had named Josephine. Albine exuded a sort of contentment, proud within her round and white little body and her full breasts stark amidst the furniture.

It is impossible to tease out what I took from this scene of massed nakedness and strange *déshabillé*. The only clothed body in the group was that of the Emperor, but he was dressed so awry that it was perhaps even more startling than the rest, though nothing could be so startling as to see one's mother in such a context, with the languorous promise of further nakedness conveyed by her posture, her ease, her air of consent.

I screamed and ran out of the room. I think it came to me in part that now there was no one on the island open to my presence, and that awareness fueled part of my impulse. It was the strangeness, the improper madness of the scene, that had devoured me, and I could hear O'Meara and my mother calling, but they were delayed by the state they had placed themselves in.

Outside, I grabbed Tom, who was grazing by the rose garden, and rode through the line of sentries, who did not try to stop me. I heard two soldiers laughing as I urged Tom on and made them stand aside. It was the laughter of utter knowledge. *They* knew what drove me.

An appropriate toxin . . .

I understood that I was riding in the wrong direction. I should have been riding to the cliffs, Tom and I going over as one creature into a trajectory to take hold of the liberty and solace of the Atlantic. Instead, I was heading to the core. I was heading to The Briars and the den of my mother. I would take poison, not to obliterate myself but to obliterate the untenable island. I would need a lot.

I bounced off Tom and let Roger take him. My sister was reading on the verandah and looked at me with tearstained eyes. She stood up as I raced past.

She said, "Betsy, I'm proud to be . . ."

But I vanished inside.

I went to the pantry to find an appropriate toxin. There were suicide trees from India on this island, but you needed to be a native to know how to use their pod correctly for the purpose. However, thanks to the island of rats we lived on, I knew there was a jug of rat poison always in the corner. I believed genuinely, and with false vengeance of theatricality, that presenting my mother with my death was the only gambit. People would think I was looking for revenge, or to induce shame. The truth was I did not know what other word to give her except the very word of myself, and to do it urgently. There was no room left within me for what I had seen in the Longwood salon. On this island of rats and goats, the Emperor and my mother had joined the beasts.

I could hear Sarah outside speaking to Alice. I took down the jug from its shelf, spread some greasy paper, and made a package of the poison I poured out on it. I imagined myself drinking it in my tea and expiring at the table in the drawing room.

Having secreted it in a pocket, I called to Sarah to bring me tea and went and sat in the seat by which I would escape the island, such a simple proposition—no involvement of flotillas, secret beaches, or the like. My sister followed me in and looked at me as I adopted the posture of a statue. I wanted her to go—I did not want her to be punished by the sight of poison taking its strangling effect.

"I am not angry with you," I told her. "You are a wonderful girl and deserve to be somewhere else. But leave me alone, please."

She made a few abortive attempts at apologetic sentiments, and when I said she had nothing to repent of, it seemed only to encourage her in uttering more regrets. She was of that character: she could not blame herself enough or do adequate penance. To her, one testy sentence, after which I had ridden away, had canceled all the years of bewildered love she had given me.

"You have done nothing wrong," I shouted. "You have nothing to come creeping around here for, yelling sorry, sorry. Now please go away."

And so she did. I was giving her a grand opportunity to live within her comfortable soul by making her tame her indulgence in guilt.

The tea arrived. I laced it with South African honey and poured the powder in and stirred it. I did not know the names of the toxins I was anxious to absorb. I did not need to make their acquaintance in that sense.

I began to drink. The concoction needed the honey. I had hoped the venoms would penetrate my throat and take my breath, but it was not like that, though there was a burning. My breath remained. It was pernicious. It wanted to argue the case with the dominant elements. I drank more to convince it that it had no case to offer.

I felt heat and cold successively possess my body. I felt dryness, and pain in my shoulders and wrists. A succession of nauseas would grip me, lift me, and depart, but these were no more dramatic, I was disappointed to notice, than spasms of biliousness or mild fever. I had designed a long fall from a great height, and ended with little more than sore ankles.

So I went back to the pantry for more and ordered more tea, and it was brought by gravid Alice, and I drank it with more of the toxin mixed in, and this time at last I felt the giddiness of a fast descent, or more, a fast dislocation from place to place, in reality or in delusion being on the floor, or at the ceiling, or looking in the window or ascending into the sky. I vomited helplessly down the fabrics at my breast, but the fumes of my delirium would not quite carry me away or extinguish me. How was it to kill rats then? I wondered. No wonder the East India Company's hundred years' war against the rodents of St. Helena had not been won.

When I lowered my forehead and closed my eyes to go to sleep, it seemed to be just that, sleeping. And true to sleep, I awoke after. The light had changed, lamps were lit, my mother and sister and Alice and Sarah were fussing about me, and Sarah had my shoulders back and was wiping my vomit off my chest.

"Surgeon O'Meara is on his way, darling," my mother assured me.

The same Surgeon O'Meara I had last seen naked, kissing her and beside a frock-clad Emperor? My mother could see the question in my mind, the one that I would ask if I had the full range of my normal strengths, and she held up a hand just for me and murmured, "He is a good man; you don't understand."

She told Sarah and Jane to leave us. Immediately her eyes were full of tears.

"Don't judge me, Betsy," she pleaded. "Tell nobody else, but there has been a plan to get the Emperor away in a woman's dress. This has led to a certain . . . silliness—even older people are capable of silliness. It's a sort of game, in which we rehearse the . . . the expedient."

I could see she was telling the truth about the proposed stratagem. But I did not believe that the *game* I'd witnessed was justified by the experiment.

"Why did you have no top?" I asked with difficulty. "Why did Albine de Montholon have no drawers?"

She shook her head, not evasive, definitely postponing. "What did you drink?" she asked. "Oh, Betsy, I'm so sorry, but what did you drink? Sarah thinks it's the rat poison."

"Wouldn't poison a flea, that stuff," I assured her. "Don't ask me things."

This last command was ferocious.

"My darling," whispered my mother, "I am a sinner. But there are things to be considered. Remember how sad we felt for him the day he showed us his room . . . and the soldiers came intruding. That little room. Such pity to it. I . . . I felt . . ."

I remembered the day, but I said nothing.

She said, "Your father, he's an honest man but a weak one. He . . . you have seen the condition of Alice? It is no excuse for me. But I began in kindness . . ."

I was not interested. Her words were like pushing around vegetables on a plate I had no intention of eating from.

Darkness fell suddenly, irradiated by a lamp in the room, and time gone and O'Meara coming in and making to inspect me with that physician's arrogance.

"Don't let him touch me!" I ordered my mother, who was in the shadows.

My father held me by the shoulders, in a grip far in excess of affection, while O'Meara forced some liquid between my teeth. I felt the bitter shaft of this antidote act like a lever on my intentions, shift the large rock of my obliteration away from the mouth of the cave in which I sought to be sealed. All my ejected ambitions came burning up through my throat and nostrils. Muck and puke and bile and acidic poison drenched my being and my bed. They were so determined to make me live on with the tableau of the salon stuck in my head forever.

Predictably enough my one recurring dream was of myself and the Emperor and General Gourgaud in a boat far out beyond the Jamestown Roads. The Emperor was rouged and had basilisk eyes, not much different from those of his real existence, except that they were marked out in a definite black, as if to enlarge them and give them a look both female yet somehow doubly martial. With him sat my drowned grandfather, though I could not explain how I knew it was him. He seemed a cheery man like his son, but I realized I had failed to grieve for him because I had foolishly thought his death happy, since he had been killed by a prince. Having been myself killed by an emperor, I knew my boatman grandfather was not consoled in drowning by the elevated cause of his agony.

Gourgaud himself had not been in the salon so his presence in the boat was baffling. If the others belonged there, in that salon of iniquities, why not Gourgaud? And I knew with my new knowledge that Gourgaud would make too much of it and see in it a pledge of utter, indivisible friendship and love, no fragment of it to go to others in the party.

As I fought with shame and poison through my long unconsciousness, the intentions of the grand military machine came to a head, or, more accurately, troop transports gathered in the Jamestown Roads in numbers adequate to take the men of the 53rd away to India. If destiny had laid down before me the generous but confusing cards represented by Fehrzen and Croad, it had in view of my unworthiness, of the combined unworthiness of our family, withdrawn them. So Fehrzen, from the quarterdeck of a transport, saw the island at whose heart I lay in stupor subside, fall down, a smaller and smaller thing, below the horizon. One of the transports was fitted as a hospital ship to take the cases of jaundice to Cape Town, where their superiors would expect them to recover in that balmy port. The rest were going on empire's business to Bengal, whose strangeness would not diminish the memory of OGF but would surely erase all else. I was quite happy to be forgotten by Fehrzen.

I woke up in a flat, slaty light, dawn or dusk. My mind was confused, and I was uncertain about the distinction between those two phases of the day—I was uncertain, indeed, as to whether the earth's entire light had taken on this dour tone. My mother's whirling oval face was close to mine and had replaced the usual celestial bodies.

"My darling," she said, "no one is more precious to me than you."

I was amazed at the clumsiness of this—it was a shot that missed the target by margins hard to calculate.

"I am a foolish woman," she said. "I am ashamed. To face you even is to be burned by a flame—not yours, darling Betsy, but my own."

I asked in the voice I had left, "Will the Emperor escape in your dress?"

She began to weep. "It will take more than that," she said. "It will take more than a dress."

"It was not your dress," I reasoned. "It was Madame de Montholon's."

She nodded and put her fingers to my mouth.

"Her child is *his*. Everyone knows it. Not her husband's. *His*. And yet still I wanted to comfort and serve him. Still I chose to. I am a foolish woman and your father is a foolish man. Marriage itself is an arena for foolishness."

My hair fell out in tufts, in those days whose light and spirit were so supine. I had set out for an utter departure and managed to look like a girl with ringworm on her scalp. They stood beside each other in that light, studying me, the foolish parents. In what sense had Father been foolish? I wondered. In what strange scene had he disported himself, with his thirst for sherry and his goodwill and his general talent for merriment? In what form had he offered the Emperor escape?

So they were together again in good imitation of a marriage, a union of intents. Good enough.

"Was the Emperor here?" I asked them.

They looked at each other as if he might have been. I remembered that the Emperor in a black suit had come into my room and said, "Hush, Betsy. We are all fools."

That seemed to be what they all universally and individually agreed upon. But I was his friend, said OGF, and he wanted nothing ill to happen to me and was sad that by some means I had been hurt, and so had hurt myself in answer, as if I were a culprit. He kept on insisting I was his friend, and there was nothing heightened about his eyes—they were not the excessive eyes of a dream in which he had also called me a friend in a less straightforward way.

Once I could stand I did not make an honest convalescent at all. I wanted to ride, and when they said no I took the chance to go hiking, with just a flask of water, up towards that cave in the great punch bowl beneath the waterfall where slave Ernest had hidden. From the rim I could see my father and Jane on horseback, and a number of the slaves, including Toby, whose liberation once proposed by OGF had been denied for now by Plantation House. They were scouring the lower ground for me. Why I came down from there instead of taking to that cave and being a female anchorite, I don't know. Except that a hermitage is something you try in the fullness of soul and in a God-filled universe, not in bewilderment and an island God has abandoned for its fatuity.

In the days that followed I heard them discussing whether I should be sent to England, and to what person there. Would Lady Holland take me? They seemed to think it a likelihood that she would look after a creature broken by the Emperor's presence. Did they feel shame and wish to remove my eyes, my judgment?

Meanwhile I was blank and sullen, though not for the sake of sullenness, but because all my pretensions at upright gestures had been blown flat in the gust that had emitted from that salon when I opened the door on the indefinable storm inside.

I was remotely pleased to find Madame Bertrand ride up one day and come striding in through the carriage gate, like a woman with sharply defined business to attend to. In meeting with me, she had obviously given the order she was not to be interrupted by my sister or mother—she emanated that message in the way she grabbed both my hands as if they were instruments of work she meant to employ. My mother was in any case prostrated that day with a fever. Bewildered, Jane kept faithfully to her timetable of French translation, needlework, sketching, and reading, and seemed nearly as sallow as my mother. She would not intrude.

"Now, you mustn't take any notice of that infantile playacting at Longwood," Fanny Bertrand told me. She waved a hand in the eastward direction of Longwood in case I did not understand. "It means nothing. The Emperor likes to play games—that is all. Would it be better if the games weren't played? It would be. I'll talk to you as a woman. I do not play along with him. But I understand those who do, from generosity of spirit. What you saw is nothing—nothing! Your mama's good nature . . . they play on it. The English are sinners, oh, yes, sinners backwards and sideways. But the French, they bring their imaginations to life and . . . it is a confection. I think the Emperor is shocked for your sake. He is embarrassed *by* me, by my anger, and he is shocked, and in a way repentant, for you. Do you understand? The Countess de Montholon is full of pride for being the Emperor's mistress, but any of us could be the Emperor's mistress—I could be. It is helpful that the countess's clothing fits him. He was always interested in clothing—the Empress Josephine used to complain that he would take hers and she could not be sure of the condition of her wardrobe. Again, it is nothing! It is the French. It is not that they do not easily confront their sins. They find them hard to identify."

I certainly did not know what to say to her, but for the first time I could perceive a key to what I had seen at Longwood. Charades. Dress-ups. Dress-downs. That could be understood. My mother's nakedness, Albine's, O'Meara's, the dress on OGF. Fanny's speech helped to diminish the mystery of it all, and the scene began to make itself proportionate to my inhabited earth.

"And," Madame Bertrand gurgled, "it is well known that soldiers like other men, through being with them in peril and in hardship. So we simply overlook that. O'Meara—a sailor, of course. And a good doctor and a nice talker. I do not find him a disgrace to the land of my forebears. We have to accept these things, Betsy, and to forgive and to discover when we are girls that there may be no more wisdom in our elders than in ourselves. That is when you become a woman, Betsy. What you saw is not a cause to take some nasty rat powders. It is the onset of wisdom."

Then she lowered her head and played with my fingers one by one, teasing them forth, inspecting the knuckles.

"They all want to own him, you know. Each one to himself. The Emperor is sometimes cool with me because I do not want to own him. He wants people to be in competition for him. My husband won't join the contest and neither will I. But the de Montholons? Gourgaud? . . . Dear God above!"

J could never escape the idea that my mother's fever was a chosen one. It was endemic on the island. It not only lay on the surface of the island ready to be picked up, but seemed to chase down its victims like a predator. It had killed slaves. It made its victims yellow and wan, far more than it killed, and to acquire it offered my mother a chance to escape and exonerate what Madame Bertrand called foolishness.

One of its chief symptoms, exhaustion, kept her at home. And, as it had in Croad, it also enhanced her melancholy. My father, at dinner, said, "Do be attentive to your dear mother, girls, I know you are."

I saw him walking with O'Meara in the garden and wondered, Does he know? Did he know the range of possible O'Mearas, including the naked one who stood by the Emperor? If he did not know, it was pitiable and I was bewildered as to whether it was my duty to tell him.

I remembered my mother mentioning Alice. Had she? Was that a phantasm? And now Alice was gone and another woman had come in to help Sarah.

"Where is Alice?" I asked Jane.

"Gone to the Hodsons' for her lying-in."

C ountess Bertrand remained a sturdy and determined visitor to me under the influence of my poison, and to my mother under the influence of hers. She would drink tea with us all, but she took no trouble to instruct Jane as she had me. Was Jane's mind of such scope that it could encompass both poles of the island, the visible by nature on the one hand and that of the salon, visible by accident? I could be the Emperor's mistress, Fanny had claimed, and I imagined how she could submerge him with her long bones and ample flesh, how she could vanquish the vanquisher. She had for me the air of an aunt who understands all the children.

Before my father set off one morning for one of his frequent meetings at Plantation House in which the orders for household goods, coming from de Montholon, were matched against my father's capacity to supply and Sir Hudson's willingness to cramp, he took me aside, grasping my hand, clapping it under his arm and leading me, weak as I still was, on a walk down the lawn.

He said, "The Emperor is concerned for you, Betsy."

"Did he visit me?" I asked. "I dreamed he visited me."

"You know he will not leave Longwood," reasoned my father. "You know he is not permitted."

"But he came to see me. He came to see me because of the wrong he did."

My father frowned. "I don't think . . ."

"Do you know?" I asked. "Do you know? Has he made you forgive him too? And has Alice forgiven us?"

"Let's not talk about Alice," he warned me.

"Do you know . . . ?" I asked. I intended to be a revelator, not a betrayer.

"Do I know what?" asked my father.

So I would be required to be the revealer. I wanted to run, but he had my arm clamped under his.

He said, "Your mother is a good woman. Some people enchant us, though, people like us. Some people are too large for us. . . . They override our minds, our normal lives, make us do things. . . . That's all. Be kind to your mother."

He seemed to think about this more than I did and then looked sideways at me.

"My God, when you think of the punishment they have put him to . . . when you think of the scope of mental endeavors they have tried to shrink him to . . . it is a wonder that . . ."

"So we must all be sacrificed," I said. Indeed, though I did not know it, he was going to sacrifice himself.

We both looked at the Pavilion and back at the day the Emperor came and asked us if he could stay here at The Briars. And my father's instinct was to say, "Of course, you are welcome, when should we make way for you?" It would have been better if we had done that, moved from The Briars to some other place. My father had said we were enchanted and his word made it truer than if anyone else, Countess Bertrand, for instance, or I, had said it.

He reached across me and took my bonnet and said, "Your hair is growing out again. You must never, never . . . It would be insupportable."

Then he was overcome by the plainest grief, the simplest tears, tears from the world before the Emperor. Tears lacking in all craft and artfulness.

"Betsy," he said, his jowls shuddering with grief, "our complaints involving you are far too regular in my book. . . . We tell you too often you displease us. But not anymore. You are my arresting child, my vivid child, the one that was up to the strength of OGF . . . the one we need above all if we're to go on inhabiting the world. . . ."

So I simply turned and, in equally plain currency, kissed his teary cheek and thought it unimportant whether he was ignorant and uncomplaining or knowledgeable and forgiving. He had brought us, father and daughter, back onto the simple field in which the usual connections of families *should* operate.

I waited by him while his horse was brought and even used a hand to help him up into the saddle, where he looked at me and sighed and smiled and rode out of the gate for the wearisome interview.

*W*hen he returned that evening, he seemed in a particularly flushed state and was inebriated by nightfall. My mother could not reach the table and so it was to Jane and my brothers and me, in a dining room sadly lacking in jovial presences, that my father announced without warning, "We are returning to England."

It did not sound like a liberation. It sounded like a sentence. Surprisingly Jane was affronted by it and asked, "How did we arrive at this?"

My father answered, "Causes. Causes."

It was so ominous an answer that Alex began to weep.

"Is Our Great Friend Our Great Enemy?" asked Jane.

I had framed that same dark question of recent days, but I found in the end that as my mother and father had been acquiescent to OGF, I had in my own way been equally so.

"Alex," said my father, "England is where you come from. You are going home."

"Is Mother well enough?" asked Jane. It was one of those questions that held a multitude of other questions within it.

When Sarah came to take the younger boys away to bed, my father said, "Of course, you realize that we have become too close to the Emperor, and Sir Hudson has been frank in accounting that a crime. And he has made sure that he depicts it as a crime to the British Cabinet."

And that was as full an explanation as anyone wanted, and we sat in silence.

"It is true I have negotiated money bills that did not go through the exalted conduit of Sir Hudson. Your mother and I . . . we have conveyed letters. We are not ashamed. The man is our friend."

I stopped myself from roaring, "But is he? Is he?"

"Fowler, Cole, and Balcombe are no longer, or will soon be no longer, the contractors for the East India Company."

And my mother had bared a breast for him as if he were a child and had contracted a fever. So much she had done.

Agreed to quit the island . . .

It would take us time to understand that the terms on which my father had agreed to quit the island were tight, like all arrangements Name and Nature made, and involved restriction on his access to assets.

It was a dismal period, assembling things that had once been treasures but had been rendered mere stuff by our going, and putting them in boxes—more than a dozen years of books and toys, clothing and island mementos. Much furniture was being left behind for the use of the new tenant of The Briars, Admiral Plampin, and so from seeing those pieces static in their places, we knew that we merely *thought* we had possessed our place in the island, and that these remaining sticks of furniture would look on with the same mute patience at the newcomer as they had brought to serving us.

Our slaves Robert and Roger were to become liverymen to another family, though one of them showed an interest in the orchard and might be appointed apprentice to Toby. My mother was nursed by Sarah, and could be called convalescent. Slaves also collected baskets and boxes of our goods on the verandah to take them to the port. Jane and I packed everyone's belongings, including our parents' clothing and items of toilette, and I marshaled our bags and sea trunks on the verandah. It was grief to look out at the garden and grief not to.

As I stood a second between burdens one morning, I thought I saw a movement in the grape arbor. For some reason I was terrified, and my extremities went cold as if the past intended to foist itself delusionally on me. I could hear from within that grotto a rustling, and approached it with some fear, worried that I might see an apparition of the Emperor and Gourgaud and Las Cases *père et fils*, all engaged in making the history of OGF, and that the confusion of the sight, as a dislocation of time itself, would prove the new unmanageable nature of the world.

I suffered no such spasm of the senses, as it turned out. It proved, when I looked, that there was a goat in there. I went in and took it by the horns and dragged it forth furiously, and kicked it until it skittered away through a fence by the carriageway. I could not quite understand my own rage against it. It had filled my head with viciousness, though, and I wanted to extirpate it and all its kind.

On the way back to the house, panting, I saw, placed like a statue at the carriageway gate, Sir Hudson in his uniform. By him stood Major Gorrequer, similarly silent. A servant of theirs, behind them, held both their horses—they would not be entrusted to our grooms. They had arrived unobserved, and watched with a terrible dispassion my struggle with the goat. The governor doffed his hat and said, "I hear that your father is in, Miss Balcombe."

I stared at him.

"Is it so?" he persisted.

"I believe it is," I admitted.

"In that case, would you let him know I wish to see him?"

I said, "He is very busy."

Name and Nature sighed.

"I'll see," I offered.

I went into the house and found Father alone at his desk in the study, distractedly looking at accounts. I told him Name and Nature was at the carriageway gate and wanted an audience. He was struck solemn by the idea but moved to instant decision. He said, "Before you let him in, send your brothers to the stables—they love it there. Jane is meantime with your mother in her sickroom. Ask her to stay there. Then lead him in here please and go to join your mother too."

I did as he asked. I went then and found that Sir Hudson stood, hat under his armpit, at the bottom of the garden stair. I told him my father would see him in his small library down the hall. So Name and Nature ascended the steps delicately, and his feet fell without militant weight in our hallway, and then he was with my father. I closed the door on them, without others in the house being aware.

I knew from my earlier detention that a ventilating shaft ran up from the cellar, through my father's library and out of the roof, and I found the keys to the cellar now and went down there and locked myself in. From the table where I had slept during my detention, I heard the entire conversation between Name and Nature and his prey, Billy Balcombe.

"So, it must be strange for you to go," I heard Sir Hudson say, in what sounded like a neighborly voice but was in fact the voice of a victor.

"It has the feeling of final days, yes."

"And your treasure of a wife?"

"She has the jaundice. You must have heard."

"The jaundice, yes," said Sir Hudson, still with inhuman calm.

"It is unfortunate," my father told him. "But I shall care for her."

Though it was the truth that he was no nurse, and that he would care for his wife to his last daughter and maid, there was no doubting his sturdy aim to care for her with tenderness. It was his answer to the suspicion of shame I had helped bring into the house by my taking of poison. And there were other suspicions he had to counter too.

"You notice I say 'treasure of a wife,' Balcombe. I have always managed to be amiable to you, but you could never quite manage to be amiable to me. I mean genuinely amiable, beyond a mere show."

My father said nothing.

Sir Hudson said, "I am an Englishman of decent but not huge reputation. No man who was utterly established in his public repute or influential in Whitehall or Horse Guards would have sought this job. It is the sort of post found for a man who has been of some service. 'What shall we do with Lowe? He was of some service at Waterloo.' Let me say frankly that my wife would have expected a more spacious government post. Nova Scotia, for example. Though I understand my limitations, I have been useful to my government, usefulness your friend at Longwood mocked."

My father muttered, "I think the Tories must be very happy with you."

"You see, you cannot even say 'our government.' You have to say 'the Tories,' as if they were an alien regime. The point is that your friend seems to wish they had sent an emperor to guard him, and a pope for a chaplain, our Divine Lord being sadly not available for the task. How absurd! And as an avowedly and self-confessed lesser man, I attract his relentless contempt."

"I am a small man and he treats me congenially," said Billy Balcombe.

"Yes, I suppose in a sense he does. But then your circumstances, Balcombe, are rather enmeshed with his."

Was Name and Nature in some way going to be explicit about the sense in which the Emperor had not been congenial? I was about to block my ears when the conversation continued on a subject I was furiously interested in as much as astounded by.

"Is there any truth at all in the story one hears that you are the by-blow bastard of the Prince Regent?"

My father laughed a little, a laugh appropriate to his good days at table.

"His Majesty would have been fifteen when I was born. It's unlikely."

"But not impossible. For there is a resemblance . . ."

"We both have gout, but that is not royal blood. That is malign crystals in the joint. The truth is that my father was a Rotherhithe boatman, killed by the Prince's yacht off the Isle of Dogs."

"But you and your brother spent time in Carlton House."

"No, that is mere rumor. Sir Thomas Tyrwhitt was secretary to the Prince and was ordered to see to our education and find us positions. He did so, in trading houses, and backed me in my efforts to be appointed to my present post. And here I am. Not a prince, not a prince's son, but a provedore, for a time, to an emperor—though sometimes embarrassed by the quality of goods I was forced to supply him."

"You rather liked the rumor of this royal connection, though, didn't you, Balcombe?"

"It appealed to me when I was in my cups. It made a plain Englishman more interesting."

"That was something of a conceit, wasn't it?"

"I fear so. Ordinary men allow themselves conceits. Without them they entirely lack color."

"Ultimately harmless, of course," said Sir Hudson, with a false air of forgiveness. "You have other tricks. I would hate you to think that all these tricks you've played, harmless or not, have placed you in a position of honor, or even of scoring points. You have been indulged by me but, believe me, at a price to yourself. You negotiate bills for the General! You bribe ships' captains to take letters! And you thought that old Lowe at Plantation House was so contemptible he would not know."

"I never said you were contemptible, sir, nor do I now."

"No, you have never so much as *said*. Your actions, however, had the arrogance of a person who believes he is not observed and not reported upon. But, my dear fellow, you were reported upon."

"Everyone on this island is reported upon."

Name and Nature ignored this. "I would let you go on with your little gestures of vanity on behalf of the soi-disant Emperor, and maintain your status on the island. And why would I do that, do you think, when you were so scornful, Balcombe? Unworldly men resort to scorn too easily—they don't understand the cost—and I think you are one of *them*. Your wife recognized that I could not be scorned. And by your malice, Balcombe, you exposed your wife. Did you think of that? That I might use her devotion to you to learn things?"

My father said, "You are trying to say something by implication. I don't like implication from fellows like you." One could tell Billy Balcombe was awed and frightened, though.

"Then I can be explicit, William. While you were being clever smuggling financial instruments and letters, I was clever in enlisting Mrs. Balcombe. She knew better than you did that you were be-having impolitically. She knew that your respectable partners, Cole and Fowler, would not be flattered to have their premises used as a staging post for the General's correspondence or to give credibility to French negotiated bills. She knew that she must protect you. And so she did, by the week. Sometimes we met at Count Balmain's and

Baron de Stürmer's, sometimes on the road near Plantation House. Always privately, so that no shame would attach.

"My wife thought that I was engaged in an affair of the heart and became jealous and, I believe, expressed some of that towards your daughter, the equestrian. I was engaged, in fact, simply in arranging a dossier. Of course, your wife tried to protect you by telling me not even the half of it, to give me harmless details that betrayed no one, even when relaying the gossip of Fanny Bertrand. But remember that the General was particular to call me, as if in contempt, 'a Prussian spymaster.' Well, it happens I was, in my role as their British adviser. I lost Capri but had a revenge on that other day, that day of all days. In my role as their British liaison, I got Blücher's Prussian Army into place beside Wellington's at a crucial hour. If I wanted to impress a village alehouse, I could depict myself to an amazed set of townsmen as the critical if barely known factor on that day. But such vanity is shallow and such consolation worthless."

"I thought you rather liked impressing the alehouse in Jamestown," my father suggested, but the blow did not even land.

"Whatever you did to spite me, whatever you considered as your exercises in worldliness and of loyalty to what you probably called the Great Man, I heard all of it in substance from an anxious and devoted wife. Think of that, Balcombe, as you return to a narrowed world."

"This can't be the case," muttered my father, but there was a silence then and it grew. I wanted, impossibly, to be able to get to my father and offer him comfort. I remembered the day we went to Plantation House to avert bloodshed, and my mother, to my surprise, had been treated coarsely by Lady Lowe.

I heard a faint scrape. It could all have been Sir Hudson taking up his hat.

I raced for the stairs and bounded up them and let myself from the cellar into the corridor. There, as he was leaving, I encountered Sir Hudson face to face.

He stood before me, composed, with a mild half smile. The splotch of dead red color in his cheek did not pulse. He had the calmness of a winner, and though he had no idea I had heard him, he would not have cared if I had. Without even forming the intent to do it, I drew my hand back and struck him across the face with a closed fist, the way men did. It made a considerable noise.

He felt it but did not touch the place. He absorbed it and moved his head back from the side, where I had smacked it, and said, "Remember me, Miss Balcombe, in your unhappiness."

*W*e were now absolutely free in our movements, since in the eye of Name and Nature they had lost all meaning. We knew we must say goodbye to OGF. It could not be avoided, and though Jane at first refused and intended, or said she intended, to leave the island without seeing him, this was in reality nearly as impossible as disdaining the air of the place. Whatever each of us, knowing what we knew, would make of the encounter, it was precisely like engaging the elements: it could not be avoided.

And so we all rode over, *en famille*, though without the boys, indifferent to the snideness of the sentries who bore the number 66. We traced the familiar route through Devil's Glen and up the escarpment where Croad had mooned over an earwig and longed for zoological renown. Fehrzen and Croad and the victors of the Peninsula and Toulon. Thank God they'd gone!

We got near the long, low manor house. Slaves and sailors were erecting a wrought-iron fence on one of the margins.

"It is to go right around," said my father.

"Of course," said Jane.

Our horses were taken and we were admitted by Novarrez, who bowed profoundly to us as if we were a corps of the victorious, the dauntless.

OGF was in the salon. The billiard table had been moved out. The map of Prussia was pinned only in three corners now Las Cases was gone. History was collapsing without that strict mentor. But OGF had been opening books with Marchand in a room where Gourgaud was no longer his attendant spirit.

"Oh," he declared. He stood up straight. He looked at all of us. I could detect the basilisk eyes of my dream behind the ones he now directed at us. "This I have dreaded!"

It might have been that people wondered about the authenticity of the Ogre's intense emotions after they had left him and had leisure to think back. But they seemed utterly real. They convinced the Balcombes and had one other unifying effect on us: we suddenly saw ourselves as part of those who had been taken from him. We had heard that Albine de Montholon was also going to Europe for her health's sake. The nakedness of men and women I had perceived here at Longwood should have overridden this meeting, but in fact OGF's bereavement did. We all wept as we embraced him. No one hesitated, not even Jane. The caresses were pure, and all of them had traveled beyond sin.

"Oh, *Cinq Bouteilles*," he said, "if I were still France, you would never want for wealth or honor, my dearest friend. You would be Comte Balcombe."

He asked forgiveness of us one by one. Jane was weeping. Her pardon came without a struggle.

Nothing memorable was said.

"Where will it end?" my mother asked. "I see Lowe is building the encircling fence . . ."

"Ah, yes, my Jeanne, but you will get well in un-walled sunshine, as you deserve. There you will hear I have died in this palisade of cliffs, and you will know at last the escape has occurred."

I felt a panic at how little could be said from our side. A world must be encompassed and yet we had only our threads of banal words. I had also given way to tears. It was the day for them. Yet I had left my handkerchief in the pocket of my sidesaddle. OGF took his, shook it out, and told me to use and keep it—to remember the sad day, he said, worthy of Talma.

"And now, at last, tears, Betsy," he said, and pursed his lips and nodded, as if he had always known they were there and it was this visit and his penitence that had brought them forth.

We went to dinner. Count Bertrand and the de Montholons attended, Albine heroically unabashed, and O'Meara and a new liaison officer from the garrison, a pleasant enough man who seemed somewhat bewildered.

Beneath the floor the rats played their rowdy game of possession. "And Guglielmo," asked OGF, "where will you live in England?"

"I believe . . . ," he said, ". . . I believe that in the first instance the Cabinet want to see me."

"Tell them all, my dear *Cinq Bouteilles*. For your own sake. There is nothing I want concealed."

My father nodded, but I knew there was much to be concealed.

"I think we might then take to Devon, the scene of operation of our patron, Sir Thomas Tyrwhitt."

"Oh, God forbid, they will rusticate you by force."

My father laughed for the first time in days, and the minutes fled. The bonbons and ices arrived. OGF urged Jane and myself to eat them up as if these were normal times. Soon we were back in the salon.

"Do not worry, my friends. No Racine tonight." And he sent for Marchand. Marchand arrived solemn, was instructed in a whisper, and went again. He came back with a bowl, a towel, and scissors. The towel went around the Emperor's shoulders. Marchand cut strands of his master's hair and put them in the bowl. Each cutting he then picked up and placed in an envelope. Four envelopes. Pouches of the essence of OGF.

"When I die," he told me, "I want my friends to be able to say they have the real hair."

Before I left, I managed to ask after the new baby, Josephine, and Albine had it brought by a maid. I looked into its wide, dark, questioning eyes for a sign of its rumored imperial blood. But then, in confusion, being unable to fit it and Albine and OGF into any acceptable model of the world, I kissed it and ran to join my parents.

Collect us at The Briars . . .

Madame Bertrand had sent a note to say she would collect us at The Briars and take us to the dock in the Emperor's barouche at noon on our last day as islanders. This journey was always a risky one because of the narrowness of the track and the steepness of the country, but the idea of Fanny Bertrand shone for my mother like a guarantee of safety and sisterly warmth. My father needed to ride—he had a gelding to deliver to one of the town's merchants.

The older Archambault brother rode postilion with another servant. When we pulled out, I did not take a last doleful scan of The Briars, for I had done that already. I had interred the house and its gardens in my mind, and no longer had any meaningful sight left to take of it. I noticed that beside Fanny Bertrand my mother looked cooler under her big hat and a net of mantua lace, as if she were suddenly the one most willing to escape the rock in the great sea. After we transited the shade of the carriageway, with Father riding ahead, and came to Hutt's Gate on the main road down to Jamestown, I had enough distance on all this geography to be dourly amused that in burying Huff at that place, as if to bury his shame, they had given his name a prominence that might last more years than had he been buried amongst the just of St. Matthew's Church on the island.

Fanny Bertrand was attentive to my mother, consolatory to my sister, and nervously tender towards me. Her gestures remained those not of formality but of unforced friendship. She made a com-

369

ment to my mother and pointed away towards her right, where at Deadwood Camp many huts had by now replaced the tents of that barren zone, and new soldiers the ones we had met in the high days. My mother turned her head to look in that direction but saw nothing to engage her.

We reached the gap in the coastal heights, where the tiers down to the port began. I sat in the barouche beside my sister, and I saw the plateau and its peaks disappear by small degrees and suffered from a sense that proved accurate—I was losing the geography for good. How convenient if the barouche, with all the questions it contained, had its wheels slip on one of the track-side precipices and we went tumbling down, our now too-knowing skulls and bodies crushed with every revolution of the vehicle's fall beyond control.

It didn't happen. I saw the redoubts at either end of the gap and their watchful cannon, and they seemed more eternal to the island than I had been.

There was some comfort in the town. A number of shopkeepers, and Mr. Porteous, were on the pavements to raise their hats as my father and the barouche rode by. At a front-floor window of the Portions I beheld the smirk of Miss Porteous. A number of army and naval officers in the street, men who had at one time dined at our table, saluted us as we passed. There was a regard for my father that was not to be despised in these gestures. He could learn from them, if not too depressed, that Lowe's view was not the island's view of him.

At the dock itself waited the Solomon family, and the Counts Bertrand and de Montholon. I think I saw distinctly in their faces the strain of *not* going, the temptation of escape that we unwillingly represented. I would have changed places with them happily: those who must go but want to stay; those who must stay but want to go. Bertrand moved amongst us with his normal air of courtly wariness. He kissed my mother's hand, ours; he even bent to Fanny's hand devoutly. He assured us in his fluid voice that the Emperor was inconsolable to lose us. More friends gone, OGF was said to have lamented. More true friends. It wasn't the day to ask with an edge in what regard the Ogre was inconsolable about my mother. Bertrand laid the softest of touches on my wrist. "He tells you, Betsy, to forgive him and then forget you knew him at all, as if you had never met."

The pious absurdity of this tempted me to crazy laughter, yet again it was not the day for such things.

"Tell him that's ridiculous," I said.

"I know," said Bertrand, "and he knows. But you might be happier if you could."

As he went to speak again to my father, Fanny Bertrand drew me aside and, enveloping my shoulders with her arms, walked me a little way along the dock. "Have you forgiven me? You know that women conceal these things for each other, and for the good of families. Forgive me before you go, Betsy."

She had the air of someone who had revelations for me. I had revelations for her, if I chose to repeat what I had overheard from Name and Nature. I held them back to pursue further about sisterly hiding of secrets.

"How long did you hide it for my mother?"

"Perhaps some months. Not six."

"And this is friendship? Or is it crime?"

"How can I answer? It was apparent the Emperor needed her so sorely."

"*We* needed her sorely. We were the ones who were her duty. She had no duty to attend to the Ogre's sore need." I felt the too familiar cruelty rise in me. "In any case, I can tell you that you were concealing nothing, since she betrayed all you said to Sir Hudson. Taking the gift of your words to *him*."

I wanted to see her shaken as I had been shaken. I wanted her to grow aghast. But she laughed without shock or enmity. "Oh, I knew that! I trusted her. She is no one's fool. Just harmless gossip, my stock in trade. And items of no consequence."

"You knew about that? Jane doesn't know."

"And no need to tell her. Yes, she told me what the Fiend demanded of her. She gave me undertakings, and then she told me what she'd told him and we laughed. For Sir Hudson has a wonderful trait: he mistakes quantity of news for quality. That is the sort of man he is."

"O'Meara says that too," I remembered in a daze.

"Yes, it is in that spirit that he guards the Emperor and weekly offends him by many new little quantities of straitening. And she gave nothing away of substance about Our Great Friend. The three of us would laugh at the things she told Sir Hudson. Since he thought his locating of her with the Emperor was a masterstroke. Even laundry lists, if she'd sent them from within Longwood, would have resonated with him. She talked, and Sir Hudson was happy."

"The Emperor too? *She* told him?"

"It was a game. It was all a game."

This made me near choke with fury. "But she did not tell her husband. My father wasn't party to all this worldly laughter and this poisonous game!"

"Well, your father is part-citizen and part-saint, and it was for love of him that she—"

"Or for love of the Ogre?"

"I think your sainted pa has absorbed that and all else with great courage. Be kind to him."

A new, revelatory suspicion rose as late as this, on a stone platform above the Atlantic, the last whisper of earth.

"Are you saying my father knew about . . . my mother and the Ogre?"

"You think that we are powerful actors in the world. But we are all hostages, Betsy, and the best people, not the worst people, are victims of pity. If your mother pities the Emperor, did you think your father wouldn't? Your mother is an honest woman and does not like to keep secrets. But she could not tell him about the monster she fed with supposed intelligence. She could confess it to OGF, but your father . . . with him there was the matter of his pride. That was a terrible thing for him to know—that he was protected from the Fiend. And it was not by his wits but by his wife."

"How could my father know the other, Fanny? How could he be calm about it?"

"That's . . . I don't know. . . . That can only be revealed if you have been through it yourself."

"I took the poison," I said. "He could be calm and I took the poison."

"I know. I know, Betsy."

"I am disgusted by you all," I decided.

"No. You have an excellent mother and an excellent father, and that must be your yardstick. They will need you in these bitter days. You should be filled with pity. One day, when you think of it, you will be."

"Not if it leads me as it's led them. I don't want to feel any pity."

But I knew it was an impossible ambition. In the midst of my ferment a cutter had landed and a coxswain was bawling for passengers to our ship, *Winchelsea*.

It meant our belongings were in the hold and our cabins awaited. We descended, I yielding, I confess and bitterly regret, merely a shake of Fanny Bertrand's hand.

As the ship left the shore, and all the way out to the vessel, I narrowed my gaze and kept my eyes down. I gave no last wave to anything. But across the water came a baritone chorus of shouts.

"Good-by-y-y-e, Pri-i-ince!"

AFTER-PAYMENT

Explaining-himself sessions . . .

hen we first arrived at the new East India Docks aboard the *Winchelsea*, my mother seemed less gray in the face than she had been on our leaving the island. I knew—since I still listened as much as I could, and because the cabins on the ships were small and gave onto a shared saloon—that my father had been solicitous during what had been by everyone's estimation an amazingly clement journey, with a pleasant four days ashore on Ascension Island, part of it spent riding from Georgetown into the verdure of the hills.

On Ascension Island we had been made very welcome by the representative of Drummond's bank, who had children about my brothers' ages. My father was mystified that when he presented a note to be cashed, the young man was embarrassed to tell him that London had placed some impediment in the way of his presenting notes, but that he should not be concerned—it would be sorted out in London, and, in the meantime, all our expenses would be settled by a Sir Thomas Tyrwhitt, and he, the banking agent, was authorized to remit my father a modest amount for incidentals. Did my father know this Sir Thomas Tyrwhitt? he asked. My father did. "I will see Lady Holland about this," said my father at table, when his anxiety spilled over. "She is a friend of the Emperor's and does not think anyone should be penalized for it."

After we left Ascension, he spent three days in his bunk, though the weather was good and he would usually have been more active on deck or reading in the saloon. I was grateful that by now we had by mutual signals decided that what had passed on the island was too grievous to consider and certainly impossible to discuss. There are some events so engorged that our only choice is to ignore them. That was the spirit in which we had resolved to face Britain. We hoped we would be permitted to be ourselves again.

In the Channel we encountered a luminous but opaque grayness, which did not disperse even a little until we were on the Thames and off Gravesend, where we could see creaky-looking buildings in the dusky air over the banks. This was my homeland, and the children running on the banks my fellow countrymen.

Entering the locks into the crowded basin of the East India Docks, we found ourselves in dizzying company, our three masts merely three trunks in a great forest. The air was hazed still, and it did not seem to be the atmosphere in which the banking issue would be settled. My father was dressed to settle it in a good navy suit and blue waistcoat. But our concern did not echo here.

From a coach at the dockside emerged the compact form of little Sir Thomas Tyrwhitt, soberly dressed and with intense, businesslike eyes but a smile I believed uncertain. He came aboard as soon as the gangplank was down. On deck he greeted us pleasantly. "I remember my last conversation with Betsy, who has grown considerably," he murmured overpleasantly (or so I think in retrospect), after praising Jane and the boys. With him was a nurse who took my brothers aside and entertained them with a card game across the deck and beyond the saloon lights, on the ship's non-business side. Jane and I strolled over there too—my father must have an earnest talk with the knight whose name so resonated in our family—and while the nurse showed some skill in entertaining the boys, we looked across the dock at the faces of warehouses, trying to find something informative in the hectic traffic of goods, wagons creaking in empty and going out loaded with everything from rum barrels to tea chests and curry powder. And through it all the male voices of many purposes rising from ship and dock and bouncing round the echoing clouds. It was so much more vastly busy than the island that it gave me the idea I did not know what haste was and so was fatally unsuited for this nation. I felt overwhelmed and doubted I could run its race.

Sir Thomas Tyrwhitt took my mother and father, who might have been able to read and interpret the scene for us, into the saloon. I wanted my father to be beside me, to read England for me—that enormous and impregnable book.

When my parents did emerge with Sir Thomas, the little knight had a look of wisdom validated. I saw a gratified reflection of his glow in my mother, but more doubt in my father. In other words, she was buoying him up. If he had had to take account of my mother's health as a motive for leaving the island, it seemed now that his was at most risk. There were solemn handshakes between my father and the knight.

There were duties and conferences my father had to attend to in town, and Sir Thomas told us we might be in London a few months before we were to go to a house set aside for us in an area of Devon in which he had business interests. Until we reached that haven or retreat or place of detention, we would live in London residences provided by him.

Our luggage was placed on the roof and back ledge of the coach. What did not fit was put in the hands of a carter and, Sir Thomas said, would be with us by that afternoon. There is so much to exercise the mind of a home-returning Briton on a gray day! More to try to discern than on a bright, revealing one—and all that without other impending issues—like money, the censure of government, the feeling that Sir Thomas was both more and less than a friend, that he was put in place by high authority to be our keeper and monitor. To add to our unease, my small brothers were stupefied by the place and its scenes and had never known the earth held this many loud fellow beings, so many vehicles, and such masses of shops and chapels and stalls and warehouses as the East India Dock Road held, and so many cries from men and women and urchins selling things in amazing ways. We watched girls dragging carts of oranges and calling, "Fine Seville oranges, fine lemons, fine . . ." There were watercress sellers, pie men carrying little portable ovens and assortments of gravies, vegetable sellers shouting their jingles in praise of cabbage or turnips, Jews crying out for old clothes. There were milkmaids, ink sellers, knife grinders, egg girls, and all of them clamorous to be heard above their vending brethren. In the coach, Alex buried his face in the hollow of my mother's shoulder and Jane herself was milk-pallid. How would my father plead cases amidst those other voices and match them for urgency?

The coach took us to a good house in a court off New Oxford Street and our spirits lifted. We did not fully understand that it was a mere holding pen for the Balcombes—I have since decided—to allow our father to be quizzed by high officers and even secretaries of state about his friendship with OGF. Sir Thomas had handed my father an amount from funds, but whether they were his funds or the government's or ours, I was never sure, and was always embarrassed to ask. The knight then called on the housekeeper to show us the house, said that the nurse was on her way to attend to the boys, congratulated my mother and father warmly on their handsome girls, and left, with a promise of future meetings.

Shown our rooms, Jane and I discussed whether Sir Thomas was a friend, a kind of parent. His care for us seemed exaggerated unless it had been ordered by a grander power still. His smile was that of a barterer—if William Balcombe and his wife behaved well, they would go on receiving it. Yet everything Sir Thomas did for us had an element that did not quite live up to the cheery benevolence he emitted. We would come to realize that there were reasons for this. There had arisen in the press a frenzy about a supposed escape plot in favor of the Emperor. This was purely to justify policy, but the claim was that Englishmen were involved. We had arrived in London at the peak of this rumor, and thus in a bad climate for my father, whose name was mentioned in some of the wilder versions. Thus we had, it seemed, landed ourselves unwittingly within the ambit of those who most wished to interrogate him. Sir Thomas was mediator between the great men who had an interest in this tale and Billy Balcombe, already a suspect. That might have explained the equivocation in the knight's smile that first day.

We seemed suddenly to be living, like the Emperor on the island, on a budget, an experience we had not ourselves had before. For causes unexplained, Admiral Plampin's rent did not arrive. Certainly we could afford bread and milk and meat, but the sense of plenty was gone, with the mangos and guavas, the nectarines and oranges. Who had made the limits of the budget for us? My father was all at once the most secretive man on that score.

Tyrwhitt remained our shepherd. Why? One thing was that Father had written too often to the Prince about the Great Ogre, which unsettled the Prince and gave him doubts—he was believed to be prone to such claims, and those around him thought it better to save him from having to encounter them. So now was my father considered disloyal, and the Ogre's man?

This was not a pleasant time under any aspect. I wondered—I wonder still—if they had used the power of the state to freeze his savings, a most un-British thing for them to do. His nominal partners, Messrs. Cole and Fowler, in the ship-provisioning business my father had run with them on the island, had—further—not wanted to communicate with him, as if they'd been warned off. Altogether, dreadful things had been done to this overtrusting, genial man. It was all a mystery. Were we truly poor or the victims of assets seized in politics' name? It seemed to me by the time we left New Oxford Street and moved out along Finchley Road, preparatory to our final domicile in Devon, that my parents had become government pensioners, and lived sparingly as pensioners do. For them, it was a new mode. My father was soured by it.

Our friend from the island, Barry O'Meara, we then heard, had been ejected himself soon after us and for similar reasons. He was now working as a dentist in Edgware Road because they had taken away his membership of the College of Surgeons. So they were certainly able to deprive my father of savings and income. My father always returned from his explaining-himself sessions wan, and then drank a lot. Later he would tell us that some of the more extreme advisers to government ministers wanted him tried for treason. I heard him, with an elevated shrill, not utterly sober voice, tell my mother, "They believed I was enriching myself by sending the Emperor's letters on. I took only enough money from Bertrand to encourage ship captains to take this or that item to France or America. How can I give them the names of the captains without betraying men who were friends of mine and sat at our table? So they think I spent it on myself." And so they would conclude that he had transmitted the Emperor's letters and money bills for pure profit, and this was a good thing since it put the likelihood of treason trials behind him, but a bad thing because it made them think of him as someone who sold his soul and relatively cheaply. His higher states of anxiety were slowly replaced by depression.

I would find out later still that he was suspected of involvement in escape plots.

A card delivered to the first house we occupied off New Oxford Street invited us to visit Lady Holland. It was an indication of her influence and insistence that the card was permitted to reach us.

When the invitation came, my father began to hope again, for Lady Holland had been threatened too for her enthusiasm for the Great Ogre and, as the absolute Empress of Whiggish England, had laughed it off—or so we had been told.

We had the use of a carriage, which had earlier brought us from the East India Dock, and on the afternoon mentioned in the invitation we set off for Holland House in Kensington more used to London now and its clamor, less frightened bowling along in sunlight through pleasanter reaches of London and well-ordered parklands.

In the coach, we were told by my mother, and my brothers were specially warned, that Lady Holland had been "a wonderful friend" to the man we had known on the island and sent him books and delicacies and had tried to persuade those in power to set him free. So, my mother explained, we must not laugh if Lady Holland seemed . . . odd. "Any more," she said pointedly, "than we would have laughed at Alex for being frightened of the city." We were very fortunate, my mother told us, et cetera, et cetera. The point was made, and it would prove a necessary one: Lady Holland was married to a great man. The pathetic thing was that we did not know which direction deliverance might come from and must expose ourselves to every chance.

Hers was a prodigious house set in a garden of oaks. As the carriage advanced towards it, I tried to count the windows, ending at forty-nine before we had reached the portico, less than halfway through the count. There seemed to be towers beyond, as if the house stretched on and on. When we arrived, footmen ran out to arrange our descent and our advance into the great hall, and then into a drawing room the size of Plantation House on the island. We were told to sit on plushly upholstered chairs and that Lady Holland would be with us very soon.

When she came in, she did so forcefully. The door swung open and she strode forward on long legs, wearing Mantuan lace over brown hair, a woman of about my mother's age.

"Oh, my heaven," she said to my mother. "You have five. Any died at birth?"

My mother, astonished, but doing her best, said no.

"But you're closing the account now, aren't you, good madam, while you still have something of yourself left? As am I. Wise woman! *Wise* woman!"

She was accompanied by a spaniel. When she told us all to sit again and she sat, it placed itself before her long legs and stared worshipfully at her face. From all I ever knew of her, extraordinary woman that she was, she was not averse to worship. Her tallness and her exceptional bluntness brought back the island, and dear Madame Bertrand, who was still on it, and who didn't mind speaking of womanly issues in front of children.

"I heard that one of you is called Betsy," she said, "my name, as it happens. Which one of you is called Betsy? Hand up."

I had met my match. I said, "It is me, m'lady."

"Well," said Lady Holland heatedly, "I am very pleased to share that name with such a pretty girl. Hair color more or less like mine, no? Ah, yes, a young woman with a future. Not that you, dear," she said, addressing Jane, "need worry for your future either."

She was more content with consigning us to unassisted destinies than we would have liked her to be. Tom began to smirk and my mother glared him down, terrifying him back into the upholstery.

More formal introductions now succeeded the raid of frankness with which Lady Holland had instituted proceedings.

"I'm sorry Fox isn't here," she told us. "He's engaged in some Whig business to do with Catholic emancipation. Not to be despised, that issue. If we are to free the slaves, we must also free the Irish. In any case, I must thank you for having been kind to my dear friend, or more accurately my admired acquaintance, the Emperor Napoleon. Fox and I were traveling in Spain and came up to Paris just after the peace of 1802, and we met him and I knew he was a new kind of man, a man Europe had not seen before. I felt I was meeting a man of the future, a man who foresaw a new Europe and a new humanity, and . . . ," she dropped her voice an octave or two, ". . . whatever his flaws, as we all have them, that he envisaged something that stood above our narrow grasp. Did you feel that way too? Meeting him? On that island, however clipped his wings?"

My mother and father both said they had certainly felt that. My mother also said, "He appreciated what you sent him, especially the books."

"Well," she said, slamming her hands down on either arm of her chair, "to neglect providing books to such an intellect . . . I hazard Sir Hudson—and Lords Bathurst and Liverpool, for that matter—can get by splendidly without books simply by following their narrow natures. But the great souls can't! Books are their breath."

"Indeed," my father agreed.

"Oh," said Lady Holland, "you have been good friends yourselves. Tell me, tell me, have you suffered?"

As we all sat there, we were aware of my father's suffering, of our own bewilderment, and perhaps it was a time when our fortune spun on the rim of a word and would fall one way or the other. And then my father, as if he came from a place like this, Holland House, as if he exercised a similar influence, moved by pure pride and the scope of the architecture, said, "No. There is nothing directed my way that I cannot manage."

Again, Lady Holland slammed the arms of her chair. "I am so relieved. Please, do you have any needs?"

I saw my mother's middle fingers caress the inside of her nose bridge by the eye as if to say, "For dear Christ's sake, tell her. *Tell her!*"

My father said, "You should not worry yourself about this. I am a lesser figure, yet I have patrons, including of course yourself, and I have no doubt that my family and I shall flourish now we have returned home."

"But no immediate wants?" asked Lady Holland, looking sideways and searchingly.

We all awaited the answer, the chance of escape from Sir Thomas's supervision and, even if by Lady Holland's appeal to the liberal spirits of Britain, from the bullying of the Cabinet.

I understand that he could not plead with her to get the intimidators off his neck. I understand it all now. But we were doomed to the monitorship of Sir Thomas Tyrwhitt from that proud point, when my father pretended he was above help. The opportunity that some brilliant writer from her salon should plant a piece about our misuse in the *Quarterly Review* and win us back the stature Sir Hudson had taken from us was one he refused to entertain. He would rather have died. And before many years, when we were sent into the far imperial province of Judea (a Messiah-less New South Wales), that was what he would do.

To whom I was married . . .

*C*uriosity *alone, as well as* chance sightings of us at church, caused a number of young men to be sociable with Jane and me. Several were clerks in the businesses of Sir Thomas Tyrwhitt. Edward Abell was not like them. He was a former soldier of the East India Company and had seen battle against those plunderers of India, the Pindaris. His stories were only in part about the great encirclement of these desperate tribesmen. Most of his conversation was about his fellow officers and their gambling contests, which tickled him so much that I in turn was tickled. For some reason he had a letter of introduction to Sir Thomas, and I first met him in the London house we occupied for a while near New Oxford Street. I should, then, have mistrusted his good manners and ease with compliments. I did know by instinct that he issued so many protestations that, like a mint producing too much currency, he was in danger of devaluing that coinage of which he was so verbally profligate—our coming eternal union. But I had been trained, by encountering great artists of the lavish, and one great artist in particular, to be both enchanted and rendered mistrustful of it; as so often happens in courtships, flamboyant compliments can outshout the calmer warnings about coming events. And as a suitor Abell, ten years older than I, was boyish enough to laugh when I played the reliable old tricks on him, the trippings-up, the skillful hiding away of oneself in the landscape, the taunts in blindman's bluff. He was a tall man of an apparently yielding temperament, was natty, and had a salary about the same as the allowance from my father's remaining wealth permitted to our family. For a young man that was not so bad an income.

Abell moved to our region in Devon, as if to consider working for Sir Thomas's enterprises there, and became a regular visitor to our damp country cottage in Exminster. He inspected Prince's Town, Tyrwhitt's prisoner-of-war camp on Dartmoor, which included the township that had grown around it while the war against the Ogre lasted. Sir Thomas had seen it as a place to hold French and American prisoners in a high-up jail far from ships. Nine thousand prisoners had once been held there, and a village and farms had grown up around the prison, to sell things to the guards and captives alike. To ensure Prince's Town would continue in existence, Tyrwhitt had gathered gentlemen into another scheme to build a Plymouth-to-Dartmoor horse-drawn railway; the act to empower it was already passed, and cuttings were being dug.

Abell had talked intermittently to my parents and me about returning to India, and my parents had said that, should we wish to marry, in these depressed times they could find no grounds to oppose it, bitter as the separation might be. Abell's eyes were alive at the chance of reviving his earlier adventures, but on the civil level. I believed I could manage him. As well as a cure for longing and possible shame, my marriage would leave my father with one less mouth to feed out of whatever seepage of funds came his way. I was in love and suddenly aware of how easy it is to succumb. When I was already enceinte with our child, who proved to be a daughter, I married Abell by license at the altar of St. Martin's, Exminster, the year after the death of OGF.

Though early in our marriage he still praised my spirited, unconforming nature, he all too quickly came to see me as merely blunt and stubborn. After an argument about his staying late somewhere and losing money at cards, he declared that I was the most vulgar woman he had ever met. When husband and wife insult each other, it's always with superlatives.

"That's the exact case why we should take a subsidized immigration to some colony," he said. "Your rawness will not stand out as much in the New World."

I can remember asking myself on one occasion why I had married such a sawney child. And soon after it was known I was pregnant, I cried out impolitically, in his presence, "What, two children to raise?"

"I was man enough to produce a child," he asserted and pleaded. And indeed he was. He was not a man lacking in vital forces. There had been delight in our connection and I should not pretend anything else.

Almost as soon as we married, he became restless about the incipient child, and anxious in a new way. Even as he mimed delight, I could tell that he saw in the imminence of this baby the beginning of a number of them, little apostles of domestic sordidness who would drag him down and weigh on his chances and his ability to wager. I saw his eyes scudding around the walls, calculating how much infantile squalor they could contain without bursting their limits and poisoning the wellsprings of all his hope.

"If you are not delighted," I told him, "I expect you to have the courage to tell me. You know there are methods—including abstinence—by which people do not have children, but you have not shown any appetite to avail yourself of them. . . ."

I did not fully understand, however, how seriously frightened he was, how certain he was of his grand error, how determined he was to amend it. And I had not realized that the island and OGF abided in me or that I troubled him with their memory. Except when he might say, "Will I always be a stranger to you because I was not on that damned island?"

Given that the shivered rock of my parents' marriage had stood up to gales and shocks and deceptions, remaining as the one creature from beginning to end, I did not expect so much fast change and volatility in my connection with Mr. Abell. But after the birth of Bessie, he was more resistant to my past than ever.

"The island is nothing!" he ranted once. "Your so-called OGF is a criminal, the greatest who drew breath, and now he is dust, and deserves to be. You will not let go of the dust, you fool of a woman."

I asked him not to awake our daughter.

"The future is with the Plymouth and Dartmoor Railway, with Thomas Tyrwhitt. The Monster is with the Pharaohs! Let them all go!"

But he would be the one who disappeared a few weeks later. He abandoned not only me but Sir Thomas's Plymouth and Dart-moor Railway, the great penitentiary buildings of Prince's Town, and any delusion he had harbored about how Sir Thomas Tyrwhitt favored us.

He also took all my jewelry.

Knocking of a polite rhythm . . .

Two years after OGF's death, and some time after the birth of Bessie, and Edward's disappearance, when I, defeated by matrimony, had moved back into my parents' house with my baby, one day knocking of a polite rhythm was succeeded by a more insistent kind from the same fist. The volume and frequency grew, like a prelude to ramming our door open, and we knew it wouldn't take much with the rattly old portal of our country cottage.

My father deliberately settled himself by the fire and picked up a copy of the *London Chronicle*—he knew it was a paper that transmitted a signal, a paper that had been hostile to Name and Nature and kindly disposed to OGF. My father no doubt wished he had a *Quarterly Review* at hand, the journal Sir Hudson really abominated.

Under the barrage of knocking, my mother pointed us to chairs where there were books for us to take up. "I shall open it," she determined.

When she did that service to the front door, she performed it suddenly and surprised the servant midpummel. "Is there a fire nearby?" she asked him. "Are you here to warn us?"

He stepped back without a word to allow Sir Hudson to occupy our door frame. She was as silent and un-amazed as she could manage, indeed as if she did not recognize Name and Nature as one of the chief determinants of our earthly welfare, though it was our first sight of him for five years. "Madam," he said, with that well-oiled air of reproof, as if he were ecstatic to find her placed behind the door his servant had just been pounding.

"General Lowe," she said. She had decided some years back that if OGF could be called "General Bonaparte," the less notable Sir Hudson could be "General Lowe," without frills such as "Your Excellency."

"It is the charming Mrs. Balcombe, no? My acquaintance Mrs. Balcombe, formerly of St. Helena?"

"Yes," she said, "you know very well it is. Was I not your informer?"

He coughed. "Ah," he said, "you did fulfill that function."

"Then I am ashamed. But I am abashed too, to say the general's visit has given me no time to attend to my toilette."

She wasn't abashed at all, of course. It was mockery, we could tell, and we were thrilled by it. Cold invaded the house through the spaces not occupied by Sir Hudson's greatcoat and small head.

"William is in?" he asked. The only good thing about him, it had to be admitted, was that his voice was melodious.

"Mr. Balcombe," she said. "Mr. Balcombe is in."

"The boys?"

"Not here. They go to a grammar school in the town."

She swung the door open with an energy itself ironic, which nearly satirized her frail self with the force she applied. "Please come in." We stood up slowly to see him in. After all, he had for a time governed the only solid earth I'd known for more than half my life and with any adequacy, from infancy until I was sixteen. But he had blighted us too. We partially asked him in to enclose him with our angry circle.

Father had stood up, but more like a man defending his hearth than exacting vengeance. He held out the *Chronicle* as his shield, and advanced a few steps. Lowe covered the distance as if grateful to meet him.

"Bill," Sir Hudson said, with concern, as if our circumstances had been on his mind—our place, the rent we paid for it, our sparse income. "May I say you deserve better than this?"

"Oh, Sir Hudson, 'deserve' is not found in the dictionary of landlords and even of patrons such as Sir Thomas."

"It's a long way from the charming Briars, I regret to say," rumbled Sir Hudson.

He took off his splashed greatcoat and looked around, but we had no one to take it.

"You may hang it on the hook," said my mother. And after a second he did so without any air of reproach. He was wearing underneath a subtle saffron suit—in fact, not far off in color from ones I later saw worn by the privately employed convicts in Sydney. He had a silk hat and brown boots the overcoat had saved from stains, and whose soles he had had the grace to scrape on the boot scraper in the garden. He took off his gloves, but no one accepted them from him, so he put them on a side table.

"You were able to attend the Emperor's funeral?" my mother asked, with sudden false interest and falser respect.

He didn't have the power to stop her using that term anymore. He had lost that, just as we had lost our hold on The Briars.

"Yes," said Sir Hudson, still standing. "He lies in one of the sweetest places on the island. Geranium Valley."

"A pity," said my father suddenly, "that his house wasn't so amiably located from the start."

Sir Hudson looked ahead with his unsteady, red-lashed eyes— they could give the impression sometimes of circling their orbits. He knew by now he would not have an easy time under this roof. That would not have surprised him.

"We all, in our different ways, served the purposes of policy," Sir Hudson said, if not pleaded. "I followed policy as crafted in Westminster. Others may have followed less solid dictates."

"Yes," said my mother, "you frequently made that point."

Sir Hudson got the idea. At least he got *an* idea. He had to set out to appease us. He turned his eyes to me where I sat across the room and said, "Yes, Geranium Valley, Betsy. You know the island better than I, I'm sure. Remember how frightened of carriages you always were, Miss Betsy?"

"It was carriages traversing heights I feared," I told him. "For I rode horses up any crag you'd name."

"Yes, I seem to remember that," he said, as if he were interested. "You won that Deadwood ladies' race."

"I did, indeed. You chastised me for using the wrong horse—the Emperor's."

My father said, "The island days are too dim for us, Sir Hudson. But it would not be right for me to deny you a welcome. Or my hand."

Sir Hudson rushed gratefully towards him. "Dear Bill," he cried, taking my father's offered hand.

Bill? Yet again. Had he ever called him Bill on the island? I could remember only "Mr. Balcombe" or plain "Balcombe." You could tell by the way he said it that he had come to do business.

Once Sir Hudson's hand was in my father's, my father held him firm and murmured, "My funds, Sir Hudson. Can you tell me anything about the freezing of my funds? A release from administration."

"I know nothing to do with that—if indeed anyone did. You were charmingly prodigal, Bill, on the island. And as for the other . . . well, the man is dead, Bill. Isn't it so? That's where we should start."

"Please sit here," said my father neutrally, and pointed to an empty easy chair on the other side of the fire. "Betsy, would you fill a pipe for Sir Hudson?"

"No, no," said Sir Hudson, sitting. "I'll take my snuff."

And, seated, he produced his snuffbox. The Emperor had given his own snuffboxes away so regularly as presents on the island—we Balcombes had three of OGF's—but this was not one of the Emperor's.

My father lit his pipe, and Sir Hudson—the sort of inhaler who spreads the snuff on the back of his hand, sniffs the powdered stimulant in either nostril and puts the box away—indulged his preference. I read my father's air of calm tolerance as arising from his suspicion that for our welfare he might have to do business with this fellow, despite all. I hoped, though in a primal way, that he might soon give us a signal to speak our encompassing contempt, as we dearly wanted to. But we were ready and hungry too for the phenomenon of promise, definite or not.

"I wondered, Balcombe, if I could prevail on your charming ladies to allow us to speak privately?" asked Sir Hudson.

We all got up. My mother and Jane bobbed in the two men's direction, having picked up the signal from my father to be mannerly for now, and I did too—a mere five-degree crimp of the knee. We made for the kitchen and, from there, flattened against a door, heard the substance of an engrossing discourse between the island's former martinet and my father.

"You must know, Bill, that our companion on the island, that Irishman . . . well, you know the Irish were all besotted with General Bonaparte and wanted him to deliver them from the Crown . . . in any case, O'Meara has written a two-volume work that accuses me of cruelty to his patient."

"The Emperor?" my father asked, my mother and sister and I joining our hands in silent applause. "I know that when it comes to Barry O'Meara you had him suspended from the College of Surgeons."

"Bill, Bill," cooed Sir Hudson, "it was the Admiralty, and O'Meara was always telling me that he was the servant of the Admiralty. I am flattered you suspect me of having so much authority that the College of Surgeons would listen to me."

He spoke in a way he had never done on the island, where his tone was always more tyrannical.

"As for the General . . ."

"The Emperor, as some of us called him," said my father.

Sir Hudson coughed. "If you wish, Bill. The point is the man is gone, and we are in private."

"I didn't hear you ever say it," our father remarked. "You never said 'Emperor.' And yet there were times during the wars when our government referred to him by that title."

"Dear Balcombe, that was necessity. The necessity vanished once we caught him. But imagine the pressure I was under. You don't know the reports Lord Bathurst and I received about intended American and French rescues of the General. If you had known that, you would understand, as the Irish surgeon fails to do for two volumes, that the General needed very close watching indeed. What was protection against enemy rescue to me might well have seemed mistreatment to you. But it was always mere prudence that motivated me, I assure you."

There was a silence. Then my father said, "And what you said to me before we left the island, that was mere prudence, sir?"

"I regret we are not always wise in choosing how things are to be said."

"I believe we can discern the difference of a wise man momentarily giving way to intemperate emotion," said my father, "and a fool reveling in malice."

My mother was pale behind the door, but I was more taken by the pure enjoyment of hearing our father give it to him square and simple. I had harbored the idea of getting favors out of Sir Hudson for a while, but it had vanished now in my delight at hearing his discomfiture at the hands of Billy Balcombe, said once to be the most jovial man on his lost island.

"Easy, sir," said Sir Hudson, in his old commanding way. But then something made him grow appeasing again. "As you know, Bill, I fought the Ogre—the man I was then ordered to confine. I have seen firsthand the disruptions he brought to the civilized life of Europe. And my reward for that is the Irishman's accusations. I had no hand at all in O'Meara's being struck from the College of Surgeons; others, mightier than myself, might have."

Silence.

Then my father spoke. "I will not impugn your word by suggesting you might have mentioned it in your dispatches to Lord Bathurst or others as a suitable punishment for O'Meara. You've said you had no hand, and I accept that."

But it was obvious that he didn't accept it.

"Look here," Sir Hudson said, "I've been treated worse by Surgeon O'Meara than I ever treated him. As for your fleeing the island, you and your family did so voluntarily—"

"To forestall arrest, or expulsion, and slanders against my wife and shaming by you," said my father, in a trembling voice.

Laudate patrem! It was curative to hear him at the height of his fury. His soul had wavered over the past years and become blurred, but now that he had his enemy in place he was arrow-straight and transfixing. And since Sir Hudson did not rant or threaten or leave, it must mean he needed the Balcombes in some way. He needed my father.

"Bill, I knew you were sending unauthorized letters for the General. And negotiating bills for him."

"I have never seen the evidence against me," said my father. "Though you were eloquent about it on our last day, as on other matters."

"Mind it, Bill!" said Sir Hudson, but even then in a moderate way without any of the fierce, manic authority he had exercised on the island.

"Get to what you want," my father urged. "It's sickening to see you pretend to be a decent man. Admit to who you are, for God's sake!"

Again, silence. And then . . .

"The thing is that Surgeon O'Meara has smeared my reputation. But I do not matter so much. I was the minister's appointment, however, and so he—Lord Bathurst, Secretary of State—is almost equally embarrassed by the Irishman's book, and that *is* significant and should be addressed.'

My father was silent. No doubt he was contemplating the embarrassment of Lord Bathurst without too profound a sympathy. My father, of course, was Whiggish, with a touch of the radical about him, whereas Lord Bathurst was Tory. Henry Bathurst was frequently publicly exercised by slavery matters, and in my father's eyes that made his appointment of Sir Hudson to control our island, and his connivance in freezing my father's assets, all the more hypocritical. Such opinions were not easily roused in my father. To earn his enmity, men had to work hard at showing their ill will. Sir Hudson had worked hard enough.

We were still united, the listeners in the kitchen as well as my father, in the expectation that there was something more to be said by Sir Hudson, that he was only halfway through some sort of proposition. And since propositions were rare in our lives, especially those that demanded apology or abasement of Name and Nature Lowe, we were appropriately breathless. Not like girls in some hollow novel—we had none of that filament-like delicacy. We had known shock and debasement too, and we drank down the scalding cup of familial humiliation.

In any case, as certain as sunrise, here came the rear end of Sir Hudson's expedient argument dressed up as a generous one.

"You were a witness to what took place on the island, Bill, and despite our differences, you were always a fair man. It would be of some service to all parties if you signed an affidavit declaring that I treated General Bonaparte as any prudent man would, placing appropriate but generous limits to his freedoms in that place. If you could indicate in your statement—which Sir Thomas's attorney will help you prepare—the time I spent, while I held the office of governor, in receiving representations from his group of exiled followers and from himself, and of my active interest in his health through frequent questionings of Surgeon O'Meara, then such a document would be appreciated not only by myself but in official quarters. And for asserting nothing but the truth, you would be rewarded with a government posting, at home or in the colonies, of a minimum of four hundred pounds per annum."

There was again a notable, weighty silence. A post like that would restore us to what we ached to become: something akin to our old selves. Then my father said, "I should order you to leave, sir. For you are inducing me to perjure myself by swearing untruths."

Sir Hudson rushed in to say, "I am simply asking you to balance out the libels of Surgeon O'Meara. And, remember, he is comfortably restored to the College of Surgeons now, and is flush with the proceeds from his slanders. Does he even come down here? Since his book was published, has he offered the hand of help to his friend William Balcombe?"

"He's a more decent man than many," my father asserted. "You have the recourse of the courts if he is so libelous to you."

Sir Hudson rushed on: "And we hope to take that course. And in that instance or any other, an affidavit from a neutral and respected onlooker would be of more immediate value."

In the kitchen, we women waited through the pause.

"I will not provide the document," said my father, with the sort of throaty sturdiness that indicated he had stood up to end this hateful discourse. "Be clear, Sir Hudson, that I do not envy Surgeon O'Meara, and I'm delighted that at least one of the two or more men who were punished for opposing you on the island has done well from it and made a fortune on the back of your despotism."

There was a large breath here to fuel a flight of aggrieved and magical oratory most people only dream of delivering. "You speak of my financial needs, but they are nothing to my spiritual ones, and I refuse to compromise the latter to put a shine on the reputation of a man like you. For you do not deserve any luster and are a fellow who proved himself in this interview as much a brigand as the Emperor always said you were. I feel I cannot thank you for taking an interest in my family or for visiting me. Do please feel free to go now."

We could hear sounds that might have corresponded to Name and Nature standing up, in dudgeon perhaps but not as deeply affronted as we would have wanted.

"Do you know," asked Name and Nature, "that O'Meara considers himself so much in the wrong concerning me that he is courting a sixty-six-year-old widow to pay his legal bills?"

We did not know this, yet also did not necessarily believe it, given its source.

"Yes," continued the Fiend, "and if that were not sufficiently absurd, Dame Theodosia Beauchamp of Montagu Square, for whom he is showing such passion, has her own absurd history. She had her fortune from her brother Sir Theodosius, a ridiculous family but, like many such, very rich! Her first husband, a Captain Donellan, was charged with poisoning Sir Theodosius and was hanged for it! I do not make up this story, sir, I assure you. After her husband swung, she married and then buried another husband, and now O'Meara is lining up to be the third consort and may well be already married to the lady. Love has strange ways, but the unkind could say that O'Meara, never vastly interested in women, has secured a buttress against loss of his royalties, and an exchequer out of which to pay for his criminal libel defense. You choose to be loyal to such a fellow, Bill?"

"Good luck to Barry O'Meara in all his endeavors," my father cried. But he *was* taken aback, and we listeners too, despite ourselves, by Sir Hudson's gossip. It was so exotic and we doubted his gifts to make up such eccentric details.

"What do you care for how the Frenchman was handled on the island, Balcombe? All those bills of his you negotiated for them behind my back. Where's your commission for that? What motive do you have for insulting a government minister like this?"

"From what I've heard," my father replied, "you may not be as close to government anymore and may carry most of the opprobrium for what befell the Ogre. This frequently occurs with overly slavish servants of the great. The gods are skilled in arranging such things."

"In the meantime," said Sir Hudson, in a voice that evoked in my mind the uneven patches of reddish color that marked his countenance, "be assured, Bill, I still retain enough influence to guarantee you a government position on a scale of income that will assure you against want. Be certain about that."

"No," said my father. "No, sir. I will not be certain."

Sir Hudson sighed in that "some people can't see the obvious" way and audibly began reaching about him for hat and cape and gloves and all the rest. Then he was heard making for the door. Just a single set of boots. My father was not going ahead of him to open it. He was *showing* him the door. We heard it scrape wide and then Sir Hudson called, "I realize why you are heated, Bill. But I think that in the watches of the night you might consider what I have offered."

After the door closed we emerged with congratulations brimming at our mouths. William Balcombe had returned to the best of his vigor. So it had sounded through the kitchen door. But what we saw gave us pause. Our father was flopped in his seat, as if all his muscular energy had gone into putting Sir Hudson down, as well as the last energy of his soul. And when we saw this gray-faced wreck, applause and praise died in our throats.

*T*he mood of our household, in the wake of my father's routing of the Fiend, was strangely wistful, even despairing. No one had ever closed Destiny's door on us as firmly as my father had, with a power and eloquence worthy of Cicero scarifying Catiline.

But not ten days after his visit, the Irish surgeon arrived in town again by the London stage—a mode that proved he had the most earnest desire to see us. He put up at Exminster's Stowey Arms and sent a boy ahead of him to ask what hour would be convenient for Mr. and Mrs. Balcombe to receive him.

Our boys, river rats with muddy boots and sloppy noses, were, despite O'Meara's earlier solemn narration of the death of OGF, excited by the news of the Irish surgeon's visit. For he had always been playful with children, and though the boys were older now—William fifteen— they too were nostalgic for the island, where O'Meara had seemed an uncle and an agent of their truest and most hectic playmate, OGF.

It was Jane who for once took up the duty of the voice of contradiction. "It's taken him long enough to come back. I thought he'd forgotten us now that he has become a literary and social notable."

So the Fiend's poison had entered her, and so had some further signs of the possible onset of consumption. And if O'Meara had a fault, of course, it *was* his little vanity that his conversations with the Emperor were unique, that he had inherited the true words. But at the same time, the Great Ogre and OGF had his own power over people to make them believe such things, to believe that each one of us was the only confidant he had. Even when I was younger, I had seen this belief at operation in so many—in O'Meara and General Bertrand, in Las Cases, destructively in young General Gourgaud, and in the de Montholons. The conviction of receiving unique trust from the Emperor had had its part in my mother's history too, and in my father's. But in my own as well. It was an appropriate delusion for the French on the island. It was a dangerous one for the English. Yet even officers on visiting ships who managed to get a two-hour audience with the Emperor would write a comprehensive history in the London newspapers, as if they too believed in the singular intensity of a confrontation where seconds were plumped out with timeless meaning, and that they had been there when the Emperor had uttered the essential revealing word.

"We will not apologize to Surgeon O'Meara for our quarters," my mother told everyone before he arrived. For he had not seen the cottage when last in the town, having stayed at one of the inns. My mother's better china from the island had taken a year and a half to reach us, her pride as a householder having traveled fragilely in boxes from the island to Cape Town, and then up the dangerous coast of Africa, on past Spain and Portugal and into the ship-shattering, let alone teacup-pulverizing Bay of Biscay and the Channel.

To the agreed hour, when the knock came, Jane opened the door with an expectancy caught from the rest of us. O'Meara was impressively dressed in black serge and a cape, a beaver hat and glimmering shoes, whose buckles were new enough not to have acquired any metallic streaking from the vapors and ordure of the streets of London and Exminster and all intermediate towns he had traveled through.

When my father stood up to greet him, we were sure suddenly that the tale of the older rich woman and her poisoned brother was a malignant fiction of Sir Hudson's, or that it could be explained in a way that shone with honor, not absurdity. My father took in the sight of the surgeon, his eyes no longer the same companionable ones of our last meeting eighteen months before, when a raggedy O'Meara, fresh from pulling teeth to allay poverty, had come to tell us from purest fraternity how the Emperor had died.

"Dear William," he said, galloping across the room to take my father's hand, and then turning to kiss my mother's.

"We are very happy, Surgeon Barry O'Meara," she said warily, "for your success."

"Ah," he said, and beamed. "Have you really read it yet, Jane?"

"We thought you had forgotten us," said my father. "In your new renown."

He sounded resentful in a way I did not like.

"I had inscribed copies of the two volumes to you but thought that as a courtesy I should ask if you would consent to accept them. They're at the Stowey Arms. I can send them round to you."

"It would be very welcome," said my mother, glancing at her husband, "to receive them from your own hand."

He pretended to be distracted by the splendor of Jane and me and uttered the normal palaver, though he must have known that the consumptive redness of Jane's face was not healthy. He slapped his hands as he took us in. "Aren't you girls the very self-same picture of delight as you were on the island? But enriched—as it were—in scale, according to your age? How is it down here in this far-off town?"

"Oh," said Jane, with a particular pointedness her answers generally lacked, but as if the Fiend had persuaded her of O'Meara's flaws, "you must understand that if we live here, it isn't far off for us."

"I have been married to Mr. Abell," I said. "My baby's sleeping in the small parlor. You can see her later."

I was tempted to ask, "Do you happen to have seen her father?"

"Yes, of course," said O'Meara in a self-chastising tone. "I had heard you were wed."

Jane went to the kitchen to make tea and cut plum cake to accompany the brew. My father, meanwhile, told O'Meara to take a seat, and, uncomfortably, knowing there was something astray in Billy Balcombe, the surgeon did it with a rare brand of obedience. He was pleased to leave the question of my father aside a moment and question me on my husband. I pretended that all was blither (I still hoped that booby would come back). I offered a few plain details about Abell's work for Sir Thomas Tyrwhitt's plans for Prince's Town, up on the moors.

"What can we do for you, Surgeon O'Meara?" my father broke in. "You surely can't be here just to visit the exiles."

"I hear," said my mother, as if to temper her husband, "that your book is in all the great London shops."

"I was fortunate, ma'am . . . Jane. The total accident of being appointed surgeon to an emperor gave me something to recount, beyond the normal adventures of the traveler."

"And are you invited to all the salons?" she asked, her chin raised, her neck extended as if to chide him with the lines of want and sadness that marked it.

"In some places, Jane, I have been fêted beyond my merits."

"And in those salons of praise," my mother earnestly wanted to know, "at Lady Holland's, say . . . who have you met?"

O'Meara blushed. He was proud of who he had met.

"My fellow countryman Sheridan," admitted O'Meara, "aging now and drinking to keep pace. Consider it like this . . . if one writes something halfway notorious, it gets puffed up to be a masterpiece. But monetary credit is still everything, and if you run out of money and leave a butcher unpaid, that is the end of all literary repute."

"And I believe the Irish leader O'Connell has sought you out."

"It is true. A great man. You cannot blame me, can you, Bill, for wanting advancement for my wretched countrymen?"

"Not at all," said my father. "But from what I hear and read, your butchers' bills are well looked after these days."

I could see then that O'Meara's success was insupportable to my father and robbed him of a brother in wretchedness. O'Meara turned to my father, nodded, and blinked as if accommodating himself to a new light. "Are you angry I've not written any letters, Bill? The truth is I kept expecting to see you in London." O'Meara's face was solemn.

"There are still some restrictions on my traveling to London," rumbled my father, refusing to meet the Irishman's eye.

"Surely Name and Nature doesn't have the power to keep you down here in the west. Surely there is freedom of movement."

"It is not, for once, Sir Hudson," my father admitted, though not yielding much. "Though he was the initiator of our condition, as he was for all of us—for you too!"

So the Irishman continued ill at ease, and though my mother was polite, my father continued to do nothing to make him feel complacent. He had been in the shadows like us but had had the wit to write himself out of them. Did my father resent that? Surely not, not like your average rancorous man. I had an instinct that he was somehow testing the Irishman, and at a deeper level than he had ever tested him before.

"I should tell you that Lady Holland remembers and asks after you both," O'Meara hurried to say.

"I imagine all her dinner guests are required to recite your book at table," sneered my father, going further than dignity should have let him. He knew it himself, and moved his lips around querulously, uncertain what tack he should now take.

"I wasn't aware," O'Meara pleaded, "that you were actually still *stuck* here against your will and was horrified to hear it said by Lady Holland. I thought when I brought you the news . . . the news from the island I was so anxious to share . . . after the death, I mean, that you would be free to . . ."

My mother and father exchanged glances. This was a man they had liked considerably, but it was as if they had spotted something slipshod in his goodwill. Jane looked at me. Despite her earlier sentiments, she had got to the stage as natural peacemaker where she believed enough bile had been expressed and wished they could all just be nice and perhaps that Father could bring out the port or brandy.

"Did you come down here just to commiserate with us?" asked my father nonetheless. "Given that we are still hostages?"

"No, no," said O'Meara. "*Commiserate* is not the word. It is too much a word of patronage, and I can't extend patronage, nor would you, from what I know of you, accept it."

"And therefore," said my mother, a good partner for my father now in keeping the Irishman on edge, "if you have not come to commiserate with us, why have you come?"

Barry O'Meara, friend of Richard Brinsley Sheridan, had been rendered markedly edgy by now. From neither side was this a normal meeting between the Balcombes and him.

He half rose. "I believed I was coming to see friends. . . . If my coming has in any way caused discomfort, then . . ."

"You have traveled a considerable way, and by road," said my mother, a bit more lenient.

"I won't deceive you on that. A personage loaned me their coach and I accepted after some insistence. It was a pleasant and illuminating journey. If one travels by coasting ship, one sees less of the character of England."

"Who is this personage?"

"A lady and dear friend who does not much travel herself."

"Is it an elderly lady whose brother was poisoned?"

"Dame Theodosia," said O'Meara, instantly. "Yes. It has been a matter of malice in some newspapers. . . . Ah, now I see what you meant earlier about butchers' bills. A little less than your normal nature and wit, William, it must be said. And, indeed, the lady is thirty years beyond me in age. But you know I am not a base fellow, Bill. . . . This is genuine affection and true friendship of the soul. The mockers do not know me and, above all, do not know her."

So my father called the game off for a while and said, "All right, all right. Sit down, Barry. It is not at all an unwelcome thing to see you, and we are not as soured as you think at your literary success."

"To which you have contributed," said Barry. "The Balcombes are memorialized with affection in the book, in volumes one and two. Betsy and the Deadwood races, for example . . ."

My performance at Deadwood had been remembered by the Fiend, too. It must indeed have annoyed a lot of people while amusing one, the watcher through the notches in the shutters of Longwood.

"You should have a share in my success, yes," said O'Meara.

"Please don't dare continue with that rubbish," said my father, but almost half-amused. "But what I resent is that in all these months of your redemption you have not written to us."

O'Meara raised his hands above his head, like a man pacifying a crowd.

"I have been in proportion forgetful, vain, flattered by attentions from those I never expected to meet, and deprived of time. And my statement that I expected to see you was no lie. I believed you, like I, would be liberated now. You have not written, Bill, when it comes to that!"

"We were still in the confines, Barry, where they've put us. A letter from us to you means little. A remembrance from you to us would be everything. To be remembered by you when all your luster and more had been returned to you. We had no light to be shed on you, but you had light you might have shed on us."

O'Meara spread his hands, nodded and nodded again, conceding the force of what my father had said.

"But this elderly dame, Barry? Is this the wisest . . . ? Well, only you will know."

O'Meara looked at my father with an intense melancholy insistence. "It is wise," he said. "It is wise but not according to the wisdom of the world."

"Do you like women, Barry?" asked my mother.

"You know me, Jane—I adore them, but not necessarily in the more accustomed sense as dear Bill."

Jane and I and the listening boys made what we could of this complex declaration. My mother and father looked at each other. "Ah," said my father, "we are not wise according to the world's wisdom too. But I love my wife above all women."

He reached for my mother's wrist, and when he took it she gleamed with joy but also a sort of shame, her face growing glossy in a cloying way.

Both my father and O'Meara took some of the plum cake. It soothed them, but O'Meara, in the middle of savoring it, put it aside and said, "I must now be honest with you all, for there are purposes I have. You guessed I was not here from motives of the purest brotherhood, Bill, as much as I should be, and you are right."

"Ah!" said my father, though without the hubris of having had an accurate nose.

The Irishman said, "It has now emerged that Sir Hudson intends to sue me over my book for criminal libel. If he wins, I could well be financially damaged but, more seriously, I could be transported. And the Fiend is able to compel a number of his lackeys from the island to say what a soft heart he had for his prisoner, and how well he treated the Emperor. But knowing their testimony could be compromised by my lawyers, he has traveled the country looking for former saints, that is, islanders, who were considered more neutral, and pleading with them, or threatening them with his secret knowledge of their island behavior, to give sworn statements about his clement treatment of Our Great Friend. I have meanwhile a handful of robust souls who have supplied me with affidavits, but no one knows the tyrannies of Hudson Lowe like you do, William. So, straight out, would you ever provide me with an affidavit? I am here of course to see you, but with shame I tell you, I am also here to plead for that sworn statement. I was for two years expelled from my station and reduced to being a tooth-puller, and the idea that my fortune should take another steep downturn—well, I could not bear it. I can offer you no inducement for this service, because it would make your testimony invalid. Though later . . ."

"No, I would want nothing," my father thundered. And then he looked around us all, frowning, as if telling us not to debate the matter. My father would choose to swear against Sir Hudson and make it certain that, as surely as when Christ's name is uttered, the name Judas lies accursed by its side, whenever the name of the Emperor was mentioned in future, Lowe by Name and Nature would reek at its side. "I must think about it, O'Meara."

"Of course," the surgeon assured my father. "You must decide on your own terms whether to give me the affidavit or not. For this is the law and there can be no coercion in the law. I would be grateful if in the spirit of our old friendship you could consider my request, but . . ."

He knew not to push too hard.

When he left, it was without the immutable self-regard of Sir Hudson. He simply kissed all of us.

It was the visit of O'Meara that triggered my father somehow, in ways I do not understand to this day. Admittedly, the departure of my husband Abell seemed to have made everything uncertain in a way Sir Hudson Lowe could not. My baby and I were back at home, and while I confess to being less than desolated to lose Abell, I was dependent again on the Balcombe resources, to which I contributed only through teaching music occasionally. As for my little daughter, she at least seemed quickly to transfer her infant affection for her father to my father and brothers.

My father, though, who had been an amiable constant on the island, seemed no longer constant. It struck me he sometimes shifted principles purely from exhaustion. He did not know how to take O'Meara anymore.

There was another illogic in his great impending decision, however—between issuing a false affidavit for Sir Hudson and a valid one for O'Meara. He foresaw that if he collaborated with Sir Hudson, destiny would remove us eastwards or westwards a pleasant few hundred miles, even to a post in Scotland or Ireland. He did not calculate that Sir Hudson might have thousands in mind. So many thousands that it would put an end to Sir Thomas's need for supervising us on behalf of the higher powers, distance becoming our chief constable.

To put it briefly, my father wrote now to Sir Hudson to get the man's terms down on paper, and an affidavit made out in favor of Sir Hudson for my father to sign, with the offer of a post underpinning it. He had been counted a man of shadows long enough. He wished to regain substance. I could understand it. His turbulent daughter and sweet granddaughter were of course on his mind. But, above all, he was trying for once to align himself with the wisdom of the world, and with no two-volume history to write, could think only of this. He had a visit from Sir Thomas, who heartily said the affidavit would be the Balcombes' salvation and our return to full stature.

Even so, the criminal libel case Name and Nature hoped to assail O'Meara with never came to court. Indeed, when Las Cases's seven-volume *Mémorial de Sainte Hélène* appeared that year, and was lambasted by Name and Nature, young Emmanuel came to London and, accosting Lowe as he left his house near Hyde Park, thrashed him with a horsewhip as he entered a coach. We could not exact such vengeance and read the press reports wanly.

A French sailor called it that . . .

The Hibernia *was a cheery* ship. Though small, it was broad-decked, with a big saloon and ample in the beam, a modern sort of ship, and a decent omen of redemption for our family. Waiting at a hotel near Holborn to board it, we nursed Jane back from a bad croup. It was the dead of winter. My infant daughter, Bessie, thrived here, would thrive even at sea, and was a sign of better things.

The captain of the *Hibernia* intended to send for us as soon as the ship was loaded and the tide propitious. My brothers were impatient to board and went chasing carriages in the streets but were happy at their colonial prospects. For everyone agreed that New South Wales was the most debased society but at the same time the one that offered the most improbable rewards.

A gentleman named Saxe Bannister, who was going out there as attorney general to my father's colonial treasurer, had told my brothers that in New South Wales boys played cricket all day, though they sometimes had to play with the children of convicts. After our hard time in the West Country, they were ready to play cricket with the devil as long as it was all day.

Meantime, in chilly Holborn consumptive girls haunted the corners of streets, and the damaged soldiery of Wellington's campaigns kept watch with them in the cold. The world would love Wellington—or at least the British world, which considered itself the world, did. But he did not seem to love his wounded remnants.

When we went aboard the *Hibernia* at the captain's summons, life seemed suddenly crisper, more definable, and snow fell on the lights of the brightly painted saloon and melted before one's eyes, as if the tropics already exerted an influence from within our ship.

It seemed that the *Hibernia* would be Jane's sanatorium. Her cabin was good-sized, especially so for that time—I believe my parents gave up their berth to her. I sat by her and read, and kept up her dosage of tonics laced with opium. I was aware she had somehow ceased to be a girl and had in a way ceased to be a woman, but instead was purely the target of solicitude. My mother was prodigal with the contents of opiate bottles when it came to Jane. If Jane, now a mild ghost with rasping breath, could be prevented from expectorating so painfully and with such richness of blood against white linen, then she would be prevented from the worst thing of all, the consuming of her system by disease.

It may have been the first ten days at sea that settled the issue, for they were wild, and we could hardly stand even in our pleasant accommodations, and lost control of ourselves, of our heads and hearts and stomachs even in a ship of those modern and luxurious dimensions. I lay a considerable time in my bunk with my baby girl, who was barely influenced by nausea.

It became apparent to us then that there was a danger of losing Jane, who had always sat so easily and lightly and benignly at the heart of the Balcombe family but whose capacity to hold us down against storms had now become noticeable. Yet Saxe Bannister, who had a soft manner with her, was suddenly and palpably a potential husband. There was no question that he was well in love with her, despite her hours of torpor, and that Jane could still prove herself a candidate for marriage and dutiful friendship with him. Saxe was a Tory and hence a voter for the government that had oppressed the Emperor and O'Meara and the Balcombes. Tory opinions were, in the midst of mighty waves, a small blemish. When Saxe knew my father had been provedore to the Emperor's household, he was as interested as anyone in my father's assessments of OGF, and did not challenge them. The world was still agog for that man. The Balcombes themselves were agog, even as we told our stories of the island, the tales we had bought at the cost of our own happiness.

We had calm weather after sighting the Azores and got to know the other dozen or so saloon guests, four of whom were settlers returning from a visit home, who had a very jaded view of colonial society but were full of practical advice on colonial life. Jane now tolerated the slack, furnace weather off Africa's huge groin, the *Hibernia* being the apex of a triangle with, away to the west, St. Helena, somehow forever our true home, and to the east, Cape Town.

On the worst night, Jane was moved up to the deck on a mattress and we all sat with her, discussing constellations and predicting more benign times. Saxe Bannister tried to sit near us and comforted my father with tales about land grants in New South Wales. "These days," he expatiated, "the governor requires someone granted a ticket of occupation to employ assigned convicts according to the scope of the country—one for every one hundred square miles."

"Do you hear these fantastic things?" my mother would ask Jane, providing her with a motive to endure. One hundred square miles at a time awaited the serial occupier in Australia. But for the moment we were in a zone beyond geography, beyond God, and the satanic heat lay in the exact partings of our hair, and between our shoulders.

"*Terre Napoléon*," I murmured.

My father and Saxe Bannister cocked their ear interrogatively.

"A French sailor called it that—Baudin. *Terre Napoléon*."

My father gave a minute shake of his head at this French presumption, yea, even unto the limits of the earth. And Saxe Bannister said, "Well, that threat was avoided, as in the end all others."

When the *Hibernia* reached the waters where the Southern Ocean collided with the Indian, in a zone beyond all claims and all explanation, Jane died quite suddenly. At the height of a piteous choking paroxysm, her amiable but perhaps too pliable heart gave way. The captain told us sympathetically that those raging winds, ice cold, had killed other passengers he had carried in the past, souls already exhausted by the passage of the Bay of Biscay and the Atlantic, then braised by African heat and, finally, unleashed into the earth's southernmost mad waters, down here, beyond the Tropic of Capricorn, the goat latitudes.

It was appalling to see such a small creature, my riding companion from the island, now strictly encased in canvas, entrusted, as one would entrust an infant to a relative, to an ocean that could not have been vaster, less predictable, less human, or more indifferent. Could it be argued that God in His magnitude, of an order even greater than this, could reach down His finger to the spot where she lay? For He who knew of the death of a single sparrow knew nothing of the Roaring Forties. The idea of His concern could not be supported there. There was not room even on the mighty, modern *Hibernia* to support it.

We were bereft, though Bessie helped us with her prattling, smiles, and crumbs of diction. She was charmingly, and sometimes relentlessly, demanding, and her demands were the footholds on which we passed the remainder of our sea days, nearly all of them rough. The children fell into high fevers, my daughter now included, recovering and relapsing, overlapping the course of each other's maladies.

The last reach, from Tasmania along the east coast of New South Wales, would ironically have had the power to revive Jane, and we grieved profoundly that she had not lingered to acquaint herself with it. It was autumn—brighter than an English summer—on that great coastline of yellow sands and surf and whales and headlands, and if no one sailed up it without doubt, no one did so without optimism. It seemed to promise that the normal rules were canceled there.

Up the hill from the seaport of Sydney stood the ample three-storey Treasury, in a street named O'Connell to honor the Irish statesman, a friend of O'Meara. Our residence sat above it. "I'll live above the shop, as a grocer should," said my father. His task was to be treasurer to the entire colony, as large as half of Russia, and to receive its incomes from customs, land taxes, and other sources. He had been allotted two clerks, young Englishmen, one of whom, Harrison, had been on the *Hibernia*, and who, to be fair, kept the books very much in order. A third, an Irish gentleman named Croke, was a convict with the same oval features as O'Meara. Indeed, Croke was permitted to dress as a gentleman and had little doubt he was one.

We lived in a fine, healthy set of apartments where at that time of year it was normal to cast the windows open and let the sparkle and breeze of the harbor in. When one took to the streets, it was normal to pass British convicts who were members of the governor's felling gangs, whose aim was to clear the country of trees, either working up hillsides, like one great tree-eating insect, or moving about the city on messages. These visible felons were called canaries, because their convict uniform always contained yellow, which stood out brightly in the street and against the background of the bush.

Let me say that the contrast was not lost on us Balcombes—this hugest island of the earth as the place of exile for small criminals, as the smallest of islands had been exile for the largest criminal or saint or hero or child or intellect of history.

Some of the convicts matched the beetle-browed, ape-like images in the London illustrated papers, but there were also fine-looking youths, and robust men, though generally given to dram-drinking. Everywhere were Irish felon women in mob caps with dudeens or clay pipes clamped between their gums and squawking in the Irish tongue. The freedom of passage many of these figures enjoyed in the town (freedom somewhat in advance of that enjoyed by Fanny Bertrand on the island) had citizens of New South Wales angered, for here there were Tories and Whigs too, and I never came to terms with Tories, since all the denial and spite and suspicion of the earth seemed to be their anthem. In any case, the relative freedom of prisoners was one of the subjects that came up at dinners when early in our colonial careers we were invited widely to them.

We were invited to dinner both by the progressive newspaper editors and evangelists, and by the larger Tory landholders and free merchants who valued their immaculate origins. For all wanted to hear about St. Helena and the Emperor, and were only slightly disappointed to discover that we had left the island before the man's death.

Billy Balcombe was a good citizen of the colony, founding the Turf Club along with others, endowing a grammar school, and all the rest. But we should have known that we had to choose, that our tales of the island would not be sufficient to appease either the Democrats, some of them the children of convicts—one the child of a highwayman surgeon named Wentworth—and the Exclusives, those settlers untainted by the judgment of any British courts. Because the other question was land, as ever, and how title would be granted to it. Nearly all the unredeemed massiveness of the place belonged to the Crown, though the Crown's citizens, being robust people, were going out and taking it from the natives, and acquiring such wealth that they could actually buy their own men in the Imperial Parliament.

So to be seen as the governor's man, as a servant of Sir Thomas Brisbane, a Scotsman who loved the stars and had brought his own astronomical equipment from Scotland with him, and who believed in such supposedly crazed concepts as granting of full rights to Catholics, was to be cut out of the company of the Exclusive part of the New South Wales polity. And yet, joining the Sydney Turf Club, my father was not considered of the strident Democrat party either, since as a servant of government he could not be full-throated on these matters, as much as the principle that a child of a convict should have equality with the child of a gentleman was one that sang to his imagination.

My daughter had a convict nursemaid, as reasonable a girl as many a yamstock, and was invited to parties and picnics. Bessie was a solemn little creature, as Jane would have been, employed on the endless endeavor to solve the earth's mathematics. But she was quick to laughter, and I was proud of her since she combined the best of myself and Jane. In a colony of taints, however, a taint of irregularity still attached to me. I could not pass myself off as a widow. I could say that my husband was vanished and could be presumed dead, but the stories were otherwise. Australia was a vast island, vaster a thousand times over than *the* island, and yet gossip rang around the sandstone walls that contained the town.

*W*e assumed that our halcyon past would reassert itself anew even after it had been canceled by so many bitter, restrictive years. My father had believed that he would hold the sort of companionable dinners in Sydney that he had in the island, but the gift for that had somehow been bullied out of him. His conviviality was no longer of the same order as it had once been. It was made edgy by what he had discovered of the world. My mother could tell it, and barely recovered from losing Jane, she lacked certainty and became shrill. Her face was lined with sadness and bewilderment and the loss of a kind of certainty about how to express herself.

So my parents were unsure hosts. They depended on me to play the piano, and nothing could compensate for the absence of Jane's tender and forgiving conversation. Our younger boys, unhappy at their grammar school in Sydney, were surly, though William, who had a post in the surveyor's office, was of an equable frame of mind. The friendship with Saxe Bannister, which might have flourished through the connection of Jane, eroded over time, and he was discontented anyhow in his stipend, and tended to complain of the governor and dine with the Exclusives. He had found there was precious little private work for him to do, even if the Colonial Office had made a big fuss about how he would be able to take clients as well as doing the government's work. He was coming under the spell, both by political temper and desire for better things, of families such as the Macarthurs, their son Hannibal, who clearly thought my father an odd fish and a radical, and might even have warned Bannister against being associated with him.

It was clear in hindsight that my father did not bring to the management of the colony's finances the calm enthusiasm he might once have done, before the turmoils brought on by OGF and Name and Nature. Sir Thomas Brisbane gave him latitude, however, and was often himself accused of being more interested in stargazing than administration—this was a jibe of the Exclusive party, in any case, who had friends in the House of Commons. The starry Scotsman was complained of and ultimately replaced. A new, strenuous soldier named General Darling, a scientific Tory, not without resemblances to Name and Nature, arrived, and immediately inquired into all government departments, and chastised my father in terms that became the subject of rumors.

The Treasury of New South Wales was a most eccentric institution. From merchants and leaseholders in remoter regions arrived the requisite payments. Some of the currency my father received on the government's behalf, land rents and customs duties included, was sterling, but some was refashioned Spanish dollars, stamped by the colonial mint to make legal tender. For more than a year the safe that contained the incomings of the revenue of the colony was located in my parents' bedroom, an oddity that made the entire Balcombe ménage look stranger than it should have. In fact, I believe, the long years of demi-disgrace and the injustice of the government's blocking my father's access to his own assets meant that, though he had great competence, he could not take the matter of colonial revenue seriously. So he had been using the Colonial Treasury, for example, to discount merchants' bills, charging a modest share of the commission for doing so for himself, according to practice, and remitting the residue of the bill, when it was at last paid, into colonial revenue.

It was the board of the Bank of New South Wales who complained about him, because they thought that discounting bills should be their business, and that he should not compete in these matters. These were ironically the people who were most akin to him, the emancipists, convicts, children thereof, supporters, founders of a bank that came to dominate colonial business.

Darling himself was the last gasp of fierce Tory-dom, before the long Tory reign of England ended, a reign that had helped mark our destinies on the island and had, before ceasing, sent Darling to New South Wales.

Curiously it was Croke who was most faithful to my father, and on whom he relied most—a man transported and apparently redeemed by the experience, after being sentenced for issuing false invoices from an architecture office in Dublin, with the design of having clients pay more than his employer knew they were, he pocketing the modest difference. I liked Croke. He never made a show of his loyalty, he just applied himself. He took the sacraments of his church, which in his case seemed a further certificate of his honesty, and he intended to marry a Sydney schoolteacher when his conditional pardon was issued. I'm sure they live now in antipodean serenity with their Australian children.

As judges and newspaper editors fought with Darling about his imperious manners—he seemed to be a colonial Charles I—my father grew more dropsical, his limbs puffing up with fluid, his ankles bloating. Yes, drinking was a problem, yet more because it no longer pumped the machine of his nature but abraded and clogged it.

Between the town and the Brickfields, where the cemetery and the brick ovens were located, was the town of the natives, where the people who had lived in their own state of nature before the penal settlement began occupied small huts and shanties or slept in the open by fires. All the town worthies were agreed that liquor was a chief peril for these people, but someone must have collaborated with them for profit, for they seemed to acquire it with ease. They were stately men and women, those former possessors of New South Wales, and their stateliness was not entirely taken away by the habit of some of their men who wore a top hat and a jacket and nothing below it. Some of the women wore convict skirts and were bare-breasted, yet were often healthy-looking, except for those who were the portion claimed by raw brandy, and the poor souls we generally did not see much of, who were poxed, and in whom, as innocent creatures, the pox flared more heinously than it did in any Briton. They and, of course, the convicts were the lesser class of humans in our polity, the people of whom we in our arrogance expected less, though the convicts seemed to think that their station was at least superior to that of the indigenes.

My father took eccentrically to showing a powerful interest in the two despised groups, convicts and Aboriginals. He would stop convict men, the more prognathous the better, or women, the more toothless and dudeen-sucking, and want to know where they were from, and was earnestly interested in what had earned them this place at the earth's end.

It became clear that my father considered himself just one more transportee, one of Britain's rejected, and was trying to find some certainty of definition for that rejection by quizzing his fellows. At home he was distracted, if not plaintively pretending to fulfill the role of paterfamilias. One night, when he had drunk considerably, he declared that he was entitled to accommodate his friends at the Bank of New South Wales and to negotiate bills, for had not *they* (the British Government) taken everything from him—a job, the flow of assets, a daughter?

"I am merely taking what the Tories owe me," he proclaimed.

My mother argued, "Dear, this might prove to be a dangerous attitude to take."

On a summer's morning more than five years after we had arrived in Sydney, when I was away giving young colonials their music lessons, as I had been doing for the past three years, my father saw an Aboriginal with an engraved metal plate on his scarred chest proclaiming his kingship of the Broken Bay natives. This was a well-known man, very sage, very earnest, named Bungaree. While it sometimes seemed that my father sought out the more incoherent men and women to interview, Bungaree was said to possess great intelligence and coherence.

Billy Balcombe discoursed to polite Bungaree for an hour, until the native was looking around, wanting to get on, an uncommon impulse in many of his kind, whose sense of time did not coincide with ours, though they could spot incipient madness as well as anyone. Very pleased after his conversation with Bungaree, my father went in to the clerks and to Croke, but when they asked him what Bungaree had said, he could not quite manage to tell them. And then, as if struck by intense recall and about to quote Bungaree's exact account, he stood with a look of growing enlightenment on his face and fell to the floor. Over the coming days he suffered bewilderment, was tormented by gout and gastric fever both, and died, exhausted by life and bloody flux.

He was the Emperor's final fallen soldier and left in my map of the earth a similar vacancy to that left by OGF. But a vacancy whose edges lacerated me with remembered fragments of his jollity, hope, and ultimate souring.

We bought a plot for him in the chief Anglican church on the western ridge above the town, and all our resources, material and spiritual, seemed drained away. My father's papers were in disorder and those of the Treasury would have been, except for the clerks. Yet now we were under polite but definite notice to leave our habitation.

Tormented by her lost love and her anxiety that she had never been kindly enough to him, my mother needed to auction landholdings my father had acquired. We had hoped at a minimum that, once we had settled all debts, Governor Darling would give us a further grant, a widow's mite in the Antipodes. But he was determined we should not have it. My mother said that we must argue our case in London.

And we did. My mother, Bessie, and I sailed back, but the boys chose to stay for the time being, addicted to the place, as I had been earlier to the island. I understood it. William had his eye on pastoral land to the southwest. The younger boys couldn't wait to join him.

My little daughter remained robust on the voyage back to England. We spoke to Lord and Lady Holland, and applied to the office of the new secretary of state for the colonies. And thus our validity was recognized. Darling, or whosoever succeeded him, was ordered to consider our case compassionately, and we returned to the remote province with better hopes of a colonial living.

Could it ever match our hopes as enlarged by OGF? Could we ever be more than pensioned ghosts in the netherworld?

But Bessie, who had not been marred by earlier things, sang childhood's songs earnestly under the Australian constellations, which shone for her without ambiguity. For she could savor any location without knowledge of what could, by comparison, belittle it or leach value from it. God be praised, she was the Balcombe who knew no better.

Some final notes on Betsy, the incompleteness of the account and remaining unnegotiable mysteries

*C*ertainly *on St. Helena there* were manifestations that could most likely be explained by obsessions, in the manner they have been. Mrs. Balcombe and, less importantly, the strange General Gaspard Gourgaud and Surgeon O'Meara may have been defamed, in which case I can merely apologize to a fine woman and to the others. As for Albine, she took little trouble in concealing that she was up for most adventures.

In the meantime, it is true that my present home, one the Balcombes occupied in the nineteenth century, New South Wales, a territory of exquisite weirdness and beauty, nearly went broke under William's administration. It is hard to say *because* of it, since it would be difficult to excuse the collapse in London wool prices and thus Australian land prices in the late 1820s. On William's death, his land grant of twenty-five hundred acres at a place named Bungonia, and his earlier purchase of four thousand further south in the Monaro, down towards Canberra, stocked with sheep and cattle bought in boom times by loans from the Treasury itself (William Balcombe's right hand endowing his left, without any other intervening authority), were handled by young William, his eldest son, barely twenty years old. William needed to manage assigned convict drovers and shepherds in rough country far from the nearest magistrate. By the time of his father's death, the countryside was brown and deprived of grass, and of the two available Australian seasons, drought and flooding rains, drought held sway. As well, when the price of Australian wool fell in London, so did many of the plutocrats, free and convict-born.

William called the farm The Briars. Alex, the youngest Balcombe, spent time with him there, and they became accomplished horsemen. It is not within the purview of this novel, but William would sell this farm and then go gold-seeking in 1851 on the Turon River with his younger brother Thomas. There, William caught fever and died of it in 1852, and was buried in an unmarked grave with two others. Thomas, the middle brother, achieved some fame as an artist of animals, married and had three children, but suffered from mental disease and committed suicide in his Sydney house, Napoleon Cottage, in 1861.

It was Alex, the child who had fed laxatives to the Emperor, who now enjoyed a more pleasant existence and, after experience of the pastoral life with his brothers on the Molonglo, moved to the Port Phillip area, the future colony of Victoria or, as Baudin would have it, *Terre Napoléon*. He married, but left for a time his wife and young children to prospect for gold, before returning himself to the duller but surer regimen of a family man and a grazier. His pastoral station was on the eastern side of Port Phillip, and here he became successful, a magistrate and a patriarch, and built a homestead that he, too, called The Briars, now a museum.

Over time the Balcombe Napoleonic relics were augmented by items bought by a granddaughter of Alexander's, the doyenne of Melbourne society Dame Mabel Brooks. Some of those same relics were stolen from The Briars in what seemed to be a steal-to-order raid by robbers in 2014.

When Betsy, her mother, Jane, and Betsy's daughter, Bessie, sailed to England, their fares were paid for by the Colonial Office, as was their return to Sydney two years later. They were in England more than a year, including the entire span of 1832. Betsy at that time met the Emperor's brother, Joseph Bonaparte—he had just returned from a long American sojourn and he dandled young Bessie on his knee.

Betsy would ultimately have less trouble receiving land in Algeria from Napoleon III, whom she would meet when, as Prince Louis Napoleon, he was sheltering in London after a failed attempt to dislodge the Bourbons, and wanted to hear from her lips that he looked like his uncle. She briskly told him, "No, you don't!" Yet he would nonetheless gratefully ascribe her the Algeria land grant that she would never see.

She and her mother needed to visit the boys once more. What they achieved at the Colonial Office was the offer of government posts for the boys, and though William and Alex were not interested, Thomas, already sacked from the colonial surveyor's office, was now reinstated.

On the ship back to Australia, Betsy enchanted a young man of seventeen named Edward John Eyre who, as an explorer, would later cross the vast Nullarbor Plain and the country of the Great Australian Bight—a heinous ordeal to put himself and his Aboriginal companion through—and much later still would become a notorious governor of Jamaica. Edward John Eyre was a mere seven years older than Bessie, but wrote of Betsy as appreciatively as any adult male admirer, describing her as in her prime, pretty of feature and "commanding in form a good figure, stylish in her dress and having a strange mixture of polish and dash in her manner, which was very captivating." Her hair was "copious and exquisite" to the young Eyre, a rich nut-brown "shot with gold in any unusual fashion."

I think he might have been the last man to describe Betsy in writing. But an artist of some note, Alfred Tidey, also left a record of her in his painting *The Music Class*, which I believe can be viewed at Worthing Museum and Art Gallery in West Sussex in the south of England. Of four figures, Betsy is teacher, Bessie, her daughter, the page turner, and two students, pianist and harpist, play at Betsy's direction. Hers is the best-realized figure in the painting.

Betsy, the glittering woman, still young as perceived by Eyre and Tidey both, is nonetheless a tragic figure. The blight and glory that entered her household on St. Helena in October 1815 both enlivened and plagued her. All else thereafter seemed almost an outfall of the good and ill fortune of her Napoleonic encounter.

Those who helped me
make this book . . .

There are many who helped, in friendship and professionalism, ensure the emergence of this novel. As ever, I am proud to say that my wife, Judy, by my good fortune a natural editor of first recourse, again fulfilled that role in the case of *Napoleon's Last Island*. The agents who believed in this narrative were Fiona Inglis of Sydney, Amanda Urban of New York, and Peter Straus and Matt Turner of London. The editors who brought it into a reasonable shape were Meredith Curnow, Catherine Hill, and Virginia Gordon of Random House in Australia, my dear friend Carole Welch of Hachette, London, and Peter Borland and Judith Curr at the Simon & Schuster imprint Atria Books in New York. The generosity of spirit was theirs while the imperfections of this text entirely belong to me.

I had generous advice about St. Helena from Ann Whitehead, especially generously since she was writing her own nonfiction version of the Balcombes and Napoleon. While I was on that island, I received every courtesy and help from the French consul, Michel Dancoisne-Martineau, champion of the Napoleonic sites of St. Helena, and from Basil George, Larry Roberts, Hazel Wilmot, and Val Joshua, saints of note. I would like to salute last of all the splendid volunteers at the Australian Balcombe house, The Briars, at Mount Martha in Victoria.

Thomas Keneally, St. Helena, 4 September 2015

A B C